WOMEN AND WAR

They left the town behind, swinging out onto a road that ran across flat, blood-red earth where the vegetation was sparser and more twisted.

'My name is Alys Peterson, by the way,' the Red Cross girl said suddenly. 'What's yours?'

'Tara Kelly.'

'Sounds Irish! In fact *you* sound Irish.'

'I am,' Tara looked at her sharply. 'But how did you know?'

'My family are English. I have a British passport myself.'

'I see.' English, she was thinking. I must be in shock not to have noticed. And not only English but upper crust English. You are out of the top drawer, Miss Alys Peterson, whoever you are . . .

Also in Arrow by Janet Tanner

THE BLACK MOUNTAINS
THE EMERALD VALLEY

WOMEN AND WAR

Janet Tanner

ARROW BOOKS

Published by Arrow Books in 1998

3 5 7 9 10 8 6 4 2

First Published in the United Kingdom in 1997
by Century

Arrow Books
The Random House Group Limited
20 Vauxhall Bridge Road, London, SW1V 2SA

Random House Australia (Pty) Limited
20 Alfred Street, Milsons Point, Sydney,
New South Wales 2061, Australia

Random House New Zealand Limited
18 Poland Road, Glenfield Auckland 10, New Zealand

Random House (Pty) Limited
Endulini, 5a Jubilee Road, Parktown 2193, South Africa

The Random House Group Limited Reg. No. 954009

www.randomhouse.co.uk

A CIP catalogue record for this book is available from the British Library

Papers used by Random House are natural, recyclable products made from wood grown in sustainable
forests. The manufacturing processes conform to the environmental
regulations of the country of origin

ISBN 0 09 953550 5

Printed and bound in Great Britain by
Bookmarque Ltd, Croydon, Surrey

For my Aunt and Uncle, Nora and Alec Mundy.

OVERTURE . . .

Tara was crouching behind the chair in the corner when Maggie and the man came into the room. She heard their voices – Maggie's soft Irish lilt and the man's coarse drawl – and tucked in as tightly as she could to avoid being seen. Like the rest of the furniture in the room it had seen better days – stuffing leaked out from the seat and hung in stringy streamers on the linoleum which covered the floorboards – but it was big enough to hide behind and Tara was glad. She should not be here, she knew, Maggie had given her a sixpenny bit and told her to go out for an hour as she always did when the men came to visit, but today Tara had not wanted to go. It was raining, soft flurries blowing ceaselessly against the windows of the cramped two room apartment she shared with Maggie in Darlinghurst, Sydney, and as she watched Maggie pull a comb through her mane of red hair and paint her lips to the bright scarlet slash that left stains on cups and cigarette ends, Tara had made up her mind. She would hide when they came back. With any luck Maggie would take the man straight through to the bedroom and they would never know she was there.

The door slammed shut. Tara held her breath. 'Wait here a minute and I'll slip into something more comfortable,' Maggie said.

'No need for that.' The man sounded impatient. 'It doesn't bother me.'

'It bothers me, dear,' Maggie said.

Tara peeped around the wing of the chair. The man was big, swarthy and untidy with a beer gut swelling above the leather belt which held up his trousers and tattoos up his arms. Tara surveyed him without much interest. He was like all the men who came to visit Maggie, more or less, and she hated all of them, partly because of the way she'd seen them paw Maggie and partly because when they came she was made to go out.

Maggie came back into the room. Tara caught a glimpse of her green art silk dressing gown, the one which showed every contour of her breasts.

'All ready then,' she said.

'Just a minute – what's that?' the man asked.

Tara squeezed tighter against the chair. A bit of fluff from the stuffing got into her nose and she was quite unable to suppress a sneeze.

'Tara – is that you?' Maggie's voice was harsh. Tara had no choice but to emerge. 'By all that's holy what do you think you are doing?' Maggie demanded.

'I didn't want to go out,' Tara began, then broke off. The man was looking at her, a strange and frighteningly unpleasant expression curling his poorly shaven face.

'Hey – who's she?' There was suppressed excitement in his voice. He took a step towards her.

'Never mind who she is,' Maggie said. And to Tara: 'Get out now, like you were told!'

'Wait a bit – how much?' He jerked his thumb in Tara's direction. 'I'll pay well . . .'

Maggie moved like lightning between Tara and the man. Her hand shot out gripping Tara's arm so tightly that the fingermarks stood out like red weals on her flesh.

'Out, Tara! Go on out!' She bundled her across the room, half threw her through the door. Tara stood on the stairs for a moment rubbing her arm. Then disconsolately she made her way down the stairs and into the street. The rain hit her like a soft veil. She had no coat, but at least it was not cold. Just as well. She would have to stay out for at least an hour. She certainly did not want to risk going back while the man was there.

Tara wandered aimlessly up the alley and started down the hill towards the centre of Sydney, a skinny eight-year-old in a faded print frock and sandals. The rain had made her hair cluster in tiny jet-black curls around her heart-

2

shaped face but her cornflower blue eyes were clouded and there was no sign of the dimples that Mammy had used to say were there because the faeries had touched her cheeks with their little fingers.

She passed a corner bar and the jangling sound of a piano wafted out to her. Tara's footsteps faltered. She recognized that tune – 'When Irish Eyes Are Smiling'. Mammy had used to sing it to her, leaning over her bed, her lovely lilting voice all mixed up somehow with the smell of her perfume and something else, something Maggie said was whisky, blending and wafting Tara to the very edges of sleep . . . Suddenly the pain was very sharp in Tara. She crept closer to the door, peeping inside. The cigarette smoke hung thickly so that she saw the people inside through a haze. But there was a woman with her back to the door, a woman in a red dress just like Mammy used to wear. Tara pressed closer, her heart beating in her throat so hard she could scarcely breathe. Could it be? This time, could it really be . . . Mammy?

The woman turned and as Tara saw her face the disappointment came rushing in, making her sick. A stranger with a garishly painted face. Not Mammy. Never Mammy. So many times Tara had thought she had seen her but it never was. At first when Mammy had gone she had walked the steep alleys of Darlinghurst until her feet were covered with blisters, waited outside the sly grog shops in Woolloomooloo and Kings Cross, haunted the taverns in the Rocks where Mammy used to sing for the sailors, but she had never come.

Tears pricked Tara's eyes and she turned away. It wasn't fair. It was not fair! Why had Mammy gone? Why, after all the wonderful dreams they had shared? They had come all the way from Ireland to Australia on the boat because Mammy had said that Daddy would be there waiting for them – the Daddy she had never seen – and they could make a new life in a land full of opportunities. But no Daddy had been there to meet them. Only Auntie Maggie who was not really an aunt at all but a friend of

3

Mammy's and from the Emerald Isle herself. Tara had not minded about not finding Daddy. What you had never had you did not miss. And they were all right, the three of them, she and Mammy and Auntie Maggie. But Mammy had minded. She had grown thinner and older and though she still sang like all the larks in the air whenever anyone would listen, more and more often Tara had smelled that something which mingled with her cheap perfume and which Auntie Maggie said was whisky.

And then one night Mammy had gone away. Dimly, as if it were part of a dream, Tara thought she remembered her bending over the bed where she was sleeping, remembered Mammy's tears falling wet onto her cheek and heard her soft brogue, so slurred it was difficult to make out her words. 'This is the best way, Tara me darlin'. You'll be better off without me.' But she could never be sure whether that part was just wishful thinking. Mammy had gone and though she had searched the highways and byways, Tara had never seen her again.

She loved Maggie of course, loved her with all her eight-year-old heart. Maggie was all she had. Maggie was kind and warm, all hugs and kisses. Sometimes Maggie would cry with her. Sometimes she would sing her to sleep. But she couldn't sing like Mammy. More often than not she would go out of tune and Tara itched to tell her son.

And too often – like today – the men would come and Maggie would send her out.

The tears pricked more insistently and as if she could out-pace them Tara began to run. Oh Mammy, oh Mammy, you used to tell me I looked as if I'd been left behind by the faeries, but it was you that left me. Oh Mammy. . . .

She ran blindly with no clear thought as to where she was going but her feet needed no telling. There was one place in all of Sydney that she loved above all others, one place where she could forget the heartache and loneliness, forget the feel of the pavement through the thin places in the soles of her sandals and the wet cling of her dress to her legs. As it came into view she caught her breath and felt the little twist of excitement shiver pleasurably through her.

The Capitol. Sydney's great variety theatre. Its light blazed out into the night and drew her like a magnet. Oh the hours she had spent here, eyes shining with wonder as she gazed at the imposing façade, at the portraits of the artistes in their glass fronted showcases, and peeped through the glass panels at the ornate gilded balcony and the staircases which swept down from it on either side between the tall lamps standing sentinel. Oh, the dreams that were bound up with the glamour and colour of it!

At first she had come here in her search for Mammy, hanging around the stage door and watching the comings and goings of the theatre people. It was a bit grand for Mammy, she supposed, but Mammy was a singer and perhaps she had come up in the world. That could be the reason why she had left Tara – because she was ashamed of her. Tara had thrust that thought aside swiftly. The days had passed and Mammy had not come out of the stage door, nor was her picture ever amongst those outside the main entrance, but still Tara went to the theatre whenever she could.

Tonight the magic of it was stronger than ever. Music wafted out through the partly opened door and with it the soaring voice of a woman singing. Tara looked at the portraits wondering which of the artistes it belonged to. One of the women was very beautiful, a lovely tilted face above bare shoulders. It was probably she who was singing, Tara decided, and as the excitement stirred in her again it seemed that the features transmuted and changed so that they were no longer the features of a stranger but her own, grown older and more beautiful.

Mammy might never have sung here but one day I will, Tara promised herself. One day it will be my picture up there, just see if it's not. And Mammy will come back to see me and I'll make her so proud of me. Oh I will, I will. . . .

5

She lifted her chin and felt the rain mingling with the tears on her cheeks. With the back of her hand she brushed them away and turned to walk back to Darlinghurst.

. . . AND BEGINNERS

The Rolls Royce purred up the wide tree-lined street in Toorak, Melbourne, turned in at a gateway marked out in the camphor laurel hedge by a pair of well-shaped cypress trees and came to a stop on the laundered gravel drive which curved between velvet lawns and flowerbeds bright with spring flowers.

From her vantage point hidden behind the rhododendron bushes Alys Peterson saw the chauffeur open the rear doors for the well-heeled occupant to disembark, and pulled a face.

Mrs Ahearne-Smythe, leading light amongst the English community in Melbourne, come to visit Mother. She had been expected, of course. An hour ago Alys and Beverley, her elder sister, had been instructed to wash and change into their best dresses and Alys had been treated to a lecture on how to behave herself like a young lady. Such lectures were totally unnecessary as far as Beverley was concerned. From her superior age of eleven Beverley was totally incapable of behaving any other way. Alys thought with disgust, while she herself seemed to roll from one scrape to another.

'You are clean and tidy, Alys, please endeavour to stay that way,' her mother had pleaded. 'And try to behave in a manner which will not make your father and I ashamed of you.'

Alys had scuffed the toe of her sandal against the leg of an exquisite Chippendale chair and said nothing. She did not know how she managed to get into so much trouble. She always set out with the intention of being good and modelling herself on Beverley. But somewhere along the way something always went wrong.

Perhaps it was because she was so easily bored. She couldn't content herself to play with dolls as Beverley did when there were so many other far more exciting things to do. Or had been, before they moved to Toorak.

Alys squirmed a little further under the rhododendron bush watching Mrs Ahearne-Smythe's plump feet, encased in their tight fitting and slightly old fashioned looking black leather shoes, move away from the car and suppressed the urge to call out something very loud and very shocking. In their old house Alys had often hidden behind the hedge and made weird noises as people passed by, stifling her laughter as they looked around to try to discover where the sound had come from. That sort of thing could not be done in Toorak, especially if your father was Daniel Peterson, banker and businessman extraordinaire, and your house was the grandest in a street of grand houses.

Toorak was the most select suburb of Melbourne, Mother said, and she was probably right. The houses here had been built in the heady days when fortunes were being made in the Victorian goldfields, she had explained to the children, and each one reflected the taste – or the homeland – of the man who had built it. For a while the fantasy of that idea had fascinated Alys and she had explored eagerly, stopping to look at a hacienda-style house with flowers in stone pots to provide bright splashes of colour against the glaring white walls, an eccentric 'wedding cake' house so fragile looking that Alys imagined the winds sweeping in from Port Phillip Bay could blow it away, and a turretted mini-castle. But Mother had not approved of Alys standing on the pavements where the cherry trees drifted pink and white blossoms like so much confetti, gazing in at the houses between the shielding spruce and chestnut, laburnum and sycamore. People were entitled to their privacy, she said. And little ladies who knew their mannners did not stare. So Alys had had to content herself with inspecting the gargoyles wearing mitres who guarded the Church of St John in Toorak Road – a much less interesting occupation.

Today, however, she was confined to the house – and now, into her prison, had come this big gleaming Rolls. Motor cars fascinated Alys even more than the fantastic array of houses had done. She could not understand that while the few boys she knew were allowed to play with cars and engines she was expected to make do with dolls. Last Christmas all she had wanted – begged for – was a toy garage, but instead she had been given a life size baby doll with a china face, a lace-hung cradle and a workbox. She still smarted from the injustice of it.

From the rhododendron bushes she watched now as Mrs Ahearne-Smythe's chauffeur lifted the bonnet of the Rolls and fiddled for a moment or two. Then he collected a large container from the boot and set out around the side of the house in the direction of the servants' entrance.

The car was unattended now, the bonnet still raised. Alys crept out from behind the rhododendron, heedless of the dirt on her knees and the bits of twig sticking to her best dress. Nobody was in sight. She could take a peep under the bonnet of the Rolls.

She gazed at the intricacies of the engine in undisguised wonder. So many parts! Carefully she leaned inside and touched one of them. Black grease came off onto her finger.

'Hey what do you think you're doing?' The chauffeur had returned, unnoticed by Alys. She jumped and her greasy fingers brushed against her skirt.

'Oh, I only wanted to look . . .'

A grin spread across his leathery features. 'You're the Peterson kid aren't you?'

'I'm Alys. Yes.'

'You like cars?'

8

She nodded enthusiastically, her bright gold hair bouncing round her face.

'Yes. But I've never seen inside one before.'

'Well, now's your chance.'

'You mean you'll show me?'

'No worries. Here, hold onto this for me . . .' He handed her the container of water, leaned inside the bonnet and fiddled. 'Now look, this is where the water goes. It keeps the engine cool . . .'

She craned closer, excitement bubbling in her, as he pointed out the workings of the engine.

'Alys!' Her mother's voice called to her from the front porch. She jumped. Water slurped from the container onto her skirt and socks.

'Oh, I'll have to go. Thank you.' She ran towards the house. 'I'm sorry, I was only . . .'

'Alys!' Her mother's voice was coldly furious, her face a mask of controlled anger. 'What do you think you have been doing?'

'Just looking at the car.'

'You are filthy! Filthy! What on earth is the matter with you? Is it impossible for you to do as you are told just once? Get inside. Go to your room and clean yourself up at once.'

'I'm sorry . . .' Alys said, looking down at her dress in surprise and dismay. 'Really I didn't think.'

'You never do. You will be the death of me, Alys.'

She turned and swept into the house. Miserably, Alys followed. Oh no, she'd done it again. Made Mother angry with her. And she did so hate it when Mother was angry. She wouldn't have her beaten, of course. She wouldn't raise a finger to her. But she would treat her to a display of cold disapproval that would last perhaps for several days. And beneath the disapproval would be outraged hurt as if the incident had been a personal affront to her. It would last until Mother was satisfied she had made Alys squirm with guilt for causing her so much trouble, until Alys was ready to cry and beg her forgiveness not simply with words but with her whole heart. And she would, in the end. For Alys, at eight, nothing in the world was more important than her mother's approval. Not even a Rolls Royce motor car.

ACT I
Chapter One

The Canary Club was dim and smoky. A bar padded with red plush ran the length of one wall; above it gilt framed mirrors reflected the rest of the room – dark glass topped tables, chairs upholstered in the same red plush, curtained alcoves, softly glowing pink wall lamps in the shape of seashells. At one end of the room a softly downbeat jazz rhythm was being played on a piano, background music only to the hum of conversation, the muted laughter and the chink of glasses, though on the small square of vacant floor between the tables a few couples were dancing, their bodies pressed into intimate contact.

The piano and a little of the dancefloor was all that Tara Kelly could see from the screened doorway where she stood waiting to make her entrance, but she could picture the rest of the club well enough, and picture it not only as it looked now to the clients who had signed in at the small makeshift desk on the landing above but as it looked during the daytime too when the light filtering down into the cellar through the pavement gratings showed up the seedy imperfections that the soft illuminations hid at night – just how threadbare the carpet really was and how worn and faded the red plush. She knew how dusty it would smell then as the cleaners beat about a bit with carpet sweeper and broom and how the stale cigarette smoke would hang in the air, impregnating the curtains and furnishings; she knew that behind the bar even these smells would pale into insignificance beside the lingering whiffs of spirits and beer, enough to turn the stomach of anyone who had drunk a little too much themselves the previous night.

She knew all this and did not care. For her nothing

11

could detract from the glamour of the place. For as long as she could remember the one dream she had cherished was that she would be a singer – and here the dream had become reality. The Canary Club wasn't the Capitol, of course, but it was a beginning.

It was two months now since she had first walked down the steep stairs where more than one drunken client had come to grief, her heart beating a nervous tattoo, her head held high in a desperate show of bravado, and she'd marched up to Ed Donelly, the owner, and announced her availability.

How close he had been to telling her he was not interested she would never know; that morning he had felt faded and hungover, worried about paying his protection money to the Sydney racketeers and the demands his ex-wife was making on what little remained of his profits. But two days earlier his resident singer had told him she was going to marry a rich punter whose house in Vaucluse gave a dress circle view of the harbour, and something about the look of the girl in the skin tight sweater and skirt had attracted him. She was young, too young for this game, but his jaded customers liked fresh youth and the dim light showed him a heart-shaped face beneath a mass of jet-black curls, eyes sparkling blue behind a fringing of sooty lashes and a well-developed figure which the tight sweater and skirt did nothing to hide.

'All right,' he had said. 'Let's hear what you can do.'

The moment she began to sing he knew he had been right to give her a chance. She had it – that mysterious indefinable something which lifted her out of the ordinary, and her voice caught at some forgotten chord deep inside him. He glanced at Chips Magee, his talented but broken down piano player, and saw that he felt it too. There was excitement in the bloodshot eyes and a lift to the pouchy face dragged out of shape by too much whisky and too many cheap cigarettes.

'When can you start?' It was the only question he asked. Had he probed further he would have learned that Tara

12

Kelly was only fourteen years old, younger even than either he or Chips had dreamed, but by the time he did discover how young she was he had merely sworn to himself and decided to forget it. Tara was good and she was pulling in the customers. He was not sure what the law would say if they discovered her on his premises but the law had never bothered Ed unduly.

Tonight, as she stood behind the screen waiting to make her entrance, Tara experienced the same thrill she had experienced twice nightly for the last two months. Chips was playing that interminable slow jazz piece that would give way to her introductory music and when it did she would move out of the darkness into the beam of the spotlight. As she waited the adrenalin began to flow through her veins like a potent drug and she clenched and unclenched trembling hands, taking long steadying breaths of the smoky air and running over the opening lines of her first number: 'My heart tells me this is just a fling / But your love to me means everything . . .'

She caught herself up as the introduction began, harnessed the adrenalin and moved out into that rosy path of light, feeling it warm upon her bare shoulders and narrowing her eyes slightly against its glare.

As soon as she was in view the sounds of chat and laughter spluttered into silence. Tara had heard it continue throughout the smutty patter of the resident comic and was always terrified that one night it might go on during her own act, but so far it never had. The moment she began to sing everyone stopped to listen and the realization of this lifted her onto a heady cloud.

The first two numbers she sang beside the piano, for the third she was expected to move slowly between the tables singing to the customers, smiling at them, making them feel good. This was the part of the act she liked least for sometimes the men made advances to her, touching her or sometimes, if they were drunk enough, trying to pull her down onto their laps. At first this had worried her – she was afraid to risk losing her job because she had slapped some lecherous patron's face – but she was not old or experienced enough to know how to deal tactfully with such advances. One thing she was determined about however – she was not going to put up with that sort of thing. She had seen too much of it when men came home with Maggie. She complained to Ed and soon the word had gone around. Molesting the singer was taboo and would result in instant ejection by the ex-boxers who guarded the entrance to the club. If the patrons wanted a girl for the evening one would be found but it would not be Tara Kelly.

Tonight, as always, she made her way between the tables moving with a slinky sideways step because her ankle-length skirt was too tight to allow her to move freely. Many of the customers she recognized as regulars and she smiled at them and sang a few lines to them. But as she moved towards the discreetly lit rear of the club, she was surprised to see Ed sitting at a table with two men she had never seen before. One was completely bald; the soft spotlight following Tara caught the film of moisture covering the crown of his head, making it shine. Yet it was the other one who, in spite of being less remarkable, somehow drew and held her attention. His face was half-hidden behind a screen of cigar smoke but she was aware of a hook nose and piercing eyes; his suit was conservative yet she gained the distinct impression of a powerful physique. Ed was smiling proudly and nodding as if to encourage her and she sang to them before moving on once more.

She was back in her dressing-room, the tiny curtained alcove halfway up the rear fire escape when the summons came, delivered by Wenda, one of the club's hostesses.

'The boss wants you to join him at his table, Tara.'

'Oh no, sure wasn't I just about to have a steak! I'm starving!' she complained, but she knew better than to refuse. She slipped on a bolero to cover her bare shoulders and went back into the club.

The men were still sitting around the table. As she

approached Ed pulled out a chair for her with a quick almost nervous gesture.

'There she is then, our little Tara,' he said. 'As you can see, Red, she's as beaut close to as she looks when she's singing.'

'Can I buy you a drink?' the big man asked. His voice was soft yet there was a vibrancy in it that commanded, just as the look of him did.

'She'll drink champagne, won't you, Tara?' Ed prompted and Tara nodded. On the rare occasions when Ed allowed her back into the club to fraternize with the customers she was expected to ask for champagne – though what she actually got was a soft fizzy drink served in a champagne flute.

'You were dinkum,' the big man said. He was looking at her through the haze of cigar smoke, eyes narrowed. 'How long have you been here?'

Ed answered for her. 'Just a few weeks. She's done well. Soon as she walked in here looking for a job I knew she'd be right.'

'Where do you live, Tara?' the big man asked.

The drinks had arrived. Busy as the bar was there had been priority for the boss's table. Tara, thirsty from her singing spot, had her glass halfway to her lips as he asked the question.

'Darlo,' she said and drank. Then her eyes widened and she pressed her fingers to her mouth as the liquid tickled unexpectedly on her tongue. That wasn't carbonated water – it *was* champagne! She glanced quickly round the table thinking she must have been given the wrong drink but the men's glasses were all whisky tumblers filled with easily recognizable amber liquid and Ed, staring at her from beneath hooded lids, was daring her to say anything.

'Darlinghurst, eh? I'd say you'll go far from Darlinghurst!' He held his cigar clamped between his teeth and his features were craggy in the dim light. But it was his eyes she was unable to ignore – his eyes on her

15

face, deep and speculative, looking at her in a way she knew only too well.

She pushed back her glass and started to get up.

'Thank you, but if you would excuse me . . .'

Ed touched her elbow, pulling her down again. 'It's too early to leave, Tara.' He was smiling but she sensed it was a forced smile with lips drawn too tightly across his teeth. 'Mr Maloney especially wanted to meet you.'

Mr Maloney. Red. The name meant nothing to her.

'I'm feeling awful tired. I'll be very bad company.'

The eyes behind the cigar smoke narrowed a fraction more; they were little more than slits now.

'Don't worry about it, Tara. Stay and relax for a little while and I'll have my car drop you home afterwards. You won't have to walk to Darlo tonight.'

There was no escape and she sensed it. On the table in front of her the champagne sparkled invitingly. Tara raised the flute and drank and this time she enjoyed the sensation of the bubbles bursting on her tongue. When the flute was half empty Red Maloney motioned to a hostess to bring more and as he raised his hand Tara saw the solid gold cufflinks gleaming at his wrist. Interested, she took a closer look and saw that his wristwatch too was gold. Obviously a man of means. But it didn't mean she liked him any better. For one thing he was thirty-five if he was a day; for another there was something vaguely frightening about him. Just what it was Tara was uncertain but it had to do with an instinct that told her he was very used to getting his own way, which was compounded by Ed's attitude. Tara at fourteen had looked up to Ed as the height of successful sophistication; to see him now so ill at ease in the presence of this big powerful man was a chastening experience.

An hour passed. The music became slower and sleepier, the couples dancing on the square of floor clung closer and the air became so thick with smoke that Tara's eyes began to sting. But strangely she found she was caring less. If this was how champagne made you feel it was rather pleasant,

16

she thought – even if her cheeks did feel flushed and the shell lights on the wall seemed to be moving in soft fuzzy circles. The company that had been forced upon her seemed more congenial too – even Ed had told one or two jokes that had actually made her giggle.

She giggled again now, lifting her champagne glass and looking down into it. 'Oh, it's all gone! What a pity!'

Ed raised his hand to summon a hostess but Red Maloney stopped him.

'No. I think Miss Kelly is ready to go home now.'

No one had ever called her Miss Kelly before. She giggled again. He stood up and she saw for the first time just what a big man he was – well over six feet tall and broad with it – but a breadth that came from physical exercise, not from sloth.

'Do you have a coat, Miss Kelly?' he asked.

She shook her head, holding her lip between her teeth because absurdly she still wanted to giggle. The bald-headed man, Jason, rose too; by the time Tara, leaning lightly against Red's arm, reached the top of the stairs a huge black Cadillac was waiting at the kerb. Red held her back in the doorway while Jason got out and opened the rear passenger door, then he ushered her into the car and got in beside her.

The fresh air had sobered her a little; she looked around surprised to find herself surrounded by such luxuries as smoked glass windows and leather upholstery. Red touched a button and when a cocktail cabinet slid out at knee level, he poured himself a Scotch.

'Want one?' he asked her.

'I don't know . . . Can I taste?'

He held the glass to her lips and the wafting smell reminded her so sharply of Mammy that she almost sobbed aloud. Then the fiery liquid was burning her throat, making her cough, and she forgot Mammy again.

The car swept past Tooheys Brewery and began climbing the steep rise into Surrey Hills. Tara looked out at the pretty terraced cottages they were passing, three tiered and decorated with wrought iron lacework like an everlasting wedding cake. She loved these houses and had always dreamed that one day she might live in one of them instead of the squalid Darlo apartment she shared with Maggie. Now, in the cocooned luxury of the Cadillac, she found herself almost believing for a moment that one of the pretty cottages was hers already.

Darlinghurst was a maze of small sloping streets and tall squalid houses. When Tara pointed down an alleyway the Cadillac slid to a stop. Red Maloney closed up his bar but made no move to open the door for Tara to get out.

'Thank you,' she said. 'Sure wouldn't Maggie have a fit if she was to go by now and see me in a grand car like this one!'

His eyes were on her again.

'I have a proposition to put to you, Tara. If you say yes you would be able to ride in a car like this all the time.'

His words sobered her even more than the fresh air had done. Did he mean what she *thought* he meant?

'Oh, I couldn't Mr Maloney, thank you kindly all the same. It's against all the laws of God's church . . .'

He laughed aloud. 'I was going to ask you if you would sing in one of my clubs. What did you think I was going to say?' She flushed and he went on: 'I have two clubs, both of them bigger and better than the Canary. The one is in . . .'

'No,' she said.

'But you haven't given me a chance to tell you . . .'

'Sure what is there to tell? I couldn't leave the Canary Club. What would Ed do?'

'He'll find someone else.' His hand covered hers and as he moved towards her she smelled again the whisky smell on his breath that reminded her so of Mammy.

'No thank you, Mr Maloney.' She fumbled for the door catch without success. The Cadillac was a prison of leather and chrome. 'Let me get out of here!' she said in panic.

'Tara!' he reproached. He caught her chin turning it

18

towards him and at first she was too startled by the vice-like grip even to struggle. So strong were his fingers it seemed to her that if he wished he could crack her jaw like a walnut. Then, still holding her face steady he bent his head to hers. She found herself looking up mesmerized into that craggy face, all lines and shadows in the half-light. Then his mouth was on hers, pressing and seeking so fiercely that she could scarcely breathe. For a moment she remained motionless then as his tongue violated her mouth she began to fight, trying to free herself. Useless. How could any man be that strong? As he raised his lips she gulped thankfully for air then, still trapped, expelled it all as a scream. At once his other hand clamped over her mouth and with the panic now making her desperate she bit at it and tasted blood.

Red swore violently and released her to suck the blood from his injured hand. Tara knew a moment's triumph that changed swiftly to fear as he lunged towards her once more, pinning her into the corner of the seat like a butterfly.

'Try that again and you'll be sorry!'

Her sob of fear turned to defiance. 'You bully!' she screamed at him. 'You'll rot in hell, so you will!'

As suddenly as he had grabbed her he let her go, leaning back with an explosive roar of laughter.

'What is there to laugh at?' she cried, mortified and not knowing why.

He shook his head, reached into his pocket and extracted a fat cigar.

'What do you want with me?' she cried in fury. 'Just get on with it, can't you, if you're going to! Don't keep tormenting me like this!'

'Oh no, Tara.' She saw the glint of a gold lighter as he lit his cigar and instantly the car was perfumed by the pungent smoke. 'You have it wrong. I don't rape little girls in the back seats of motor cars.'

She stared at him, trembling. She did not understand and not understanding made her more afraid than his aggression had done.

'Do you know, my dear, that I own three brothels in this town, with the best girls in the whole of New South Wales? They're not whores. They are courtesans. I can visit them whenever I choose. Oh no, I don't need to rape anyone and if I did I assure you it would be in comfort.'

'Then what . . . ?

I can afford to wait for what I want,' he said and the note in his voice chilled her. 'You'll come to me in your own good time.' He leaned over then tapping the glass that separated the rear of the car from the driver. 'Open the door please, Aldo.'

The door slid open. Tara gaped at it, too surprised to take advantage of her way of escape now that it was offered.

'Well, aren't you going?' he said. 'Or have you decided to come home with me already?'

She moved then with all the speed and agility that her tight-fitting dress would allow, tumbling out into the street and running on her spike-heeled shoes down the alley. But it was not until she reached the flight of uneven stone steps leading up to the front door that she heard the engine purr into life and glancing fearfully over her shoulder saw the Cadillac slide away.

*

Maggie was asleep when Tara came bursting in, hennaed hair spread in violent disarray across the pillow. The room smelled stale and Tara guessed that Maggie had had at least one visitor that evening.

'Maggie . . .'

'Ugh?'

'Maggie, please wake up! There was a man . . . a man at the Club. He brought me home in his car . . .'

Maggie rolled over. 'Mm – all right for some . . .'

'It wasn't what you think . . .' Tara broke off realizing the futility of it.

'A car! Think yourself lucky,' Maggie mumbled and was promptly asleep once more.

Tara sighed. She straightened up, kicked off her shoes and stood for a moment hugging herself with her arms. Then she peeled off the skin tight dress, the wisp of suspender belt and stockings, turned back the sheets and climbed in beside Maggie.

Maggie was wearing a nightgown, a creation in green art silk which had been given to her by one of her gentlemen friends. Her body heat burned through in waves but ignoring it Tara curled close to her back. Before long Maggie would probably lash out, tell her to 'Give me some air, for Chrissakes!' But for the moment Tara felt in need of comfort and Maggie, unwilling or not, was the closest she could come to that.

*

The next evening when Tara arrived at the Canary Club she was summoned at once to Ed's office. He sat behind his desk sweating slightly and dabbing at his face with a silk handkerchief.

'Tara, I'm sorry, I don't know how to tell you this so I might as well come right out with it. I can't have you working here any more.'

Her jaw dropped. 'Why not?'

'I'm under orders to get rid of you.'

'Whose orders?'

He dabbed at his face again and replaced the handkerchief in the pocket of his tuxedo.

'You know who that was here last night, don't you?' Her face darkened. She did not answer. 'It was Red Maloney,' he continued. 'Well, Red wants me to get rid of you.'

Her chin came up.

'Red wants! Well, why the hell do you have to do what *Red* wants?'

Out came the handkerchief again. Ed dabbed at his profusely sweating forehead.

'It seems you upset him last night.'

'So what?'

'I'll tell you so what. Red wants you out of here. And in case you didn't know it what Red says goes. I don't want to lose you – you're the best draw the Canary has ever had. But I don't want the place done over either. I can't afford that.'

'And Red will do it over if you don't get rid of me?'

'That's right. Oh look, Tara, you still don't know who he is do you? He's only the most powerful man round here, that's all. He runs clubs, brothels, protection rackets, dial-a-bloody hit man, the lot. He has the sly grog shops sewn up, and the gambling dens. He's trouble, for Chrissakes. And I can't risk him putting the finger on me. I'm sorry, kid, but there it is.'

'I see.' Tara was trembling. 'And I don't even get to sing tonight – just this once?'

'Sorry kid. I'll have to make my apologies to the punters. And you'd better get along home.'

Tara went, tears of anger at the injustice of it pricking behind her eyes. She knew why he'd done it all right. She could hear his voice still as clearly as if he was beside her saying what he'd said last night. *You'll come to me, Tara, in your own good time.* But she wouldn't. She wouldn't! There must be another way . . .

Oh, why did he have to come to the Canary Club last night? she asked herself. Why did he have to take a fancy to me?

But on one thing she was determined. Whatever happened she was not going to allow this big shot to ruin her career before it had even begun. Somehow she would play him at his own game. And somehow she would win.

*

'Tara – is that you?' Maggie called.

Tara, climbing the last few stairs to the tiny apartment after her latest disappointment, sighed. Once she had used to run up those stairs, feet flying with the eagerness of

22

youth. Now the weight of despair that ached inside her seemed to have got into her limbs too and her feet dragged on the stairs like the feet of an old woman.

A month had gone by since Red Maloney had come to the Canary and still she had been unable to find another job as a singer. All over Sydney she had tried and all over Sydney she had been refused. It was not for lack of talent, she knew. She had sung for too many bar owners and known they were pleased with her only to see their faces change when they learned who she was. In desperation she had tried lying about her name but her reputation – and her Irish accent – had scotched that. Still she had been turned away and she knew it was all Red Maloney's doing.

'Tara?' Maggie called again and Tara's heart sank still lower. Surely Maggie didn't have someone with her this early in the day? If she had to go back out and wander the streets until Maggie had finished with them, she didn't think she could bear it.

'Sure it's me,' she called back. 'Can I come in?'

'Course you can. It didn't sound like your step, that's all.'

Tara pushed open the door and sighed at the sight that met her eyes. Although it was midday the apartment was still in a state of early morning chaos – a milk bottle in the middle of the table, dirty dishes piled on the draining board, the bed unmade. Maggie had still been asleep when Tara had gone out; at least she was up now though she was still wearing her dressing gown and last night's stale make-up made garish streaks on her puffy face.

'What's the matter with you?' Maggie asked.

Tara did not answer. She crossed to the stove and lifted the kettle, testing it.

'There's tea in the pot,' Maggie said. 'I just made some.'

Tara rinsed out one of the cups and poured tea from the brown tin teapot. It looked, and smelled, stewed, but she sipped it anyway, glad of the comfort it brought.

23

'No luck again?' Maggie asked.

Tara shook her head. 'No. Oh Maggie, it's just not fair! I'm good – I know I am. And I could have made it – I could! – if it hadn't been for *him*. I don't understand it really. Why should anyone want to ruin my chances . . .'

Maggie reached into her dressing gown pocket for a packet of cigarettes, took one out and lit it.

'He doesn't want to ruin your chances, Tara. You know what he's doing as well as I do. You know what he said to you.'

'That I'd come to him in my own good time.'

'That's right. He wants you and he reckons if you can't get work elsewhere he'll get you.'

Tara set down her cup with a bang, slopping tea onto the table.

'Well, he won't! I wouldn't work for him if he was the last man in Sydney.'

Maggie drew out a chair and sat down. 'He is, isn't he?'

'What?'

'The last man in Sydney – as far as you're concerned. You might as well face facts, kid – he's got it sewn up. Either you go to sing for him or you don't sing at all.'

Tara picked up her cup again, went to drink, then pushed it abruptly aside as the bitter smell assailed her nostrils, suddenly revolting her.

'There are other places where Mr Red Maloney can't reach,' she said stubbornly.

Maggie leaned back in her chair arching her back and crossing her legs.

'Oh Tara, don't be such a fool. Why go chasing off all over Australia when you've got the chance of singing in the best clubs right here in Sydney? I don't know why you've stuck out against it so long. It's your mother in you, I suppose, determined to be independent. But there's no point fighting it. You're only hurting yourself.'

'But Maggie . . .' Tara's hands clenched to fists. 'You know what he wants, don't you? He doesn't just want me to sing.'

'Oh Tara, Tara . . .' Maggie drew on her cigarette, blowing smoke towards the doorway then looking back at the young girl with eyes that were half amused, half sad. 'I thought you were a woman of the world.'

Inexplicably, Tara felt her knees go weak.

'You mean to say you've been around the clubs all this time and nobody has had you?'

Tara shook her head. 'Ed said anyone touching me would get thrown out.'

'And Ed didn't . . . ?'

'No.'

'Well, well. And what about boys? Surely in some back alley . . . ?'

'Oh, sure they've tried. But they don't go on trying very much when you've given them a good kick where it hurts.'

'Well, well, Tara,' Maggie said again, blowing smoke in a thin steady stream. 'No wonder Red Maloney fancies you. If you've any sense, my girl, you'll get in there double quick while you've still got what he wants. All it takes is someone to get the better of you, kick or no kick, and you won't be such desirable property anymore. Use what you've got, Tara. Use it well. All men want the same when it comes down to it. You might as well sell to the highest bidder.'

'Holy Mother.' Tara pressed her hand against her mouth as the bitter tea she had drunk turned in her stomach.

She felt trapped suddenly, as if she stood in a darkening room with the doors slamming shut around her one by one. Men were all the same, Maggie had said and she supposed that was true. But to give in, to go crawling back to Red Maloney . . .

It was all right for Maggie. Maggie was a whore. Tara had known that since she was just a child though she did not think about it more than she could help. Maybe Mammy had been a whore too. Tara's lip trembled at the thought and she caught it firmly between her teeth. No. Mammy had been a singer and *she* would be a singer too — a really successful one. Somehow.

'Have a bit of sense Tara,' Maggie pleaded. 'You'll lose it one day anyway. Might as well have something worthwhile in return or you'll end up just like me. And that would be a pity.'

Tara looked at her, at the bloated, mascara-smudged face behind the curling cigarette smoke, at the tangle of red hair that had not yet seen a comb though it was past midday. Maggie's dressing gown had fallen open slightly so that one of her crossed legs stuck out between the folds of cheap art silk – a once shapely leg, now notched and streaked by varicose veins, as bright a blue as her painted toenails were red. Once Maggie had been going through an old trunk and shown Tara a photograph she had come across – a photograph of herself as a young girl, not much older than Tara was now. And she had been a beauty. The highly coloured studio portrait had shown that. But now . . .

'Take my advice, Tara. Aim high,' Maggie said. And quite suddenly Tara knew what she was going to do.

If this was the way her cards had been dealt then this was the way she would play her hand. She owed it to Maggie, she owed it to Mammy, and most of all she owed it to herself.

'I'll make a pot of fresh tea and then I guess I'd better go out again,' she said.

And though neither mentioned it both of them knew exactly where it was that Tara intended to go.

*

As Tara had discovered Red Maloney owned two night-clubs, three brothels and a high class restaurant, besides all his other interests. He also owned a mansion in Elizabeth Bay, built on colonial lines and furnished with every luxury money could buy. As she approached the colonnaded front door down a path flanked by meticulously kept beds of marigolds and roses Tara was overawed – and trembling with disbelief.

She had misunderstood Red Maloney surely! For what would someone who lived in a house like this want with her?

It took all her courage to ring the bell and when the door was opened by a large, hard-faced man who she realized must be one of Red's bodyguards, she almost turned and ran. She gave her name and he left her standing on the doorstep while he went to announce her arrival. Then, just as she thought she would be there forever, the door opened again and the hard-faced man showed her into the house.

Too nervous to look around Tara was nonetheless aware of a breathtakingly large entrance hall, big enough to fit the whole of their apartment into, she told Maggie later, with chandeliers, more flowers and a sweeping staircase with gilt handrails.

'This way.'

She followed the bodyguard through a maze of corridors. He pushed open a door padded in black leather with more gilt and to her surprise Tara found herself in a room equipped as a gymnasium. For a moment she stood uncertainly looking around at the benches and the weights, the punchbags and the exercise cycle. She had never seen a gymnasium before and could hardly believe that anyone would have one in their home. Then the double doors at the far end of the gymnasium swung open and Red came in. He was wearing a blue towelling robe, monogrammed in gold on one shoulder, bare feet were thrust into flip-flop sandals. A white towel trimmed with the same blue as the robe was thrown loosely over his head and beneath it Tara could see that his hair was lanky wet and his face misted with moisture.

'Well, Tara,' he greeted her. 'I've been expecting you.'

In her pockets her hands clenched so that the nails drove hard into the palms.

'You don't look as though you were expecting me.'

He laughed, the same laugh she remembered from that nightmare night in the back of his Cadillac.

'I've been working out. And after a good workout I always like to treat myself to a sauna and massage.' He slipped the white towel down onto his shoulders so that it lay around his neck like a stole. 'So – tell me why you're here.'

She looked at him, at the casual power of him, and hated him. He wasn't satisfied that he had brought her to this. He was going to make her crawl. For a moment she was tempted to turn and walk out of this house – this monument to wealth – away from this powerful arrogant man. But she knew that if she was ever to fulfil her ambitions she could not afford to.

'You know very well why I'm here, Mr Maloney,' she said.

Chapter Two

At the mansion in Toorak, Melbourne, Beverley Peterson's engagement party was in full swing. In the banqueting room the crystal chandeliers shimmered light onto the scene, the men immaculate in their evening suits and their ladies bright butterflies in jewel-coloured silks, floating chiffons and glittering lamés with diamonds, emeralds and rubies glinting at their throats and on their well-manicured hands as they danced with genteel enjoyment to the strains of the five piece orchestra which had been imported for the occasion; the waiters moving smoothly amongst them to offer chilled Dom Perignon in crystal flutes; the buffet table laden with every imaginable delicacy; the ferns and flowers banked against the walls so thickly that the party could have been taking place in a garden rather than inside the house. There were portraits on the walls, gilt framed oils of stern looking men and grand ladies. Some were of Frances Peterson's aristocratic English ancestors – part of a line which could be traced back unbroken to the 14th century; some had been purchased at auction though the Petersons would never have admitted such a thing.

But there were no portraits of Daniel Peterson's family. Daniel was a self-made man. He had left a father and mother in England who occupied a small house behind the family bakery business in Darlington, to come to Australia to make his fortune – and make his fortune he certainly had. His primary business interest was in import and export, but he had a finger in a dozen pies besides – banking and finance, real estate and shipping. He owned a store and had shares in almost everything that made money from vehicle manufacturing to alluvial mining and cyaniding, from textiles to the companies which worked the immense brown coal deposits in the Latrobe Valley. Even the racehorse he owned was seldom anything but first past the post. Everything Daniel Peterson touched seemed to turn to gold and the ties with the family back home in Darlington had now been severed forever – except for a fat cheque which fell through the letter box onto the tiled floor of the bakery along with the bills at the beginning of each year.

In a corner close to the french windows Alys sipped champagne and did her best to remain invisible. Had it not been for an exceedingly large potted palm this would have been a task of almost insurmountable proportions for Alys at seventeen was truly stunning. She was a tall girl with bright red-gold hair and a slender figure which had no need of the contraptions of satin and elastic known as 'the girdle' and 'the corselette' into which her mother was continually trying to force her, and for all that she spent as little time as possible on her appearance a year at a Swiss finishing school had taught her to choose her clothes wisely. Tonight her gown of turquoise crêpe almost perfectly matched her eyes, the halter neck laid bare creamy shoulders and from beneath a wide sash the skirt skimmed smoothly over her hips to end in a fishtail flounce which reached from knee to ankle. Daniel had commented that the gown was too old for her but Alys had become immune to their criticisms. Whatever she did it seemed she was unable to meet with their approval.

They wanted her to be a carbon copy of Beverley, she knew – Beverley who was content to amuse herself with flower arranging classes and helping her mother with her endless charity fund raising functions and who had now made a suitable match by announcing her engagement to Louis Reilly, youngest son of a prominent Melbourne family. That had been very much to Frances and Daniel's liking – Louis was a worthy and earnest young man who had already gained himself a foothold on the ladder of success in his family's bank. But privately Alys thought him a bore and a drip and the prospect of settling down to spend the rest of her life with a clone of Louis terrified her. She could not – would not – do it. There had to be more to life, surely, than learning and then using the social graces; there must be room for something between being a daughter and then a wife.

Just what it was she wanted to do Alys was not sure. She only knew that deep inside her was a restless unfulfilled yearning and the same aching dissatisfaction which had filled her that Christmas long ago when she had begged for a toy garage and been given a beautiful china doll. She had tasted freedom briefly in Switzerland and now, back in the claustrophobic atmosphere of her parents' world, she wished with her whole heart that she had made more of the chance to explore her own avenues and develop her own personality.

Perhaps Beverley was happy to be the daughter Frances wanted – a genteel young lady without a thought in her head beyond making a 'good' marriage – but Alys knew she could not bear to follow in her footsteps. She glanced at her now as she hung onto Louis's arm, a pale insipid girl whose light brown hair frizzed unflatteringly around a face turned a delicate shade of salmon by the heat and excitement, and felt the claustrophobia stir again. They would force her into the same mould if she stayed here, she was sure of it, but what was the alternative?

'Alys, what are you doing hiding away here?' Alys turned at the sound of her mother's voice, her heart sinking. Frances' mouth was set in a social smile but there was no mistaking the gimlet anger in her eyes. 'For heaven's sake can't you make the effort just for once to behave as we would wish you to? This is your sister's engagement party. You must circulate.'

'Yes, Mother,' Alys said.

'Well do it then!' She glanced around. 'Look – there is Clarence Davenport all by himself. He was asking after you a moment ago. Go and speak to him – make him feel welcome. You know how shy he is.'

Alys smiled wryly. She could have told her mother that when she had found herself alone with Clarence Davenport at a family gathering last Christmas he had been anything but shy. Spotty and unattractive he might be but it had not prevented him from trying to force himself upon her in a way she had found quite revolting. But to say as much would be little short of heresy. Like Louis, Clarence was, in her mother's eyes, a 'suitable' young man.

'Please, Alys!' Frances commanded sharply.

Obediently Alys moved away from the shelter of the potted palm. On her way across the floor she was accosted by a friend of her mother's who commented on how grown up Alys was looking this evening and wanted to know what she would be doing now she had returned from Switzerland and when she, like Beverley, would be announcing her engagement. By the time Alys escaped Clarence was no longer alone – he and another young man were engaged in conversation. Alys was about to return gratefully to her corner when the stranger turned and she stopped, arrested by the look of him.

He was not a tall man but the athletic proportions of his body made him appear so and the stark black of his dinner jacket was flattering to his springy fair hair and tanned skin. His features were good – a strong nose and jaw line and a well-shaped mouth – but there was something unusual about his face as if perhaps he had Jewish blood in his veins in spite of the fair hair. Alys felt a stirring of interest and crossed to where the two men were standing.

'Hello, Clarence.'

'Alys!' Clarence's voice was high pitched, competing with the music. 'I was just saying I wondered where you were. Thought you couldn't be missing from your sister's engagement do – wouldn't be quite the thing, would it? People might think you were jealous!' He laughed, carried away by the daring of this remark.

'I should hate anyone to think that,' Alys returned smartly. 'For one thing I'm not the jealous type, for

32

another . . .' Her voice tailed away meaningfully and she swivelled her eyes as if becoming aware of Clarence's companion for the first time. 'Hello. I don't think we have met.'

Brown eyes met hers. The smile in them made her tummy tip.

'Oh sorry, Alys – awfully rude of me. This is Race Gratton – Race, Alys Peterson, daughter of the house.'

'Nice to meet you.' She liked his voice as much as the rest of him. His accent was stronger than she was used to but he was making no effort to hide it and there was no awe in his tone as there so often was when strangers were first introduced to one of the Peterson family.

'Nice to meet you too,' she said.

'Alys – your glass is empty. Can I get you another drink?' Clarence wittered.

Alys, who had swopped a full glass for an empty one on her way across the room, glanced down and affected total surprise.

'Oh so it is! Thank you, Clarrie, that would be lovely . . .'

Left alone they looked at one another again and Alys felt the colour rising in her cheeks. Then both spoke together.

'Do you live in Melbourne . . . ?'

'Lovely place you have here . . .'

They broke off, laughing.

'Go on, you first,' he said.

'All right. I was just asking if you live in Melbourne. I thought I knew all Bev and Louis' friends.'

'My sponsor does business with Louis.'

'Your sponsor? I'm intrigued.'

He smiled. 'If I told you what I do you wouldn't believe me.'

'Oh, go on – I would! I promise!'

'All right. I drive racing cars.'

'You don't!'

'You see – I knew you wouldn't believe me!'

33

'Oh how exciting! What did you say your name was – Race . . . ?'

'Gratton. But you won't have heard of me – yet.'

'I've never met a racing driver before! I know a couple of jockeys – Daddy has a racehorse – but a racing driver . . .' She caught sight of Clarence picking his way across the room carefully carrying a champagne flute. 'Oh gosh, here comes Clarrie. Is he a friend of yours?'

'Not really.' A corner of his mouth quirked and she felt as if he was reading her mind. 'Do you want to dance?'

Their eyes met like conspirators and she felt a giggle beginning inside her. 'Yes. Shall we?'

They moved quickly onto the floor to be swallowed up by the twirling couples and in her delight Alys had to control the desire to giggle again as she spotted a bemused Clarrie looking around for her.

Race danced well, moving like an athlete with lazy grace and she liked the way he held her, not too loosely, not too close, with no suggestion of the pumping action that amused her with so many of her partners. She longed to ask him more about his career but felt that to be too enthusiastic might make her appear childish.

'Night and day . . . you are the one!' the orchestra played and Alys hummed along with it. No one had ever made her feel this way before. There had been a young man in Switzerland – a student – but the reason she had gone out with him had had more to do with not wanting to be the only girl in the school without a boyfriend than it had with her feelings for him. But this – this was different; exciting and exhilarating, it bubbled inside her like the champagne. Yet only an hour or so ago she had been bored, restless, convinced that nothing wonderful could ever happen to her here!

'This is quite a party, isn't it?' he said later. They were at the buffet table, helping themselves with all the vigour of their youthful appetites to smoked salmon canapés, chicken in aspic and deliciously decorative salads.

'Hmm.' Alys mumbled, her mouth full.

'You don't sound very thrilled by it,' Race said.

She swallowed the mouthful and dabbed her lips with a lace-edged napkin.

'I'm not. Parties are colossal bores – especially the big ones.'

'Familiarity breeds contempt!' There was a strange expression in his eyes. 'But actually I thought you were enjoying yourself.'

'Yes, tonight I am!' She popped a radish sculpted into the shape of a water lily into her mouth. 'I *have* enjoyed myself tonight.' Then, realizing what she had said, she held the napkin to her lips again in an effort to hide the flush of colour that was reddening her cheeks. 'Oh, that radish was hot!'

'Why don't you like parties then?' he pressed her.

'Oh – having to be polite to a lot of boring people. See – there's the Hon. Mrs Nancy Fielden looking now – she'll be after me in a minute. "How you've grown, Alys!" ' she mimicked. ' "And how was Switzerland?" They all say the same, like a gramophone record that's stuck. The only way to escape from them is to dance. And I'm not really that keen on dancing.'

'But you dance well.'

'Liar!' she giggled. 'Anyway, it's just that I can always think of so many things I'd rather be doing.'

'Like what?'

'Like driving. Oh, I do envy you!'

'Yes, I guess I am lucky, but then . . .' His eyes flickered around the room and to her surprise she thought she saw something like envy mirrored in them. Race had not seemed the type to be interested in material things. 'Do you want to see my car?' he asked suddenly.

Her own eyes widened. 'You have it here?'

'Not my racing car, though actually they did use to race in them. It's a Morgan – a three-wheeler. You'd really like to see it?'

'You bet!'

They slipped out. The night air stung slightly with the

last chill of winter and Alys wished she had brought a wrap. The cars of those who had driven themselves to the party had been parked in the broad drive behind the house and moonlight gleamed coldly on Bentleys, Mercedes, and a Lagonda. Race led the way to his Morgan, parked in the deep shadow of the outbuildings. Smart yellow, smoothly beautiful, it was in no way outclassed by the other vehicles. Alys touched the bonnet reverently.

'Oh, it's marvellous! Where did you get it?'

'I inherited it.' He paused, slightly awkward. 'It's a long story.'

'It was your father's?' she pressed him.

'No.' Another pause. 'I'd offer to take you for a spin but I'm not going to be able to get it out until the others move. There's no reverse gear on the three-wheeler. But, perhaps some other time . . . ?'

She nodded excitedly. 'Oh yes, I'd love that! Can I just sit in it though? Just for a minute?'

'You have to climb over the side.'

'Oh – I'll never do it in this skirt!'

'Come here, I'll lift you.'

He swung her up into his arms and she was amazed at how strong he was. So slim yet so strong! As she hung onto him she could feel the hard muscle in his shoulders through the immaculate cut of his dinner jacket and went weak inside again.

When he had deposited her on the seat he climbed in beside her. Above the rooftops the moon was a perfect crescent and the stars were sharp and bright, a million pinpricks in the velvet dark. The music of the orchestra wafted down to them on the slight breeze. She shivered and, noticing, he took off his jacket and placed it around her shoulders.

Happiness sang in her veins, as haunting and melodic as the music so that she felt somehow as if she was no longer real but living a romantic fairy tale. Race was talking, telling her about the car, about his ambitions, about what it was like to drive at breakneck speed with the wheel juddering in your hands and the metal straining and the huge wheels holding the track as you cornered, driving, not braking, through the bends, and she thought she could go on listening to his voice forever. But in spite of his jacket the cold night air was beginning to get to her and when she shivered again he noticed.

'Come on, we'd better go back inside before you catch pneumonia.' He climbed out and came around to help her out. She put her arms around his neck where the hair grew soft yet springy down to his collar line and jarred her cheek against his chin. It felt ever so faintly rough and a tiny corkscrew of excitement twisted inside her. It was as if there was something of the forbidden about that touch, innocent though it was, and it added a new dimension to the magic of the encounter.

He put her down and she was almost surprised to find the ground solid beneath her feet. For just a moment his arms went around her beneath his jacket holding her so close that she thought she could feel the beat of his heart before she realized it was her own, thundering against the wall of her chest. Then his lips brushed hers, lingered for a brief caressing moment and were gone.

'Come on, I don't want to get into your father's bad books for keeping you out here to catch your death of cold when you should be inside doing your duty. After all, it is your sister's engagement party.'

'Oh my goodness yes! Suppose they do the formal announcement and I'm not there! What's the time? Is the music still playing? Come on!'

Light spilled out of the house and onto the lawns in a golden flood. Hand in hand, laughing, they ran towards it.

*

'Who is this young man you are going out with?' Frances asked.

Alys, fixing her ear-bobs in the dressing table mirror,

looked up to see her mother standing behind her.

'Race Gratton.'

'I know that,' Frances said sharply. 'There's no need to be impertinent.'

'I wasn't being. I was just telling you . . .'

'I know his *name*. We would never have countenanced you going out with someone whose name we did not even know. In fact, if we were still in England he would have had to come to see Daddy and give a full account of himself before we allowed it. No – what Gratton is he, I'd like to know? I don't think we have come across any Grattons.'

'He comes from Yallourn.'

'Hmmm.' Frances' lips tightened a shade. 'The thing is, Alys, I'm not at all sure he is the sort of boy we want you associating with. There are some very fine families in Melbourne. The Davenports to name but one. Clarrie is keen on you I know. And one knows where one is with one's own sort of people.'

Alys swivelled on her stool, looking up at her mother pleadingly.

'Please give him a chance, Mummy! I'm sure you'd like him if you got to know him!'

Frances lifted her chin, holding her shoulders very stiff and still.

'I very much doubt if it will last long enough for that,' she said.

*

Race Gratton had been born twenty-two years earlier, the son of a miner who worked the huge brown coal deposits around Yallourn. His father, a hardworking but unambitious immigrant who had modified his almost unpronounceable surname to the more easily handled 'Gratton', had expected nothing but that his son should follow him in his occupation. But, from the moment he had pushed his first toy car, carved for him by his father from a block of wood, across the scrubbed wood floor of their tiny but spotless kitchen, Race was set firmly on a very different course.

He was just four when he went missing from home and after his frantic mother had alerted the neighbourhood he was eventually found in the town garage sitting on a pile of tyres and watching, fascinated, while Fred Holder, the proprietor, tinkered under the bonnet of a farmer's ute.

At twelve he paid his first visit to the Motodrome in Melbourne and there, excited to fever pitch as he watched the cars race crazily around the concrete bowl, he had recognized for the first time the ambition that was burning within him. This was what he wanted to do – drive a car with the skill and courage these drivers displayed, smell the oil, feel the surge of power that as a spectator he could only hear, see the dust spew up from the gravel track. He had told his father that night what he wanted and had been hurt but not discouraged when he was laughed down.

Someone else to whom he confessed his ambitions did not mock, however. Fred Holder had retired now, but his son Jeff who had taken the garage on had warmed to young Race's interest in all things mechanical. He encouraged Race, gave him jobs to do and taught him everything he knew. At Fifteen Race was driving anything on wheels – two, three or four. At sixteen he owned his first motorcycle, saved for from the money he earned working for Jeff. From there it was a short step to racing motorcycles at the Motodrome – mostly hybrids made up of parts Jeff was able to acquire and put together with his help.

Race's ambition was still to drive cars but they were becoming too fast for conditions in the death-defying Motodrome. After several drivers were killed car races there ceased, though the motorcycle races continued and Race was able to keep on riding. Then, when he was twenty years old, his big opportunity came. Midget car speedway was introduced at the Motodrome and Race

39

was right in there in his fast and noisy little car built around a motorcycle engine.

His daring and skill paid off; before long he was one of the heroes of the midget car racing. But still it was not enough for him. With the backing of Jeff Holder he acquired an Austin Nippy, working on it every spare minute, testing it, modifying it, fitting cannibalized parts, souping it up. Now at last it was almost ready – in time for the start of the spring and summer season. This year the Grand Prix was to be held at Bathurst, over the border in New South Wales, and Race was determined he would be there lined up with the others, the enthusiasts like himself in their hybrids, and the rich boys, backed by money that came from wool and farming, in their MGs.

Nothing, he promised himself, would stand in his way now. And no one, especially beautiful and rich young ladies, would ever ask 'Race who?' again.

*

Alys leaned back in the passenger seat of the Morgan lifting her chin and half closing her eyes as the wind whipped her hair across her face and blew breath back into her throat.

'Oh, this is heaven! Will it go faster, Race? Make it go faster!'

He glanced sideways at her, laughed, and pressed his foot down hard on the accelerator. The car surged forward on the arrow-straight road so that the trees which lined it sentry-like shot past in a green blur and the g-force seemed to stick her navel to her backbone.

They had been to the garage where Alys had met Jeff and seen for the first time Race's pride and joy, the Nippy. Once through the wooden doors and into the workshop the men had hardly seemed aware of her existence but she had not minded. She was happy to watch them work, though she had laughed at the sight of Race's legs, divorced from his body, poking knees bent from beneath

40

the car – and the smell of the petrol and oil had excited some deep chord within her that none of the ladylike pursuits she had been forced into had ever done. She had nosed around the garage ignoring the pin-ups on the walls and oblivious to the grease smudges that had somehow transferred themselves from her fingers to her nose and also the pocket of her dress. The language she could not ignore – a mixture of interesting technicalities and ripe adjectives she had never heard before but knew instinctively she would never dare to use. But not even that had bothered her. Being with Race would have been enough – being part of this fascinating world of his was better than she had ever dreamed possible.

Up ahead a pub at the roadside indicated the first outpost of another sprawling small town and Race slowed to pass through it.

'You've never told me how you got this beautiful motor,' Alys shouted above the roar of the engine.

'I told you – I inherited it.'

'Yes, but who from?'

'An old guy who used to come into the garage. He was a farmer – he had no use for it really – kept it locked up in a barn fifty weeks of the year. I used to go out and see him – well, it was to see the car really. He knew how I felt about it and he left it to me in his will. He had nobody else. Just a daughter who thought he was crazy. He told me once he didn't want to think of it just being used to take her kids to school and back. So I got it.'

'You must have been really surprised when he left it to you.'

'Yeah,' Race said but something in his tone jarred on her slightly.

'I'm learning to drive,' she said, changing the subject.

He looked along at her. 'Do you want to have a go then?'

'Oh not in your car! I couldn't! I might do something dreadful.'

He smiled at her. 'You wouldn't. I wouldn't let you. Go on, try it.'

41

She caught her lip between her teeth. 'Well, if you're really sure . . .'

He pulled the car in to the side of the road, climbed out and went around to the passenger side.

'Move over then.'

She did, trembling with nervous excitement, and under his guidance drove the car along the road. At first, she was horribly conscious of the responsibility then she began to relax and enjoy herself, thrilling to the surge of power and the heady feeling of being in control of this handsome, monstrous machine.

'That was very good,' Race said when she eventually pulled in on his instructions. 'You're a natural. You just need proper teaching. You have to love the car, understand?'

'Oh, I do!'

'But you have to treat it like you love it!' He put his arm along the back of the seat catching her shoulder and giving it a little squeeze. 'Don't look so worried! You'll soon get the feel of it.'

Her eyes were shining. 'You mean I can try again?'

He nodded. 'Yes. As long as you do what I say and not what somebody else tells you.'

'You teach me then!' she said boldly.

'All right.' He caught her eye and grinned. 'You're sure there's nothing else I can teach you while I'm at it?'

Sharp excitement corkscrewed inside her. It reminded her of the g-force she had experienced when he had accelerated the car. She pursed her lips and looked at him primly under the long lashes. 'What can you mean?'

He laughed and pulled her towards him. 'One of these days, Miss Peterson, you will find out. For now, I think I'll have to make do with this!'

She felt his breath warm and fluid against her wind-cooled cheek. When he kissed her, his hand cupping her breast beneath her blouse through the thin material of her brassiere, she thought that wonderful as driving and being driven fast was, this was perhaps better.

*

It was hot and noisy in the Motodrome. The sun, high overhead, poured down into the concrete bowl and reflected back from it in waves. The crowds, vying for the best view of the circuit, gave off a heat of their own and the smell of sweat mingled with engine fumes and the pungent whiff of oil. Their cheers and shouts of encouragement were drowned out by the screaming of the motorcycle engines which powered the midget cars, but though their throats were dry from the clouds of dust that spewed from the track they still cheered, borne along on the thrills and spills.

Alys, squeezed between a fat man in a sweat-stained shirt and a sunbronzed rouseabout, cheered with them. She guessed they thought it was odd – a girl on her own at the Motodrome. But she did not mind. She felt special – and very proud. That's my boyfriend down there, she longed to tell them. But of course she said nothing, just went on cheering.

A car veered suddenly and the crowd gasped as it skewed across the track, clipping the rear of another and sending it broadside into the barrier. Alys screamed involuntarily, clapping her hands across her mouth. Race! Look out! But it was all right. He was past the danger, swerving and manoeuvring with all the skill that was making him a leading driver, and her frantic heart, beating so hard that the echoes of it throbbed in her throat, swelled again with pride.

Was he going to win? Come on, Race! You can do it! Come on – come on – yes! He was over the line and she was leaping up and down, unable to contain her excitement.

And then he was out of the car and looking up, looking for her, one face in the crowd. He could not see her of course, she knew that. But as he clasped his hands high above his head, acknowledging victory, she felt for all the world as if the gesture was just for her.

43

*

Afterwards, though, when he drove her home, he was unusually subdued.

'I thought you'd be high for hours after winning like that,' she said. 'What's wrong?'

'Nothing.' But the lightness of his tone was false and she knew it.

'There is. You can't fool me,' she said.

He sighed, holding onto the steering wheel and shifting himself on the fat leather seat. 'All right, if you really want to know. It looks as if I won't be driving in the Grand Prix after all.'

Her eyes widened. 'But why, Race?'

'The money has run out. I heard today. I didn't want to think about it before I drove but now the adrenalin has stopped flowing there's no way I cannot think about it.'

She gave her head a little shake. 'Race, I don't understand.'

'Jeff is going bust. That's it in a nutshell!' He looked along at her, smiling wanly. 'He's too soft, that's his trouble. Too many people owe him money and now his creditors are going to pull the rug out from under him. That not only means I shall be out of a job, it also means there's no money to do what still needs doing to the car. So goodbye Grand Prix – for this year anyway – maybe forever if I can't find someone else to back me.'

She chewed on her lip for a moment. 'Race – ask Daddy!' He half turned towards her; in the fading light his profile was very strong and it caught at that jagged nerve deep inside her. 'Ask Daddy to back you!' she said.

'Oh, I don't think I could do that . . .' But there was a note of uncertainty and perhaps a glimmer of hope in his voice.

'Of course you could! He's not an ogre. He owns a racehorse – why not a racing car?' She reached out, covering his hand on the steering wheel with her own. The

44

tendons felt taut and stretched beneath her fingers. 'Look – I'll come with you. We'll ask him together.'

'No!' he said harshly. 'I've got to do this myself.'

'All right, if that's what you want. But do it, Race. You can't give up now. I won't let you!'

*

Alys pushed the meat around her plate with her fork. It was saddle of new season's lamb, pink and succulent enough to melt in the mouth, but tonight she had no appetite. She speared a pea, popped it into her mouth and looked up, wondering if perhaps this was the right moment to say what she had to say.

At the head of the table Daniel Peterson was eating heartily, a large white damask napkin tucked into the neck of his waistcoat, while at the opposite end Frances was helping herself to more baby carrots from one of the bone china tureens. Beverley, across the table from Alys, appeared to be in a day dream – planning her wedding again, no doubt.

Alys swallowed the pea and took a deep breath.

'Has Race been to see you, Daddy?'

'Race? Hmm – no.' Daniel's reply was short because his mouth was full but even without turning to look at her Alys was aware of the frost that emanated from Frances at just the mention of his name.

'Why should Race want to see your father?' she demanded.

'Because I suggested he should.' Alys laid down her fork. 'Daddy – Race is desperate for somebody to back him. He's been setting everything on driving in the Grand Prix and now it's all gone wrong. He still has work to do on his car and the garage he's involved with is going bankrupt.'

Daniel Peterson washed his meat and vegetables down with a great gulp of wine. 'And what do you expect me to do about it?' he asked.

'I thought maybe you . . .'

'So that's it!' Frances said sharply. They all turned to look at her. 'I knew there had to be a reason behind that young man's behaviour and now we know what it is. He's simply after your father's money, Alys.'

'That's a ridiculous thing to say!' Alys retorted. 'Please, Daddy, it isn't like that at all! It was my idea, not Race's.'

'And I suppose it was your idea that he came here in the first place.' Frances' lips were tight, her eyes cold.

'No, of course not. I didn't meet him until the party. He was a guest of Louis' . . .'

'Hardly!'

'He was! He said . . .'

'It's true he knew Louis vaguely but he would never have been invited if he hadn't pestered Louis and wormed his way in. It's true, Alys, whether you like it or not. Tell her, Beverley.'

Bev had come out of her dream world. She bit her lip uncomfortably.

'What I say is true, isn't it?' Frances persisted. Bev nodded slowly. 'You see?' Frances trumpeted. 'The boy is nothing but a scrounger. And now we've found out what he's after. Money to indulge his hobby.'

'You've got it all wrong!' Alys protested. 'He's not playing at it. He is a really good driver.'

'If he is, no doubt he will find someone else willing to put their money behind him, but after the way he has tried to take advantage of you, it certainly won't be us.' Frances said coldly. 'Now, let's close this unpalatable subject and enjoy our meal, shall we?'

'Daddy . . . ?' Alys appealed.

But Daniel only helped himself to more potatoes.

'It sounds to me as though your mother has a point,' he said, and Alys realized it would be useless to argue just now.

She scraped back her chair and got up. 'I think you are all being jolly unfair!' she said, tears of anger stinging her eyes. But even then she did not dare to voice the thought that was edging in at the corners of her mind.

In the world of business Daniel might be a driving force and an influence to be reckoned with. Here at home he was as much in the sway of the redoubtable Frances as everyone else.

*

Alys, terrified Race might call at her father's office next day and walk straight into a frosty reception, managed to put a call through to him at the garage.

'I'm really sorry. I've put my foot in it now and spoiled everything,' she explained.

For the first time ever Race snapped at her.

'Why didn't you do what I said and leave it to me?'

She glanced around to make sure no one was in earshot.

'I was afraid you wouldn't ask, and I thought that Daddy . . .'

'I know. You thought you could wind him around your little finger like you do everyone else.' He sighed. 'Ah well, it's too late to worry about it now. I've got the afternoon free. Shall we go out somewhere?'

Alys thought briefly of her mother's freezing disapproval, weighed it against the pleasure of being with Race, and made up her mind.

'I'd love to. Will you pick me up?'

'Yes. About half past two.'

'All right. I'll be looking out for you so that you don't have to face Mummy.'

It was a perfect afternoon with a brisk breeze blowing puffs of white cloud across the sky, blue as morning glories, and whipping up matching white frills on the sea. In St George's Road the English trees provided patches of shade but the sun shone bright and harsh on the houses, bouncing off roofs and stuccoed white walls with a brilliance that was hurtful to the eyes.

'Where are we going?' Alys asked as Race turned the Morgan down over the hill and the vista of Melbourne, roofs and spires, patches of green amid the grey, spread out beneath them.

He executed a racing change. 'I had thought of Phillip Island – to see the fairy penguins and the seals.'

'Oh yes, they're sweet . . .' She broke off. 'Wait a minute – you're the crafty one, aren't you? The penguins don't parade until dusk, on their way back to their burrows in the sand dunes after a hard day's fishing. That's just an excuse. You want to go to Phillip Island because of the race track!'

He laughed. 'No, honestly, I hadn't given it a thought. Though I have to admit it's because of the race track that I know about Phillip Island. People from my background don't have as much time to go out looking at wild life as you do.'

There was a tiny, awkward silence. It was the first time he had mentioned the difference in their lifestyles.

'On the other hand,' Race said, 'we could just go up to the Dandenongs. But wherever it is, we'd better make the most of it. This could be the last time for outings in the Morgan.' She turned to look at him in alarm and he gave an elaborate shrug. 'It's the one asset I've got. If I can't get the money from anywhere else, I shall have to sell the Morgan.'

'Oh Race, you can't do that!' she protested.

'Don't make it harder for me. I don't want to, of course. But I'm damned determined to get into Grand Prix racing and if the only way I can do it is to sell the Morgan, then the Morgan has to go.'

His tone frightened her. Yes, she had known he was determined but never before had he struck her as ruthless. If he could get rid of the Morgan which he loved so much then he would sweep aside any obstacle which he found in his way. Admirable, but also a little scary.

'Anyway, let's not talk about it now. Why spoil a lovely afternoon? And let's make it the Dandenongs, shall we?' he said.

They left Melbourne heading east and with the wind in

her hair Alys felt herself relaxing. The country, open and green, not yet scorched to match the colour of the sandy earth, quickly became rolling hills fringed with forests. Race turned the Morgan into a narrow track where the sun, filtering through the high and spidery branches of the trees, made sparkling patterns of heat on the dusty ground. On and on it went, winding now and then around a knoll of higher ground, rising and dipping, then suddenly opening out to reveal a reserve where the bush, virgin in appearance, surrounded a small clear water lake. Race pulled the Morgan off the track onto a patch of scrub and turned off the engine.

'Who wants to go all the way to Phillip Island when it's nice so close to home?' He put his arm around her, his touch light on her warm skin. 'Anyway, it's you I want to see, not a penguin, fairy or otherwise.'

Warmth trickled through her veins, but she smiled at him teasingly, pulled away and clambered nimbly over the side of the Morgan.

'Come on, I'm going to paddle!'

The brush grew thickly around the lake, covering the shingly soil. She ran through it feeling it tug at her skirt and whip her bare legs and not caring. At the water's edge she kicked off her sandals and plunged in, wading out until it reached her knees and though she bunched up her skirt with her hands the hem hung down into the water at the back. Beneath her feet she felt the pebble floor of the lake and she wiggled her toes against the shifting surface, laughing and looking around for Race who was running through the bush after her.

'Come on in!' she called. 'It's lovely!'

He was wearing shorts and he paused only to kick off his shoes before plunging into the water.

'Come on!' she urged, then as he splashed towards her, she backed away again.

'Look out!' he warned.

'Why?' She was still laughing as her foot touched the edge of a trough where the bed of the lake fell away in a deep shelf. The loose pebbles crumbled beneath her and she went under, water flooding into her mouth, wide open with surprise, and billowing her skirt up around her. A moment later, she surfaced, gasping and coughing.

'Are you all right?' Race was swimming towards her.

She trod water unable to speak for a moment then as she got her breath she swam a couple of strokes back onto the shelf and stood up. Her dress clung to every curve and hollow of her body and water streamed out of her hair and ran in rivulets down her back. She shook her head and rubbed her eyes with the back of her hand.

'Oh jeepers, what a shock!'

Race was beside her, half concerned, half amused.

'I thought you said you were going for a paddle, not a swim!'

'Beast! How can you joke . . . !' She hit out at him and almost lost her balance again. He caught her by the arms and pulled her towards him.

'What are you trying to do – drown us?'

'No – I'm . . .' But his lips were too close and she broke off. His arms slid around her, holding her there, then as their bodies touched with nothing but the thin clinging wet layers between she felt a tremble run through the length of him and an answering thrill echoed deep within her own body. She stood quite still while he kissed her, his lips warm after the coldness of the lake water, though the sensations she was experiencing made her want to cling to him as closely as the sodden clothing. His hands moved from her back, tracing the curve of hips and thighs as a blind man might and everywhere his hands touched came to tingling, singing life. Her lips responded first, moving beneath his and parting slightly, then her hands, tracing the lines of his back which felt clean and hard beneath the wet cotton. Their hands reached hip level simultaneously and he pressed her to him. The sizzling desire exploded then and she melted, the softness of her body moulding to the hard strength of his.

Their lips became hungrier now, kissing not only each

other's mouths but any bit of flesh they could find and Alys felt the breath catching in her throat as the water had done a few minutes ago. Half panicking, she twisted her head and her breath came out with a sobbing sigh.

Without speaking Race bent to slip his arm beneath her knees and scoop her up. Her arms went around his neck and for a moment he stood quite still, kissing her again before wading towards the shore with her. On the bank he lowered her gently to the ground, sinking down beside her.

Beneath the pressure of his lips and body she lay slowly back into the scratchy bush. It gave to admit them then closed around them once more. It seemed that already they were not two but one, glued together by their soaking clothes.

'Oh Alys!' It sounded like a moan of pain, and strangely it injected a note of harsh reality.

'Race – no, we mustn't! Stop it, please . . .'

'Just a little, Alys. I won't hurt you. It'll be all right . . .'

'No! Mummy would kill me if she knew . . .'

He rolled away from her a little though their heads were still close.

'I don't suppose they'd let us get engaged, would they?' he said.

'Umm?' She had heard what he said, but thought she must have imagined it.

'Engaged – married. Do you think they'd let us? Oh, I want you, Alys!'

She could not answer. He wanted to marry her. She had ruined everything, spoiled his chances of Daddy backing him and still he wanted to marry her. She felt herself melting, relaxing beneath him and even when the pain came, so sharp that it made her tense and arch her body and dig into his back with her nails, she did not care. She loved Race, loved him, loved him – and he loved her. He must do!

Afterwards she lay with her eyes half closed looking at the clear blue sky above the gently waving tracery of brush.

The pain still throbbed between her legs, dulled now to a burning sensation. Race lay beside her but not touching her and a tiny finger of fear pierced her through. She turned her head so that she could see him.

'Race, did you mean what you said about us getting married?'

He did not answer. 'Race?' she said again.

He shifted a little impatiently.

'Of course I want you, Alys. And getting engaged seemed the only way, But . . .'

She stiffened. 'But what?'

'It's not that easy, is it? This is real life, not a fairy story. To begin with I don't suppose your parents would agree to it.'

She rolled towards him, frightened suddenly and wanting the comfort of his nearness.

'I don't care what they say! Oh, they would probably disown me, it's true. They already said as much, because they've got this terrible idea that you are only using me to get at Daddy's money. But they can't keep us apart if we love each other.'

'Christ, Alys, if they cut you off what the hell do you think we would live on? I can't keep myself, let alone a wife.'

'I'd live anywhere with you, Race, I'd do anything . . .'

He broke away from her, sitting up abruptly.

'You don't know what you're talking about Alys. You've always had everything you wanted. You haven't got a clue what it's like to have nothing.'

'Race!' She sat up too. 'Don't you understand? I've had money and possessions all my life and none of them has made me half as happy as I am with you. The way we feel is something money can't buy.'

He reached for a blade of springy grass, snapping it between his fingers and staring straight ahead of him.

'Race, you do feel the same way I do, don't you?' she said. A light breeze whispered through the brush and as it touched her wet back she shivered. 'You do love me, don't you?'

'Of course I do!' But his tone was impatient and he made no move to touch her. Suddenly, she was painfully aware that he had never said the magic words she so desperately wanted to hear. She leaned towards him urgently.

'Say it, Race, please!'

'Say what?'

'That you love me.'

There was an awkward pause. He threw the twisted grass away. 'I love you.' But it was stilted, cold. She looked at him, hurt, and he said apologetically, 'I've never said that to anyone before.'

Oh, she wanted to believe him, wanted to believe he loved her and was embarrassed to say so. But she didn't know anything any more. Tears stung her eyes and she turned away, pressing her hands to her mouth. After a moment she felt his arm around her shoulder.

'Alys, I'm sorry. It's just – it's all such a bloody mess, isn't it?'

'Is it?' she said through her fingers.

'Yes, I didn't mean to hurt you, honestly . . .'

She jerked her head up, blinking the tears away.

'That's all right then isn't it? Race . . . I think perhaps we ought to be going home.'

'Yes,' he said.

They walked back to the car in silence and Alys could feel the great pool of sadness deep inside because something that should have been special had somehow gone wrong and there was no way that she could ever turn it around and make it different.

*

Alys raised her head from the basin, wiping the bile off her lips with the back of her hand. As she straightened she caught sight of her reflection and was shocked by it – cheeks drained of colour, hair lacking its usual bright lustre and great dark smudges beneath her eyes. Hardly

53

surprising really – in addition to the nausea and sickness she had scarcely slept for the last week, not since she had realized that her period had not come. At first she had lain awake willing herself to feel the first niggling ache which usually warned of its onset, then as the days went by her brain had begun chasing in great terrifying circles. But still her period, never usually late, had not come. When the nausea had first begun she had told herself it was because she was so worried, but as it continued she was unable to deceive herself any longer.

Pregnant. The very word frightened her. There was such an awful finality to it, like the clanging of a dungeon door, shutting out light and air and leaving her in a morass of terrifying darkness.

Alys ran some warm water into the basin and washed her face, trying to will the sickness to go away. Yesterday it had not. It had persisted all day. And when she felt so dreadul there was no way she could even begin to think what she had to do. Every ounce of concentration had to be used up in pretending that everything was quite normal. But it could not go on like this. It was early days yet, because her period was usually so regular and because of the sickness she had discovered the truth much sooner than she might otherwise have done. But that did not alter the facts. Sometime, somehow she was going to have to tell someone.

The thought sent a fresh pang of nausea through her and she bent over the basin retching again. Oh God, it was horrible, horrible! Just like a nightmare. And she was so terrifyingly alone. If she had been able to see Race and tell him it would not have been so bad. But she had not seen Race since she had been certain. He had sold the Morgan now so he had no transport to get over from Yallourn to Melbourne and in any case he was working every spare moment on his racing car to get it ready for the Grand Prix.

And when she did tell him – what then? Another shudder ran through Alys as she remembered what Race had said that day in the Dandenongs – the day it had happened. Suppose he still reiterated that he could not afford to support a wife? Worse – suppose he was simply using that as an excuse because he did not want her for his wife? The niggling fear was constantly there now at the back of her mind that perhaps there had been some truth in what Mummy had said – he had only used her as a way of getting at Daddy's money. Unwillingly, Alys found herself remembering how reluctant Race had been to talk about how he had come by the Morgan. Could it be that he had cultivated its owner in the same way, 'wormed his way in' as Mummy had put it so that it was bequeathed to him in the old man's will? If so and if the same was true for her, then . . .

At this point Alys always tried to pull her train of thought up short because to let it go on led her to something quite unthinkable. That Race had not only used her for her money but for other reasons too. Why had he mentioned marriage that day by the lake if it seemed so truly impossible to him? Because he had momentarily fooled himself into believing it could work? Or because . . .

A tap at the bathroom door interrupted her reverie.

'Alys? Are you all right in there?'

She grabbed a towel, holding it to her mouth for a moment, then gulping deep breaths of air into her lungs.

'Yes. I'm fine,' she called back.

There was a little silence and she thought that Mummy had gone away and the awkward moment had passed. Then Frances tapped once more.

'Open the door, Alys.'

'No – I'm all right, really.'

'Do as I say. Now!'

Alys ran a quick, tidying hand through her hair. She could not disobey. There was no point. Frances would simply stand there and knock until she got her way. Alys turned the key and stepped away from the door, turning her back and bending to busy herself arranging the towel on its rail. The door opened and Frances came in.

'What have you been doing in here all this time?' she asked suspiciously. Alys shrugged without turning round. 'What do people usually do in bathrooms?'

For once Frances did not chide her daughter for impertinence.

'That towel is perfectly tidy, Alys. You may turn around and look at me. I'm not Medusa. I won't turn you into stone, you know.'

Slowly Alys turned. Though she did not raise her eyes she was aware of her mother's shocked expression as she took in Alys' ravaged face. 'For heaven's sake, child, what is the matter with you?' she demanded. Alys did not answer. She could think of nothing to say. 'The way you look anyone would think you were . . .' Frances broke off, catching herself as the full meaning of what she had been about to say came home to her. 'Alys,' she said more quietly, 'you're not pregnant, are you?'

Still Alys could not reply. It was not only her tongue which seemed frozen but the whole of her thought processes. She stood with her arms hugging herself as if to protect that tiny life which she wanted so little.

'My God!' Frances said. 'You are pregnant, aren't you!' She stepped forward, involuntarily bringing her palm up to strike Alys a swingeing blow on the cheek. 'You dirty little whore!'

Alys' head jerked up, her eyes wide and staring. She lifted a hand, pressing her fingers to her stinging face, and as she did so the nausea stirred again. The bile rose, bitter and burning in her throat, and she dived past her shocked mother to reach the basin.

*

Alys jammed the gearstick of the Morris into top and pressed her foot hard down on the accelerator. Ahead of and behind her the road was ribbon straight and open – any other traffic could be seen miles away – but Alys kept checking her mirror nervously all the same, half expecting to see a police car following and closing in on her. But mile after mile of the road came and she began to relax a little.

Perhaps she – and the Morris – had not been missed yet. And even when they were there was no reason to suppose Daddy would set the police on to her. They did not know where she was going, after all. They would probably simply think she had decided to go out for a drive. It would never occur to them that she had been out on the highway since long before dawn, heading as fast as the car would take her towards Bathurst and the Mount Panorama motor racing circuit.

Steadying the wheel with one hand Alys glanced at her watch. It would take her another two or three hours nonstop motoring yet to reach Bathurst. Would she make it in time? She did not know. She was not even sure when the Grand Prix was due to begin. But even if she did not make the start at least she would be there some time today. The important thing was to see Race. And she did not intend to tell him until afterwards, anyway. He did not want something like that on his mind when he was driving.

What was he going to say? she wondered anxiously. But whatever it was, even if he disowned her, she had to tell him and tell him soon, otherwise matters would be out of her hands and her chance gone.

She pushed the accelerator even harder into the floor and as the car surged forwards to its maximum speed she seemed once more to hear her mother's voice in the roar of the tyres on the road. 'We have decided, Alys, the best thing to be done with you.'

She had come to see Alys in her room; since admitting the truth Alys had scarcely left it. Frances had stood with her back to the window looking at her daughter who sprawled miserably on the bed. 'We are going to send you to Darwin.'

Darwin! The top end of the continent with the whole dead centre between her and Race. Alys had jerked up, bringing her cushion with her, to gaze at her mother with horror-filled eyes.

'Your father and I have decided it's the best thing. I've been in touch with Sylvia and James Crawford and asked if they would be willing to have you until it is all over and then . . .'

'You've told Aunt Sylvia about me?' Alys had interrupted, shocked.

Frances had given a tight little laugh. 'My dear girl, if we don't get you to Darwin and out of the way, before very much longer everyone will know. No, I've spoken to Sylvia, told her of the predicament we are in and begged for her help. As you might expect, she has been marvellous. You are to go there now – next week. I shall tell people that you are travelling. Sylvia has promised to arrange for the adoption – in her position as organiser for the Red Cross it's something she knows all about – and you will be able to come home again in a year or so and no one here will be any the wiser.'

Alys had hugged her pillow.

'Adoption?' she'd repeated. 'You mean you want me to give my baby up?'

Frances' lips had tightened. 'What other choice do you have? You don't seem to realize the position you are in, Alys – a young girl, unmarried, having an illegitimate baby. The practical considerations are enormous, and leaving those aside, think of the shame of it!'

The shame, Oh yes, she had hardly been able to avoid thinking of that, what with Daddy not wanting to look at her and Mummy talking about 'letting herself down' and Beverley in floods of tears saying she had ruined the wedding and she, Beverley, would never be able to face any of her friends – or Louis' family – ever again.

'No, by far the best thing is for you to go to Darwin – right away,' Frances had said firmly.

'And what about Race?' Alys had asked.

'Him!' Frances snorted. 'The least said about him the better!' Then, as she saw Alys' face crumple, she sat down on the bed beside her, taking her hand in a way which oddly Alys found more embarrassing than comforting.

58

'Forget him, Alys. See the unhappiness he has caused you. Just accept that I know what is best and everything will be all right.'

Alys had said nothing. She knew from past experience it was useless to argue with her mother who, as usual, had come up with a solution which, looked at logically, was as foolproof as any could be in the circumstances.

Except that it did not take account of her feelings. It did not take account of the terrible way her heart dipped at the thought, even now, of giving up her baby. And it took no account of Race at all.

He had to be given the chance to have some say in the matter, Alys decided. After all he was the father. And oh – it gave her the excuse to see him again if nothing else.

The thought spurred her on now and keeping her foot flat to the boards she raced the Morris on towards Bathurst.

*

Mount Panorama, Bathurst, had been a New South Wales beauty spot long before motor cars had been invented let alone raced, but now the scenic driveway which skirted it had become a road racing circuit, host for the first time ever to the Australian Grand Prix. The rises, shaded through every imaginable hue from palest yellowy green to the deep rolling turquoise of the ocean, echoed to the sound of engines revving and tyres squealing and the kookaburras had a new range of sounds to imitate as they scornfully watched proceedings from the branches of the gums. At the highest point of the rise, some 800 feet, the air was normally thin and clear; today it was weighed down with the smell of petrol and oil, scorched rubber and hot metal.

In the area set aside for the pits the cars had pride of place and the men who had brought them crawled around them like worshippers doing homage, tinkering with an engine to bring it to the finest last minute tune, changing a wheel, checking an axle, revving a motor. They looked hot and dirty in their overalls and the smell of grease emanated from them. Alys picked her way over discarded spare wheels and various tools lying on the road and scanned the cars and the waiting trailers looking for Race. He was nowhere to be seen. One or two men looked at her curiously but no one asked who she was and she guessed rightly that they were all too preoccupied to be interested in anyone else, even a lone woman.

Suddenly a shout claimed her attention and looking around she saw Jeff Holder waving to her. Enormously relieved she picked her way over to him. 'Where's Race?'

Jeff rubbed his face with an oily hand and indicated towards the track. 'Gone for a practice lap. He won't be long. What are you doing here?'

'I had to see him.'

Jeff grinned. 'Yeah, well, this is his big day and no mistake. He's worked and sweated to get this far. You don't know what he's given up to be here today.' His last words were drowned out by the roar of an engine and Jeff gesticulated wildly. 'Here he is! Hey, Race, look who's here?'

Race steered the Nippy in. He was bareheaded and grinning from ear to ear, a bright turquoise scarf knotted around his neck streamed out behind and there were already grease stains on his clean white overalls. His face, too, was dirty – how dirty Alys did not realize until he removed his goggles and revealed two clean circles in the midst of the dirt.

'That was great, Jeff . . .' He broke off, his face lighting up still more as he saw her. 'Alys! I never expected . . .'

'Race.' Suddenly, foolishly, she was close to tears. Oh, she had wanted to see him so badly and now . . . She caught her lip between her teeth, eyes brimming.

'Alys!' His delight changed to alarm. 'What's the matter? Hey, love . . .'

With a massive effort she gulped back the tears, forced her lips to smile. 'Nothing's the matter. I'm just pleased to see you, that's all. It's been so long.'

'Christ, don't I know it!' He levered himself up and climbed out. 'She's doing just fine,' he said to Jeff. 'Just needs the fuel topping up. Can you do it while I have a breather – and a word with Alys?'

Jeff pulled a knowing face. 'Oh yeah, go on with you! Don't go distracting him too much though will you?' he warned Alys.

'Want a drink, love?' Race asked her. She nodded and he went on, 'It's only cold tea now before the race, but afterwards – well, it could be champagne, who knows?'

'You bet!' She could not trust herself to say more. One part of her wished she had left seeking him out until it was all over, but it was such a huge relief just to be with him that she did not think she could have waited another hour.

He put his arm around her guiding her across to a patch of scrubby grass where a fallen tree formed a makeshift seat. 'Here, sit down.' He poured some cold tea from a thermos into a mug and gave it to her. She drank thirstily and when she lowered the mug she saw that he was looking at her. 'What the hell is wrong, Alys?'

'Nothing, I told you.'

'Don't give me that shit.' Here on the track his language had degenerated to the kind she had heard him and Jeff use at the garage. 'You look terrible. What the hell have you been up to?'

'Nothing, honestly. You don't want to worry about me.'

'Not much! You look as though you haven't slept for a week. What is it? Have your parents been on at you?'

'Yes, that's it. I'll tell you afterwards.'

'You'll bloody well tell me now – or I swear I won't get into that car!'

'Oh Race . . .' She was trembling now, torn with indecision. 'I can't! I didn't mean to . . .'

'What for Christ's sake?'

And suddenly she could keep it back no longer. 'I'm going to have a baby.'

She saw his face change, saw him turn white beneath the dirt. 'Christ!'

The tears were in her eyes again; angrily she blinked them away. 'I'm sorry, Race. I didn't mean to tell you now, honestly.'

He was staring into space, not saying anything. She caught at his arm. 'Look, you don't have to worry. It'll all be taken care of. I'm being sent to Darwin and that will be the end of it but I just wanted you to know . . .'

'I should bloody well think so too!' He turned to her – she had never seen him so angry. 'Look, I can't think about it now, Alys. I've got to concentrate on this race. But afterwards we'll sort something out. OK?'

She was numb, too numbed to feel or think. The tears were running unchecked down her face now and she could only nod.

'Why the hell didn't you tell me before?' he demanded. 'Well, never mind that now. Just make sure you're here when I finish.'

'Yes, Race.'

'I've got to go now – it's nearly time. But everything will be all right, you'll see.' He squeezed her hand, kissed her and tasted the salt of her tears. 'I love you, Alys.'

'And I love you.'

'See you.'

'Yes.'

She watched him walking back to where Jeff was still fiddling with the Nippy and it felt like a load had been lifted off her shoulders.

Oh, there would be problems God alone knew. They had not gone away. But Race loved her. He had not been using her. The knowledge was so wonderful that she believed for a few glorious moments that now, at last, she could face anything.

*

The race was half over. From the vantage point Jeff had selected for her, Alys had watched the cars hurtling past along the mile-long straight he had told her was called

62

'Conrod' and she had seen more than one come to grief – an engine exploding here, a tyre bursting there to send the car veering crazily off course, off the road and onto the surrounding waste land. But Race was still there, in and vying with the pack, though the clear leader was the bare headed Englishman, Peter Whitehead, in his B-type ERA. He was going to win, no doubt about it, his car was so far superior to anything else on the track, but if Race could only stay with the others and acquit himself well then perhaps at least someone would see his potential and be prepared to give him the backing he so desperately needed.

Watching the cars pass in an endless roar, Alys felt the adrenalin pumping wildly through her veins. It was like being on a knife edge, she thought, minute after long minute, time suspended to mean nothing but how often the car she was watching for passed by below her. How many times had she seen the turquoise scarf flying in the slipstream as the Nippy gathered speed along the straight? She had lost count. But he should be past again at any moment now. There was the ERA, there the bunch of MGs, now . . .

The first faint buzz of alarm made her muscles tauten. She craned forward straining her eyes down the straight. Was that him? Yes! – No! No, it wasn't. Oh Lord, had something gone wrong? If he had had to pull in for some reason he would never make it up again.

She waited, anxiety mounting. The ERA flashed past again and the MGs. Her fingers were in her mouth now, her teeth tearing at the skin around her nails. One quick began to bleed but she did not even notice. Where was he?

Then, faintly borne on the breeze, just audible above the roar of the cars she heard what sounded like the jangle of an ambulance bell and amongst the watching crowd she heard the first excited murmurs. A crash. Someone had crashed. Her body convulsed again as she strained forward. Race, where are you? Yet again the ERA roared past and she made up her mind. She could not stay here any longer waiting. She had to find out.

She began to run on legs that trembled, running while her breath came in harsh gasps and her heart, pounding in her throat, made her feel sick. As she ran she kept her eyes on the track, still watching, still hoping, though somehow she knew it was in vain.

When she reached the pits there was no sign of them. No Race. No Jeff. No Nippy. Wildly she looked around, grabbing the arm of a surprised marshall and begging for information.

'Race Gratton?' She saw his face darken. 'He's out of it. Ran out of road up on Skyline.'

'Oh God!' Her hand was clapped to her mouth, the track seemed to spin around her. 'Where is he?'

'He'll have been taken off to hospital by now. He was hurt pretty bad.'

She grabbed his arm. 'Oh please, could somebody take me? Please . . .'

He shook her off. 'Look-ee here young lady, we're all pretty busy. There's a race going on here.'

'Please!' She was half hysterical before she remembered her own car. 'Where is the hospital? At least tell me that!'

A touch on her arm, a quiet voice beside her. 'Calm down, love. You're in no fit state to drive. There's enough of us here looking after my pal's car. I'll take you.'

She didn't know him, never seen him before, but he was like an angel of mercy now. 'Oh thank you, thank you!' she wept.

'Don't thank me yet. We may be too late,' he returned grimly.

*

They were too late. By the time they reached the hospital Race was dead. As the marshall had said he had crashed on the terrifying drop called Skyline where the road falls away so steeply that the skyline is all the driver sees as he goes over it. Race had driven over it and into a patch of oil spilled by another car. He had spun off the road. The

Nippy was shattered – and so was his body. He had been barely alive when they got him out and into the ambulance but he had died before reaching hospital. Jeff said he had spoken one last word on his dying breath.

Alys.

*

They sent her to Darwin and she no longer cared. If Race was dead it did not matter to her where she was. Guilt added to her grief – she should not have told him about the baby before the race. Perhaps it had made no difference but she would never know that now. She would go to her grave wondering if perhaps his concentration had been that little bit less than it should have been and, as he went over Skyline, he had had things other than driving on his mind.

Only one hope was left to her – that perhaps when the baby was born she could find a way to keep it. For she could never give up Race's baby, she knew that now.

Awash in her grief she scarcely noticed one day that the ache that never left her had shifted a little, localized, become physical. It was only when it sharpened to a tearing agony that she became alarmed, and by then it was too late.

One sweltering summer night the legacy that Race had left her slipped away, borne on a tide of scarlet pain, and Alys knew that the decision had been taken out of her hands.

Chapter Three

Tara came through the connecting door from the en suite bathroom into the bedroom, crossed to the dressing table and perched herself on the low stool in front of it drawing a gilt-backed brush through her curls, tangled and damp from the steam of the bath.

In the mirror the room was reflected – a flamboyant room, as flamboyant as Red himself. For all that Tara had shared it with him for the past five years there was not a single concession to her femininity in its decor. The walls were deep red, covered in heavy flocked wallpaper, the curtains rich matching velvet. The scroll lacework at the head and foot of the kingsized bed was gold plated, the sheets were black silk and the gold coloured wall to wall carpet echoed the scroll design. Only Tara's brush, powder bowl and perfume spray on the dressing table and her scarlet silk negligée laid out on the bed gave any indication that she, too, slept, rose and made love in this room.

Red was already in bed lying half propped up against the pillows, arms folded behind his head as he watched her complete her toilet.

Five years had changed him hardly at all. His face was still as hard and craggy, his body as firm and muscular without so much as a hint of a paunch. For a man who had made his money out of almost every degrading vice known to humanity he looked remarkably healthy. But Red was a keepfit fanatic and had been for twenty years. Each day he spent at least two hours swimming or running, weight training or shadow boxing and the persistence had paid off.

It was Tara who was barely recognizable as the pathetic child of the slums who had put on her powder, paint and too-tight sweater to play at being grown up. The beauty that had promised at fourteen had been more than fulfilled – good food had filled out the skinny frame to womanly curves, regular exercise in Red's gymnasium had ensured she remained firm and supple, and with time and money to spend Tara had acquired the clothes and the trappings of glamour to complement the charms with which nature had endowed her. Yet despite all she had, Tara still experienced pangs of restless discontent just as she had in the days when she had shared two sordid rooms in Darlo with Maggie, and her ambition to become a professional entertainer was as far from being fulfilled as it had ever been.

When she had first come to Red, crawling on bended knees for a chance to work in the Sydney clubs he either owned or controlled, it had suited him to humour her. He had given her plum spots in each of his two best clubs and sat back to enjoy the sensation she caused there, this young and talented girl whose discovery he took credit for and who went home with him at night to his mansion in Elizabeth Bay. But before long he discovered that the green-eyed monster which dogged his life was once again rearing its ugly head.

For Red, although he knew that no one would be foolish enough to cross him, was a jealous man – jealous of his position as king in the shady world of nightclub and bar, jealous of his reputation as the hardest, the toughest, the fittest, and jealous, most of all, of his women. To begin with he had regarded Tara and his conquest of her as an amusing diversion, but very soon he realized she was much more than that. His almost paternal desire to protect her developed into full blown possessiveness and Red found himself obsessed by her.

She was his, this funny, fiery little Irish girl with the streak of vulnerability alongside the brashness that reminded him sometimes of a child dressing up in her mother's high heels and lipstick. He had never before had a woman who could induce him to heights of passion on a

Saturday night, responding herself with all the warmth and fire of her unfettered nature, only to leave his bed on Sunday morning because, in her words, not to go to Mass was a sin. He had never before seen a rosary jumbled in a drawer with make-up and jewellery only to be taken out and lovingly fingered when some minor catastrophe threatened. He had never known such a mixture of innocence and worldliness and it captivated him totally. Tara was his. Let anyone else lay a finger on her and they would encounter a couple of heavies waiting for them in an alleyway some dark night.

'If ever I catch anyone messing with you, Tara, I'll have him killed,' he said and the calm cold tone of his voice convinced her it was no idle threat.

The problem was that when she was singing at the club, Tara was a magnet for every man who came through the doors. At first Red managed the situation by insisting that each night after she had performed Tara should return to his table, and when business decreed that he could not be there himself he ensured two of his henchmen were there to do the job for him. But as his possessive jealousy increased he began to feel he could not even trust his henchmen. There was only one thing to be done and that was to reduce Tara's spots at the club from nightly to twice-weekly and then to special occasions only. He was sorry as Ed had been for Tara was good. But she was more to him now than just a pretty and talented singer. She was his woman. He had even thought once or twice about marrying her but conscious of his image he had decided against it. Better to keep things as they were and the black-haired colleen with the wicked dimples on his arm where she belonged. He bought her rings with diamonds, emeralds and sapphires 'to match your eyes', but they were for every finger but the fourth finger of her left hand.

Tara did not know whether to be glad or sorry about the change in her status and eventually settled for an emotion midway between the two. She missed singing but she enjoyed the advantages of being Red's woman too. That was like playing a part in a way for she had to walk right, talk right, behave as he expected in a variety of situations. It was, she thought, almost as much fun as performing on stage – and a great deal more lucrative!

As for her place in Red's bed, that had never been as bad as she had expected from her observations of Maggie's life – not even that first time when he took her to his scarlet and gold bedroom dressed just as he was in the monogrammed towelling robe with his hair still wet from the sauna. Red, who held most of the hardest men in Sydney in a grip of fear, was a tender and generous lover – and the luxury of those black silk sheets and a tub of scented water to relax in afterwards removed all feeling of having been used.

She enjoyed, too, the schemes she could weave in order to get her own way. It was a sport to find ways of winding Red around her little finger and she liked the feeling of power when she scored a small victory.

Tonight, however, as she sat at the dressing table the thoughts that occupied her were too serious for any game. There was a certain subject she wished to broach and she was unsure of the best time to do so – before making love or afterwards. Red was impatient for her. She could tell from the way he watched her every move as he sat propped against the pillows. If he was impatient he might cut her short whilst afterwards there would be all the time in the world and if she worked at making it good for him he would be in a rosy glowing mood, able to refuse her nothing. On the other hand, he might simply go to sleep before she finished telling him what she wanted whilst now he might agree to anything in his eagerness to have her.

She drew the brush through her curls again, raising her arms so that her breasts thrust enticingly against the silk wrap and watching his reaction in the mirror.

'Oh Red, it's so lucky I am! Sometimes I just can't believe anyone can be as lucky as me.'

'And what brought that on?' He sounded amused but she knew he was pleased.

'It's when I get reminded of how I used to live – when I see friends deep in trouble and think it might be me.'

'And what has reminded you just now?'

She avoided the question. She was not quite ready for it yet.

'I just wish with all my heart that I could do something to help. Just a little thing to ease the suffering . . .'

She was watching his reflection from beneath her lashes and was not altogether pleased to see one corner of his mouth twist upwards.

'Come on, Tara, what is it you want? Out with it and then perhaps you'll be ready to come to bed.'

She put down the brush and ran over to plump down on the edge of the bed, resting a hand on his chest. 'It's Maggie. I saw her today and . . .'

She felt him stiffen and knew she had chosen the wrong moment.

'You know I don't like you seeing Maggie,' he said shortly.

'Oh Red, please don't be angry!' she begged. 'She's my friend – she practically brought me up after Mammy ran off and left me – she's been more like a mother to me ever since. And she's ill Red, really ill!'

'I'm not surprised, living in that squalid room,' he said. 'And that's not all. If she escapes food poisoning she's liable to get a dose of the clap.'

'Red!' she admonished. 'It's nothing like that.'

'What is it then?'

'If you ask me I think she has a growth – cancer. It doesn't bear thinking about, she looks so bad.'

'Where did you see her?' he asked.

She hesitated. As he had said he didn't like her visiting Maggie in Darlinghurst, she went when she could sneak across town undiscovered and for some time she had been concerned by the look of Maggie. 'You're not eating enough – you look so thin!' she had told her repeatedly and Maggie had just laughed and replied that if she was putting on weight like some people, then Tara would

70

have something to chide her over.

But today there had been no jokes. Tara had found her in bed, too weak to get up, and though her thinness was hidden beneath the tumbled sheets the dark circles beneath her eyes and the hollows in her cheeks were more noticeable than ever. Horrified, Tara had questioned her and for the first time Maggie had admitted just how ill she was.

'Red, please!' she begged now. 'She needs medical attention – the best. If she doesn't get it I dread to think what will happen to her.'

He shrugged. 'Maggie is not your problem, Tara.'

'Red . . .'

'And she is certainly not mine. Good God, if I was expected to help every sick down and out and whore in Sydney . . .'

'Not every one. Just Maggie.'

'If she has got cancer I doubt whether money would help anyway. It would just be wasted.'

'No!'

'Yes.' He reached out spreading his hand around the back of her neck and drawing her towards him. 'Forget about Maggie and come here.'

'But Red . . .'

'Come here I said!'

Obediently Tara tipped her face to his kiss, twining her arms around his neck and thrusting her breasts enticingly upwards. But inside a little knot of anger was growing. How could Red be so callous? To dismiss Maggie that way with less consideration than he would give to one of his dogs . . .

His hands were on her breasts easing them out of her wrap and running down across her belly and, for a moment, she stifled a manic urge to thrust him away and scream her anger and disgust. But as his fingers moved downwards, lingering with long gentle strokes on the soft inner part of her thighs, she began to forget her anger as the first stirrings of desire sent weakness coursing through the deepest parts of her.

71

How could he do this to her? she wondered. When she was hating him so, how could he make her feel so good? She moved her knees restlessly and he tugged at the sash of her robe, loosening it, then pushing the silk back over her hips.

'Come here,' he said, his voice vibrant with desire.

She twisted round and half rose to turn back the sheet and get in beside him and as she did so the robe slipped back exposing one knee and thigh. Seeing it snapped her back to cold reality for it was as if she was seeing Maggie's leg that day when she had told her to go to Red, that same day when she, Tara, had decided she would do anything to escape the fate that was stalking Maggie. An aching emptiness flooded through her and with it the compulsion – she must do something to help Maggie. Whatever Red said, she must!

Automatically her body obeyed his dictates while her mind raced. Perhaps she had chosen the wrong moment. Perhaps afterwards she could try again. He had so much – surely he could not continue to deny Maggie just a little . . .

The silk sheet slid sensuously across her back as he turned her, then his muscular bulk was towering over her, and she felt again the surger of inner weakness. As he thrust into her, her sensitized flesh rose to his and she moaned softly, unable to resist, unable even to keep her mind detached any longer. Red was power – power – and she was his! If he was cruel and hard it did not make any difference. It was *him*. And it was so good to be his woman – so good . . . !

But afterwards, when she lay languorous and still sticky from the heights of passion, the wretchedness began to creep in again, a heaviness that began in the pit of her stomach then swelled like leavening yeast until there was no room within her for any other emotion.

She must help Maggie. She would. Somehow, whatever it cost her, she could not allow Maggie to suffer and die. Throughout the weeks that followed Maggie was constantly on Tara's mind and the first creeping anxiety turned gradually to frantic worry and then to despair. She had hated Red when he had said money spent on trying to cure Maggie would be wasted, but before long she was forced to admit that it would be a miracle if a cure could be found.

Her later attempts to persuade Red to help had been no more fruitful than the first – Red was as stubborn as he was hard and nothing Tara could do or say could induce him to part with a single penny piece for Maggie – not her pleas, not her tears, not her wiliest wiles or her most ardent loving – and eventually the state of his temper when she raised the subject made her realize that it would be wise to allow it to drop for a while at least. But that did not mean she had abandoned Maggie – far from it. Tara's determination to do the best she could for the friend who had taken the place of her mother burned more fiercely than ever and she made up her mind that if Red wouldn't give her the money to help Maggie she would get it elsewhere.

In spite of her spoiled status in Red's household Tara had no access to ready cash – whatever she wanted he paid for, so she had to explore other avenues, and the one that came to mind first was her jewellery. During the five years she had been with him Red had showered her with gold and gems of every description – now she decided that if she were to sell a few he would never miss them.

Sneaking away from the bodyguards one day she took them to a downtown jewellers and was shocked by how little she was offered for diamonds and sapphires she knew had cost Red thousands of dollars. But argument proved to be useless and Tara took what she could get and left. It was something for Maggie – enough to get her away, perhaps, to a doctor who could do something for her.

But Maggie, when Tara told her this, only shook her head and laughed, a hollow parody of the shriek of merriment that had used to fill the apartment.

'No point wasting good money on fancy doctors. Mac the Knife is good enough for me.'

'He's a drunken old fool!' Tara had said hotly.

Maggie's face turned grey as a spasm of pain creased through her. 'Drunken he might be, but he's no fool,' she said as it passed. 'I've trusted him since I was your age, Tara, and believe me there have been times when he's saved my neck. If Mac says there's nothing can be done, I'll take his word for it.'

'No!' Tara urged desperately. 'I can't just let you get worse, Maggie, and not even try to do something for you! There must be a way! If you were rich . . .'

Maggie smiled sadly. 'Even the rich have to die, Tara.'

'No!' Tara could hold back the tears no longer; she threw her arms around her friend, burying her face in the now-scrawny breasts. 'No, Maggie, no!'

'Oh sweetheart!' Maggie stroked Tara's hair with a thin hand – she, who was sick, was the comforter now. 'I'm not afraid. But I don't want to be carted off to some fancy hospital to die. I'd rather be here in my own home. And it's not as if I'm alone. I've got Jack now.'

Tara nodded silently swallowing her tears. Yes, at least Maggie had Jack. He would not have been Tara's choice but who was she to judge? Jack was a seaman who had jumped ship. He and his mate, a big brawny Irishman named Mick O'Neill, had visited Maggie one night and had grown friendly with her, attracted by the fact that she too was Irish. She had given them both a roof over their heads and then, as a relationship developed between her and Jack, Mick had moved on, while Jack had stayed to share her bed and her life. For a little while Maggie had become almost respectable. Jack had objected to her way of life saying he was no pimp and he would walk out before he would take advantage of a penny piece she might have earned in that way, and Tara had teased her that after all this time she was actually going to settle down.

'See how lucky I am, Tara,' Maggie had said. 'Having someone to spend my old age with. I never thought that would happen to me. I always thought that when I lost my looks I'd be alone.'

But that had been before the illness struck her down – a pitifully short time before. Now it looked as though Maggie would not have an old age to spend with anyone – or to be alone.

Tara wept tears of frustration and premature grief, but nothing she could say would induce Maggie to change her mind. Not being allowed to pay for the best treatment for Maggie did not mean not being able to help her at all, though, and Tara was determined to remain firm on that point. All her life Maggie had lived from hand to mouth. Now she could not work there was no money coming in and none put by either, while Jack, though able bodied and willing, had been unable to find employment.

'It's not his fault, Tara,' Maggie said. 'There just aren't enough jobs to go round any more – and Jack has to be careful he isn't seen around the harbour. If they caught up with him and took him away from me now, I don't know what I'd do.'

Tara had turned away swallowing at the tears. Her mind was made up. She would make Maggie's last weeks comfortable if it was the last thing she did. So a few more items of jewellery found their way into the downtown jewellers and a few to the pawnshop and Tara was able to buy the things she wanted for Maggie – some delicacies in a vain attempt to persuade her to eat, perfumed soap to try to wash away the smell of death, and a silk nightgown to replace the cheap art silk.

'Oh Tara, all my life I've wanted a real silk nightgown!' Maggie said when she saw it.

Mac also had to be paid and the drugs that were needed to keep Maggie's pain under control did not come cheap. And there had to be enough, too, when it was over, to bury her properly.

All this had to be kept from Red and Tara planned her visits to Darlinghurst with military precision. At first, when she went only once a week, this was not too difficult but as Maggie's strength failed Tara wanted to visit her more and more often. The house in Elizabeth Bay became like a prison to her and she paced the rooms, fretting and thinking of ways she could get over to see Maggie. Even when Red took her out she was preoccupied. There seemed something obscene about wining and dining at one of the clubs when her friend lay dying and the music and laughter echoed in her head like a manic nightmare.

Red does not need me, she thought with a touch of bitterness. He almost ignores me when we are at the club – I'm nothing but an adornment to him. But Maggie . . .

Maggie was always so pathetically pleased to see her. Her face was drawn and grey all the time now, the circles and hollows so pronounced they made Tara shrink inwardly just to look at them, and the lines of pain were clearly defined around her mouth. But when Tara came around the door her eyes always brightened, tiny twin orbs that no amount of suffering could extinguish. Tara did not stay long, she dared not if Red was not to become suspicious.

They never talked now of Maggie's illness or the fact that she was failing fast, but when Tara left Jack always walked to the end of the road with her so that he could tell her how the day had been.

'It's been terrible today,' he said one night. 'Maggie won't give in – and she won't let on to you how bad it is, either. But I don't think Mac's stuff is working properly any more.'

Tara went cold. She had forced herself to come to terms with the fact that she was going to lose Maggie, but she could not face the thought of her suffering.

'Oh Jack, what can we do?' she groaned. 'Isn't there something stronger he can give her?'

'If she has anything stronger it will hasten her death.'

Tara's eyes filled with tears. 'God knows I don't want that, but I don't want her suffering either. She must have whatever it takes, Jack.'

He nodded, a big man bewildered by the situation he found himself in – and by his own emotions.

'Yes. I just didn't feel it was my place to say so, Tara. After all I've only known her a matter of months while you . . .'

'Jack!' Tara caught his hands, looking up into his rugged, agonized face. 'You have every right. You have been marvellous – not many would have done what you have done for their own wife. And you've made her happy in her last weeks. That's worth a great deal too.'

He bowed his head. 'I suppose I love her.'

'You do.' She stood on tiptoe and kissed his cheek, rough and unshaven. 'I'll come again as soon as I can, Jack.'

The next time was three days later and Maggie was worse. She lay seemingly not even aware that Tara had come, sunk into a world of pain and drugs. Tara sat beside her bed holding her hand, thin, veined, with traces of scarlet nail varnish still growing off the tips of her fingernails from the last time she had felt like prettying herself up.

'Next time I come I'll bring some stuff to get that red off your nails.' Tara told her friend and Maggie seemed to rouse a little.

'Still determined to make a beauty of me, eh, Tara? It will be an uphill task now!'

'That's rubbish and you know it. You're as lovely as you ever were,' Tara lied. 'I'm going now but I'll see you soon. Right?'

'Right.' And Maggie drifted off again.

Tara's eyes were full of tears as she left the apartment. Dimly she was aware of Jack following her down the stairs and out into the street.

'I don't think it will be long now,' he said when they reached the street.

She shook her head, looking at him through blurred eyes.

'I don't think it will. Oh Jack, I'll miss her so!'

He shuffled awkwardly. 'How would I let you know, Tara, if . . .'

'Ring me. The minute anything happens.'

'But I thought . . .'

'It won't matter any more then, will it? He can't prevent me coming to see her when she's . . . And I have to know. I couldn't bear it if I thought something had happened and I didn't know.'

'All right. I won't stay talking tonight. I don't want to leave her.'

'No, you get back, Jack.'

She pressed his hand and turned to walk away up the steep valley.

There was a car parked opposite the apartment but she was too upset even to wonder what it was doing there. Cars, people – what did they matter when Maggie lay in that miserable room dying? She walked on, head low.

And suddenly the quiet of the night erupted. Gunfire, sharp and cracking, seeming to go on forever. Roosting birds rising, flapping into the reverberating air. The roar of a revving engine, a car speeding past her, screaming around the corner on two wheels . . .

Shocked, bewildered, she swung round.

And then she saw him lying crumpled halfway up the stone steps.

'Jack!' she screamed.

Her trembling legs carried her back down the alley, then she drew up short, cold through and through as she looked down at him.

He was clutching his chest, his eyes, wide and surprised, staring back at her. Blood was pumping between his fingers. Then as she watched his body convulsed violently, his legs threshing out, head jerking back. And he was still.

'Jack – for God's sake . . . ! What . . . ? Why . . . ?'

But she knew. Even in that shocked moment when her body, cold and trembling violently, refused to obey her, even as her conscious mind ran in wild frightened circles, deep within she knew.

This was Red's doing. He had threatened her once that

78

he would kill any man she tangled with. Now Jack was dead, gunned down by Red's hired killers. Not for anything he had done but because of Red's insane jealousy. She must have been seen with Jack. Red had had her followed and he had jumped to the wrong conclusion. And Jack, innocent of any crime but that of loving Maggie, had paid the price.

'Oh my God, my God!' she whispered, twisting this way and that, hands pressed to her mouth. What to do? What to *do*? Jack was beyond help. Any moment people would come – the police – and . . .

Maggie. She must go to Maggie.

She ran past the sprawled body, up the stairs, into the apartment. Maggie lay as she had left her, inert, sunk once more into coma. She had heard nothing. Well, thank God for that at least.

Tara's trembling legs would support her no longer. She sank down beside the bed, fumbling for her rosary. Maggie's hand lay on the sheet. Tara took it and began to gabble the words that from her childhood had been comfort, refuge, salvation.

'Hail Mary, full of grace, the Lord is with Thee . . .'

*

When the police came blundering into the apartment she was still there. They stopped in the doorway, shocked by the scene before them.

'Oh Christ – what . . .'

Tara got up slowly, stiffly.

'It's all right. She's dead.'

'Sorry, Miss, there's been a shooting . . .'

'I know,' she said. Her voice was steady with conviction and with the determination which had grown during the last long minutes when she had sat here beside Maggie and known what it was she had to do. 'I know all about it and I can tell you who was responsible. I can tell you everything.'

79

When it was all over she knew she had to run. Throughout the trial they had afforded her 'protection' – keeping her at a 'safe' address with a police guard twenty-four hours a day. But they could not protect her forever.

At night lying sleepless in her bed Tara lived and relived the scene in the court room on the last day of the trial and trembled.

The trial had lasted for two weeks. Each day she had gone to the court because afraid though she was she could not stay away – she had to keep this last vigil for Maggie.

She had thought that giving her evidence would be the worst part. She was wrong. That was relatively easy – a little like being on stage. Even answering the fierce and searching cross examination by Red's counsel had not caused her any great distress. Trying to read the meaning behind his sharply phrased questions and staying one move ahead of him became a game and his inferences as to her morals and lifestyle failed to worry or embarrass Tara. No, it was afterwards when she took her place in the court room to listen to the remainder of the trial that the torment began.

To sit in full view of Red and see his eyes burning hatred and the threat of revenge, to look away from him and feel his presence, his command, his power over her; she hated him for what he had done to Maggie's man, despised the jealousy that had driven him to it and yet still was aware of the hypnotic attraction that had kept her with him for more than five years, even when he had made it clear he would no longer allow her to sing in his clubs. More than once she was almost torn apart by the overwhelming desire to run to him even now, to throw her arms around his powerful frame, to beg him to forgive her. She longed to touch his face, so expressionless it might have been carved in stone, run her fingers over the hard bunched muscles in his back and shoulders that rippled through the silk of his handmade shirt. And then she would remember Jack, whose only crime was to love Maggie, the lifeblood pouring out of him as he lay dying in a Sydney gutter, and the hatred would return, so fierce it took her breath away, so scaring that her body burned with the agony of it. Jack had died because of her, Tara, because she had deceived this monster. She did not think she would ever forgive either of them.

Yet even at the end Red had held in his hands the power to draw one more emotion from her – total blind terror. It had come when the judge had passed sentence with the stern words: 'For the sake of this whole community I feel it is my duty to make certain you are removed to a place of detention for a very long time.'

Tears had blurred her eyes suddenly so that she did not see the guards moving in to take Red away, did not see him move forward. Then his voice had filled the court room and she had raised her eyes to see him looking directly at her, fists clenched threateningly.

'Watch out for yourself, Tara. I'll get you for this. Don't think there is anywhere you can hide away from me. If it takes the rest of my life I'll make you sorry for the day you did this to Red Maloney!'

It was a moment of pure melodrama. The next day the newspapers were full of it. 'Gangland boss threatens former Moll' read one banner headline. If Tara had not been so shocked and afraid she might have laughed. As it was she had no energy left for anything but fear.

'An idle threat,' the police told her. 'He's safely behind bars. He can't harm you now.'

Tara knew better. Red would not make idle threats and Red would not forgive. In prison or out he would find a way. And if he was set upon revenge, one way or another he would have it.

*

Where could she go where Red would not find her? He had

friends everywhere; his power was enormous.

Mentally Tara drew a map of the continent, picturing the wild and desolate outbacks and deserts where no clubs and sly grog shops were to be found and no racketeer or gangster could live a life of luxury on the strength of his ill-gotten gains. A possibility. But sure, I could never survive in the wilds, Tara thought in panic. I'm a city person. I need people and buildings around me.

Darwin. It came to her in a flash of inspiration. Darwin – frontier town of the wild and untamed Northern Territory. Darwin – outpost of Australia. Perhaps she would be safe there.

With no thought in her head beyond escaping Red's vengeance, no thought of what she would do when she got there, Tara fled.

ACT II
Chapter One

Alys Peterson zipped up her Red Cross uniform skirt, neatened her tailored blouse and went out onto the louvred veranda of the spacious clifftop house where James and Sylvia Crawford were at breakfast.

It was a beautiful February morning. Later, the heat haze would close in and the rain begin to fall in a steamy suffocating cloud as it did each day in this season of the year, but as yet the sky was clear and the sea was an unbroken band of broad blue below the scarlet-leaved crotons and banana palms, vibrant bougainvillaea and fragrant frangipani that rioted along the edge of the clifftop.

Alys breathed in the perfumed air and felt she breathed contentment with it. She loved this place and it had repaid her by working a miracle in her life. When she had arrived here three years ago she had believed she had been sent to the last place on God's earth and she had not cared. Race was dead. Her child was dead. It no longer mattered to her where she was or even whether she herself lived or died. She had woken each morning to a well of misery so deep that not even the miseries of the steamy hot Darwin climate or the fact that a continent separated her from everything and everyone she had ever loved could make things worse.

And then slowly, subtly, things had begun to change. Sylvia had had much to do with it, she knew. Sylvia who, although she never probed or asked awkward questions, seemed to understand so well. In her brisk no-nonsense way she had set about encouraging Alys to take an interest in life again and she had unerringly selected as a starting point the very thing which Alys found irresistible.

'You're a very good driver – if you were to learn vehicle

maintenance you could be very useful to us,' Sylvia had said and there was no hint of either sympathy or reproof in her voice, only that enthusiasm and energy which she had brought to everything she did.

'What do you mean?' Alys had asked. In all her life no one had ever before suggested she might be useful.

'There is a war coming. Heaven knows it may be soon. And when it does come we shall need every able pair of hands we can get. You can drive an ambulance for us, Alys.'

'Oh!' Alys had been too surprised to say anything else. She knew, of course, that Sylvia was one of the mainstays of the Red Cross here in Darwin – in fact her whole life seemed to revolve around it. But it had never occurred to her that she might become involved herself. 'I don't know anything about First Aid,' she said lamely.

'You can soon learn,' Sylvia said briskly. 'That will be a damn sight easier than me trying to teach one of my nurses to drive. And it will do you good. No sense moping around here by yourself all day.'

Alys had taken the bait unenthusiastically at first then with growing interest. For so long she had been aware of a lack of purpose in her life, now suddenly she had found one. As Sylvia bullied and chivvied her into shape she found herself marvelling that this busy little woman could ever have been a friend of her mother's – in attitude and lifestyle they were light years apart. Where Frances had expected ladylike decorum, Sylvia demanded devotion to duty and a willingness to roll up her sleeves, literally as well as metaphorically; where Frances had tried to rein her into a tight narrow well-ordered world, Sylvia opened new horizons.

For the first time in her life Alys found herself looking forward to each day as a challenge. The pain of Race's death and the loss of her baby were still there but she no longer had so much time to think about them. And as her new life helped to mend her broken heart and set her new goals, Alys found that she was falling in love with this strange wild frontier town. She loved the feeling of space and lack of convention, loved having the sea spread out at her front door and the wild wide desert of outback at the rear. She loved the sneaky treacherous way that golden sand turned to muddy mangrove flats, loved the smell of the pure salt air that sometimes carried on it a sharp whiff from the iron ore loading jetty or the bitumen plant, loved the rioting tropical greenery and the huge spreading banyan trees. She loved it so much she felt she never wanted to leave it – even when the war that Sylvia had predicted had become reality and letters began to arrive from Frances urging her to come home.

'My dear Alys, I am so worried about you,' Frances wrote. 'I cannot sleep for worrying and your father is afraid I shall make myself ill. Sylvia means well I know, keeping you occupied, but she doesn't understand you are not used to that sort of thing. She is hardy – she always was – while you . . . Please Alys, do as your mother asks and come home immediately.'

Alys had tucked the letter away in her handkerchief drawer with a wry smile. It was not Sylvia who failed to understand her, she thought. The Red Cross was busier than ever and she was enjoying the sense of urgent purpose which filled her days. Besides the war seemed so far away, in France and Belgium, Syria and Egypt. What on earth was there for her mother to worry about? But then Frances would always worry – and advertise the fact if she thought it would help her to get her own way.

As the months passed the letters from home became more urgent and in spite of herself Alys was forced to admit that perhaps there was after all something in what Frances had to say. The war that had seemed so distant was creeping inexorably closer and daily it seemed the news grew ever more grave. Half of the cream of Australia's troops in Crete had been safely evacuated after fighting a brave but losing battle – what had become of the other half? HMAS *Sydney*, pride of the Australian fleet, was sunk and all aboard her lost – all those gallant young men who had so recently marched with pride in their tropical white uniforms through the streets of the city for which their ship had been named. And then Japan was involved and the world rocked to the news that her planes had decimated the US fleet in Pearl Harbor and attacked Hong Kong, Singapore and the Philippines. When that happened a telegram had been delivered to the clifftop house in Darwin: *Come home at once stop Frantic with worry stop Mother.*

Again Alys had smiled, perhaps more because for the first time in her life she was beyond the reach of her mother's jurisdiction rather than from amusement. But six days later she had stopped smiling.

She had been in the cinema that evening, Tom Harris's Star Theatre, known locally as Tomaris's Place, watching a gangster film, when the air raid siren had begun to wail, louder even than the gunfire and sounds of a car chase on screen. She had scrambled out into the hot dark night almost unable to believe the impossible was happening yet swept along by the panicking crowds who had appeared on the streets – the entire audience of the cinema, swarms of Chinese from the gambling dens and dives of Cavenagh Street, families who had fled from their homes – all making for the only place that might be safe from the threat of Japanese bombs, the beach beneath the protective shelter of the high cliffs. With them she had spent an uncomfortable couple of hours plagued by the mosquitos and sandflies who hovered in constantly moving clouds above the warm sand until it became clear that no Japanese planes would come tonight. But with the relief had come a new and frightening realization – tonight the siren had sounded a false alarm. Next time it might not. Next time it could be for real.

Alys was not the only one to see that what had seemed like an empty threat could be on the point of becoming reality. Next day the evacuations began, evacuations that had been planned for many months by the administration and zone wardens for just such an eventuality. Women and children were ordered out of Darwin, leaving by road and by sea, some unwillingly, some only too anxious to escape the vulnerable north coast.

But Alys had resisted. For one thing she was needed here – and was not Aunt Sylvia too insisting that she remain for exactly the same reasons? For another she was unwilling to leave the scene of action. Afraid and uncomfortable as she might have been that night on the dark beach, she had also felt strangely alive, the vibrancy of fear awakening in her new and exciting sensations. Never before had she been on a knife edge of danger; it was an exhilarating experience. To leave now and run for the safety and claustrophobic boredom of home was not what Alys wanted.

During the weeks that followed that first air raid warning Darwin took on the appearance of a town under siege. Barbed wire entanglements appeared on the beach, concrete machine gun emplacements were built and armed, the streets, almost cleared now of civilians, thronged with soldiers. Fresh food and liquor were in short supply; petrol became as valuable as liquid gold. And the letters from Melbourne became more frequent and more insistent than before, in spite of the fact that Alys had written home stating that she had every intention of remaining until she was forcibly carried out.

This morning as she crossed to the breakfast table where the Crawfords were already seated she saw there was another one – but this time it had been addressed not to her but to Uncle James. The pages covered with her mother's unmistakable hand were spread out across this morning paper and as Alys approached he riffled them together and looked up at her over the rim of his gold-framed spectacles.

'Morning, Alys. Your mother has been writing to me again. She is very concerned about you, you know.'

Alys helped herself to a piece of toast.

'I wish she would stop worrying. I have explained to her that I am needed here. But Mummy can be extremely obtuse when she chooses.'

James Crawford hid a wry smile. He had spent his life, he thought, wrestling with deliberately obtuse women. At the Darwin branch of the United Bank of Australia where he was manager he was thought of by his clients and staff alike as a man to be reckoned with but in his own home . . .

'I happen to think she is right.' James settled himself back in his chair, dabbing at his military-style moustache with a damask napkin. 'Darwin is no place for women just now.'

'Oh do stop nagging, James!' Sylvia Crawford said with a touch of impatience. She was a daunting woman in her own right, features sharp and clear in a face still smooth in spite of having survived almost fifty Australian summers, pepper and salt hair curling irrepressibly from the kirby grips which attempted to tame it. 'Alys is needed. She is the only girl here who can drive the Red Cross ambulance – and she is a great help with the police canteen too. If she went I don't know how I should manage.'

James Crawford sighed and poured himself more coffee.

'Alys' mother and I are not alone in thinking Darwin is a dangerous place to be,' he said testily. 'The administration have deemed it sensible to evacuate women and children. It's almost two months now since the order and most people have had the sense to obey it.'

Sylvia snorted, an explosion which somehow still managed to sound ladylike. 'What order? Oh, they've tried to get us out, but you know as well as I do they have no real power. Just let one of those jumped-up wardens try to force *me* to evacuate. I'd soon send him packing!'

'And no doubt you have already done just that,' James said drily. 'I know you are an impossible woman, Sylvia. I've learned that to my cost in the thirty years since I married you. But, because you are determined to stay here and get yourself killed, it's no reason to encourage Alys to do the same. We have been lucky so far. But it can't last. I think Alys should go immediately.'

'Just because of my mother's letter, I suppose,' Alys said biting into her toast.

'No. Not just because of that.' He moved the letter aside and tapped the newspaper. 'Singapore has fallen now. Singapore – the one place everyone thought was impregnable. Now it will be only a matter of time before Australia is attacked – and Darwin is right in the front line.'

'Fiddlesticks,' Sylvia said briskly.

'Have you taken a look at the harbour this morning?' James demanded, waving at the panoramic view laid out beneath them. 'Can't you see all those ships?'

'The harbour is always full of ships. That's what it's for.'

Not like that. There must be close on forty of them – corvettes, sloops, tankers, a minesweeper. There's even a hospital ship. Look, you can see its red cross.'

'Which reminds me that I have work to do.' Sylvia stood up smoothing her uniform skirt which had wriggled into a web of horizontal creases across the widest part of her plump thighs. 'We have a consignment of comforts to get to that ship, Alys.'

James brought his fist down sharply onto the table making the china rattle.

'Will you listen to what I am saying, woman! Amongst those ships is a convoy of transports. It was on its way to reinforce Timor but the Jap bombers drove it back. It came running back here for safety. I heard about it at the Club Hotel last night. Now look, if the Japs have followed it in they might have another crack at it here in Darwin. If they can do it in Pearl Harbor, they can do it here.'

'Sometimes, James, you sound exactly like an old woman,' Sylvia said calmly. 'Are you ready, Alys? Let's get your ambulance on the road.'

'Yes, I'm ready.' Alys stood up too, pausing to drop a kiss on James' sandy head. 'Don't worry, Uncle. We'll be all right. And you are still here, after all, aren't you?'

James watched them go and sighed. He had done what he could. Short of ordering the army to cart them away there was no more he could do. Well, very likely they would be safe enough. Pity the Jap who thought he could take on the pair of them!

With a small shake of his head he returned to his paper. At the top in black ink the date stood out clearly.

February 18th, 1942.

Chapter Two

The kitchen of the Savalis' Darwin boarding house was stiflingly hot in spite of the lateness of the hour and the large twirling ceiling fan. The heat emanated in waves from the big old range and to a lesser degree from the central lamp, bounced off the shutters, firmly closed to enforce the blackout, and wafted in to join that central pool of suffocating air which moved slowly up, stratum by stratum, to be dispersed temporarily by the fan and begin the same inevitable round again.

At the range Tara Kelly was stiring gravy in a large cast iron frying pan. Perspiration was trickling in small steady rivulets down her neck and her hair, usually a mass of tight springy curls, felt damp against her hot face. Irritably she raised a hand to brush it away and the pan, no longer steadied against the violent rotations of her wooden spoon, slopped thick floury-looking liquid onto the range where it spat and bubbled for a moment before congealing into an evil-looking crust.

'Damn,' said Tara.

The kitchen door opened and Dimitri Savalis' face appeared. It was not an attractive face – a fondness for the bottle had made it too florid and paunchy – and now it glistened with sweat. His lips were large and loose, his eyes too small behind the folds of flesh, his hair hung in a greasy lock across his forehead.

Tara tightened her own lips in disgust and turned away.

'Is it ready yet?' Dimitri asked, his tone betraying impatience. 'The guests are all waiting. They finished their soup long ago.'

'Give them a drink to fill in time then,' Tara snapped.

'A drink? You know drink is in very short supply in this town right now.'

91

'Oh, come on, Dimitri – I know you've got enough in your cellar to float a battleship! It might help to keep them from noticing how few vegetables there are anyway. They're in short supply too in case you hadn't noticed.'

Ignoring her, he continued, 'Just be as quick as you can. I have a reputation to keep up, you know. Savalis' is one of the best rooming houses in Darwin and gives a good value for money evening meal too. Don't you know the Captain of the *Fortuna* and two of his officers are eating here tonight? Oh, when my Tina was here to run the kitchen things were different! My Tina is a wonderful cook. My Tina . . .'

'Well, she isn't here now,' Tara retorted. 'I'm doing my best and you're just holding me up. It's ready now anyway.' As she lifted the pan from the range her thumb slipped onto the hot rim and she swore. 'Ouch!'

'Don't drop it! Don't drop it!' Dimitri's body followed his head into the kitchen – a body as paunchy and unattractive as his face. When Tara had first fled to Darwin and taken a job as maid of all work in the Savalis' boarding house she had marvelled that a girl as nice as Tina could not only have married Dimitri but had four babies by him; now that she and the children had been evacuated south, Tara could only think it must be a great relief to her to be able to go to bed and not have to face the prospect of that disgusting lump of lard climbing in beside her and crawling all over her.

Yet Tina had protested vehemently when the authorities had ordered her to leave. It had been in December, immediately after the first air raid warning, and Tina had pleaded with their zone warden to be allowed to remain at least until after Christmas. Without success. The warden was adamant – Darwin was not safe for women and children and Tina, likely to give birth at any moment, was one of the first who must go. She and the children had been loaded onto a coastal trader and shipped south out of the danger zone and Tara had been left to carry out Tina's jobs as well as her own at the boarding house – and to take the brunt of Dimitri's bad temper and constant complaints.

I'll take the steaks — you bring the rest,' he said as she put the platters side by side on the table. 'Ah! But they are so small!'

'That's because I had them cut in half to make enough,' Tara told him. 'You're lucky to have any at all with the food situation as it is.'

'*I'm* lucky!' He thrust his face across the table so that it sweated and glared just a few inches from hers. '*You* are the lucky one. When I can't feed my customers any more and I have to shut up the place you will have to go like all the other women. That is the only reason you have been allowed to stay, because we are providing a service here.'

Tara's chin came up and her eyes blazed back at him. 'And what makes you think I want to stay in a dump like this?'

Dimitri's lip curled unpleasantly. 'You think I don't know, huh? You think I don't know you are running away? Darwin is a good place to hide. The back of beyond. So! You stay as long as you can. Ah, I know . . . I know!'

She snapped upright as a finger of fear touched her spinal cord. Then common sense and reason came rushing in. He didn't know. He couldn't. Maybe he had worked it out that she had come to Darwin to hide. But he did not know who it was she was hiding from and why. If he had done he would never have taken her on to work for him, never allowed her to become friendly with his wife, never have kept her on here when Tina was evacuated. No, not even if it had meant a choice between closing down altogether or running the place by himself. Some of her usual confidence returned.

'Are we going to take this food into the dining room or not?' she enquired acidly.

'Yes, yes — we take . . .' He held the door open with his foot while she went through with the laden dishes.

The dining room was on the front of the house as far from the kitchen as it could be, a big square room furnished with scrubbed wood tables and chairs, one large enough to seat six or eight, the rest for fours or twos. Once, in an attempt to bring the look of the Greek islands to Darwin, Tina had covered the tables with bright checked cloths, but Tara had abandoned that idea. The scrubbed wood was more functional and it saved washing. And the men didn't seem to mind. As long as the food was good and they were still able to shout a beer, that was all that seemed to matter to them.

She set down the dishes and looked around. Three men in naval uniform were occupying one end of the long table, chatting and smoking while they waited to be served – the three officers from the *Fortuna* Tara guessed. Another group she knew to be the bosses from the ice works were laughing loudly over some joke, and sitting alone at a corner table, a copy of last week's *Northern Standard* spread out across his sprawled legs, was a dark-haired, rakishly good-looking young man. As she noticed him, Tara's lips tightened. Sean Devlin, typically wild Territory born and bred, who had set himself up in Darwin as an electrical contractor. He came to eat regularly at Savalis' and that fact, coupled with his Irish immigrant ancestry seemed to give him the idea that he had the right to be familiar with her. What was worse was that when she put him in his place he retaliated with the kind of mocking manner which made her feel he was laughing at her.

Of course the trouble was he had no respect for anything or anyone, Tara thought. Take the way he dressed now. Not that there was anything unusual about wearing shorts – the men from the ice works were also wearing them. But they had the decency to team them with knee-high socks and smartly polished sandals, while Sean Devlin – or Dev as she had heard him called – displayed bare legs covered only by an indecent amount of black hair – like a monkey! And the shirt, open at the neck to reveal more dark curling hair. It was about time Dimitri set standards of dress for his establishment and if it wasn't wartime she would tell him so. He would never lift the place above the hoi polloi this way.

But then that was Darwin all over, the frontier town.

Rough tough men perhaps running as she had run, misfits and vagrants, gamblers whose stakes were their lives, men for whom civilization was a straight jacket, jokers wild, all of them. And all the time this damned weather setting them at one another's throats, provoking arguments and irritation, making them go troppo if they were not used to it, driving them to fight and sometimes to kill. And Dev . . . who looked as if he could kill quite easily . . .

As if sensing her eyes on him he looked up from his newspaper.

'Evening, Tara. Not left Darwin then? You should do while you have the chance.'

She shrugged. 'I'm not interested in running away.'

The men from the ice works had stopped joking to listen.

'Everybody else seems to be going,' one said. 'The typists from the Government Administration Offices went today. They flew them out. Things are looking bad if you ask me.' He looked over his shoulder at Tara. 'You must be pretty well the last woman left in Darwin.'

Tara spooned cabbage onto a plate. 'I should hardly think I'm that.'

'She wouldn't mind anyway would you, Tara?' Dev drawled from the corner.

Tara did not answer but she was thinking: No, I wouldn't mind. She had always preferred the company of men to that of women. Unless of course it was Tina – or Maggie. But Tina had gone south and Maggie was dead. Tara's heart fell with the familiar sick jolt as she thought of the woman who had meant more to her than any other. Strange, sometimes it was almost as if she had forgotten Maggie was dead and then it would hit her all over again, the grief and the aching sense of loss, as vivid and agonizing as ever.

With a conscious effort now she put her memories aside and set about serving the vegetables. Leaving the men to eat their meal she went back to the kitchen where several pints of custard had to be made and a stack of dirty pans were waiting for her attention. As she stirred the custard the heat from the range made her burned thumb throb and she thought for the umpteenth time since Tina had gone how she hated domestic work.

When I make my fortune, vowed Tara, I'll never cook another potato or wash another dish as long as I live. I'll have someone to do it for me just as I did when I was with Red. Only next time I won't be beholden to any man. The servants will be there because of *me*.

The men in the dining room worked their way through the menu to the coffee and still she was washing up, drying one lot of clean dishes to make room for the next on the draining board. Dimitri had long since disappeared – stopping to yarn with the men, she supposed. She was scouring a pot, attacking the gluey residue in its cracks with a last spurt of desperate energy, when he put his head around the door to drawl: 'More coffee, Tara!'

More coffee. Do it yourself! she thought. But she was too tired now to argue any more. All she wanted to do was go to bed, to sleep, and it was barely ten o'clock. Weary dimples tucked suddenly in her cheeks as she thought of how late her bedtime had used to be – never before one or two in the morning, sometimes not until dawn unless of course there had been a good reason to go to bed! How things had changed!

But I had no choice, she thought. No choice but to do what I did. It won't always be like this. Holy Mother, if I thought it would be I believe I'd go clean round the bend!

She carried the coffee through to the dining room. The men from the ice works had left now but Dev had joined the naval oficers at the big table and one of Dimitri's bottles, already half-empty, was occupying pride of place. Tara smiled to herself wondering how much profit Dimitri had managed to make on it. A hundred per cent? She would not be surprised. Dimitri took some persuading to unlock his cellar door and with Darwin as dry as it was at present the sky would be the limit regarding prices.

She poured the coffee and was about to leave when Dev stopped her.

'Would you like a drink, Tara?'

She shook her head. 'No thank you.'

'You look tired.'

'I am.'

He pulled a chair out. 'Sit down for a minute.'

'No, I can't stay.'

'Yes, you can. I want to talk to you. And there's no need to look like that. I'm not about to attack your virtue.' He grinned ruefully. 'You'll probably tell me it's none of my business anyway. But with our shared Irish ancestry I can't help feeling responsible for you.'

She snorted impatiently. 'Your ancestors were convicts, no doubt. Still, I have to hand it to you, you've done very well for yourself. I've seen the ute with your name on it running about Darwin.'

'Correction. I *was* doing all right. The war is putting paid to that. There's no petrol now for running a ute about even when I'm on government business. Darwin is a dead city. And that's what I want to talk to you about.'

'Don't think I can get you any petrol!' she scoffed.

He tipped his chair onto its two back legs.

'What we were saying just now, Tara – you really ought to get out while you can. This is no place for a woman now. This war is hotting up and Darwin is right in the firing line.'

Tara tossed her head so that the dark curls bounced.

'Why should anyone want to attack Darwin?'

He reached for the bottle, refilled his glass, and pushed the bottle towards the naval officers. 'To begin with there's a harbour full of ships down there – thirty or forty of them. Then there's a convoy of transports that was on its way to reinforce Timor when it was attacked by Jap bombers. It ran for safety, back here to Darwin, and got in yesterday. Now ask yourself what sort of a tempting target that would make if the Japs decide to follow it in. Oh, it's all too easy to get complacent after a few false alarms. But one time when that siren goes it will be for real. One time, my beauty, when you run for the cliffs or the slit trench there will be a Jap bomb after you or a fighter drilling holes in the ground behind you . . . bang, bang, bang!' He drew an imaginary line in the air with his forefinger.

Tara snorted, 'Oh, I haven't got time to listen to this!'

The naval captain reached for the bottle but his eyes were on Tara. 'Maybe you ought to make time.'

The seriousness of his tone stopped her.

'How do you mean?'

'I mean if you leave it much longer you could be too late. The Japs could cut Darwin off, no sweat, if they took over the seaward side. And it's no good thinking you can make a run over land. The Track is impassable half the time during the Wet.'

'Sure don't I know it!' she said, thinking: That was why I chose Darwin, after all. Impassable. Cut off. The last place in Australia where Red would start looking for me . . .

The *Fortuna*'s captain leaned forward on his elbows. 'As soon as I've unloaded I'm sailing for Perth. There's a berth for you if you want one.'

She gathered up the empty glasses. 'Sure thanks, that's very nice of you.'

'I mean it.'

'Think about it Tara,' Dev said. 'But don't think too long. You heard what he said. He's sailing as soon as he's unloaded.'

'This sounds like a conspiracy. It's trying to get rid of me you are!'

'That's true enough. But for your good, not mine. Dimitri will be gunning for me when he knows I've talked his home help into leaving!'

'I am *not* his home help!'

'Well – whatever you are. Take this offer up, Tara, or you may live to regret it.'

'I'll sleep on it,' Tara said.

She could still hear the men's voices coming from the dining room as she passed the door on her way to bed and she shook her head with a twist of impatience that was half-rooted in jealousy. They were the ones who would have the thick heads in the morning!

The Savalis' house was one of the few two-storey buildings on the street and Tara's room, small and cupboard-like, was at the rear of the upper floor. A double bed too old and stained to be used now for the guests, took up almost the entire floor space and a tiny chest, topped with a cracked mirror, had been squeezed in alongside it.

On one wall a sampler worked in cross-stitch announced that 'Home is where the heart is'; from the opposite wall a pre-Raphaelite Christ, complete with lantern and crown of thorns, surveyed it with solemn dignity. The pictures had been hung to cover the state of the walls, Tara suspected, and she had added a touch of her own – a wooden crucifix – on a nail above the head of the bed. When she had first come an out-of-date calender, minus its book of dates, had hung there but she had quickly effected the change – 'Sure wouldn't I hate to sleep with time gone hanging over my head!' she had joked to Tina.

The window was small and high up and no one had bothered to finish it with curtains. From its lofty position it looked out over the rear garden and sometimes Tara would clamber up onto the bed to view the tropical plants that rioted there, for even after almost a year in Darwin they were still a novelty to her. Tonight, however, the shutters were closed to enforce the blackout and the room was like an oven, singing with heat.

Tara hesitated for a moment then took the stick that stood in the corner beside the bed and reached up to unfasten the catch on the shutters. She would not be bothering to light the lamp tonight so there was no danger of the ARP warden thundering on the door to demand total darkness. And she had managed to repair the holes in the meshing well enough to keep out all but the most persistent mosquitos. As the shutter swung open the smallest hint of a breeze kissed her cheek and died again. The air outside was as humid and heavy as that inside. There was no way to escape it.

Wearily she unbuttoned her dress and slipped it off. The faint odour of cooking wafted up from the material and she wrinkled her nose. Tina had always smelled of cooking and Tara had thought it revolting. Now the thought that she smelled the same depressed her still further.

She tossed the dress into the corner of the room ready for washing and followed it with her underwear. Even forgetting the cooking smells clothes still had to be changed every day and sometimes not even that was often enough in this sweaty heat. Standing quite naked Tara could still feel the sticky patches between every fold of skin and the thought of lying down like this on that rough bed was more than she could bear.

Tired or not she would go down to the bathroom and have a cool wash, she decided. She reached for her wrap, lying discarded across the foot of the bed, and put it on. In daylight she had thought how incongruous it looked lying there, palest blue raw silk contrasting wildly with the once bright but now faded patchwork counterpane. Now, in the dark, she merely luxuriated in the cool smoothness of the silk against her hot damp skin. At least she had Red to thank for this!

The bathroom was downstairs at the back of the house and next door to the kitchen – for ease of plumbing she imagined. As she approached the door to the dining room a roar of laughter told her the men were still there and making a night of it and she hurried past anxious only to have her wash and get back to bed.

With the door shut safely behind her she slipped out of her wrap, filled the basin and buried her face in the water. Then she patted her cheeks dry with the cleanest of towels and began to soap her body. The cool water against her hot skin made her shiver but she only threw her head back and smiled, luxuriating in the soothing touch of her own hands. Every inch of her body she soaped, her pale thrusting breasts with the nipples pink and roused from the shock of the cold water, small taut waist, hips rounded to balance those curving breasts, legs shapely if, to her mind, a little too plump. Dark-skinned as she was Tara tanned easily and her legs, arms and shoulders were all a rich brown in contrast to the whiteness of her body.

One day I'll find somewhere I can sunbathe without a stitch of clothes on and get this brown all over, Tara promised herself.

Her wash completed, Tara put on her robe again and started back to her room. In the passageway she heard the men's voices louder than before and realized they must just be leaving. Hastily she slipped back into the kitchen. She didn't want to walk into them half dressed as she was – let them go first.

For a long while it seemed they remained in the veranda doorway while someone told a joke, perhaps, for after a little silence there was a raucous laughter. Then she heard them calling goodnight and the sound of the door slamming and the bolts being drawn. Relieved that she could now escape to bed she emerged from the kitchen to see Dimitri disappearing back into the dining room. Her heart sank. Oh, he wasn't going to expect her to help him tidy up tonight was he? Why hadn't she had the sense to stay in her bedroom out of the way!

As she passed the doorway he looked up and saw her. 'Ah, Tara!'

'Oh, leave it can't you, Dimitri?' she pleaded. 'I'll get up earlier in the morning and do it then. I'm just so tired . . .' He did not answer. 'There's no one staying tonight,' she went on. 'We won't have to do breakfast so I . . .' Her voice tailed away.

Dimitri had not moved except to straighten up from the chair he had been repositioning but there was something about the way he was looking at her that was disconcerting – no, worse, downright unnerving. Tara had seen that look before and knew what it meant. But never before had she felt so totally paralysed as if she had no will of her own to move away from those bright intent little eyes that were mentally stripping her of every stitch of her clothing.

She stood mesmerized while those eyes moved slowly and lasciviously from the V of tanned flesh at the neck of her wrap down over the swell of her breasts to her waist, neatly defined by the tie-sash, and down over her hips, belly and legs where the silk clung to her still-damp skin. Then he jerked his head, flicking the greasy flop of hair off his forehead and the movement broke the spell. Tara raised her hand to pull the robe more tightly around her, horribly aware that beneath it she was totally naked, and backed away a step into the passage.

Still Dimitri did not move. His tongue had crept out a fraction; it curled over his lower lip pink, moist and somehow obscene. His eyes were fixed on her face now. Half hidden as they were in the folds of flesh they were nonetheless compelling. She took another step backwards and her shoulders encountered the wood panelling of the wall.

'Tara . . .' His voice was thick, very foreign.

She drew herself up. 'You have had too much to drink, Dimitri. And I am going to bed.'

She turned with a flounce of composure she was far from feeling, marched along the passage and up the stairs. Only when she was back in her own room with the door closed behind her did she crumple, her breath coming out on a sigh, her whole body shuddering with distaste.

Ugh, but he was revolting – a great fat slug – and the way he had looked at her made her feel like washing all over again. Strangely, it had never occurred to her before that she might have to be wary of him and now she cursed herself for being a fool. Just because he was married to Tina didn't mean he had no eyes for anyone else – she of all people should have known that. But circumstances had made her forget – perhaps because, drudging in the kitchen as she had been since coming to Darwin, she felt so dreadfully unattractive herself. It had not occurred to her to worry when Tina and the children had been evacuated and she was left alone with Dimitri – no, not even tonight when she had paraded in front of him wearing nothing but her robe. She had hidden in the kitchen so that the other men should not see her but she had stopped to speak to Dimitri without giving it a second thought.

With a sense of shock Tara realized how foolish she had been to forget Dimitri was a man – a man who had not seen his wife for almost two months. Well she would not forget it again. She untied the sash of her robe and began to slip out of it, then changed her mind and refastened it around her. Since coming to Darwin she had always slept nude – in the heat it was the most practical way. But tonight she did not want to. Hot or not she was going to keep her wrap on.

She turned back the single rough sheet and lay down, pulling the silk across her legs. For a moment it reminded her of the silk sheets she had used to sleep between. Something halfway between regret and nostalgia stirred a haunting chord within her and with it a rush of loathing for this room, so different from the one she had shared with Red.

What had she come to, she who had sworn that she had finished with squalor and poverty? She had drifted back to it because she had been afraid. But now . . . maybe the time had come to stop being afraid and to move on. She had been given the opportunity tonight by the Captain of the *Fortuna* – perhaps she should take it. Perth was a long way from Sydney just as Darwin was and possibly a good deal more pleasant. And what if Red did find her there? He could only kill her as he had threatened to do – and the life she had now was barely worth living in any case.

And yet . . .

I can't go without weighing it all up and I'm too tired to do that tonight, Tara thought. Already a delicious drowsiness was beginning to creep over her making her limbs leaden and entwining silly nonsensical thoughts with the coherent ones. Tomorrow she would be up early and she would think then what she would do. The *Fortuna* would not be sailing too early. Red would not let it. No – not Red – the Captain. Red was in prison so there was no need to worry about him. No – wrong. There was every reason to worry. He was in prison because of her. And a man with his influence could still find a way to reach her.

Oh Red, Red, you were power, she thought, and then she was drifting again with sleep weighing down her eyelids.

*

Suddenly, shockingly, she was awake once more. Someone was in the room with her. As she opened her eyes to see the bulky form between her and the light she screamed and a hand covered her mouth – a hand smelling of beer and tobacco and sweat.

'Quiet! Do you want to wake the whole of Darwin?'

She wrenched her mouth free of the hand.

'Dimitri! What the hell do you think you are doing?'

The bed dipped as he lowered himself onto it.

'Come on, Tara, don't play games with me. We're on our own, both of us. And you like me, don't you? I'm not so bad!'

He rolled towards her. Heat seemed to flow from him in waves and the rank body odour turned her stomach. As his hand slipped through the opening of the loosely tied robe she rolled away across the narrow bed deftly missing the chest. He followed her but less adroitly; his leg caught the corner of the chest, rocking it, and he swore violently.

'Argh! Bitch! Where do you think you are going? Come back here!'

He lumbered towards her, trapped between bed and wall. The pain of his barked shin had inflamed his passion still further; weeks of frustration burned in his blood and crawled on his greasy skin.

'Keep away from me!' she warned him.

The rasp of his fevered breathing came closer and his bulky shadow blotted out the pale light filtering in through the window. He reached for her, closing in, and as he did so she brought her knee up in the time-honoured defence she had learned in the back streets of Sydney. It was a trick she had not used since those long-gone days but it had never failed then and it did not fail now. As her knee connected with his groin he caught his breath and doubled up in agony. Contemptuously she pushed past him.

'Now get out of my room!' she ordered.

'You bitch!' he growled, still holding himself.

'Get out this instant unless you want Tina to know what you've tried on. Out!' She threw open the door and stood waiting for him to go.

'OK, OK, I go. But you've been asking for this. Begging!'

'Out, you old fool!'

He lumbered past her still groaning and she slammed the door after him leaning her weight against it. He wouldn't try anything else tonight. But there would be other times when they were alone; other nights. If she had been undecided before about whether to leave Darwin or stay, now her mind was made up. She would not spend another night under the same roof as that dirty old goat.

Tomorrow, as soon as it was light, she would pack her things, go down to the wharf and take up the offer of the passage on the *Fortuna*.

Chapter Three

Tara was just finishing her packing when Dimitri pushed open the door and walked in.

'Hey, come on, we have work to do . . .' He broke off. 'What do you think you are doing?'

Tara slammed down the lid of the expensive pigskin suitcase that had been a present from Red.

'I'm leaving. I've decided to take up the offer of a berth on the *Fortuna*.'

'Leaving! You can't! What am I supposed to do without you?'

'I don't know, Dimitri. But if things are as bad as everyone says they are you won't have a business here much longer anyway.' Tara turned to collect her few trinkets from the small chest. 'Look, I'm sorry, but there it is. Tina went, didn't she? You didn't try to stop her. And I may not get a chance like this again.'

'Of all the ungrateful . . .' Dimitri waved his hands expressively. 'I have treated you like one of the family, Tara.'

'Huh!'

'It is true!'

'You're over familiar with me if that's what you mean. Barging into my room without knocking for one thing – and as for that episode last night . . .'

He coloured. 'I had been drinking. Men do many things when they have been drinking.'

'I don't want to hear your excuses,' she said.

'It's not an excuse. Besides, I had every reason to think . . .'

'Because you kept me working here, I suppose. For that I am supposed to fall into bed with you out of gratitude. Gratitude! For the privilege of being treated like a drudge!'

106

'You can't go!' he protested. 'I won't let you!'

She picked up her suitcase. 'Try stopping me. And you owe me two weeks' wages, by the way.'

'Two weeks . . . !' He was almost speechless. 'I can't pay you just like that – and I wouldn't if I could! You see – you'll have to wait. Don't go until the end of the week.'

Tara sighed. 'If I wait until the end of the week I shall have missed the boat. No, I shall just have to let you have a forwarding address when I get wherever I'm going and trust you to send it on to me.'

'You'll be lucky!'

'Yes, I thought you would say that. Still there are sometimes things which are more important than money. I'm going now – if you would please get out of my way.'

'No!' As if suddenly making up his mind he positioned himself in the doorway. 'No, I refuse to let you pass. Soon the boat will sail and then you will have to stay.'

'Out of my way you old fool or you'll get more of what I gave you last night!' She moved towards him purposefully and he sidestepped smartly.

'Tara . . .'

'Goodbye, Dimitri, I'm sure you'll manage without me.'

His reply was in his native language but without the help of an interpreter Tara still knew what he meant to convey and she smiled to herself as she ran down the stairs her suitcase bumping against her leg. Dimitri was not well pleased! Well, tough luck. If he had been fair with her she might have taken her chances and stayed to help him out. As it was he could look for someone else to do the cooking and washing up and share his bed. She was not going to stand for it any longer.

She let herself out of the house and into the small garden. The sky was clear as yet, the sun high and bright in defiance of the lowering clouds that would soon gather and thicken to herald the daily downpour, but the air was heavy with the bitter sweet scent of henna and Tara felt the beginnings of a headache, legacy of an almost sleepless night, throb in her left temple. She walked down the path between the crotons, garish almost in their bright autumn hues, and hibiscus, red and pink against the lush green foliage. Pawpaws overhung them in pendulous clusters and Tara reached up and picked one, biting into its delicious juicy flesh.

How long would it be before she ate again? She did not know but it was the least of her worries. She was leaving Darwin, she was leaving Dimitri, and she was leaving the threat of invasion. If she was putting herself in danger from Red once more, well, there were only so many things a person could worry about at any one time.

*

As she drove her ambulance along the Esplanade with yet another supply of comforts for the hospital ship *Manunda*, Alys had a perfect view of the harbour but the sight of all the ships gathered there did not disturb her as they had disturbed James Crawford.

War is terrible, Alys reminded herself. But it made no difference to the way she felt – the sharp needle edged thrill, half fear half something else – a primeval emotion handed down from the beginning of time and conjuring up a dozen pictures coloured in the green and gold of glory, the scarlet of freshly spilled blood . . . Roman legions marching, Royalists and Roundheads clashing in sunlit clearings, cavalry at full gallop heads held high and unafraid . . . *Into the valley of death rode the six hundred . . .*

War is terrible, she reminded herself. But at the same time she was honest eough to admit that it had brought her alive in a way that nothing had ever done before.

On the Esplanade Alys stopped her ambulance outside the post office, a solid stone building where so much of Darwin was timber and corrugated iron. The previous evening she had written a letter to her mother explaining why she was not coming home and she was anxious to post it as soon as possible. But there was a long queue waiting to be served and Alys thought she had better not wait. She was already running a little late for she had been delayed at Red Cross HQ while a missing consignment of comforts was located.

The clock in the post office said 9.45 a.m. Alys waved to Iris Bald, the postmaster's twenty-year-old-daughter, who was just passing through with a library book under her arm, and wondered why she was not at her desk in the Taxation Office where she worked. Then she stopped for a moment under the veranda to check her private mailbox and turned back to her ambulance. Get the comforts delivered and then she would come back to post her letter.

She was driving towards the harbour when she saw the aeroplanes. At first she took no notice. There was always activity in the skies over Darwin – if it was not the Aussie Wirraways it was the American planes who used the base. Then something in the sound of the engines made her uneasy. They did not sound like Wirraway, Kittyhawks or Hudsons. They sounded heavier and more ominous . . .

And suddenly there were objects besides the aircraft in the sky – slender objects catching the light of the morning sun as they fell. Alys gasped, jamming on her brakes and feeling a slow sharp edge of terror slice up her spine. It couldn't be a raid – could it? There had been no warning.

At that very moment the siren began to wail.

*

Tara was on the wharf when the Japanese bombers came. It was an ugly and inconvenient structure supported on steel and wooden piles which jutted out into the harbour from Stokes Hill then dog-legged through an angle of 90° to run parallel with the shore and provide berths for two ships, a large one on the outside and a smaller one on the inner. On the landward end of the wharf a locomotive pulled the trucks to and fro, but it could not negotiate the acute angle of the dogleg and to overcome the problem a turntable operated by a donkey engine had been installed.

109

Trucks were shunted onto this turntable two at a time then pushed by hand one at a time to the waiting ships.

As on the previous day the harbour was crowded. Two vessels were unloading and it was for one of these that Tara was making. Back in the docks she had enquired for the *Fortuna* and the man she had asked had pointed to the ship tied up at the outside berth. At the time it had seemed like good fortune not to have to find a launch to take her out to the *Fortuna*. Now, as she lugged her suitcase along the seemingly never-ending length of the pier, she was not so sure.

Oh, it was so hot! Early as it was the atmosphere was suffocating, made heavier, it seemed, by the clouds of steam rising from the hardworking locomotive and impregnated by the sharp whiffs from the iron ore loading jetty and the bitumen plant. Tara's head throbbed with every step she took, her arm ached from the weight of her suitcase and she thought she was starting a blister on one heel.

At the dogleg angle of the wharf she paused, setting down her suitcase and idly watching the engine shunt a couple of trucks onto the turntable. Two wharfies were waiting for them, swarthy little monkeys of men in vests and shorts, their muscles hard and rippling beneath skin tanned to burnished leather by constant exposure to the sun.

As the trucks angled off onto their section of rail they took charge, calling their intentions to one another then man-handling them on their way with the ease of toys.

'Smoke-oh!' A shout close at hand startled Tara and she turned to see another wharfie standing in the open doorway of a shed which also occupied the dogleg. He was a larger man than either of the ones working on the trucks, with a beer pot which hung over the top of his shorts and heavy, unshaven jowls. The one who got out of manual work as much as possible, obviously; the self-appointed tea-maker. 'Smoke-oh!' he bellowed again, then leered at Tara. 'You want a cup, darlin'?'

Tara shook her head and picked up her case once more. Wharfies were drifting down the jetty now in groups, making for the recreation shed; they ogled and whistled at her as they passed. As she came closer to the two ships that were tied up she felt the first niggle of doubt. The smaller one on the inside berth was a freighter, the *Barossa*. But the other was a much bigger ship than she had expected. Officers from a ship as impressive as that one did not usually dine at the Savalis' place, for all Dimitri's delusions of grandeur.

Another wharfie was heading towards her and Tara approached him.

'Excuse me, is that the *Fortuna*?'

'*Fortuna*? Naw. She's not in yet.' The wharfie rolled a wad of tobacco across his lip.

'But I was told that was her,' Tara said, pointing out the ship at the end of the wharf.

He shook his head. '*Neptuna* that is. She's unloading explosives.'

Tara swore. 'Oh, you don't mean I've got to go all the way back!'

The wharfie grinned and picked up her case. 'Come on, I'll give you a hand. I've got to go back that way myself.'

His last words were almost drowned out by the drone of approaching aircraft. 'More of those noisy Yankee bastards,' he yelled above the roar.

Tara looked up and saw a sky full of planes. He was right, the Yanks were everywhere now. Then, more in surprise than alarm, she registered something wrong. Yankee planes did not fly with gaping holes in their bellies and those markings . . .

Simultaneously she heard the wharfie yell a warning.

'Christ – look out! It's the bloody Japs!'

He grabbed her arm pulling her down towards the decking. She hit it with her knees and experienced a moment's searing pain. Beneath her the wharf vibrated, all around the thick air echoed with the throb of engines. Then a high-pitched whine threatened to split her car-drums. Instinctively she covered her head with her hands. And the world seemed to explode around her.

*

She came back to consciousness like a drowning man surfacing through choppy storm waves with the ground rocking beneath her and the trembling air torturing her ear drums with a sharp stabbing pain that was both physical and aural. Thuds and explosions jarred through every one of her senses, each preceded by the piercing whine that made her clap her hands across her ears. Yet nothing could shut it out, nor the screams and the shouts, nor the crackle of gunfire.

Acrid smoke drifted past her filling her nostrils and stinging her eyes and she arched her body coughing, only to gulp in more of the smoke so that for a moment she thought she would choke. The sensation frightened her more than the mayhem around her and she struggled to a sitting position, hawking and gasping. Then, as her streaming eyes took in the scene, she froze in utter horror.

The whole of the harbour, it seemed, was ablaze. Clouds of smoke, thick and black, obscured some ships, others listed at crazy angles. In the water men struggled and screamed, small boats dodged, patches of oil blazed. And still the planes threatened overhead, not the high level bombers now – they had done their work – but dive bombers and fighters, swooping in, attacking.

Near the wharf edge a swathe of scarlet fluttered; Tara recognized it as one of her own skirts. She rolled over to reach for it and saw her suitcase bobbing in the water below, blown open, with the contents spread over a yard-wide area. Beside it, face down, was a body blackened by oil – the wharfie who had been helping her. A scream bubbled in her throat and died, then she was on her feet stumbling back the way she had come into the drifting cloud of smoke.

A few yards she ran, then drew up sharply with all the

tiny hairs on the back of her neck pricklingly erect. Something was wrong, terribly wrong. She hesitated. Then as the smoke swirled away she saw what it was. The dogleg angle of the jetty had been destroyed. Just a few feet in front of her the steel and timber ended abruptly and there was nothing but the sickening drop to the oil blackened water below. Another step and she would have gone plunging down.

For a moment Tara stood frozen unable to believe her own eyes. The turntable, the locomotive, the recreation shed where the men had been gathering for smoke-oh – all gone – blown to oblivion by a Jap bomb. Then as her mind cleared like the drifting smoke she realized the full implications of the destruction.

She could not get off the wharf. She was trapped on an island of debris in the middle of the harbour with no means of escape. And still the Japanese planes swooped in overhead so low that the pilots' grinning faces were clearly visible, still the bombs fell and the guns fired, still everything burned around her.

As Tara stood there, staring down into the void, the air screamed again and she threw herself down as the wharfie had thrown her, burying her head in her arms. The world rocked not once but twice and the explosions deafened her. As they died away she rolled over, looking over the shelter of her arm and gasping at the sight which met her eyes.

The ship she had been making for in error – the *Neptuna* – had suffered a direct hit. The bridge was gone, a pall of black smoke mushroomed up into the already thick atmosphere. Then, as she watched, the flames leaped orange and scarlet against the black, Dante's inferno here before her eyes.

Tara scrambled to her feet again – but which way to go? There was no escape. Someone caught at her arm and she turned to see a burly seaman.

'Come on, love – we shall have to jump to get off here!'
She shrank from his touch. 'No – I can't!'

113

'Come on I say! We're effing good targets up here!'

Leaving go of her arm he launched himself, disappeared then bobbed up again. As he did so a bomb hit the water and a wave, feet high, erupted. The force of it lifted the man like a toy, hurling him at one of the struts. He crashed into it and fell back into the water thrashing feebly and fighting for breath, his lungs crushed by the explosion.

'Oh Holy Mary!' she sobbed. Blindly she turned back towards the end of the wharf and as she did so a Jap plane sprayed a line of machine gun fire alongside her. Once again she threw herself down but a man running in front of her fell, blood spurting scarlet from his leg. He missed me on purpose, she thought, but she knew she could not rely on the next one doing the same.

Her searching fingers found the edge of the wharf. Perhaps she could climb down the struts and shelter underneath, she thought. It wouldn't save her if a bomb scored a direct hit, but it would keep her out of the way of flying debris and machine gun bullets. Concentrating totally on the effort Tara scrambled over the edge and sought a foothold. Slowly down, one foot then the other, hanging onto the edge of the wharf with hands that bled. Something whistled through the air close by and she flattened herself until she heard it splash into the water below. Then she lowered her foot carefully onto the next strut – and screamed as it splintered and gave way beneath her. For a moment it seemed she was bound to fall, then her searching toes found a ledge and she scrambled onto it, hanging out like a bow from the shattered structure of the jetty.

She could think of nothing now but the physical effort of hanging on; the attack was merely the background to the nightmare. Her fingers were slipping, slipping, every muscle screaming a protest. Then above the roaring in her ears she became aware of a voice she recognized calling her name.

'Tara! For God's sake! Get down here!'

With difficulty she twisted round enough to see a

launch in the water below her and there in the bows was Sean Devlin.

'Come on – move!' he yelled at her.

She was hanging onto the strut for grim death. 'I can't!'

'Yes you can. Jump! We're here! We'll catch you! Come on!'

She did not answer. She couldn't do it – let go of this strut and fall towards the water! Holy Mary, she couldn't!

'For Chirst's sake!' he shouted angrily. 'You've got to get away from here. The bloody *Neptuna* is going to go sky high in a minute. Can't you hear it?'

Hear it? Hear what? Words meant nothing. She had been able to think of nothing but that fall. And then, through the cacophony of other sounds she heard it – a low and threatening rumble that seemed to come from the very core of the earth, shaking the air, reverberating along the wharf, entering her body through her fingertips as well as through her tortured ears. Vaguely she remembered words that seemed to have been spoken in another life – the wharfie who had died telling her 'The *Neptuna* is unloading explosives' and saw again as she had seen with her own eyes the two crippling bombs that had torn into that ship. She saw it and heard it and suddenly it all came together in one terrifying flash of realization.

The *Neptuna* was going to blow up. If she remained where she was she would almost certainly be killed.

Tara swung round. Beneath her in the launch, arms outstretched, was Dev. For just a second she hesitated, then pushed herself away from the wharf and into thin air. She screamed as she fell, Dev caught her and they rolled over together. In panic she tried to cling to him, but without even asking her if she was all right he extricated himself, returning to the bows of the launch and yelling instructions to the three others who were crewing with him.

'That fella there – see him? He's alive. Fish him out!'

Horrified, Tara clawed at him.

'But the ship is going to explode – you said . . . !'

He shook her off. 'Get a line to him – quickly now!'

She watched as the man was pulled in. He was black with oil and there was an ugly hole where his eye should have been. It gaped scarlet in the midst of the black slime. Tara turned away clapping her hand over her mouth to stop the rush of bile. One of the Chinese seamen swimming in from stricken ships was pulled out of the water too.

'Let's get out of here!' Dev yelled and as the launch turned to head for shore the breeze brought Tara a whiff of a strange and overpowering smell reminiscent of roast pork. But with patches of blazing oil being blown towards the swimmers she knew it was not.

*

They had just reached shore when the *Neptuna* blew up. She went with an explosion that rocked the entire harbour, chunks of metal and lengths of rail launched like toy rockets into the vast billowing cloud of smoke, planks of wood and even the main mast tossed like matchsticks. The launch was set rocking madly and Tara thought they would capsize, then as it steadied she was amazed to see the air still full of pieces of falling debris showering towards the sea, foreshore and other ships. One fragment, white hot, landed in the water close by. And above the stricken ship the first dense black cloud continued to mushroom up and out, a gigantic, awesome memorial.

As the water settled Dev brought the launch closer to land and when he told her to Tara jumped over the side, the water splashing up her legs, and struggled towards the beach. Dev and one of the other men followed, supporting the badly wounded seaman between them. They set their burden down in the shelter of the towering cliffs and Dev turned to Tara.

'You can look after him now.'

All Tara wanted to do was crawl into a crevice of the cliff and hide until the raid was over.

'Me? But what can I do?'

'Get him to a hospital, first chance you get. help will come – as soon as the raid is over.'

'Couldn't you take him?'

In his rakish face his eyes were very dark, very hard.

'We have other work to do.'

She looked out over the harbour. It was like a scene from hell.

'You'll be all right now.' He turned to his friend. 'Come on, let's get this show on the road.' And without a backward glance they went back down the beach, splashing through the water to the launch. The engine was still running and soon they were just another bobbing dot amid the debris, half obscured by a curtain of smoke. Tara felt a moment's admiration, swiftly followed by disbelief. Her own sense of self-preservation was so strong she could hardly believe that anyone would go out into that holocaust risking horrific death if they did not have to.

Beside her the injured man moaned and Tara glanced at him, half impatient, half repulsed. She would help him to a safer spot beneath the cliffs and leave him there, she decided. Then, when the raid was over, she would find someone with transport and tell them where to find him.

Trying not to look at his face she put an arm around his shoulders and immediately recoiled from the slimy touch of the oil. She moved out of the cleft but a burst of gunfire from a fighter plane made her skip back again.

Oh, it was like the end of the world! Tara's fingers went to the rosary she always wore around her neck, clutching at the cross with shaking fingers. The injured man moaned again, mumbling something unintelligible, and Tara looked at him in despair. She was trapped. Trapped with this – this *thing*. Shapeless, slimy, stinking black and that terrible gaping wound like raw meat on the butcher's slab . . . she could not bear to look at it a moment longer. If she had to stay here she must at least try to cover it up. But with what? She had nothing. Except . . . Tara found

117

herself remembering countless movies . . . her petticoat. She hauled up her skirt looking with regret at the fine cotton lawn, the nicest petticoat she had ever owned and nicer even in her opinion than the flame-coloured silk that Red had bought to go with her basque. But the petticoat was already muddied and torn in one place where it had caught on a wharf support and in any case at that moment Tara would have sacrificed anything to hide the gaping wound from view.

She ripped off two strips of material then gritting her teeth, tried to clean the oil away from the edges of the wound and bandage over it. Several times she had to turn her head away, taking fresh air, such as it was, into her lungs and deliberately steadying herself. The man was semi-conscious, but when she finished tying the strip at the back of his oil-caked head with a neat bow he muttered something once more and leaning forward she caught a name.

'Roma.'

Oh Holy Mary, he thinks I'm his wife or something, Tara thought, horrified, but she found herself leaning closer and summoning the courage to wipe the oil away from around his mouth too.

'It's all right, we'll have you in the hospital soon enough, so we will,' she said, and told herself: Whatever he looks like this is *not* a thing. It is a man. And you, my girl, would do well to remember it!

Chapter Four

Just when it seemed they never would the Japanese planes went away. As the All Clear sounded the shocked people of Darwin emerged from their hiding holes, the drainage ditches, open sewers and sheds where they had taken refuge, and Tara, along with dozens of others, was able to creep out of the shelter of the cliffs.

All she wanted to do was to run – as far from Darwin as she could before the planes returned – but she was held back by the thought of the wounded man. He's not my responsibility she told herself, but it was no use. The pieces of her petticoat bound around his face somehow *made* him her responsibility.

I'll have to make sure he's all right before I leave him, Tara thought crossly. I'll have to see he gets proper treatment or I'll have nightmares about him. Well, I'll probably get the nightmares anyway!

She bent over the man again. The stench of oil and blood assailed her once more but at least it no longer made her feel sick.

'I won't be long,' she said. 'I'm going to find help.'

His fingers fluttered on her arm and she made herself squeeze them.

'Stop worrying now. The worst is over.'

The dock road was in chaos. Vehicles, pressed into service, hooted and honked above the jarring grind of engines that refused to start, the injured staggered drunkenly, clutching their wounds with something like disbelief, the frightened ran and milled, their faces ugly with panic as they fought to jump aboard anything that moved. Frantic to get away herself Tara ran this way and that looking for someone who could help her, but for all the attention she was able to attract she might as well have been invisible.

On one side of the dock road a man was bending over a heap of rubble, shifting it stone by stone from the roadway. His hair had flopped limply down across his face as he worked but Tara recognized him as a customer of the Savalis' place. Heart pumping with relief she ran over to him.

'Griff! Thank goodness!'

He glanced up at her, his face red and running with perspiration, then bent to move another block from the heap of rubble, tossing it with seemingly senseless precision to a new heap a few feet away.

'Griff, you must help me, please!' She caught at his arm, trying to get through to him, but he shook her off with a fury which startled her.

'Cut it out for Chrissakes!'

'Griff – I've got a wounded man . . .'

'Deal with it yourself. I've got other things to do.'

'But Griff . . . !'

He broke rhythm long enough to look up at her, rubbing the perspiration out of his eyes. 'Mate of mine is buried under this lot. Either lend a hand or fuck off,' he snarled.

Tara backed away. It was hopeless. No one was going to take the slightest notice of her – too many people had been killed or wounded whilst she, though dirty and dishevelled, was unhurt. Turning her back on the chaos she ran back to where her charge was sprawled under the cliffs.

'Could you get up, do you think, if I help you?' she asked him.

An imperceptible nod told her he had heard. Bracing her back against the cliff she got an arm around his waist and began to lever. Oh, but he was a dead weight, slipping and slumping all over the place!

'I can't do it unless you help me,' she said and her tone if not her words seemed to rally him. She felt him struggle and increased her own effort, then somehow he was on his feet though as she took a step or two forward it felt to her as if the whole of his weight was on her arm.

120

Like two drunks they staggered towards the road. I can't make it, Tara thought. In just a moment my knees will give way and I shall just sag down like a sack of potatoes with him on top of me.

The thought of being pinned down, unable to escape his trickling blood and the choking oily smell that emanated from his every pore gave her the strength to struggle on though her goal – the end of the dock road – seemed farther away than ever.

She heard the engine of a motor vehicle behind her, tried to veer clear and could not. A horn honked loudly and mentally Tara echoed the exhortation Griff had used to her. Fuck off. If the driver wanted to get by he would have to do some manoeuvring. Tara certainly could not.

The horn honked again and a voice – a female voice – shouted: 'Hi! You!'

The vehicle was almost alongside her. With an effort Tara turned her head and saw it was white-painted with a prominent red cross on the side. An ambulance – and leaning out of the driver's window was a young woman, whose hair gleamed red-gold in the strong sunlight.

'Hey! Do you want some help?' she called.

Tara could do nothing but nod her head gratefully. The ambulance stopped, the driver's door opened and a pair of long legs emerged.

'Hold on. I'll be right with you.'

A slimly built body followed the legs. The girl was wearing the uniform of the Red Cross; she paused for a moment to pull her rucked up skirt down to her knees.

'Damned skirts! You'd think they'd give us trousers! Right, I'll give you a hand and we'll get him in. Can you make it round to the back doors?' she asked Tara's charge, hauling his free arm up around her shoulders and releasing some of the weight from Tara. 'You'll have to sit up, I'm afraid – I'm full already. But I guess it's better than walking.'

As she spoke she was unlocking the rear doors of the ambulance. The stench of burned and blistered flesh

121

wafted out and someone moaned. Half a dozen men sat or half lay on the stretcher beds and between them the two girls manoeuvred Tara's charge into the only remaining space.

'Right, fellas, we're on our way,' the Red Cross girl said cheerfully, and to Tara, 'You'd better sit up in front with me – there's no room here.'

'Oh, I don't want to come . . .' But the girl was already on her way back to the driver's cab and Tara followed not wanting to be left alone again.

The girl had left the engine running; as Tara climbed in beside her she knocked it into gear and pulled away with a jolt.

'Damn.' She changed up. 'You'd think they would make a vehicle like this to run smoothly, wouldn't you? Instead of jolting the patients just when they don't want to be jolted.' Another swift change. Then she said conversationally, 'Well, that was a hell of a raid, wasn't it?'

Tara nodded. Her teeth were trying to chatter now from reaction and she knew if she spoke she would be unable to control them.

'Where were you when it happened?' the girl asked.

Tara set her jaw. 'On the wharf.'

'Nasty! You are lucky to be alive. They got the *Manunda*, didn't they?'

Tara looked puzzled.

'The hospital ship. You'd think they could have seen her red crosses – they're big enough for heaven's sake!' She broke off to steer around a bomb crater. 'The town's a complete mess, you know. God knows how many people have been killed. The post office got a direct hit. No one there would have stood a chance.'

'What about the Savalis' rooming house – is that all right?'

'Couldn't say. I haven't been out that way. Look out!' She swerved to avoid a man wavering dangerously on a damaged bicycle and gave a small resigned shake of the

122

head. 'I suppose they'll all start running now. Can't say I blame them.'

Tara stared in silent horror at the devastation all around – buildings reduced to piles of rubble, bits of curtain fluttering in the breeze, ruins smouldering. And everywhere the sense of barely controlled panic; panic growing with the sweltering heat of the sun as it climbed in the heavens.

'This isn't the way to the hospital is it?' Tara asked presently.

'We're not going to the civilian hospital. That had a hit, I believe. I don't know how bad it was – only that I've been told to take patients to the AGH – the military hospital.'

They left the town behind, swinging out onto a road that ran across flat, blood-red earth where the vegetation was sparser and more twisted.

'My name is Alys Peterson, by the way,' the Red Cross girl said suddenly. 'What's yours?'

'Tara Kelly.'

'Sounds Irish! In fact *you* sound Irish.'

'I am.' Tara looked at her sharply. 'But how did you know?'

'My family are English. I have a British passport myself.'

'I see.' English, she was thinking. I must be in shock not to have noticed. And not only English but upper crust English. You are out of the top drawer, Miss Alys Peterson, whoever you are . . .

'Hang on!' Tara's train of thought was interrupted as Alys stood on her brakes, almost catapulting Tara through the windscreen. 'Looks as if somebody else needs our help.'

The man at the roadside was partially doubled up, his face hidden; but Tara got the impression of crumpled flannels and a none-too-clean shirt and a wide brimmed hat pulled well down onto his head. Alys leaned out.

'What's wrong? Are you hurt?'

'Naw, I . . . need a ride.' His head was still bent so that his drawl was almost indistinguishable.

'We've no room,' Alys said. 'Sorry.'

What hapened next took them both by surprise. With lightning speed the man yanked open the ambulance door and grabbed the wheel from Alys.

'Out – both of you!' His voice was dangerous. 'That side – move!'

Tara was about to obey but Alys' squeal of fury stopped her.

'How dare you! This is an ambulance!'

'Get out I say! I'm warning you . . .' The sun glinted on steel. Oh my God, he's got a knife! Tara thought and in the same instant: But she won't give up her ambulance. Not if he kills her she won't.

Wildly her eyes skittered around the cab and fell on the small fire extinguisher in its holder. All her backstreet instincts of self preservation asserted themselves and without stopping to think she grabbed it, pointed it and aimed. The foam caught the man full in his unshaven face and he staggered back, the knife falling harmlessly from his hands as he clawed at his eyes. Without waiting to close the door Alys drove her foot down onto the accelerator pedal and the ambulance shot forward while the extinguisher still pumped foam across her lap and out of the open door.

'That's one patient someone else will have to take care of.'

Tara laughed shakily. 'Heaven only knows the damage I could have done!'

'He asked for it. Looters, cowards, they all crawl out from under their stones when this sort of thing happens,' Alys said. She slammed the ambulance door. 'No more stops for anything until we reach the hospital. Right?'

'Right!' Tara agreed with feeling.

*

'Here we are then – thank God!'

Alys Peterson swung the ambulance around a lush green island and pulled hard left into a track, worn hard and wide by the passage of numerous wheels. Surprised, Tara watched the trees thin into a man-made clearing and the track broaden into a sweeping drive edged by coconut palms and new young saplings. Five concrete and corrugated blocks had been built end-on to the drive on the right, their clean washed appearance witness to their newness, and two large square buildings faced them from the opposite side. A flag pole centred the drive: Alys missed it by inches, swinging a wide arc to the second of the five blocks.

'Casualty Department, known here as Inspections and Admissions,' she explained. 'Not bad as military hospitals go, is it?'

'It looks brand new,' Tara said.

'It is, almost. 138 Australian General Hospital are a lucky crew.' She leaned heavily on the horn again and two orderlies appeared, making their way amongst the stream of casualties who were going in and out.

Inside the hospital looked exactly what it was – a battle clearing station. In the clinging heat that had descended when the power for the ceiling fans had been lost men sat or slumped, holding pads to cut faces and nursing wounds of every conceivable kind. The more serious cases were taken directly to treatment rooms where a team of doctors and nurses worked constantly, cleaning, stitching, repairing and arranging for those in need of surgery to be whisked over to the block that housed the operating theatre.

A slightly built girl in the uniform of a sister of the Australian Army Nursing Service was in charge of admissions. Her face was pale and she wore no make-up, light brown hair straggled untidily from a few hastily applied pins. She looked, Tara thought, as if she had just got out of bed. Then, as she caught sight of her own reflection, she could not help smiling – at least the nurse was clean!

The patients were brought in and Tara's charge was whisked away to a treatment cubicle. It was a relief to see him go, to feel the burden of caring for him lifted from her shoulders, but Tara felt lost suddenly. She had wanted to get away but now that she was free to do so there was nowhere to go. Alys had disappeared – Tara had last seen her talking to one of the medical staff – and as Tara stood aimless and alone the admissions sister came bustling over to her.

'I'm Sister Kate Harris – and you'll be the new Voluntary Aid. Glad you're here! Could you begin by cleaning some wounds? You'll find everything you need . . .' She broke off, a slight frown creasing her forehead. 'You *are* the new VA, aren't you?'

Tara shook her head.

'But she's going to lend a hand anyway,' Alys said from behind her. 'Look, Tara, I've just been asked to go up to the RAAF aerodrome for some supplies they're desperately in need of here. You could come with me if you like, but to be honest I should think you'd be more use here.' She smiled at Kate. 'She's a dab hand with a fire extinguisher!' she added.

Tara opened her mouth to plead with Alys to take her with her to the aerodrome. Anything – anything rather than stay here with all these wounded men, being expected to dress messy wounds and dispense cheerfulness and courage. But Alys was already on her way.

The AANS sister smiled; Tara recognized the sympathy in that look and inwardly squirmed.

'Well, if you haven't any nursing experience you can still be useful to us,' she suggested. 'The electricity has been off since the raid. But if you think you can get the old fashioned primus stove to work, you can make us all a nice cup of tea!'

*

She was in the pokey kitchen struggling with the primus when she heard the aeroplanes returning.

She froze, listening almost in disbelief to the thunder of engines as it grew louder, vibrating in the air and shaking every stone and sheet of corrugated iron in the hastily built hospital. Every moment she expected to hear the whine of falling bombs and the crash of exploding earth and masonry, but the thunder reached a crescendo as the planes passed overhead then began to die away and the dreaded thuds when they came were muted by distance.

Tara dumped the matches and ran out of the kitchen. The admissions hall was in chaos. Those who could walk milled around the entrance pushing and shouldering one another in an effort to get out, while two frightened looking nurses were trying to rig up a makeshift shelter of mattresses around some of the more seriously wounded. The atmosphere of barely controlled panic was contagious and Tara twisted this way and that looking for a path of escape. It had been bad enough on the wharf with bombs falling all around; somehow here, hemmed in by four walls and a mass of people who smelled of blood and fear, and with the memory of the last raid still agonizingly fresh to all her senses, it was much, much worse.

'Hold it everyone, please!'

The voice was loud enough to make itself heard; authoritative enough to command attention. The hubbub faded and died and every eye turned towards the speaker – a tall white-coated figure who had emerged from one of the treatment cubicles.

'That's better.' He raised a hand and ran his fingers through thick fair hair which had receded slightly at the temples. 'We are not being attacked. They have headed up towards the aerodrome. There's no need for panic.'

'Who says?' someone called jeeringly.

'Panic gets us nowhere. I suggest those who are fit enough to walk make their way to the slit trenches in an orderly fashion. You'll find them to the rear of the hospital – behind the nurses' quarters. The rest of you take what cover you can in case of attack. And medical staff – let's

127

get on with the job, shall we? We may have another influx of casualties when this raid is over.'

He turned away, going back into the treatment cubicle, and for a moment there was complete silence before people began talking once more. But amazingly his words seemed to have had the desired effect, the panic had become an uneasy calm, an orderly queue filed out through the door and those unable to move lay with resignation rather than terror in their eyes as they listened to the distant sounds of the attack. Tara, feeling slightly ashamed of herself, returned to the kitchen. She could, she supposed, join the queue and file out to the trenches. But what was the point? A bomb could fall on a trench just as well as a hospital.

I believe if I had been meant to die I would have caught it on the wharf, Tara thought. And only pausing to cross herself and whisper one hurried Hail Mary she filled the kettle and jammed it onto the spluttering primus.

*

In years to come Tara was never able to able to recall the details of that second raid. Time became meaningless and each facet blended into one tumbled whole – a bad dream from which she was unable to waken – so that it seemed she stood outside of herself watching a stranger inhabiting her body. This other Tara made tea and took it round, guiding the cup to parched and trembling lips, supporting it for those whose hands were too badly burned to hold it for themselves. That task completed – and it seemed to take forever – she was pressed into service as an auxiliary in the treatment rooms – holding dressings in place, snipping the sodden and scorched rags that were all that remained of clothing from tortured bodies, easing men into clean hospital pyjamas and trying not to wince when they winced or cry at their protesting screams. The faces of the other players in the drama were indistinguishable too, those of the nursing staff pale and anxious blobs

128

above grey cesarine uniform dresses and white medical coats; while those of the patients were sweating, dirt-streaked reflections of agony.

Only the doctor who had appealed for calm stood out from the rest and Tara found herself drawn to him as to a lifeline. Holding a dressing to one vicious wound while he stitched another she watched him, watched his quick clever fingers moving deftly over the ruptured skin and taking a kind of comfort in their success. Long, strong fingers that did not shake despite the droning of the aeroplanes overhead; fingers that reminded her a little of Chips Magee, the most talented pianist she had ever known. But with the fingers the resemblance ended. Chips had been a small man, with shoulders hunched from too many hours of stooping over the keys and legs bandied by poor nutrition when he was an infant. This doctor was tall and straight, six feet of well proportioned muscle and sinew, and beneath that slightly receding hairline his face was strong boned yet handsome, with a fine nose and long jaw, forehead high and angular, lips narrow but well defined. And his eyes . . . He glanced up to ask for an instrument and Tara found herself looking directly into them – blue eyes, as blue as her own, fringed by lashes thick as a girl's.

As she looked at him Tara felt a falling away in her stomach, a sudden strange lurch which took her totally by surprise.

Crazy, crazy! she thought. You stand here with a raid going on, doing horrible things you never thought you could do, and look at a man's eyes and hands! You, of all people! But crazy or not it somehow seemed the only reality in a world turned inside out.

Captain Allingham was his name – she heard someone call him that and slotted it into her mind alongside the other realities, something good, something solid to hold on to, like the image of those strong deft fingers and the blue, blue eyes.

Eventually, the planes went away, droning back across

the coastline and leaving a new trail of devastation in their wake, but the stream of casualties continued. Tara, who had slept little the previous night and been up since the crack of dawn, began to feel weary, but it did not occur to her now to ask if she might go. She worked like an automaton helping one patient after another, seeing them come and go, not knowing where they went or even if they existed outside the confines of the treatment cubicle.

Towards the middle of the afternoon a nursing sister poked an anxious face into the treatment cubicle.

'Captain Allingham, I'm sorry to interrupt but there's an emergency just come in – I think she ought to be seen immediately.'

The doctor straightened his tall frame.

'It's all right. I've just finished with this patient. Have the emergency brought in here, Sister.'

Two orderlies wheeled a stretcher into the cubicle. Tara's first impression was of blood, more blood than she had ever seen in her life. Then she raised her eyes to the face, ashen white beneath blood-caked hair, and caught her breath as she recognized it.

'Alys Peterson!' Sister Kate Harris said, her voice mirroring Tara's shock. 'She was asked to go up to the RAAF aerodrome for supplies, wasn't she? She must have got caught in the raid.'

Mentally Tara crossed herself. Holy Mary, she looked more than half dead already . . . Slyly she edged away so as to be able to watch what Captain Allingham and Sister Harris were doing without being too closely involved. They seemed to have forgotten she was there and she was glad. For a few minutes they worked quietly, speaking to one another in tones too low for Tara to catch what they were saying, then she heard Sister Harris say, 'She's lost a lot of blood.'

'And she'll lose more unless we operate immediately.' Richard Allingham looked up and Tara thought that the strain was beginning to show in his eyes. 'Is the theatre free?'

'I believe so. Major Parks has been operating but I think the most pressing emergencies have been dealt with.' Kate Harris' voice was quiet and calm, no longer betraying any of the emotion Tara felt sure she must be experiencing. 'Thank God we are equipped to carry on without power! It's one of the blessings of a purpose-built hospital.'

She placed a clean blanket over the unconscious girl then exclaimed softly, 'Hey, wait a minute – what's this? She's wearing a medical information bracelet!'

Tara leaned over to get a better look and saw the heavy silver chain around Alys Peterson's wrist. She had noticed it in the ambulance, she remembered, and assumed it to be an identity bracelet. Now Kate Harris lifted the inert hand to look at the lettering on the bracelet and groaned.

'This is a blood group alert bracelet. She's AB rhesus neg!'

Captain Allingham, who had been washing his hands at the sink, turned sharply and swore. 'That is a complication we could do without! I'll bet we haven't any AB rhesus negative here.'

'We'll have to send down to the blood bank at the civil hospital,' Kate suggested.

'No good. I believe it's been hit.' He finished drying his hands and tossed the paper towel into the bin. 'I'll go with her to theatre. Can you hold the fort here?'

'Yes, of course.' Kate Harris was every inch the efficient AANS sister. As two orderlies wheeled Alys out of the cubicle she shook her head. 'That is going to be touch and go. Thank goodness I noticed the bracelet, though. If she had been given the wrong blood . . .'

Tara said nothing. Ever since the bracelet had been identified she had been listening intently; now she mentally completed Kate's sentence for her. A transfusion of the wrong blood would have killed Alys.

Tara knew all about rare blood groups. It was a subject she preferred not to think about. But Donald Mackintosh – Mac the Knife as Maggie had called him – had explained it to her once in what she had found sickening detail.

'Will they be able to get her some?' she asked.

Kate crumpled a used paper sheet with more than usual force.

'I hope so. She certainly needs it – more than one unit I should say. But you heard what Captain Allingham said – the blood bank at the Civil Hospital has been hit. The best thing would be to find a donor. But there aren't that many people walking about with AB rhesus negative blood in their veins. Marvellous, isn't it? All the work the Red Cross do with blood, and when she needs some herself . . .'

'I am,' Tara said in a small voice.

'I have a feeling you can use the O or B negative groupings in an emergency,' Kate continued, then stopped abruptly. '*What* did you say?'

Tara was shaking. Blood – she hated it. And injections terrified her. Now the thought of feeling a needle go deep into her vein and seeing the warm scarlet tide flow from her own body into a clinical bottle made her feel physically sick with fear and loathing. If it had been anyone else in need Tara honestly believed she would have remained silent and learned to live with her conscience. But she felt a strange inexplicable kinship with Alys Peterson. In a shared half hour's drive something had grown up between them and Tara knew that to give way now to her own fear would be to betray not only Alys but also herself.

'I am AB rhesus negative,' she said more loudly.

Kate's face registered surprise and disbelief mingled with relief.

'You are? Are you sure?'

Tara nodded.

'Well, that is the most incredible coincidence! Listen, go straight over to the operating theatre – it's in the next block – and tell them there . . . no, wait.' She cast a quick look around the newly tidied treatment room. 'I'll come with you and show you the way.' She smiled at Tara. 'You know you might just be able to save Alys Peterson's life.'

'Yes, I suppose I might,' Tara said faintly.

It was a thought to keep hold of.

Chapter Five

Captain Richard Allingham bent over the basin and splashed water lavishly onto his face. The water was tepid – nothing in Darwin was ever cold unless it had come directly from the ice-works – but against his taut skin and eyes that burned with tiredness it felt refreshingly cool. He reached for a towel blindly and felt it rasp over the stubble on his chin.

How long was it since he had shaved? Two days? Three? He had lost count. Since the raids, day and night had merged for he had worked around the clock patching up burned and broken bodies and snatching only a few hours' sleep where and when he could. In all that time he had not been out of his clothes except to change from perspiration-soaked into fresh, nor sat down to eat a proper meal. His body ached from napping in awkward positions when weariness had completely overcome him and his brain felt as fugged and feverish as if he had been a patient suffering from sleeping sickness or malaria.

Perhaps today would see an easing of the situation, he thought, snatching at the prospect with more desperation than hope. The hospital ship *Manunda* had been in the harbour at the time of the raid and although she had been hit by two bombs one of which had killed a nursing sister and eleven others she was still seaworthy. It was intended to move her to the safety of Fremantle and some of the patients of 138 AGH were to be evacuated with her. At present it was barely possible to walk through a ward without climbing over the mattresses laid end to end on the floor to accommodate those patients for whom there were no beds and the pressure on the nursing staff had been unbelievable.

It had been inevitable, of course. Besides the casualties

who had been brought in during the aftermath of the raid there were the patients evacuated from the other hospitals more in the firing line than 138. They had arrived together with the medical staff in a convoy of ambulances and staff cars on the night of the raid and somehow 138 had stretched to accommodate them. There had been no choice and Richard accepted that fact without the slightest hint of resentment. This was war and in wartime one was not allowed the luxury of adhering to normal standards.

That did not stop him from pondering ruefully how very different it was to the way he had expected his carefully planned career to progress. He had thought he had almost done with the bone-racking tiredness of seventy and eighty hour weeks as he approached the end of his apprenticeship as a resident at the Royal Melbourne Hospital, done with being dragged from bed after only a few hours' sleep to pronounce on a patient who had taken a turn for the worse, done with being a small and helpless cog in a machine that ran relentlessly on the same power that had propelled it for generations. He had looked hopefully towards a future when he would be able to enjoy his chosen profession – enjoy it as opposed to surviving it – and use the skills he had learned and inherited without being so damned tired that he lived in terror of making some ghastly mistake.

The war had changed all that and dreams and ideals had been placed in cold storage. War meant doing what had to be done and doing it to the best of one's ability, whether it was in Tobruk or Darwin. War meant carrying on, knowing that even a tired and inadequate doctor was better than no doctor at all, trying to put the failures out of one's mind and barely pausing to savour the triumphs.

But triumphs there were, nonetheless. Triumphs such as saving the life of Alys Peterson.

Drying his face on the rough cotton towel Richard thought of her and her desperate condition when she had been brought in with her life's blood pumping out of a gaping wound in her stomach. The sight had shocked him – he had seen plenty of men with wounds as bad and worse during his time in Tobruk, and had dealt automatically and almost without emotion with the other casualties of that dreadful day in Darwin – yet none of it had prepared him for the rush of anger he had experienced when he saw the young Red Cross girl on the stretcher, red-gold hair in glorious disarray framing her deathly white face, uniform skirt in blood-soaked tatters. She had been almost awash in her own blood in spite of the attempts of the orderlies to stop the flow, her legs stained with red streaks, her motionless hands caked with it. At first glance he had thought she was past help, yet somehow his own skill and the skill of Bob Parks, the surgeon, had been able to save her and this had started a glow of pride and satisfaction that played warm fire on the cold remote place inside him which had begun with professionalism and been frozen to numbness by the death and destruction he had witnessed.

Not that they alone could take credit for saving her, of course. Their skill would have been useless without the transfusions of lifegiving blood. Thinking of it now Richard shook his head, marvelling at the twist of fate that had put another young woman with the same rare blood in the hospital – and not only in the hospital, but right on the spot so that she was able to volunteer her blood without delay. The hand of God, his mother would call it, but Richard, a confirmed agnostic, preferred to think of it as one of those strange coincidences that happen from time to time. Yes, Alys could certainly thank Tara Kelly for her life. She had done all that anyone could ask of her and more, insisting that she should give a second unit as soon as it was safe for her to do so. Under any other circumstances Richard would never have allowed it. Taking two units in so short a time, especially from a slim young girl, was not something to be done lightly. But these were not ordinary circumstances. Tara might be weak and woozy as a result of the transfusions, but she was in good health and it would not kill her, whereas Alys . . .

Without Tara's blood and the subsequent top ups from other compatible donors she would certainly have died. As it was she now stood a good chance of recovery.

Richard tossed the towel down and went outside. The rain had not yet started for the day but underfoot the earth was still a cake of red mud and beneath the coconut palms at the edge of the drive the bougainvillaea and hibiscus ran riot. Midway across the drive stood an ancient baobab tree which no one had had the heart to cut down when the ground had been cleared for the hospital to be built; as he passed it Richard glanced up at the sky between the branches that fanned out from the huge gnarled split-parsnip shaped trunk, estimating how long it would be before the downpour began once more. If it were possible to get the stretcher cases out and on their way to the *Manunda* whilst it was still dry then so much the better. His boots squelched in the soft earth and he smiled wryly remembering the strict hospital regimes he had been raised to. His father was one of the most eminent surgeons in Australia – what would he think if he could see the conditions under which the sick and wounded were cared for?

A room had been made available for Alys Peterson and Tara Kelly in the administration block – the two wards had been needed for the dozens of male patients. Richard entered the block, returning the greeting of the two clerks in the outer office. As he walked along the corridor a storeroom door opened and Tara Kelly backed out, a jam jar containing a bunch of wild flowers held carefully between her uplifted hands. She turned and saw him, her face brightening.

'Oh, good morning!'

'Morning, Tara. What have you got there?'

A faint pink flush tinged her cheeks. Good, he thought, she still has enough blood left in her to blush.

'I picked a few flowers to brighten up the room. It's so bare in there, so it is! But Sister wouldn't allow them to stay there overnight. Something about the oxygen, she said.'

He smiled, a half-ironic smile with the irony directed at himself. Perhaps not quite all the conventional hospital standards had gone by the board. Trust the sisters to keep up discipline. It had been the same in Egypt. They had tried to run their wards in the ways they had been trained to, as well as making their quarters as homely as possible. Tobruk had not been the same after they had been pulled out.

'How are you feeling this morning?' he asked.

She pulled a mischievous face. 'A little bit as if I'd had too many nights on the town.'

'Tired?'

'Uh huh. But I'm fine really, considering. It takes more than the loss of a couple of pints of blood to grind down an Irishwoman.'

'I can see that.' But he was remembering the fear in her eyes when he had taken the first unit from her – fear that she had been determined to hide – and the stubborn determination with which she had insisted she stay around in case more of her blood was needed to save Alys' life. One thing Tara Kelly did not lack was courage – and her pride was equally fierce.

'And how is Alys?' His tone softened almost imperceptibly but she heard it and the dimples in her cheeks tucked and hardened.

'Oh sure, you'll have to see that for yourself. You're the doctor.'

'True.' He lengthened his stride.

'Oh, it's all right, don't worry. She's still alive,' she said drily.

The two beds had been squashed into the small room at right angles; the one in which Alys lay was beneath the window. The bright sunlight flooding in was harsh on her pale skin but illuminated her hair, fanned out on the pillow so that it gleamed like burnished copper. She had turned her head away from the window to escape the glare of the sun; now as she heard the footsteps and voices she opened her eyes and smiled. The tiny movements appeared to cost her tremendous effort and Richard was aware of a twinge of alarm, sharper than he would have expected in the line of duty.

'How are you doing?' he asked.

'I'm fine.' But her tired voice belied it.

'Hmm.'

'I am! At least I'm alive – thanks to you and Tara.'

'To Tara mainly.'

'Sure I didn't do anything much,' Tara said almost irritably. 'Look, here are your flowers. I suppose that witch of a sister won't make me take them away again now it's morning – though how flowers can do you anything but good at *any* time I can't imagine.' She turned to Richard. 'I suppose you want me to go now so that you can examine her.'

'No, you can stay and help me. That will save me having to call a nurse over. Now, let's have a look at you, Alys.'

He crossed to the bed, checking the record chart then lifting Alys' hand which lay inert on the coverlet. The skin looked pale and transparent with veins and sinews clearly visible, and her nails, devoid of varnish, appeared quite colourless. He took her wrist between his fingers feeling for the pulse. Still faintly irregular and not as strong as he would have liked. Then he pulled back the covers, gently eased off the dressing and examined the wound to her abdomen. It was deep and angry though not as large as the first sight of her had led him to believe. She had left her ambulance to take cover under a clump of gums when the Japs had come – just as well for the ambulance had been hit. A piece of jagged metal had caught her and was responsible for her wound. Carefully he probed it. It should be all right now – provided it healed. The trouble was that in this steamy heat things did not heal, or if they did they took a very long time about it. Unfortunately, it was all too easy for wounds to putrify. He thought of the hospital ship sailing tonight for the south. She would have a better chance of recovery there – if she could stand the journey. He stood deep in thought, his handsome face furrowed with concentration and haggard with tiredness. Then he bent his long back to sit on the edge of the bed.

'The *Manunda* is leaving tonight. I think we should try to get you a berth. You'd be far better off in the south.'

A hint of rebellion flickered in her eyes. 'I'd rather be here. I have work to do. Aunt Sylvia . . .'

Richard smiled ruefully. He had come across Sylvia Crawford once or twice – a formidable lady, tough as old boots and twice as stubborn. Could it be that Alys took after her for all that she looked so vulnerable now?

'How much work could you do in your condition?' he asked reasonably. 'Besides, Darwin is going to be a garrison town from now on. Almost all the civilians have gone – and the ones who haven't soon will. Even your redoubtable aunt. There won't be a Red Cross unit here any longer – it will have to be run from Katherine or The Alice.'

He did not add that many enlisted servicemen had joined the exodus, going 'bush' or running south down the gravelled road to the Adelaide River which locals knew as 'the Track'. Some had thought in the frenzied aftermath of the raids that they were under orders to disperse, some had simply taken the opportunity to desert in the mayhem. Nor did he add that Darwin was in a state of chaos with private houses as well as businesses being looted, food eaten by hungry wharfies and seamen, furniture carried off to add comfort to mess rooms or to be sold for cash. The bank managers had gone – Alys' uncle, James Crawford amongst them – in a commandeered 3-ton truck, taking with them all the cash, securities and records of their banks by order of the Administrator. And most of the rest of the population had gone too, any way they could – by bicycle, on horseback, in cars or on foot. Soon, he believed, the hospital would be evacuated back down 'the Track'. Darwin, always untamed and a law unto itself, was no longer a safe place to be. In a few short hours the marauding Jap planes had proved that.

Alys sighed and moved her head on the pillow and something caught and twisted deep inside him, he warned himself. You have a golden rule never to let personal feelings intrude into professional relationships – don't break it now.

'I suppose if there is no one left in Darwin I'll have to go,' Alys said resignedly.

'Come on, don't sound so fed up about it,' he teased her. 'I would have thought you'd be glad to go home. Melbourne, isn't it? The centre of civilization.'

Her eyes flicked up and he saw the spark of interest in them before the drowsiness claimed them once more. 'You know it?'

'I certainly do. I trained at the Royal Melbourne. And I don't mind admitting if I had the chance to walk up Bourke Street now I'd take it.'

'Bourke Street.' There was a dreamy tone to her voice as if she was drifting in time and her eyes began to droop.

'I'll see what I can do,' he said. He smoothed the counterpane across her shoulders and as his fingers brushed the tangle of her hair he let them pause for a moment. So fine. So delicate. She looked like a wax doll lying there. Would he be doing the right thing by having her moved? But as he had said, everything and everyone bar the military would be leaving Darwin soon. A few more days and she might have to endure a jolting ambulance ride down the track with a wound festering from the steamy heat. No, better that she should go on the hospital ship tonight.

He straightened up and saw Tara watching him. He had almost forgotten she was there, now he remembered that she too was still in Darwin – and there because of what she had done for Alys. If she had not insisted on being on hand to supply more blood should it be needed, she would have been safely on her way south by now.

'You should go too,' he said. His voice was slightly raw now from tiredness and it came out sounding harsh. He saw her eyes darken then look away and he stood up.

141

'I may be able to arrange for you to go on the *Manunda* too.' He crossed to the door. She did not speak until he reached it, then her voice, still softly lilting yet oddly urgent, stopped him.

'I don't want to go.'

He turned, surprised. She was standing with her hands clenched into tight fists. 'I don't want to go,' she said again. 'I'd rather stay here in the hospital. I could help. I'm not a trained nurse, I know, but I'm learning. And there are so many jobs to be done . . .' She broke off.

'That's true, but . . .' He shrugged his shoulders wearily. 'I don't have the authority to take on staff. And you're not a VA, are you?'

The dimples tightened a fraction, blue fire flashed in her eyes.

'Nobody stopped to ask if I was a VA when they left me to look after that man with his eye blown away. Or when I gave blood to Alys.'

'No, but then . . .'

'I've learned a lot in the last few days,' she went on. 'I could have taken to my bed and stayed there – the Lord only knows I felt like it often enough! But I haven't, only to rest for a little while. I've done all the odd jobs around here and the nurses have been glad enough to let me. They've been under pressure enough. I've learned to change dressings and make beds the way they like them done. I've sterilized bed pans and made tea. Oh, not very skilled jobs, I admit, but somebody has to do them. And I've been glad to do it. So couldn't you *please* put in a word for me?'

Richard passed a hand across his aching eyes. Why anyone, a girl in particular, should be so anxious to remain in this hell hole he could not imagine, yet here were two of them and neither of them wanted to leave. In a way, he could understand Alys' reluctance to go. She had been working for the Red Cross for months now, since before he had been posted to Darwin himself and he could imagine her feeling that she was deserting her post. But

Tara . . . why on earth should Tara be so anxious to remain in the Territory? Did she have some pressing personal reason? He looked at her intently now trying to read what lay behind those sparkling blue eyes. But they gave him no clue. Perhaps I am wrong, he thought. Perhaps she simply does want to help. Certainly she had worked as hard as anyone on the day of the raid, tackling one unpleasant task after another until she had been forced to stop while her blood count recovered, and he had to admit her pert good looks and her personality has been good for the morale of the patients. Despite all this, could he take her on? She had no qualifications, not even the First Aid and Home Nursing Certificates that were asked of a girl who wanted to enlist as a VA. But he had the feeling that this was shortly to be waived. The services were desperate for as many women as they could get to release men for the front.

'Well . . .' he began.

Her face brightened and the dimples played in her cheeks.

'Oh, you can fix it for me! If anyone can fix it, it's you!'

He smiled, tiredness forgotten. Perhaps if the redoubtable Sylvia Crawford were still here – and he suspected she would stay to the last – she might be able to help. After all, the Red Cross was represented on the Joint Council.

I'll see what I can do,' he promised.

*

The *Manunda* sailed that night and Alys Peterson was aboard her. She lay in her bunk, weak and dizzy after the performance of having been moved by stretcher and ambulance and stretcher again, feeling far removed from the bustle about her.

A nursing sister paused by her bunk, leaning over to neaten her blankets.

'What is happening?' Alys asked. 'Have we started moving?'

Her voice, though weak, was taut. The sister smoothed a strand of red-gold hair away from the ashen face. 'Don't worry about a thing. You're going to be fine. You are on your way home now.'

Home. On the way home. The words echoed in her ears repeated by the lapping of the waves. But there was no comfort in them. She did not want to go home. Darwin was where she belonged now. Aunt Sylvia was still here in spite of the raids, hanging on to the last because she hated the idea of abandoning her responsibilities and was determined to fight for them, although Uncle James had been forced to go to ensure safe passage of the bank's cash reserves and records. Everything she had come to care about was here. Not to mention the rather attractive Dr Allingham. Whilst Melbourne . . .

At the thought of it Alys felt as if sinewy fingers had tightened around her heart and all the bitter memories came flooding in to swamp her. And not only the more recent ones, either. The claustrophobic boredom of growing up there was as vivid now in her mind as the pain of Race's death, and the fear of finding herself once more under the domination of her mother pressed like a weight on her chest. Already, she could imagine Frances' cautionary tones: 'I knew something like this was inevitable. If only you had taken notice of me, Alys, and come home as I asked none of this would have happened. I only hope it will have taught you a lesson.'

A lump rose in Alys' throat.

'We are on our way,' the sister said. 'Try to get some sleep now.'

Alys could not reply. She turned her face into the pillow and felt the weak tears trickle down her nose.

*

Tara closed the door of Matron Swift's office behind her and stood with her back pressed against it, eyes half closed, drinking in deep breaths of pure air. It was a trick she had used when she had been a singer, a way of steadying herself after a performance – and what she had just given, she thought, was the performance of her life.

'Well – and how did it go?'

At the sound of his voice her eyes flew open and she jerked upright.

'Captain Allingham! I didn't hear you coming.'

'It's these damned gumboots we have to wear.' He glanced ruefully at his rubber shod feet amply splashed with red mud. 'But you haven't answered my question. How did you get on at your interview?'

'All right, I think,' she said in a low voice. 'But we'd better not talk here. These doors aren't very thick.'

He smiled. 'You're right – this place is Jerry built. Come on, we'll find somewhere a bit more private.'

He turned to walk along the corridor with long even strides and she followed feeling her heart pump strangely the way it did every time she looked at him.

Oh, but he was handsome – the handsomest man she had ever met. And a gentleman too, that was obvious from the way he spoke and the easy grace with which he wore his uniform. Even in gumboots he still managed to look well-bred. And that was not all. Tara felt a quirk of excitement as she remembered the cool way he had taken charge on the day of the raids and the skill and compassion she had seen repeated day after day in his work since then. The pace of life in the hospital had been hectic, every facility stretched to breaking point. In addition to the casualties who had come to them direct, the entire RAAF hospital had been evacuated to 138 AGH, as had part of the civil hospital, and many of the staff were cracking up under the strain. But not Richard Allingham. He remained as cool and efficient as ever, managing to carry on with apparently effortless ease.

He even remembered it was my interview today, Tara thought, gratified, though of course his remembering probably had more to do with the fact that he had arranged it for her than it did with any real interest in the outcome . . .

Richard threw open the door of one of the vacant offices and stood back for Tara to enter.

'That's better. No one will be able to eavesdrop now. So, how did it go?'

Tara perched herself against the edge of the desk. 'All right, I think. But it was nerve racking! There were two of them . . .'

'Matron Swift and Sylvia Crawford.'

'Is that who they were? They were both rather large . . .' Tara broke off picturing again the two women who had faced her across Matron's big oak desk. Perhaps it was the fact that they both wore uniforms that had made them so daunting – Matron in her cesarine, crisp and fresh in spite of the humid conditions, Mrs Crawford smart in the dress of an officer of the Red Cross – while Tara could manage only a blouse and skirt borrowed from Sister Kate Harris for the occasion, since all her own clothes had been lost in the raid.

It could simply have been that it was so very important to Tara that they should consider her suitable to become a Voluntary Aid that had made her so nervous. Waiting to go in for the interview, willing her knees not to knock, she had realized just how much it mattered. If they took her on it meant she had a place to stay – somewhere Red was very unlikely ever to think of looking for her, if not, she would be forced to move on – but where? She did not know. And besides . . .

Perhaps hiding from Red was only part of her reason for wanting to stay. Perhaps it also had something to do with Captain Richard Allingham.

'What did they ask you?' he enquired now.

Tara raised her eyes to heaven. 'What didn't they ask! They wanted to know just about everything about me.'

'And they were satisfied with what you told them?'

'Oh, I think so.' She did not add that the answers she had given bore very litle resemblance to the truth. 'It was funny really. Matron put the fear of God into me, but the other lady Mrs Crawford did you say her name was? – I would have quite liked her if I hadn't been so darned scared!'

'Yes, she's quite a lady.' Richard's eyes softened almost imperceptibly. 'She is Alys Peterson's aunt, of course. Alys has been living with her while working for the Red Cross.'

Tara noticed, but was determined to ignore, the change in Richard's tone. Alys had gone now, shipped south on the *Manunda* and she had no intention of worrying about a rival who was far away.

'Maybe that's why she wasn't so bad to me,' she said. 'Maybe she thinks she ought to do something for me, seeing I saved her niece's life.'

Richard dug his hands deep into the pockets of his white coat. 'So what was the final outcome?' he asked.

Tara grinned mischievously. 'I think I got the thumbs-up, though they did say the final decision lay with the CO.'

'Colonel Adamson,' Richard said thoughtfully. 'Have you got to see him?'

Tara looked alarmed. 'They didn't say so. Do you think . . . ?'

'I shouldn't worry, I expect he will rubber stamp their decision. He's too busy personally to vet every VA and orderly in 138, whatever he may like to pretend to the contrary.'

'That's true enough. Besides he's a man.' Some of Tara's natural ebullience was returning. 'If I can get past two old biddies, I'm quite sure I can get past a man.'

The moment the words were out she regretted them. She glanced quickly at Richard wondering if he had noticed what she had said, but if he had he was too much of a gentleman to remark upon it.

'Well, I should imagine we shall soon be taking on a new addition to our voluntary staff,' he said dryly. 'So hoping I'm not being too premature – welcome!' He extended his hand and she took it, going weak inside again as those strong deft fingers wrapped around hers.

147

'Thank you, Captain Allingham.'

The corners of his mouth lifted; those blue eyes looked directly into hers. 'I'd much rather you called me Richard,' he said.

Chapter Six

Tara pushed the trolley into the clean room, rammed it into a vacant corner and sank down onto the single upright chair, spreading her elbows outwards on the small scrubbed wood table and laying her head on her arms.

Tired, tired – she could not remember a time when she had been so tired. Even her days of working for Dimitri Savalis seemed like a holiday compared with this. Her legs were leaden with exhaustion, her eyes stung and burned with it, every muscle in her body ached and she felt faintly nauseous.

Why in the world did I let myself in for this? Tara wondered. I must have been mad. But her brain was too furred by exhaustion even to begin to answer the question. All she could think of, all she wanted in the world, was to fall onto the narrow bunk in the quarters she shared with the AANS and masseuses and sleep. But that was out of the question. It was only half-past eleven in the morning and Tara's working day stretched endlessly on towards evening. At eight, if she was lucky, she would be relieved. Last night she had not been lucky. An aborigine woman had been admitted in labour late in the afternoon and there had been no other female auxiliary staff on duty to cover the room that was used for deliveries. Every time she was left alone the woman set up a hollering that echoed through the concrete and tin blocks, upsetting all the patients and setting the nurses' nerves jangling, but the sisters could not spare the time to do more than to make regular checks on her progress and the male orderlies, mostly rough stockmen who had enlisted to become soldiers and were disgusted to find themselves detailed for hospital work, were hardly the best choice to look after a woman in labour. So Tara had been asked to remain on duty.

The birth had proved to be a difficult one. It was almost two when the baby finally put in an appearance. Then, on her way back to her quarters, Tara had been waylaid by Sister Kate Harris. The seaman she had brought in on the day of the raid had taken a turn for the worse. She thought Tara would like to know. For a moment Tara had wrestled with the ridiculous sense of responsibility she felt for the man, then she had submitted. She had sat with him until he died two hours later and when she eventually fell exhausted into her bed she was quite unable to sleep. Now though . . .

A strident voice in the corridor outside brought her awake sharply. Sister Anastasia Bottomley – coming this way. Tara had no desire to be caught by her sleeping on the clean room table.

Of all the AANS sisters at 138 AGH, Bottomley was the one Tara liked the least. Some, like Kate Harris, had been helpful and tolerant, teaching her to take temperatures and blood pressures and how to make a bed with hospital corners. Others had been impatient, taking pleasure in handing her the most menial jobs and expecting her to work tirelessly. Tara had done so without complaint, knowing it was the price she had to pay for remaining with the hospital. But Anastasia Bottomley was the one person who could make Tara feel she would prefer to take her chances with Red rather than stand her unpleasantness for another single day. She was a sharp-featured woman with a manner to match, tall as a man, with thin shapeless legs which Tara privately described as 'gum sticks' and strawlike hair cut short and square.

The door swung open and Anastasia Bottomley came in.

'Ah, Kelly, what are you doing in here?' She did not wait for a reply. 'There is no time for idling, we have a great deal to do. I've just been informed that we are on the move.'

There had been rumours ever since the raid that the hospital would be pulled back away from the vulnerable

150

Darwin to a site deep in the wilds of Northern Territory, but Tara had not expected it to be so soon.

'Where are we going?' she asked.

'Adelaide River. It's ridiculous if you ask me, leaving new purpose-built accommodation for tent wards on the banks of a river. Some people will run scared from everything. Take the day of the raids when the authorities freed the prisoners from Fanny Bay Gaol – some of the girls were scared stiff of being raped in their beds. I'd like to see the prisoner – or the Jap – who thought he could rape me!'

Tara hid a smile. Personally, she could feel nothing but relief at the prospect of being pulled back out of the danger zone. But one thing was nagging at her – when she had fled Dimitri and the Savalis' house she had left her crucifix hanging on the wall over her bed and she hated the thought of leaving Darwin without it. For all she knew the house might not have survived the raid, but if it had . . . the crucifix had belonged to Mammy and meant a great deal to Tara.

'Do you think there might be a chance of me getting into Darwin?' Tara asked.

'I really couldn't say. Depends when we go, I suppose. And I expect we shall be the last to know when that will be. Now, we have wasted enough time in chit chat, Kelly. We have work to do . . .'

'Yes, Sister,' Tara said obediently.

*

Three days later Tara was in the small store room at the end of the ward sweltering in the afternoon's heat as she packed box after box of sterile dressings into crates ready for transportation. Now that the decision had been made to move the AGH no time was to be wasted; the first convoy of patients and staff was to leave the following day and Tara was glad she was to go with it. Frequent alarms were fraying her nerves and an afternoon raid on the

RAAF building, Daly Street and Myrilly Point had been the last straw.

She still regretted, however, that she had been unable to get into Darwin to retrieve her crucifix. She had tried without success to find a way but ten miles might as well be a hundred when she had no transport. Now it seemed likely that she would have to decamp for the Adelaide River leaving it behind.

'Hey – nursie!' The low whisper came from the open window. Tara spun round to see a cheery face topped by a mass of curly hair. 'Word on the grapevine is that you've been looking for a ride into Darwin.'

It was Private Maxwell, one of the soldiers employed on general duties at the AGH and well known as a Mr Fixit. Besides his official chores Maxie organized card schools, ran a book on anything that moved and managed to come up with an unending supply of black market goods to defy the shortages.

'Oh I am, Maxie. It's just one little thing I want to do before we leave. Can you help?'

'I might be able to. Charlie and me are going in tonight. Just two conditions. One – keep quiet about it. Two – you've got to be ready to come back when we are. We can't hang about. Got it?' He tapped the side of his nose meaningfully.

Tara nodded. This trip was strictly unofficial but that was probably just as well. She wasn't at all sure Sister Bottomley would sanction her going if she were to ask permission. And nervous as she was about venturing into town under the present conditions she did so want her crucifix.

'Where will you pick me up?' she asked.

'Nine o'clock – camp gates. Are you sure you want to risk it now? Darwin is full of looters, they say. And you never know, there could be another raid.'

'Oh, stop it! You're the cheery one, aren't you? If you can go, so can I!'

'All right then. Suit yourself. We'll see you later.'

152

Maxie's face disappeared from the window and Tara went on with her packing.

*

The humid darkness was heavy and unbroken, the rigorously enforced blackout obliterating any remaining signs of life. But, as a fitful moon emerged for a moment from behind the blanket of cloud, Tara was able to see the stark silhouettes of bombed out buildings, one wall perhaps out of four left standing, and the piles of rubble defining the lips of bomb craters.

Somewhere in the darkness a dog howled – abandoned by his fleeing owners and as yet defying attempts to round him up and destroy him as hundreds of other pets had been destroyed – he bayed his loneliness, hunger and fright to the uncaring night. The sound made Tara shiver. Then the sound of a truck engine drowned the howling and Tara drew back sharply into a shop doorway, her feet crunching on broken glass.

A truck might mean sharp-eyed provosts who would at best bully and delay her with their questions and at worst place her under arrest. Stories concerning the behaviour of the provosts were legion for though martial law had not been declared they had taken it upon themselves to act as though it had, rounding up civilians like cattle and forcing them out of town at gunpoint. One man who had come into the hospital to have a nasty flesh wound dressed had claimed that it had been inflicted by a provost for 'stealing' – after two days' travelling without food and with precious little water and unable to join the army however hard he tried, he had eventually succumbed to temptation and eaten a handful of peanuts from an open sack on the railway platform!

The truck sped by and Tara recognized it as a US Army vehicle. Its headlamps were blazing a bright path in the blackness; beyond them the shattered buildings were dark dancing shadows while ahead the beam revealed an obstruction – barricades of barbed wire placed across the road. As the truck turned off into a side street Tara left the shelter of the doorway and approached the barricade more slowly looking for a way around. She found one – by keeping close to the wall there was room to slip past. The barricades had been erected for the purpose of impeding the progress of invading troops not one lone girl and she had not come into Darwin to be turned back at the first obstacle.

Tara quickened her step, hurrying past a shattered shop front where a tailor's dummy lay sticking out of the rubble looking for all the world like a stiffened human body. She did not have much time – an hour at the outside – and she must be back at the agreed place or Maxie would leave without her.

To her relief the Savalis' house was still standing. There was a utility truck parked outside the house – no, not so much parked as abandoned, Tara decided. No one *parked* a ute at that angle. The gate stood open and between a crack in the blackout curtains at the dining room window light showed, golden yellow. Tara followed the path around to the rear of the house where the bittersweet scent of the henna still lingered in the air and the pawpaws hung above the crotons and hibiscus.

Up the veranda steps she went and opened the door. The kitchen was in semi-darkness. No delicious cooking smells came from the stove, only the stomach-turning odour of something-gone-off. Tara pressed her fingers across her mouth in disgust.

The sound of men's voices was coming from the dining room and she followed it. Then, in the doorway, she stopped abruptly. The men, three of them, were sprawled around two tables which they had pushed together within the circle of light thrown by a handful of candles and a once highly polished brass and glass tilly lamp. The air was thick with cigarette smoke; the remains of a meal lay like garbage amongst a scattering of Dimitri's precious bottles; one man's booted feet were propped on the table.

'Well, hello there!' The man with his feet on the table pushed his chair further up onto its back legs, looking at her down the length of his face through eyes narrowed against the cigarette smoke.

Tara returned his stare coldly. He was a tramp of a man, unshaven and with shirt-sleeves untidily rolled back to reveal swarthy tattoed forearms.

'Who are you?' she demanded.

The man laughed unpleasantly.

'We might ask her the same, mightn't we, lads?'

'We might, but why bother? She's a sheila, ain't she?' The speaker had a weaselly face across which his hair hung in greasy strands. 'All we needed to make the party complete was a sheila – what do you say, Rico?'

'*Mamma mia!* Rico say *bellissima!*'

'*Bellissima!*' they ribbed him, but their teasing did nothing to reduce the atmosphere of threatening tension. It hung in the air with the wreathing cigarette smoke.

'This wine is sure as hell *bellissima*,' the man with his feet on the table observed and he wriggled forward, his heels scoring the surface as he reached for another bottle. The sight of it fired Tara's ready temper.

'Just what do you think you are doing?' she flared. Another roar of laughter drowned her but she continued angrily: 'Does Dimitri know you are here? I'll bet he doesn't!'

More laughter. 'Who's Dimitri when he's home?' one of the men asked.

'Who cares?' another rejoined. 'He ain't at home, is he?'

'No, he is not, but I am!' Tara was trembling with indignation. 'Get out of here, all of you. You have no right . . .'

'Right?' The man with his feet on the table lowered himself down so that the front legs of the chair landed on the floor with a crash. 'Now let me tell you somethin', lady. There's a war going on if you hadn't noticed and when there's a war on things is diff'rent. Finders is keepers, for one thing. There ain't much food left in

Darwin and what's here they won't want. They've gone, ain't they? Run like bunnies. And what ain't eaten will only go off anyways – rot on the tables where they left it and in the fridges for want of power. We're hungry – we might as well fill our bellies with what we can find. What's wrong with that?'

'Nothing I suppose – so long as it's only food you're taking.' Tara wheeled around pointing at the Italian who was holding a porcelain figurine belonging to Tina in his swarthy hands. 'But you can put back anything else you may have taken a fancy to here and now. That ornament for a start!'

The rubbery face turned sour and the Italian half-started to his feet.

'Who you talking to – huh?'

'You!' Tara was beside herself to see Tina's precious possessions so carelessly mauled and the anger made her oblivious to any fear. 'Eat if you must but don't steal things that don't belong to you. If you do I'll . . .'

'Yes, what will you do?' the monkey man taunted.

'I'll report you to the police. Or the military.'

'Much good will that do you!' they jeered. 'The police have gone, all bar one, and the military are doing their eye good same as the rest of us!'

The man who had had his feet on the table tipped his chair onto its two back legs again to reach backwards for the door.

'Hey – Wally! Come on down here a minute and see what we've got!' he called, grabbing Tara's skirt.

'Take your hands off me!' she flared.

The Italian moved in, his weaselly face eager, and she lashed out at him. There was a crash and Tina's porcelain ornament lay in a thousand fragments on the floor.

'What is it, then, my old cobber? What have you got?' The man called Wally appeared in the doorway. He was wearing an army uniform – was he a deserter Tara wondered? – and in his hands was Tina's trinket box. The lid was open and cheap bead necklaces dangled carelessly out as if he had been rifling through to find anything of value.

'Well, well, where did you spring from?' The soldier's interest in Tina's trinkets was waning as he eyed Tara. 'I didn't think there were any sheilas left in Darwin!'

Tara tried again to pull away from the man who was holding onto her.

'Let me go, you oaf! Don't think you're going to get away with this!'

'And who's to stop us, eh?' One hand gripped her thigh, the other caught her arm, pulling her roughly down onto his lap. 'Who's first then – me?'

As his slobbering mouth sought hers she lashed out and her nails drew blood in scarlet bars down his cheek.

'You bitch!' he roared.

He grabbed her by the wrists pinning both together with one huge hand and ripped at the neck of her dress. A cheer went up as he tore it open exposing her breasts, then he rucked her skirt thigh high and scrabbled between her flailing legs. Tara fought wildly, biting and kicking, but she had still not recovered completely from giving two units of blood to Alys and her strength was failing. The watching faces were a blur to her and the ugly laughter echoed in her ears. Then, louder than the laughter came a crash and the sound of splintering wood and into the moment's startled hiatus a voice, unmistakably outback Australian, roared: 'Which of you bastards pinched my ute?'

Dev stood framed in the doorway. A week's growth of beard covered his chin; his shirt, stained with sweat and oil, looked as if it had not been off his back since the raid.

'Come on, which of you was it? I want to know!' His tone was fiery.

The soldier, Wally, levered himself away from the wall, throwing down a bottle from which he had been guzzling.

'It ain't your ute any more. It's the Army's.'

'Who says?'

'I do,' the soldier swaggered, his words slurring

together. 'I've requisitioned it. It's mine now!'

Dev crossed to him, two short steps. 'Think again, soldier.' His forefinger stabbed Wally's chest in time with the words. 'It's my ute. And until your CO tells me different that's the way it stays. So you can sod off back to your camp and tell him so.' He swung round to look at Tara, struggling to disentangle herself from her assailant. 'Are you all right?' he asked roughly.

'No, I'm not!' she returned hotly. 'This filthy beast was about to rape me. You got here just in time.'

His lip curled with a flash of his old humour.

'The ninth cavalry to the rescue again. Lucky for you these thieving swine left my ute where I couldn't miss it. Come on – I'll give you a lift before some other bugger takes a fancy to it.'

He held out his hand to help her up but as he did so the soldier took a swing at him. Dev must have seen the punch coming for he ducked it, turning sharply and throwing a punch of his own, low and deadly accurate. As the blow caught him hard in the stomach the soldier doubled up, winded, and Dev hit him again. He reeled back across one of the smaller tables, crashing with it to the floor, and Tara's assailant weighed in. His fist caught Dev square on the chin and as he staggered the man closed in. Tara screamed a warning and Dev hit the wall, rebounded and lashed out, all in one fluid movement. For what seemed to Tara like an age they stumbled around the room trading punches, gouging and kicking and she watched breathlessly, aware of a sneaking edge of excitement and admiration. She had not seen anyone fight like that since she left the back streets of Sydney. Tables and chairs crashed over and the watchers yelled their support. Then there was the sound of breaking glass and the man had a bottle in his hand, the neck sheared off to make a jagged weapon. Tara gasped in horror as he lunged towards Dev, but the man from the outback was too quick for him. He side-stepped, kicking out at the same time. The other man fell heavily and blood spurted scarlet as the glass cut into his own face. From behind Dev hooked him up by his collar, turned him and cracked him under the chin. Then, as he subsided, Dev kicked him again for good measure. He doubled up, beaten, and Dev straightened, breathless yet high on the powerful drug of victory.

'OK – who's next?' He advanced on the Italian. 'Do you want to play this game?'

'No – no . . . !' The weaselly face was a picture and he fell over himself in his eagerness to put distance between himself and Dev.

'How about you?'

The other man turned away with a sickly grin, pretending indifference.

Dev turned to Tara. 'Come on then – unless you want to stay here and tend to the wounded.'

'Not likely!' She was about to follow when she remembered the reason she had come here tonight. 'Wait just a minute though, would you?'

She ran up the stairs. Her crucifix was still hanging on the nail over her bed – obviously it had not been flamboyant enough to attract the attention of looters. She unhooked it and ran back downstairs. Dev had the door open and was looking watchfully at the men he had beaten. He thought they had had enough for one night, but that was not something it was wise to take for granted. As she went past him down the veranda steps the night air was warm and damp on her face and bare shoulder and she hitched her dress to cover it.

Dev crossed to the ute which she had noticed on her way in.

'Nothing's safe now. But lucky for me the fool was so damned cocky he left the keys in the ignition. Now, can I drop you off somewhere?'

'Yes . . .' She glanced at her watch and groaned. 'Oh Holy Mary, if I haven't missed my lift! They'll be gone by now for sure! I'll be for it!'

'Where are you headed?' he asked.

'The Army Hospital. I'm nursing there.'

'You? Nursing?' There was no concealing the amusement in his voice.

'Yes, me, and why not? Didn't you expect me to take care of that man on the day of the raid? You went off and left me with him then soon enough. What's so funny about me nursing, anyway?'

He paused to look at her, ruefully dabbing with a handkerchief the corner of his mouth where one blow had caught him.

'I suppose it would be too much to hope you might nurse *me*?'

She lifted her chin, annoyed because she knew he was laughing at her.

'Indeed it would, Sean Devlin.'

'There's gratitude for you,' he said ruefully. 'I save you from a fate worse than death and all you can do is be rude to me. And it's the second time I've saved you too, remember. It's getting to be quite a habit.'

'A habit I intend to break.'

'Oh, so you're going to get all the way out to the AGH by yourself, are you?'

'Oh!' He had started the engine; summoning what dignity she could she swung herself up into the ute. 'I'll let you run me home this time seeing as how you'll want to make sure they've done no damage to your ute. But we are moving south tomorrow so no doubt it's the last you'll see of me.'

He let off the handbrake and pulled away from the kerb.

'Is that a threat or a promise?' he teased and in the darkness she had no way of seeing the look in his eyes as he said it.

*

They had already begun moving the hospital out the next day when an ambulance turned into the drive beneath the coconut palms, its wheels churning and spraying out red mud.

160

'Not more patients, surely!' Kate Harris groaned. 'I'd better get over to the MI room. There's no-one on duty there this morning. We thought we'd done with admissions.'

'Do you want me?' Tara asked.

'No, you carry on here. We want to be ready to go as soon as we can.'

Tara watched her go regretfully. Richard Allingham was the doctor on duty – practically the first time their duties had coincided. Such high hopes she had had when he had put himself out to help her get the post – and when he had asked her to call him Richard she had been convinced their relationship was moving in the right direction. But since then she had scarcely laid eyes on him and things had skidded to a depressing halt. Now she glanced out of the window hoping she might catch a glimpse of him but all she saw was Kate squelching back across the drive.

'Tara!' she called from the doorway. 'Can you look out some dressings and pop over with them? Half the stuff in the MI room is packed up ready to go.'

A smile spread over Tara's face. Lucky for her she had done a good job packing away the dressings! She selected a pack and crossed to the door. Kate was kicking off her boots and looking uncharacteristically annoyed.

'Take them over, there's a good girl, and give Captain Allingham a hand. It's nothing you can't handle and I have a lot to be getting on with here.' She straightened up, brushing a stray end of fair hair off her forehead. 'Wouldn't you think we had enough to do with casualties of war without having to pick up the pieces of silly personal grievances!'

Tara was pulling on her own boots. 'What do you mean?' she asked.

'This bloke who's just come in disrupting everything. He's been beaten up. I ask you! Some men just seem to like fighting. Hurry up, now, the sooner he's dealt with the sooner we can get on with things that matter.'

Surreptitiously Tara tidied her hair and retraced Kate's steps to the MI room. For all her eagerness to see him, she felt unaccountably nervous at the prospect of having to practise her newfound skills under the watchful eye of Richard Allingham.

He glanced up as she went in and her knees went weak at the sight of him. Never in all my life have I felt like this about anyone before, Tara thought with a sense of shock. Never before have I looked at someone and wanted them so much I could die for them . . .

'Ah – Nurse Kelly.' His voice was pleasant but perfectly normal. How could he look at me and not know what I was feeling? Tara thought, stunned by the strength of her emotions. 'You have the dressings, I see. Good. Now, I think he has some fractured ribs . . . amongst other things.'

'What would you like me to do, sir?' Tara was amazed to discover her own voice sounded just as it always did. Sure, I deserve an Oscar, she thought dryly.

'Just hand me a swab . . .' He bent over the patient again and Tara went across to do as he asked. Then she checked, shocked, as she looked at the man on the inspection bed. His face was a bloody mess, lips swollen and split, cheeks grazed, one eye already closed. But beneath it all she could still hardly fail to identify it.

Her hand flew to her own mouth and she stared down in horror. One of the bruised eyes opened a crack, the swollen lips moved with difficulty. But when he spoke there was still a trace of amusement in the unmistakable drawl.

'The bastards got me in the end, Tara. But you can see what it means, can't you? You won't be getting rid of me as easily as you thought!'

Chapter Seven

The last of 138 AGH's trucks, with Tara squashed ignominiously in beside the driver, rolled around a bend and headed down the valley to the Adelaide River. It was well into the evening and the journey had been hot and tiresome – sixty miles of uneven track, still flooded and only just passable in places, deeply rutted in others where heavy service vehicles had churned through in the wettest of the weather and the heat had dried the red earth into long patterned hillocks and troughs. Twice the truck had become bogged down in thick mud. Tara glanced ruefully down at her feet, squeezed together under the dashboard and caked ankle-deep in red slime, and wondered how she had managed to do her share of pushing without falling flat on her face.

'Nearly there,' the driver said. 'That weren't so bad now, was it?'

Tara bit on her lip and refrained from offering her opinion. The driver was a steady tempered stockman from New South Wales with prematurely leathered skin and eyes as patient as one of his own sheep. His equanimity had been comforting when they had first set out but now, five hours later, Tara found it merely irritating.

'What do you think of that then?' the driver continued in his slow drawl as the truck rounded the last bend and the camp came into view. 'Pretty, ain't it?'

Tara, about to bounce once more with impatience, caught her breath at the sight. *Pretty*! Trust a stockman to understate! It was beautiful!

The camp had been hastily erected by the advance party in a clearing, a gaggle of tents beneath the trees. But the tropical evening had magicked it with a shrouding of river mist pink-tinted by the diffusion of light from the full

163

moon which hung suspended within it like a huge orange balloon. Looking at it Tara was reminded of the old aboriginal legends of Dreamtime, the days when the world had been young, here in Northern Territory. Easy to see how they had begun, possible almost to believe in them even now, just as she had believed in faeries when as a child she had stood on the edge of an Irish bog and watched the lights dancing over it in the darkness.

The driver killed the engine and the night was alive with the sounds of nature – the chirp of crickets, the hum of mosquitos, the croak of the frogs. Tara sat very still, feeling her tiredness and irritation melt away. At times like this the war and all its horrors and hardships seemed very distant; Red Maloney was an unreal character from another life. She tried to picture his face and failed; even his towering personality threw no shadow here on this enchanted land.

By the next morning, however, reality had once more intruded and daylight showed the camp for what it was – a hastily convened and incongruous hotchpotch of facilities which could only have sprung up in time of war. Tents provided most of the accommodation – ridge tents for wards, a bell tent for the Sisters' mess room, another for Matron Swift, even a tent for the CO, Colonel Adamson. What solid buildings there were were made of corrugated iron sheets, unlined, with tin roofs and shutters for windows – the operating theatre, the X-ray block and the huts that provided sleeping accommodation for the sisters and masseuses. Inside, the heat was stifling and the few fans, mounted on their long poles, made the kind of constant whirr that had the patients begging for them to be turned off for a few minutes' peace before the heat had them begging for them to be turned on once again.

A dirt track bisected the settlement, limping past orderly rooms and offices, canteen and kit store, but the recreation hut was placed at as safe a distance from the line of wards as was the isolation ward, and the water tanks – those ugly necessities – were situated on a slight rise on the river side of the hospital. Like much of the remainder of the hospital they were screened by trees, for all around was the bush – the paw-paws, the gums and the lush tropical vegetation.

To her own surprise Tara found her surroundings exhilarating. There was a feeling of freedom here on the banks of the river, a restless expansiveness which dreams could feed on. In Darwin she had begun to despair of ever getting the opportunity to make an impression on Richard. Their duties had rarely coincided and there had been no time for anything but working and sleeping. But here surely it would be different – this place was made for romance. This could be our special place, Tara thought, and the notion excited her strangely, making her yearn not only for Richard but to be a tiny part of this wild and beautiful country which stretched from here to the very heart of Australia, growing ever more desolate and awesome as the eucalyptus grew more stunted and the vegetation gave way first to open meadows, barren and uninhabited, and then to the parched red earth of the Never-Never, the dead centre where it could not rain.

How far away that seemed though! Here, the rain fell in the same torrents as it fell on Darwin, rushing down the slopes and rising as thick steam from the ground to gather as clouds once more. There were electric storms that made night into day and rent the sky with lightning, both forked and sheet. And the wildlife was as prolific as the vegetation. Creepy-crawlies of every imaginable type were everywhere – beetles and crickets, spiders and grasshoppers.

And the birds! Flocks of brilliant green budgies and dove-grey cockatiels, dumpy Dollar birds calling harshly as they performed their sunset aerobatic displays, sacred kingfishers diving for small fish in the river and swooping from their vantage points on the branch of a tree to gobble up some unsuspecting insect. There were bronzewings, too, normally running and hiding in the grass if disturbed, but occasionally taking to the air with a noisy clapping of

165

their wings. They sometimes fed on the seeds of the box poison plant and though they did not harm the birds, the poison got into their bones and entrails so that any predatory animal eating them died in agony.

In this magic place tempers improved and petty irritations were forgotten – even Anastasia Bottomley seemed less sharp than she had done in Darwin. Tara struck up a friendship with Kate Harris who, unlike some of the sisters, tolerated her mistakes and helped her to learn the correct way of doing things. She was a Victorian girl, brought up on a small farm in the flat fertile valley between Bendigo and Echuka, a very private person who never mentioned her background nor pressed Tara to talk about hers. But Tara had the unmistakable feeling that Kate Harris nursed some secret sorrow – it was there in the shadows around her eyes and the expression on her face when she thought no one was watching her.

The hospital was as busy as ever it had been – busier – for now the Northern Territory was alive with servicemen, Yanks as well as Aussies, as reinforcements poured in to the Army, the RAAF and the US establishments, bomber and fighter strips were built and supply installations had sprung up.

There were aborigines, too, who had been rounded up and confined in control camps in the bush. Until she had come to Darwin Tara had scarcely set eyes on an aborigine, now it seemed they were everywhere. Each day, the men were bussed in to the hospital to help out with the manual jobs which soldiers could be ill spared to do – driving trucks and cutting timber, working on the sanitation and helping with the stores. One was even employed as a kitchen hand – Tara nicknamed him Spud because each morning he was to be seen sitting beside a huge pail in the bright sunshine peeling mountains of potatoes, his face split in the friendly, contented grin that was the trademark of the aborigine.

Busy as they were Tara saw little of Richard Allingham. He was friendly enough when their paths did cross, treating her to a smile and a wave or a friendly word. But the opportunity to be with him and to make some progress in their relationship seemed as distant as ever – while as an orderly Tara saw a great deal more than she would wish of the infuriating Sean Devlin.

Hospitalization had dampened him not one scrap – the moment his wounds began to heal he was as impossible as ever. One day, finding the ward suspiciously empty, Tara had discovered him running a card school for all the walking-wounded patients behind two judiciously arranged screens; another time she found a half-bottle of whisky which someone had smuggled in to him hidden beneath his bedclothes and was just able to conceal it behind a box of bandages before Sister Bottomley and Matron stalked into the ward to do their daily inspection. But though she tried to smooth his path for him, he still took every opportunity to tease her just as he had done in the days when he had been a patron of the Savalis' place and she had waited at table.

One morning, she was busy filling the boiler that was used for the sterilization of instruments when Kate Harris popped her head around the flap of the tent.

'When you have finished here, Tara, perhaps you would give Mr Devlin a blanket bath.'

Tara pulled a face. 'Surely he's fit enough to get up and wash himself.'

'I don't know that he is,' Kate said seriously. 'Today he's complaining that his ribs are very painful still. He's well strapped up so there shouldn't be any problem, but I think I'm going to ask for another X-ray and until we get the results I don't want to take any chances.'

It was already hot in the tent-ward, the groaning fans making little impact on the heavy humid air. Tara collected a screen and arranged it around Dev's bed.

'Well, well, what a beautiful morning this is turning out to be!' he remarked heartily.

'For a man supposedly in great pain you seem very cheerful,' she returned tartly.

'And who wouldn't be with the prospect of a blanket bath from the best looking girl in the hospital? Sorry – *nurse* I should say!'

Tara's suspicions hardened and she shot him a look under her lashes.

'You'd better behave yourself now or I shall get one of the male orderlies to attend to your toilet.'

The still-swollen lips twisted into the semblance of a grin.

'Oh, I promise to behave! How would a sick man like myself manage to do otherwise?'

Again she shot him a suspicious look, again he met her eyes with that same amusement. She slopped water into the basin and began washing him vigorously. At first he said nothing then grumbled a protest.

'Ouch! You're very rough, Tara, with a man in pain.'

'I'm sorry if you're feeling so tender. I'm doing my best.'

'Are you indeed? Well, I wouldn't mind betting you would find it in you to be a little more gentle if the doctor was around!'

Her face flamed. The truth of it was impossible to deny but to have him say it like that . . .

'If you must get into fights you must expect to get hurt,' she snapped.

'Of all the gratitude when I got my wounds defending your honour!'

'You most certainly did not!'

'Well – as a result of.'

'It was another day entirely. And in any case it was not my honour you were fighting for – it was your ute!'

'Much good that did me. It's in their hands again now. No, a totally wasted exercise. Let's hope I was more successful where your honour was concerned.' He shot her a wicked look.

She stood back, glaring at him. 'What do you know about my honour?'

'More than you might expect! But don't worry, I won't

tell the good doctor,' he said wryly. 'No, not a word shall pass my lips!'

Her face was flaming again and she was as annoyed to think he would be able to see it as she was by his remarks.

'How dare you!' she flashed.

'Ah, come on, Tara, there's no point in getting mad! I've seen the way you are when he's around. I just wish you'd put on an act like that for me! Not that you need to, mind you, when I know and love you just the way you are. But it would be good to think you felt like making the effort.'

She reached for the sponge and stood over him threateningly.

'Perhaps I should point out that whilst you are incapacitated it would be wise of you not to try to antagonize me, Mr Devlin.'

He raised a hand in mocking surrender. 'All right, all right, I'll say no more. I've too much respect for my own comfort. And my ribs are very painful. I'd be an easy victim for you, Tara.'

But his eyes were still full of laughter and he had touched on too many tender spots for her to be able to put the episode aside.

'What's wrong, Tara? You don't look your usual merry self!' Kate said as she met Tara on her way to dispose of the basin of soap-scummed water. 'You've not had trouble with Mr Devlin, I hope?'

'Humph!' Tara snorted so vigorously that water slopped over the rim of the basin and made wet stains on her uniform skirt.

'Not worse, is he?' Kate asked anxiously.

'Worse? I don't believe there's anything wrong with him!'

And with a lift of her chin and an angry sparkle in her eye, Tara stomped off across the rough ground.

*

Tara plodded resolutely up the gentle slope that rose behind the camp following the path of one of the numerous creeks that watered the hills. This early in the year it was still a sizeable flow; soon, as the dry weather took a hold, it would reduce to a mere trickle and eventually dry up altogether.

It was a beautiful March afternoon, the sky a clear rich blue above the myriad tropical greens and the ground firm enough to make for easy walking. But Tara did not like walking. In fact she disliked it intensely. Only the determined bullying of June Day, one of the masseuses, had persuaded her to join this afternoon's excursion and already, with the camp still in sight, she was regretting her moment's weakness.

Not only that – this morning before she had come off duty she had fallen foul of Anastasia Bottomley when she had been rash enough to disregard a 'Nothing by mouth' sign on a patient's bed. She had felt sorry enough for him to allow him a sip of water; unfortunately, the patient had allowed his thirst to get the better of his good sense – he had snatched the glass and drunk half of it before she could stop him. The implications had been far reaching. The patient's operation had had to be delayed, Sister Bottomley had been furious and Richard Allingham had been detailed to reprimand her. Now, remembering his reproachful manner, Tara's cheeks burned dully once more. That sort of encounter was hardly calculated to make the impression she intended on Richard.

'Oh, the hell with it!' Tara said crossly.

Kate Harris, walking alongside her, glanced at her curiously. 'What's up with you?'

'Oh nothing. I might well ask the same of you,' Tara said sharply. 'You look as though you haven't slept properly for a week.'

It was true – the circles around Kate's eyes seemed to grow larger and darker every day and the distance Tara had sensed in her manner was more marked.

Kate did not reply and Tara shrugged. She, of all

people, respected a person's right to privacy. They walked in silence some distance behind the rest of the party and Tara's mind was threatening to stray once more to her embarrassing interview with Richard Allingham when Kate said suddenly: 'It's my fiancé.'

Tara turned, startled. 'I beg your pardon?'

'I'm worried to death about him,' Kate said. 'He was in Singapore with the 2/4th Anti-Tank Regiment. I've heard nothing from him since the surrender.'

'Oh, I see.' Tara could not avoid feeling gratified that she should be the one Kate had honoured with this confidence. 'Was he taken prisoner?'

'That's just it. I don't know.' Now that she had begun talking about her private worry the words came tumbling out. 'I don't know whether he's alive or dead or if he's been wounded. If he has, God alone knows what medical treatment he will have received. It will be tropical conditions there much like it is here in the Wet, I imagine, and you know what happens to wounds or even mosquito bites if they aren't treated properly. Tropical ulcers, gangrene, malaria, dysentery, fevers of every kind – you name it, our boys in Malaysia will have it.' She rubbed her face with her fingers. 'That's the trouble with being a nurse. It makes you too damned aware of the worst possibilities.'

Tara was silent for a moment. Then she took Kate's hand urgently.

'Listen to me now – you must say a rosary to our Blessed Lady. Do you know the Hail Mary?' Kate shook her head. 'Wait now and I'll show you.' Tara fiddled beneath the neckline of her uniform and pulled out the beads, set in their decades and hung with the crucifix. 'This is the Our Father and this is the Glory Be and each of these you use for a Glory Be too . . . Oh Kate, I can see you think it's strange but She will hear, you know.'

Kate smiled and shook her head. She had been raised strict Methodist, not allowed any reading matter but the Bible on Sundays, packed off and sent regularly to Chapel in her Sunday best.

171

'My grandmother would have a fit. She'd call it worshipping idols.'

'That's nonsense! When we pray to the Blessed Virgin it's asking her to intercede we are. And who better than Her to do it, for isn't She His own Holy Mother? If I were you I would say a rosary every night and ask Her to pray to God to keep him safe . . .'

She saw hope flicker briefly in Kate's eyes and die again.

'No – no, I couldn't. I don't suppose it would do any good anyway.' She gave her head a little shake and Tara knew the moment for confidences had passed. 'The others are miles ahead. We'd better hurry and catch them up, don't you think?'

Tara shrugged and tucked the crucifix back inside her uniform. Some people would never understand the truth if you waved it under their noses. Well, it was their loss. But Tara felt a moment's compassion for Kate who had a boyfriend who might be dead or in enemy hands and had no faith to sustain her.

I'll say a rosary myself tonight for his safe return, Tara thought. Then, forcing her tired legs into action, she plodded along behind Kate.

Chapter Eight

Tara was dreaming. She was back in Sydney in the Canary Club. It was dark – too dark to see anything but the spot illuminating the centre of the stage, the spot which was waiting for her. The piano had played her introduction and she knew she should be leaving the sanctuary of the darkness and stepping out into the blinding pool of light. But her limbs seemed to be frozen by fear. She could hear the audience becoming restless. Gathering all her strength of will she moved and her legs felt as heavy as if she was ploughing through water.

What was she afraid of? She did not know. Only that there was danger out there in the darkness and terror too great to contemplate lurking at the core of her memory, grasping the edges of her mind.

The pool of light was very close now. One more step and she would be in it, with the brightness making her glow, catching every facet of the diamonds round her wrist and at her throat. She stepped forwards but the light seemed to move with her and draw her on – a strange tantalising will o' the wisp full of hidden menace.

And then suddenly someone else was in the light. A figure – just a dim silhouette, but she did not need to see the face to know who it was and why she had been afraid.

'Red,' she said and the name brought the silhouette to life. She could see his face clearly now and he was smiling, but it was not a pleasant smile.

'So you came, Tara,' he said.

She nodded.

'Come closer,' he said. 'You must come closer.'

Her lips were dry. 'Why?'

'Because, my dear, I am going to kill you.'

His hands flashed beneath his jacket and she knew he

was going for his gun but she could not move. Transfixed she waited, knowing how it would feel even before the gun cracked, smelling the acrid smell of spent bullets, feeling the sharp pain, the burning sensation, the certainty that her head would burst wide open. And still the gun cracked – again and again – and she was falling . . . falling . . .

Slowly, she came through the layers of sleep. For a moment she lay motionless, her body bathed in sweat. Then suddenly the whole hut was brightly illuminated and the loud crack which she had believed a moment ago was coming from Red's gun came again, volley upon volley, echoing around the corrugated iron sheets that formed the walls of their quarters.

Oh, Holy Mother, not another raid! she thought, sitting bolt upright. Then, as the rain began hammering down onto the tin roof like a hail of bullets, she awoke sufficiently to know that the noise was neither a gun nor an air attack.

Thunder and lightning and rain. A thunderstorm.

Goodness only knew she liked storms little enough. As a child she had clung to Maggie when they came and Maggie had been no help at all for she had been as afraid as Tara. In fact, Tara thought, maybe it was Maggie's fear that had planted the seed for her own. But just now the reality of the storm had paled into insignificance compared with the horror of her dream. Even awake she could see Red's malevolent face, hear his voice – 'I am going to kill you' – and a fresh sweat broke out on her already clammy skin.

It had been just a dream this time, but next time it could be real. Oh, she had hidden herself as well as she possibly could without leaving Australia altogether. But Red had friends – and enemies – everywhere. Sooner or later he would catch up with her and then the dream, horrific as it was, would become the reality.

She shivered, pulling the sheet up over her as if to shut out her fears but there was no escaping them. They were there in the dark beside her, so real that she expected to

174

see Red or one of his henchmen there beside her as the lightning illuminated the hut, gun at the ready as it had been in her dream.

Almost directly over her bed a leak developed in the corrugated roof and water began dripping through with monotonous regularity. But Tara scarcely noticed it. Determined to exorcize the demons she reached beneath her pillow and pulled out the rosary which Kate had spurned. Then, counting the beads between finger and thumb, she began to pray.

*

Tara filled the kettle and set it to boil on the ring in the ward kitchen. She was on night duty now and, as usual, tired out. The previous few days had been hectic ones – the rain which had accompanied the thunderstorm had continued remorselessly for twelve hours, lashing down furiously to lie in pools on the sodden ground and seeping into every nook and cranny. The downpour had delighted the frogs who frequented the camp – and particularly the toilet tents; they seemed to multiply in the space of a few hours and their croaking could be heard even above the lashing of the rain. Eventually, the river had threatened to burst its banks and there had been talk that the entire hospital would have to be moved to higher ground.

'Sure why didn't they think of that before they chose their site?' Tara had asked Kate and was unfortunate enough to be overheard by Anastasia Bottomley.

'If you spent more time learning to be a good nurse and less in criticising the decisions of others you would be a great deal more help to us!' she had snapped.

The rain had stopped now but the river was still high and would be until the Dry came but that, everyone said, could not now be far off.

As she waited for the kettle to boil, Tara set out the cups and poured milk into them, but she did so absent-mindedly. Since the night of the storm she had been

175

unable to get Red out of her mind and the vividness of the dream was as real to her now as it had been then.

How much longer would it be before he was released from prison and came looking for her? His sentence had been a long one but with Australia now so involved in the war she wondered if excuses might be found to empty the gaols of as many prisoners as possible. Even in time of peace she could not imagine Red remaining in prison very long. It was only surprising he had been sent there in the first place considering his power and his friends in high places.

Perhaps it would be wiser to get out of Australia altogether, Tara thought. Though where on earth could I go with half the world fighting?

The kettle boiled and Tara was pouring the water into the pot when a low whisper from behind her made her jump out of her skin.

'Hello there, nurse!'

She swung round, kettle still in hand, to see Dev grinning at her.

'Sean Devlin! What are you doing out of bed? You should be asleep!'

He pulled a mock frown. 'Don't be such a spoilsport! I'm a big boy now.'

'Not so big you won't be in a deal of trouble if Sister catches you wandering about in the middle of the night!'

'She won't.' His eyes twinkled. 'Col Dempsey is making a fine job of keeping her busy for a while.'

'Col Dempsey! When Sister Harris was called to his bedside a minute ago it was made to sound as if he had taken a turn for the worse. Are you telling me now there is nothing wrong with him?' Tara exploded.

Dev put a finger to his lips. 'Shh! You don't have to tell the world, do you? I just wanted her out of the way for a minute or two and Col is a sport. He obliged.'

'And why did you want her out of the way? Because you could smell the teapot I suppose and fancied a drop. Well, it's wicked of you!'

176

'Tara!' He laughed and put a hand on hers. 'Just listen for a minute. I didn't come for a cup of tea. I came to tell you I've been discharged. I go in the morning – if I can get transport out of this place.'

'Oh!' she said and wondered why she felt unexpectedly bereft.

'I didn't want to go without saying goodbye to you – and ask you the little questions I couldn't in front of a wardful of wounded men, like when can I see you again?'

Something sweet yet sharply painful twisted deep inside, disturbing her. She lifted her chin.

'And what makes you think I'd want to see you again? Haven't you been the bane of my life ever since I clapped eyes on you?' she demanded.

He pretended to wince. 'I was afraid you might say something like that. Ah Tara, you're a hard-hearted woman. I suppose it's still that damned doctor standing in my way.'

The reference to Richard Allingham brought her upright, all the old fire blazing in her eyes. 'And what business is that of yours?'

'None I suppose. I just wish you'd come to your senses and realize he's not for you.'

Inexplicably she had begun to tremble. 'What do you mean by that?'

'He's not your type, Tara. Now ask me how I know and I'll tell you. He is a little bit better than the rest, isn't he – out of the top drawer as they say. You can tell it the way he speaks, the way he walks, the way he wears his uniform even. And you, my love? Well, you aren't out of the top drawer, are you. Oh, you might put it on a bit when he's within earshot and pretend you're something that you're not, but how long can you keep it up, eh? Not long I reckon. It would be a terrible strain, even for you.'

She was trembling in earnest now. 'Of all the nerve! Putting me down that way and all the while thinking yourself so good . . .'

He laughed. 'Not in the least. We're the same, Tara, out

of the same mould. That's why we'd be so good together.'

She ignored this. 'And supposing he does come from a better background than I do – what's wrong with that? why shouldn't I better myself?'

'No reason – if you can get away with it. I just don't think you would. He would ask you all kinds of awkward questions, Tara my lovely, and if he didn't it's a pound to a penny his highly proper family would.' He paused, looking at her under his eyelashes. '*I* wouldn't ask you a single awkward question, like who you are or how you made your living before you came to Darwin. And that's a solemn promise.'

For a second he had her almost nonplussed. No one had ever been that frank with her. Red Maloney had been cruel and cutting on occasions, but his minions had been made to respect his woman. And Dev wasn't being cruel – merely mocking. Scenes of her early life flicked before her eyes – and a few more recent ones too – and then her ready instinct for self-preservation asserted itself.

'I don't know what you're hinting at, Sean Devlin, but if you must know I was in show business.'

One corner of his mouth lifted – an easier movement now that his face had recovered a little from the onslaught of fists and boots.

'Just as I thought.'

'It is *not* what you thought! I was a singer and if the war hadn't come along to spoil everything I'd be a star by now.'

He leaned back against the table eyeing her lazily. 'In that case I am surprised you're not doing your bit to entertain our long-suffering patients. They could do with something to brighten their lives.'

She looked at him intently, her annoyance forgotten.

'I think you should organize a concert,' he went on. 'I'm sure you'd find there are others about with talents of one sort or another and you could be the star – you'd like that!'

'What a wonderful idea!' She was too excited even to be annoyed by his last remark. 'But where could we put it on? There's no spare tent.'

'The Dry is coming. You could have a stage out in the open. Somebody would be only too pleased to build it for you, I'm sure, and there would be no restriction on the number you could seat. They'd come from miles around if I know anything about it – all the camps like a concert.'

'You're right!' Her eyes were shining. 'But it would be at night. What would we do for lights?'

'I could do those for you. I'm an electrician by trade.'

'But you won't be here.'

'I could always come back. I mean – if I can be of service to our gallant soldiers, sailors and airmen . . .'

'You are the craftiest man I ever met!' she said, but she was laughing.

'How about it then? Do I get the job?'

'You certainly do – if I can get permission for the concert that is. Now listen – Sister Harris will be back in just a moment and if she finds you here you'll be for it, especially if she's been taken for a ride by Col Dempsey.'

'Don't I get a goodbye kiss?'

'What are you thinking of? You really would be in trouble then!'

'Like I said, you're a hard woman! Well, in that case, Tara, I'll bid you goodnight.' He paused in the doorway. 'Don't let the tea stew now!'

'Get away with you!' But she was smiling and the smile lasted on her lips until Kate returned, grumbling about that hypochondriac Col Dempsey, and deep inside her for much longer than that.

*

Colonel Adamson, CO of 138 AGH, stretched his large frame carefully against the canvas back of his chair hoping as he always did that it would not collapse beneath his weight and deposit him ignominiously on the ground. The folding chair was the only concession to the fact that his office was now a tent – desk and filing cabinets were all solid enough, even his aide had a real chair, even if it was of the compact straight-backed variety. Colonel Adamson made a mental note to get on to Stores again about it, but he knew already what the answer would be and the thought of being denied such a basic need made his voice brusque when he addressed the young woman in VA uniform who was facing him across the desk.

'Yes?'

Tara hesitated briefly. Now that she had got as far as the CO himself she wanted to be sure she was presenting her plan to him in the best possible way.

From the moment Dev had suggested a concert to her she had thought of little else. Even her obsession with Richard Allingham had been dwarfed by it. To sing again – oh, the longing it had started in her! At once, Tara had begun putting out feelers and already she had mustered more support than she had dared hope for – an orderly, a carpenter in civilian life, who had offered to construct a stage and some scenery; a junior MO whose friends vouched for him having the best voice ever heard in the showers and a surgical officer who was known for the clever conjuring tricks he could work with a pack of cards and a length of string.

Matron Swift had proved the greatest barrier so far. A big bustling no-nonsense woman she had viewed the idea with some scepticism but eventually Tara had persuaded her to allow her to put the scheme before the CO.

'You must realize his decision will be final,' Matron said. 'If he raises any objection then that will be the end of the matter. This is a hospital, not a variety theatre, and Colonel Adamson may very well feel as I do that we have quite enough on our hands without playing at concerts.'

'Thank you, Matron,' Tara had said demurely, all the time thinking. If I can get it past a grumpy old woman like Matron I can certainly get it past the CO!

Now, as she confronted him, she consciously gathered all her charms and smiled at him, the wide sparkling smile which lit her eyes to blue pools and made the dimples play in her cheeks.

Well?' Colonel Adamson said again but this time his tone was noticeably softer. 'What can I do for you, Miss Kelly?'

'If you won't have me court-martialled for saying so it's what I can do for you, sir, and all the others here in the camp,' Tara said pertly.

The Colonel raised his eyebrows, great sandy thatches which seemed to meet across the bridge of his rather thin nose.

'I'm an entertainer you see – or I was before I came to Darwin,' she went on quickly. 'I'd like your permission to put on a show for the hospital. I could sing myself and I'm sure there is far more talent right here than you would ever dream. It would be so good for morale to have a concert, don't you think?'

'A concert, eh?' The CO boasted a fine sandy moustache to match his eyebrows; now he fingerd it softly, smoothing it outwards from the fleshy curve of his lips.

'I could do it – I'm sure I could!' Tara pressed on enthusiastically. 'I would need help with setting up a stage of course but that would be no problem . . .' She broke off, biting her tongue as she realized it would not be very tactful to let the Colonel know she had already sounded out one or two people before seeking his approval. 'I could arrange the programme myself and rehearse the acts, and I am sure if I could count on you for backing, sir, everything else would fall into place too.'

'Hmm.' The subtle compliment had gone home; Colonel Adamson began to forget his collapsible chair. 'A show is certainly good for morale – and we don't get any concert parties up here. Too far from civilization for them, I dare say.'

'Oh yes, that's so,' Tara agreed. 'To most people the Top End hardly exists.'

Colonel Adamson leaned back, still playing with his moustache and eyeing her appraisingly.

He had not been keen to take her on board. When Sylvia Crawford had asked him to, he had been on the point of refusing. An eminent surgeon who had cut his military teeth in the Army Medical Service during the Great War and kept his hand in by remaining with the militia afterwards, he had little time for women aids on active service. The sisters of the AANS and the masseuses were an asset, he knew, but when it came to orderly work there were so many jobs a man could do which a woman could not – lifting and carrying, chopping wood, a hundred and one heavy jobs. But Sylvia was both an old adversary and a valued friend and he had given in to her request. Now he looked at Tara and felt his earlier misgivings about her stir again.

Was it better for the men's morale to see a girl as attractive as she was about the place, or did her presence merely cause tensions, frustrations and petty jealousies? Probably a little of each, but at least while the men were ogling her they were not getting up to more serious trouble. And if she really was capable of organizing a concert then it certainly would be a morale booster.

Once again his eyes ran over her, lingering a little too long on the trim flare of her hips and the curve of her breasts and by the time they had moved up to the full pout of her lower lip, pink and inviting and rucked slightly back by the grip of small even white teeth, his own mouth felt slightly dry and the palms of his hand moist.

'Very well,' he said, arranging the papers on his desk into a neat pile to hide the faint tremble of his hands. 'I approve the idea, in principle at any rate. See what you can do and if there is anything you need or if you encounter difficulties of any kind, be sure to report straight back to me.'

He was rewarded by seeing her face light up so that her eyes danced like blue pools.

'Oh thank you, sir, that's very kind of you!'

'Not at all!' Beneath the beetling sandy brows his own eyes narrowed slightly. There would be, he decided, just enough difficulties to make Tara a regular visitor to his tent.

Chapter Nine

Late summer sunlight filtered through the leaves of the big old plum tree in the walled garden at the rear of the Toorak mansion, making dappled patterns on the grass and on Alys' face as she sat in the lounging chair which had been carefully positioned for her within the patch of shade.

Oh, it was so good to be out of the confines of the house for a little while, good to smell the faintly cidery odour of the orchard, hear the buzz and whirr of insect life in the rioting end-of-season flowers, feel the sun warm on her skin. Her mother had not wanted her to come outside, of course. 'I don't think you should attempt to walk, Alys. It's very foolish!' she had admonished, but Alys had persuaded Morrie, the chauffeur and her greatest friend amongst the servants, to carry the chair out for her and then give her a helping hand across the lawn so that she could sit in it. The effort had taken its toll on her far more than she had expected – the pain still made her grit her teeth as she hung onto Morrie's arm and crossed the lawn, step by careful step – but oh, it had been worth it! And nothing was going to spoil her pleasure in this longed-for excursion back into the normal everyday world – not her mother's disapproval, which would replace her claustrophobic loving concern for the next twenty-four hours at least, not the prospect of the painful trek back across the lawn when the sun began to go down, and certainly not her sister Beverley who had brought out a sun-lounger to sit beside her.

Alys cast a sidelong glance at her sister, lying with the skirt of her cotton sundress draped delicately around pale freckled legs that had managed to survive yet another Australian summer without a trace of tan, and gave her head a small shake. She did not understand Beverley. She never would. It wasn't that she did not love her, she did, she supposed, and when they had been the breadth of a continent apart she had thought of her quite fondly. But when they were together they seemed to rub one another up the wrong way continually.

This afternoon for instance. Beverley visited regularly once or twice a week bringing Robyn, her little daughter, with her and when she did she always spent the entire time in the house talking to Frances. Not so today. She had joined Alys in the garden – at Frances' suggestion, Alys suspected. She had said as much to Beverley.

'I suppose Mother has sent you out to make sure I behave myself and don't start jitterbugging all over the lawn!'

But Beverley had not seen the funny side.

'Don't be silly, Alys. Although,' she had added slyly, 'I wouldn't put it past you.'

Determined not to spoil her enjoyment of the afternoon Alys had bitten back the swell of irritation. Let it go. It did not matter.

A breeze stirred the leaves of the plum tree making the pattern of shade flicker on the girls' faces. As if touched by a sudden finger of doom, Beverley sat up abruptly looking around with obvious anxiety.

'Robyn! Robyn – where are you?

'She can't be far away, Bev. There's no way she could get out,' Alys soothed.

'Yes, but . . .' Beverley swung her legs over the edge of the lounger. 'Oh there she is! Robyn, come out of that sun, darling. You'll burn or get sunstroke. One or the other.' She got up, crossing the lawn to where a shiny golden head was just visible over a clump of purple dahlias, scooped up the child in one arm and the wooden horse on wheels she had been playing with in the other and carried them back to the shade of the plum tree.

Robyn, who had been enjoying herself in her secret world, yelled lustily as Beverley dumped her beside the lounger.

'Here we are, Robyn, you can play with Dobbin here.'

'Don't want to,' Robyn grizzled. She struggled to her feet, a small round pink bundle in sundress and floppy hat, and began to toddle back towards the dahlias.

'Robyn, no!' Beverley jumped up again, brought Robyn back once more and stood over her threateningly. 'Stay here or Mummy will be cross.'

Alys began to feel a little like an oyster when the speck of grit invades its shell.

'For heaven's sake, Bev. You shouldn't namby-pamby her.'

'I did not!'

'You do. She wouldn't get sunstroke. She's got her hat on and the dahlias are much bigger than she is anyway. You just like her where you can keep an eye on everything she does.'

'And what's wrong with that?' Beverley asked hotly. 'She's my baby – I should think it would be strange if I didn't want to look after her. You're not a mother – you wouldn't understand.'

A sharp little pain that had nothing to do with her wound shot through Alys. Strange how it could still hurt – to have carried a child, even for such a short time, and to have lost it. Strange, too, that others should assume she had no feelings in the matter – as if being seventeen and unmarried had rendered her immune from normal maternal emotions.

'When I have children of my own I shall make darned sure I don't wrap them up in cotton wool,' she said after a moment. 'And when they are old enough to have lives of their own I shall let them fly the nest, too. You've got to let them go. There's nothing worse than imposing your will on grown-up children.'

'You would think like that,' Beverley said crossly. 'You've always been a rebel.'

'Wrong,' Alys said, 'Oh, I admit I've never conformed and acted out Mummy's every whim the way you have, but I certainly wasn't a rebel. You have no idea how much I wanted their approval!'

185

'You had a funny way of showing it. And you haven't changed much either. Take this business of insisting you are going back to Darwin the moment you are fit. It's worrying Mummy to death I know. Surely for her sake . . .'

Alys sighed. Oh yes, impossible to spend an afternoon with Beverley without disagreeing about something. And the bone of contention this time was to be her future plans. She should have known her mother would have told Beverley about the fuss that had ensued when she had mentioned her intention of returning to Northern Territory and her Red Cross work as soon as she was fit – and known too that Beverley would raise the subject at the first opportunity.

'Why should I be made to feel guilty about wanting to do my bit for the war effort?' she demanded.

'You could do your bit for the war effort from here.' Bev made a grab for Robyn who was on the point of toddling off once more. 'Mummy does sterling work raising funds. She would be only too pleased for you to help her. So you have no excuse – none at all.'

'Look, Bev, just because you are happy to stay here and fit in with Mother's idea of what her little girls should be doesn't mean I have to,' Alys said. She was beginning to lose her temper, since she had been ill it seemed to be on a very short fuse. 'I don't want to raise funds. I want to work in the field, doing what I'm good at. In any case, all this is a bit premature, isn't it? It's all I can do to walk across the lawn, never mind driving an ambulance out of Katherine or Alice Springs or wherever the Northern Territory HQ is now that they have been evacuated from Darwin.'

'Just as well to make up your mind now that it wouldn't be wise even to think about going back,' Beverley said sanctimoniously. 'For heaven's sake be sensible, Alys, and think of someone other than yourself for once . . .' She broke off, turning to look across the lawn towards the house. 'Oh, here is Mummy now, and Dr Whitehorn too. They're probably looking for you.'

Alys followed her line of vision and saw Frances crossing the lawn with Donald Whitehorn who had been both family physician and friend since the Petersons had come to Melbourne more than fifteen years ago. Frances appeared animated and she greet Alys almost gaily.

'You see, Alys, you have been caught! I told you it was not advisable for you to leave the house and now here is Dr Whitehorn to see you.'

'I can see her perfectly well out here, Frances,' Donald Whitehorn said equably. He was a small compact man whose receding hairline gave a look of mature wisdom to his pleasantly ordinary face. 'The fresh air will do you good, Alys.'

'I suppose you will want us to leave you alone in that case.' Beverley got up from the lounger, managing both to look and sound the perfect martyr. 'Robyn – now where are you, darling? Auntie Alys wants some privacy.'

Frances perched herself on the edge of the sunbed Bev had left vacant. 'I don't suppose that applies to the patient's mother, does it, Donald?' Her playful tone was more marked than ever. She was actually flirting, Alys realized with a shock.

'It's up to Alys.' He smiled at her. 'I have no objection.'

Alys lifted her chin a fraction. 'I'd rather see Dr Whitehorn alone, Mother.'

A tiny frown puckered the bridge of Frances' nose. 'What on earth do you mean, Alys? I'm concerned, naturally, about your progress. I'd like to hear what Donald has to say.'

'Mother, please . . .'

'Just a few minutes, Frances, and then I'll be happy to take up your kind offer of a cup of tea.' He patted her hand, the soul of tact, but Frances was bristling.

'I can't think why you should want me out of the way, Alys. But since you do – I'll be in the house.' She rose. 'Come along Beverley. Let's leave your sister with the doctor.'

Alys watched them go and sighed. Why couldn't they

let her be? Why should they make her feel awkward and uncooperative simply because she wanted the basic privacies which were her right?

'How are you feeling, Alys?' Donald Whitehorn asked. With Frances out of the way his manner had become more professional.

'Oh, not too bad. Improving, I think. At least I made it out here – though I must confess it took more out of me than I would admit to Mother.'

'Ah-hah!' He smiled. 'Was that what you didn't want her to hear?'

'Not especially. I just wanted to be able to talk to you . . .' She took a quick breath. 'How do you see the future for me, Doctor?'

'You're doing well. You're a strong young woman and you should make steady progress now back to health. I wouldn't like to say exactly how long it will be but it's my guess that before the end of the year you will be good as new.'

'Are you sure about that?' Alys asked quietly.

'No, I just said I wouldn't like to make a definite prediction as to how long . . .'

'Not how long,' she said. 'How completely good as new?'

She saw the muscle in his cheek tic and suddenly his eyes were avoiding hers. She saw it and felt her stomach fall away.

'Well, Alys . . .' His tone was hesitant.

'It's all right,' she said with a brightness she was far from feeling. 'You don't have to keep the truth from me. I think I have guessed it already.'

His eyes met hers again but the cheeriness had gone from his face.

'In that case I may as well be straight with you, Alys. Your injuries were such that although you will be able to resume a normal life in all other spheres, I am afraid it is almost certain you will never be able to be a mother.'

She had known it yet somehow it still managed to come

as a shock. The soft sounds of the afternoon went on around her – the crickets still chirping in the grass, the wasps humming in the pear tree; high in the sky an aeroplane drew a white vapour trail; out on the road a car honked its horn. And closer – somewhere between here and the house – Robyn's voice, clear and childish, called: 'Mummy! Mummy!'

She heard it all and felt far removed from it as if she was separated from that other world by a wall of crystal. Only Robyn's voice had the power to touch her, make the bridge between the pool of dangerous stillness within her and reality. Harsh cruel reality. Once she had borne a child who would have been just a little older than Robyn. But that child had been lost to her. Now there would never be another.

'Thank you, Dr Whitehorn,' she said and was almost surprised to hear her own voice so cool and controlled. 'Thank you for telling me.'

'I am sorry, Alys,' he said. 'But you wanted to know. And I do believe that in every other respect you will be able to lead a perfectly normal life.'

She nodded. 'Oh, yes, I shall make certain of that.' But there was a catch in her voice now.

When Donald Whitehorn left her to go back to the house and drink tea with Frances she sat for a long while in silence. It was not fair. Oh God, it was not fair. Even now, before the rawness of the truth had fully come to her, she knew there would be times when the knowledge of her incompleteness would be almost too much to bear. But thinking like that was useless. She had suspected as much and tried to prepare herself for it with the cliché she knew deep in her heart to be no less than the truth. At least she was alive. At least she still had two arms and two legs, her sight and her hearing. And one day soon she would be strong enough to take up her life where it had left off. It was a great deal more than many thousands of poor souls caught up in this war had been left with. And as a price to pay for her freedom Alys knew she would do it all again.

Chapter Ten

Tara stood on the newly constructed stage gesticulating wildly with her arms to indicate to Dev just where she needed the spot to fall. 'Here! No – here! That's it. Now, is my face in shadow or can you see it clearly?'

'I can see it – and very pretty it looks too!' Dev's voice called back from the darkness.

Tara's dimples tucked in annoyance. Couldn't the wretched man take this seriously for even a minute? But she bit back the sharp retort that hovered on her lips. Dev and his lights were a necessity if the concert was to go on and really he had been a tower of strength. She couldn't afford to upset him now.

'Right. Block that one in then. And then give me another pool over here . . .' She moved stage left, close to the steps up which her performers would make their entrances. 'No, here – *here*! Not on the front row of the audience!'

'She's not only pretty, she's bossy as well!' Dev's voice remarked.

'It's bossy I have to be if this show is ever to get off the ground!' she retorted. 'We haven't got this far with nothing but moonshine, I'd have you know!'

He manoeuvred the lights to the position she wanted them, blocked them in on his chart and walked down to the stage.

'No, credit where it's due, Tara, and you're making a fine job of it,' he said, serious at last. 'Who would think a couple of weeks ago this was no more than a twinkle in my eye?'

It was true. In the four weeks since Tara had gained the CO's approval, arrangements for the concert had gone ahead by leaps and bounds. An orderly who had been a sign writer in civilian life had offered to paint the scenery as it was built by the carpenter and several tins of paint to do the job had mysteriously appeared one morning. Would-be performers, too, had offered their services and besides the tenor and the conjuring surgical officer, Tara had auditioned the camp dentist, who recited the poems of Banjo Patterson with the drollery that he maintained came from spending his life looking 'down in the mouth', and a masseuse who was a wonder when it came to playing the spoons. In an effort to provide variety Tara had persuaded two of the medicos to work up a comic drag routine.

By far the most important member of the company, however, was a US airman who was a patient at the hospital. He was a talented pianist and ancient and worn-looking as the camp piano was, Joe the Yank was able to jangle it to tuneful life, playing by ear any melody required of him.

There had been hitches, of course – Tara would have been surprised if there had not been – but the CO had been as good as his word in ironing them out. When white ants threatened to eat through the stage supports, it was Colonel Adamson who signed for the release of the corrugated iron that was needed to reinforce it; when Sister Bottomley refused to allow her to change duties so as to be able to rehearse with her cast, an appeal to Colonel Adamson quickly changed that. Even the paint had necessitated a visit to his tent office when Tara learned that he had been discreetly responsible for its appearance.

'I must say the CO has been a great help,' she said to Dev now.

Dev replied with a non-committal grunt.

'It's true,' Tara insisted. 'Anything that goes wrong, I have only to see him and it is all worked out for me.'

'I'll bet it is,' Dev said sarcastically.

Tara's eyes narrowed. 'Now why are you putting the CO down? You wouldn't have that nice scaffolding for your lighting box if it wasn't for him. Sure didn't he send for me and offer it himself?'

Dev swung himself up onto the stage beside her.

'Has it not occurred to you, darlin', that he's being a bit too helpful?'

'Certainly not! What are you saying, Sean Devlin – that the CO . . . ?'

'He's a man, Tara. And you are a very attractive woman.'

'Oh fiddlesticks! It's a prude that you are!' Tara snapped, all the more tartly for the finger of guilt that prickled up her spine. Perhaps she had turned on the charm a little. She had thought of the Colonel as a staid senior officer, the very epitome of respectability, and she had played up to him a little without a thought as to the consequences. You are slipping, Tara Kelly, she told herself. You of all people should know the way it can be . . .

'What is it to you, anyway?' she asked tartly. 'If the show is a success that's all that matters, surely? You're always putting me down and pointing the finger at my morals – what's the point of having a reputation if you don't make use of it sometimes?'

'I ought to put you across my knee and spank you,' Dev chided but there was an undertone to his joking which suddenly made Tara uncomfortable.

'Never mind the CO, let's get back to what is really important – this concert!' she said sharply. 'Now, I am going to arrange for chairs for the walking wounded but everyone else is going to have to bring their own seats. And we'll pray the weather stays good.'

'Oh, it will,' Dev assured her. 'This is Northern Territory, remember, and there is nothing drier than the Dry here!'

'Oh, Dev!' Tara said, solemn suddenly. 'I'm so scared something is going to go wrong! I never realized before just how many things could. None of my turns are pros – they could dry up with stage fright or anything. Then there's the stage – I know it's been reinforced but those white ants will eat anything they can get their teeth into – it could give way beneath the lot of us. Your lights could catch fire. And me . . .' She broke off, pressing her hands across her mouth. 'It's so long since I sang maybe I can't do it any more!'

'Of course you can.'

'How do you know that?'

'Because you are a trouper, Tara. Come on, I have to be getting back to Darwin.' He swung himself down off the stage and turned back to her. 'Are you coming or do you intend to stay out here all night worrying?'

'I'm coming.' But when she reached the edge of the stage she drew back. She was trembling a little from exhaustion and nerves and the ground suddenly looked a long way down. 'Oh – I can't! It's too high.'

'Wait a minute, I'll lift you.' He put his hands one each side of her waist. She hesitated for a moment but the bunched muscles in his arms looked comfortingly strong. She placed her hands on his shoulders and felt the taut ridge there also, bracing to lift her as easily as if she weighed no more than a child.

'All right?' Her feet touched the ground but he did not release her. The pressure of his fingers through her thin blouse seemed to be raising tiny warm vessels beneath her skin and sending sharp prickly needles through her veins. Her eyes flicked up, surprised, and met his – hazel eyes flecked with green, dangerous as a tiger's and very bright in his dark tanned face. Breath caught in her throat; she could not look away. His eyes hypnotised her; for a moment it seemed that everything in her was stilled and waiting, every muscle, every nerve cell, every thought even, and the world had reduced until it held nothing but the two of them standing there just outside the beam of the lights like cardboard cut-out characters against a picture-scope. His fingers tightened on her waist and the sensitized area around them grew and spread so that the whole of her body seemed to be suffused with warmth.

193

'Dev!' she tried to say but no words would come. He was drawing her closer, she could feel his nearness through every pore in her body and his face was going out of focus. Then his lips were on hers and she was no longer thinking, only feeling.

After a long moment he pulled away, holding her by the arms. She opened her eyes to see him looking down at her but his expression was masked by shadows. 'You see, Tara, how good we are together? Didn't I tell you that's the way it would be? And to think now I won't be seeing you again until the night of the show.'

Her brow puckered. 'What are you talking about?'

'I won't be able to get down again until then. I have business that will keep me tied up – you know I'm doing some work for the Government? They want it finished in a hurry.'

His words had sobered her and Tara became aware of sounds in the shadows telling her someone was there, only yards away. She jerked her head around, wondering who it was and whether they had seen her and Dev, and embarrassment made her tone sharp. 'You're not going to let me down, are you?'

'Now, would I do a thing like that? I'll be here in plenty of time to set up for you, darling.' He was still holding her by the arms. She gave a little shake but he held her fast. 'Come here.'

'No!' She glanced over her shoulder into the soft dark. 'Will you let me go? There's someone there!'

'You didn't seem to mind that just now.'

'I don't know what I was thinking of just now. Please, Dev, will you stop it!'

His mouth twisted into an ironic grin. 'Oh Tara, Tara, what do I have to do to make you see?' He let go of her arms. 'Ah well, next time maybe. Because there will be a next time, I promise you! Now, if you like I'll have one last look at my lights just to make certain they won't catch fire, if that's what is worrying you.'

He strode away across the dark clearing, a stocky purposeful figure.

*

Tara watched him go, letting her breath out in a long controlled 'Whew!' She felt shaky, still, her knees weak, and a nerve was jumping at the base of her throat. It was not the fact that he had kissed her that had shocked her so – but her own reaction.

What in the world came over me? she thought. It was as if I was possessed. I've never felt like that before – never – as if I was being swept away and had no will of my own. It must be because I'm overwrought with worrying about this damned show!

But somehow the explanation did not seem very convincing, even to herself.

*

Tara slipped off her uniform dress, hung it in the open-ended cupboard at the foot of her bed which she shared with the sister in the bed on the opposite side of the ward and fumbled in the darkness to find her pyjamas. There was a thud as a shoe fell out of the locker and a voice from across the aisle grumbled: 'Keep it quiet, can't you?'

Tara pushed the shoe back into the locker and straightened. A slight breeze kissed her sticky skin and she noticed that someone had opened the shutters a crack to let the air in. Fair enough – as long as they were not plagued with mosquitos. Even now she could hear them humming in the soft dark. Without bothering to search any more for her pyjamas, Tara turned back the single cool sheet and slid under it. But tired though she was sleep had never been further away. Every nerve ending in her body tingled and crawled and her mind ran in endless circles – around and around and always back to the same point.

Dev.

It wasn't possible – it simply was not possible – that Dev should have had that electric effect on her. He was the bane of her life, wasn't he? No. Not strictly true. She had told him he was the bane of her life, countering his teasing and banter with some of her own. In fact, if she was truthful she had a great deal to be grateful to him for. He had been on hand to get her out of trouble on more than one occasion and he was helping her now far more than she had any right to expect – without him and his electrics there would be no show.

And he was without doubt a very attractive man. Not beautiful in the way that Richard was beautiful, but magnetic and virile. Dev was all male. She thought of him now, his dark muscular body, even white teeth and lips that could be as sensuous as they were mocking, and those hazel eyes with the dangerous green flecks, and in spite of herself felt the niggle of excitement stir again in the pit of her stomach.

Funny she had never noticed it before. Funny it had taken something like this, totally unexpected and unasked for, to make her see him as more than a friend who loved to tease and needle her and who just occasionally had her best welfare at heart . . .

The hut door opened and closed and Tara saw a shadowy figure move between the beds blotting out the moonlight as she passed each unshuttered window. One of the sisters, just off duty and heading gratefully for bed. It was no wonder it was almost impossible to get a good night's sleep with all the comings and goings of the different shifts, Tara thought. But she knew that tonight she would have found it difficult to relax, however few the disturbances. She turned over, moulding her head into the hard pillow and stretching her body sensuously.

Oh, why couldn't it have been Richard who had grabbed her like that, kissing her until her head spun? But then, of course, Richard never would. He was too much of a gentleman. I'll bet he has never grabbed anyone in his life, Tara thought. And he would certainly never grab me! Dev is probably right, damn him, and I am just crying for the moon. He never seems to notice me – I don't think he knows I exist. As for Dev . . .

I must make very sure I don't get into a situation like that again. It's just as well he won't be coming back until the night of the concert. I've proved I can't trust myself and I certainly can't trust him. Now, for heaven's sake get some sleep, girl, or you will be no use to man nor beast in the morning.

*

Two days before the concert Joe Hanks, the Yankee pianist, came to see Tara.

'Hey, hon, we've got problems.'

The smile of greeting died on Tara's lips. 'What sort of problems?'

'Big ones. I've been told I'm fit to be moved out to a convalescent hospital.'

'When?'

'Today, the quack said.'

'Oh, Holy Mother!' Tara's hands flew to her mouth. 'They can't do that!'

'They are doing it.'

'But I need you!' She stood for a moment chewing on her lips as she thought it through. Any of the other performers they could have covered for one way or another. But not Joe – there was no way they could manage without Joe. He was needed for continuity and to accompany almost all the acts, her own included. Tara pulled herself up very straight. 'I won't let them move you. Not before the concert, anyway.'

'How are you going to stop them? You know the army. All red tape and bullshit.'

'I'll stop them. Don't worry about it.'

She tidied her hair, applied a little of the lip gloss that made her lips shine without looking painted, and made

197

straight for the CO's tent.

Outside she was met by the quartermaster, who looked at her strangely.

'Just a minute – where do you think you are going?'

'To see Colonel Adamson.'

'Hang about now. You can't just waltz in like that. The CO is a busy man.'

'He'll see me,' Tara said confidently.

'We'll see about that. Wait here.'

Tara waited, tapping her heels impatiently. A few moments later the quartermaster was back.

'All right, you can go in.' His tone was short.

'Thank you very much,' Tara replied sarcastically.

The Colonel rose as she entered, coming around his desk to greet her.

'Tara, my dear. Not more problems, I hope.'

'I'm afraid so.' She went on to outline what had happened. 'Without a pianist we won't have a show,' she concluded.

The CO smiled, his eyes twinkling darkly beneath the sandy brows. 'A few more days of treatment will take care of the matter I presume?' He turned to a corporal who was sorting papers at the filing cabinet. 'Do the necessary will you, Seaton? No transfer for Joseph Hanks just yet. I will put it in writing if needs be, but if the paperwork has not been completed yet there should be no need to make it formal.'

'Yessir!' The corporal, a fussy little man, scooted out of the tent, leaving Tara and the Colonel alone.

'Well, my dear, and how is it all progressing?' he asked her. 'The stage is completed, I see. Had a look at it the other evening. Most impressed. And you have got the lights from somewhere?'

'Yes, sir. An electrician from Darwin working on a Government contract.'

'Capital. No problems?'

'I don't think so.'

'Good. Now Tara, my dear there is something else I

198

wished to mention to you.' He put his arm around her shoulders in avuncular fashion. 'I have been most impressed with the way you have arranged this concert – it seems to me you have considerable powers of organization that are totally wasted in your present classification. You are a nursing orderly, are you not?'

Tara nodded.

'Yes.' He paused thoughtfully. 'I can't help feeling there are other jobs which would suit you better.'

'What do you mean?' Tara looked up at him, genuinely puzzled. Then she saw the tiny beads of perspiration standing out on his lip just below the lines of his moustache – and understood.

'I believe I could make use of your skills myself.' Colonel Adamson smiled, his eyes narrowing beneath his beetling sandy brows. 'I dare say we would have to list you as "clerk" but what I have in mind is that you should take responsibility for organizing recreational pursuits. Now the good weather is here there are all kinds of things that could be arranged – chop picnics, picture shows, sports – you know what I mean.'

Yes, Tara thought, I know what you mean. And it is not only the sports and recreations of your members of staff that you have in mind, either.

'I don't know whether Matron would be agreeable,' she ventured.

'I'm sure she would raise no objection.' He patted her shoulder amicably. 'We have worked together very well on this concert, haven't we? I see no reason why we should not work together well in other areas. Especially when we get to know one another's little ways.'

Tara hesitated. She would not be sorry to be relieved of all the messy chores which went with being a VA nursing orderly. She did not care if she did not change another bed as long as she lived, or boil up water for sterilizing instruments, or spray water on packed earth floors to stop the red dust rising. It would be wonderful never to have to face another bedpan or dress a festering wound. She wasn't a nurse and she never would be, no matter how hard she tried. But working for the CO would mean she would see less than ever of Richard – and she saw little enough of him already.

Moreover, she was not so naive that she didn't know why Colonel Adamson wanted to take her on board. It would be all too easy to become the CO's personal assistant in more ways than one and the inevitable gossip would spread like wildfire around the hospital. Already the quartermaster must be suspicious. And if Richard got to hear the stories he certainly would want nothing to do with her.

'It's very kind of you, sir,' Tara began in an effort at diplomacy, 'but I don't think . . .'

The CO's fingers tightened on her shoulder, his smile was no longer avuncular.

'I'm sure you won't refuse, Tara, after all I have done for you,' he said meaningfully.

Her heart sank. So this was what it came down to. Blackmail. Do as I ask or I'll scupper your show, his expression said more clearly than any words could and for a moment she was transported back across the years to when she had been a star-struck youngster in Sydney. It had been Red then who had held the reins of power to make her do what he wanted – but here in 138 AGH the CO was just as powerful in his own way. He could make life difficult for her if he chose – even get rid of her. The place was different, the circumstances were different, but the moral, in the end, was just the same.

'Thank you sir, it would be a wonderful opportunity,' she said demurely.

*

The night before the show Tara scarcely slept at all for worrying about the hundred and one things which could go wrong and whether there was anything she had overlooked. By lunchtime she was feeling sick with nerves, and by the time darkness fell the adrenalin was pumping so hard it was almost impossible to think straight any more.

And she needed to be able to think straight to sort out the inevitable hitches. They had been occurring all day – not serious, but trying. First, one of the balloons used by the drag act to form a whistle-worthy bosom had accidentally burst. Tara begged a spare brassiere from the bustiest of the AANS sisters and stuffed it full of surgical dressings. Then, an over zealous corporal managed to knock down half the greenery decorating the stage. Most worrying of all were the cracklings and whistles that came from the loudspeaker system each time the microphones were switched on.

'If we can't cut that noise we might as well give up and forget the whole thing!' Tara snapped at the technicians.

An hour before curtain up Dev had still not arrived. Holy Mary, where is he? Tara wondered frantically. What in the world will I do if he doesn't turn up? Maybe I'd better have a look and see if he's left it so that someone else can carry on if the worst comes to the worst.

She clambered up to the lighting box on the rickety ladder made of creepers. Everything seemed to be where he had left it but there was no sign of any lighting plan. Without that it would be impossible for anyone else to attempt the programme she had asked for. She flicked a switch or two and the lights came on, bathing the whole scene in bright light and, unbidden, the imp of terror leapt inside her again.

In less than an hour the stage would no longer be empty. The acts she had got together would be taking it in turns to perform in that brilliantly lit rectangle of isolation. *She* would be performing there . . . her throat closed with fear at the thought.

Down below in the clearing the first members of the audience were beginning to arrive, determined to gain the best positions for the blankets and cushions they had brought to sit on. The sight of them panicked Tara still

201

further. She flicked the light switches off and went to climb down the swaying ladder again.

'Hey – what are you doing up in my lighting box?' a voice enquired from behind her. She jerked her head round, still hanging onto the creeper rungs for dear life.

'Dev! I thought you weren't coming!'

'I told you I'd be here. Everything is ready – I've nothing to do but work to the plan I made. You haven't touched anything, have you?'

'I only put a couple of lights on to make sure they were working . . .'

'Why couldn't you leave it alone?' he chided. 'If you've messed anything up . . .'

'I'm sure I haven't! And where were you, anyway? It's unforgivable turning up so late. I was having kittens in case you didn't come at all.'

'Oh, stop fussing, woman!' he exploded. 'And do you mind getting out of my way? I can't do anything until I can get up to my box, now can I?'

Tara jumped down the last two rungs, steadying herself on landing by hanging onto the ladder.

'There you are, then. Don't let me hold you up, for goodness' sake.'

He touched her shoulder lightly yet somehow it was almost a caress.

'Make it a good show, Tara. Good luck.'

Nerves jangling she thrust him aside. 'You mustn't say that!'

'Mustn't say what?'

'Good luck. You mustn't say it. You say break a leg.'

'All right – break a leg!' He sounded amused.

But Tara had already gone and he did not know if she had heard him.

*

More than halfway through and it was going well. Still so tense she was almost afraid to admit it yet beginning to flush with cautious relief. Tara stood at the side of the stage and watched Kath Rice rattle the spoons in an astonishing rhythm accompanied by Joe Hanks on the piano. She was good – she really was good – and a born performer too, milking her audience for every last scrap of applause. Which was more than could be said for the drag act, Tara thought a little crossly. The two medicos, overwhelmed by stage fright, had rushed through their routine so quickly that much of the humour of it had been lost. But then the audience didn't know what they were supposed to have done and they had simply lapped up the spectacle of two respected doctors prancing about in skirts.

The loudspeaker system was working reasonably well now – it only gave the occasional whistle if someone got too close to the microphone and Tara had done her utmost to impress upon all the performers not to do that. And the lights were a dream – well done, Dev! thought Tara and – Oh, Holy Mother, don't let me be the one to let the show down!

After the spoons it was the turn of the tenor MO. He made a false start, coming in on the wrong note, and Tara's nails dug into her palms as she whispered frantically to George Marshall, the dental officer who was compèring for her. But Joe Hanks, thumping the true notes so loudly that only a deaf man could fail to hear them, got him back on the right track and Tara breathed again. He did have a good voice, all he lacked was confidence, and with an audience as big as this one it was enough to give anyone stage fright.

She craned forward to look at them – nowhere in the clearing was there a square inch of space to spare. Soldiers and airmen from nearby camps had arrived by the truckload and every patient who was fit enough had been brought out of the wards too. Please God we don't have a raid, Tara thought. But the coast watchers had not reported any enemy activity and raids did not penetrate this far inland.

The tenor finished his first number 'I Dream of Jeannie' and a burst of applause rose like a bubbling living roar from the massed audience. It was an ovation such as Tara had rarely heard for a professional performer, and this MO, though his voice was pleasant enough, was scarcely a virtuoso. It's because they want to enjoy it, I suppose, she thought. They would applaud anything. But though it eased her anxieties about the show it did nothing to lessen the spiral of tension that was tightening within as her own spot approached. The other performers were amateurs – they were allowed a little leeway. She was a professional. She had to give the performance of her life. More. She had to prove herself again. And the moment when she had to do it was coming closer and closer. One more song from the tenor, a five minute spot by Sister Grace Dunwoody on the harmonica and she would be on!

'Tara!' The urgent hiss from the darkness behind her caught her jagged nerves and she turned sharply as one of her backstage helpers caught her arm.

'What's wrong?'

'It's Grace Dunwoody. She's collapsed.'

'Collapsed? What do you mean – collapsed?'

'She hasn't been well all day, it seems. But she's said nothing to anybody because she was so keen to do the show. Now she's fainted.'

'Oh no! Is somebody with her?'

'Of course. The place is crawling with doctors. But she was due to go on next, wasn't she?'

'Yes. Yes!' Tara was icy cool suddenly. 'I'll have to go straight on. Find George and tell him. He was here a minute ago. And Joe . . . can you get a message out to Joe?'

'Sure.'

'Now! This minute.'

'Yes.'

'Go on then.'

She climbed the rickety steps to the side of the platform and stood behind fronds of greenery, hands clenched into damp fists, heart beating so hard it echoed in every pulse and nerve. Calm down, Tara. Deep breaths! The tenor was coming to the end of 'Granada', thoroughly enjoying himself now. The deep breaths drew a path of calm through her panic. Almost time. Almost. Where the hell is George? Another moment of threatening panic. Don't be foolish – George will be here. All he has to do is introduce you instead of Grace. Another deep breath. Applause for the tenor, like the roar of the sea in her ears, and George was there beside her, totally unruffled and smelling of alcohol.

'All right, sweetheart?' She nodded, unable to speak. He squeezed her arm. 'Here we go then!'

This is it. The moment of truth. They are waiting for you.

She stepped out onto the stage and was no longer afraid. She felt the anticipation of the tight packed audience and Dev's lights hot and bright on her face, heard Joe's piano tinkling out the bars of her opening number. As she began to sing all the nervousness she had bottled inside her acted as a cataclysmic force, generating power and electric magnetism. Her voice rose sweetly in the clear soft night: 'Yours – till the stars lose their glory . . .', and it was not only the purity of her tone which entranced but the force of her personality. On and on she sang, one war song after another, carrying them with her. And when at last she came to the end of her programme it seemed they would never let her go. They clapped, they cheered, they whistled, they stamped their feet. She came back for one encore – 'Wish me luck as you wave me goodbye!' – determined to do no more. First rule of the variety theatre – leave them wanting more! But after she had left the stage, they were still yelling and cheering and she stood in the darkness beyond the pool of light, hands pressed to her mouth to contain the bubbling excitement, savouring every moment of her success.

Oh, this was what she could live for! If there was nothing else – nothing – it didn't matter. As long as she could feel this thrill, ride this breathtaking wave, she could ask for no more . . .

Arms caught her around the waist, swinging her round.

'And who is the cleverest girl in the whole of the Northern Territory?'

'Dev!' She hugged him, laughing and almost crying. 'Oh Dev, what did you think?'

'I just told you. You want to hear it again? You were wonderful.'

'And the rest? The rest was all right, wasn't it?'

'The rest? Oh yes, the rest was fine. The audience enjoyed it, anyway. But there was only one star for me.'

'Oh!' She kissed him, a quick warm kiss on the lips. 'That is to say thank you for all you did. Your lights were marvellous.'

'Good. So how about coming for a beer to celebrate?'

'Oh Dev, I still have so much to do here . . .'

'Come on, leave it.'

'Oh, I don't know . . .' He felt her stiffen suddenly, drawing herself upright, and her eyes, narrowed slightly, were no longer meeting his but looking at something – or someone – behind him. 'I don't think . . .'

She sidestepped his arms. He turned and swore softly.

'The good doctor.'

She seemed not to hear him. Her sparkle was still there, shining out of every pore, but it was no longer for him. If it ever had been.

'Richard! Did you see the show?'

'I certainly did! It was splendid. I had no idea we had such a talent in our midst!'

The cultured tones annoyed Dev; he felt irritation begin to ferment in the pit of his stomach. 'Careful you don't give me a swollen head, sport,' he said with biting sarcasm but no one was listening to him.

A couple of backstage workers came past carrying one of the pieces of scenery from the drag act; Richard stepped back to let them past and into the pool of brilliance thrown by one of the lights Dev had left on. In it his hair shone like molten gold, a halo above the perfect lines of his face.

'Tara, I'm not only here on my own behalf,' he said

with the easy manner that twisted Dev's irritation another knot tighter. 'I'm also speaking for my brother officers. We have a bottle of something rather old and special in the mess and we would be most honoured if you would come and share it with us.'

'Oh yes – thank you!' She was too high still on excitement even to hesitate. First the thrill of the concert's success, now Richard asking her to the mess for a drink – it was all too much. She felt intoxicated already. 'Have I time to do something about my face? I've caked on all the make up I could find because of the lights . . .'

As if the mention of lights had reminded her of Dev she turned, half embarrassed. 'Oh, look, I should introduce you. This is Sean Devlin – Dev – who did all the electrics. He's been marvellous . . .'

'Congratulations, Mr Devlin. Fine show.' Richard was smiling but the bright lights showed it for a polite smile. 'Perhaps you would care to join us too.'

Sod you, mate, Dev thought. Aloud he said: 'Thanks, but I'm sure you don't want me.'

'Nonsense.'

'Thanks all the same, but I have all my equipment to dismantle and get out before the army requisition my ute again.'

That caught Tara's attention. 'Oh Dev, they're not going to do that, are they?'

'' 'fraid so. I've had great difficulty persuading them to let me keep it this long.'

'Oh no! You mean if I do another concert I'll have to do it without your lights?'

'Well, well, it's a sad life!' he said mockingly. 'Here was I beginning to think that at last I was wanted for my own charming self and all the time it was my lights she was after.' He patted her shoulder. 'Don't worry, Tara, I'm sure it will all work out for the best. The army will probably requisition my lighting equipment too!'

'Oh Dev, you're impossible! He is impossible, isn't he, Richard?'

207

There was no mistaking the way her eyes were shining. And to think that for the last couple of days he had been harbouring the illusion that he had made her see the pair of them in a different light! Ah well! The knot hardened in the pit of his stomach. I shall land a punch right on his well bred nose if I don't get the hell out of here, thought Dev.

'I'll leave you now,' he said dryly.

She turned quickly, guiltily. 'Dev . . .'

He caught one of her curls between finger and thumb and tweaked it down behind her ear. 'Have fun, Tara.'

Then he turned and walked away.

Watching his stocky frame disappear into the darkness Tara was aware of a tiny falling away deep inside her, a strange, poignant, anonymous ache. Then she turned to see Richard smiling at her and the excitement of the evening returned, bubbling in her veins like champagne.

'Just give me ten minutes to make sure everything is being taken care of here and I'll be with you!' she said.

Chapter Eleven

The clearing was empty now. The stage stood deserted and ghostly in the light of the moon and the air was full of the smell of crushed grass. Tara closed her eyes and lifted her chin, breathing it in and imagining she could still hear the roar of the crowd.

Oh, what a night – what a night! And it hadn't ended there. The adulation had extended to the mess party where the officers young and old had vied for her favours, flattering her, teasing her, falling over themselves to buy her drinks. Finally, the CO himself had made an appearance and staked a claim.

'She's my find, this one!' he had declared putting an arm around her and pulling her uncomfortably close. 'The moment she came to me for help I knew we would have a winner on our hands. And splendidly right I turned out to be!'

Tara dimpled him a sideways smile while her eyes skeetered around the room looking for Richard. Tricky! She couldn't afford to offend the CO but neither did she want Richard to think she was leading him on.

Richard was at the bar; at the very moment she saw him he turned to look at her and she managed to mouth at him with her back to the CO – 'Help!' His expression did not alter but the slight narrowing of his eyes told her he had understood. She saw him lean forward to say something to his companion, then make his way across the mess in her direction. Her lips twitched as she suppressed a smile, wondering how he would handle it.

'How about an encore, Tara?' It was casually elegant – so natural!

She hesitated, feigning modesty. 'Oh, I don't know . . .'

'By special request! Round the evening off with a song.

What do you say, sir? We'd all like to hear her again, wouldn't we?'

The CO nodded. His movements were slightly deliberate and above the sandy moustache his face was rather flushed. 'Capital idea! Go on, my dear, favour us with a song.'

'Well, all right, just one,' Tara conceded. 'Then I really think it's time I left. It's been a very long day.'

'Quite right. And if you will give us the pleasure of this one song, I will see you get back to your quarters safely afterwards,' Richard said.

Tara smiled demurely but she felt like laughing out loud. It had worked!

'What on earth am I going to sing?' she asked Richard as he steered her across the mess.

'Does it matter? I'm sure whatever it is will be splendid.'

He clapped his hands for quiet and announced her. I'd never do this normally, she thought. No rehearsal, no accompaniment, but tonight . . .

Tonight was special. And she knew just the song. Too new yet for any pianist to have the music but she had heard it on the wireless and learned it by heart – a song from a new Hollywood musical:

> A journey to a star would not be very far
> As long as I'm alone with you,
> Romantic as we are a journey to a star
> Could start before the dawn breaks through.
> You're right beside my heart,
> We're just about a kiss apart
> And we could make a dream come true,
> A moment of your love would have the feeling of
> A journey to a star with you.

As she sang her eyes found Richard's. The room was crowded but she was singing to no one but him. When she finished the applause and the calls for more were deafening but Richard moved in front of her holding up his hand for quiet.

210

'Perhaps Tara will do us the honour of singing for us again some time but for tonight, sadly, we must let her go.'

He took her elbow, steering her towards the door. As it closed after them she turned to him, smiling.

'Thank you! That was an inspiration. I didn't know what to do. I could hardly be rude to the CO, could I?'

Richard smiled back. 'Glad to have been of assistance. He's had a little more to drink than is good for him. Normally he's a perfect gentleman.'

No, she wanted to say – you are the perfect gentleman. The only real gentleman I've ever met – the only one I want to meet.

The night was warm and still. In the undergrowth the crickets chirped, a constant symphony. They walked close together but not touching and Tara was sharply aware of his bare arm swinging just a few centimetres from her own.

Outside the door of her hut they stopped.

'Tara, I'd like to see you again,' he said. After all her hopes, all her plotting, the directness of it took her breath away. 'I know there's not a great deal here on offer – no theatres, no restaurants, no civilization – but maybe we could find a way to make up for that. There are some quite pleasant walks and . . .'

Suddenly, ridiculously, Tara was laughing, the mirth bubbling up in her though she scarcely knew why. For a moment Richard looked shocked then he too was laughing.

'Oh, I'm sorry,' Tara said when at last she controlled herself. 'There's nothing funny really. It's just the thought of grand opera or something out here in the middle of nowhere. And when I started to laugh I just couldn't stop . . .'

'Stay just as you are, Tara.' His voice was low now, vibrant with something that was certainly not laughter. 'Keep everyone's spirits up while this damned war lasts.'

She looked at him sharply but his face was in shadow.

'Tomorrow, then?' he said.

She nodded. 'Yes, I'd like that.'

He touched her arm lightly. 'Go in now. Get some sleep. You must be exhausted.'

'Yes,' she said. 'I am.'

But she knew that she was far too excited to sleep. She waved until the darkness swallowed him up then leaned against the corrugated wall of the hut, hands pressed over her mouth as the happiness welled up within her.

I'll never sleep, she thought. Not for hours and hours – not now. I'll only keep everyone awake with my tossing and turning. I think I'll go for a little walk.

That was how she had come to find herself back in the clearing, scene of her earlier triumph, deserted now yet still seeming to echo softly with the music, the laughter and the applause. Tara stood at the very perimeter remembering and relishing every moment. And the pleasure in the memory was heightened because of what had followed.

Richard! Oh, Richard! He noticed me! He asked me out! We laughed . . .

With the joy bubbling in her she began to laugh again. Soft happy laughter blending with the sounds of the night! Then the laughter died in her throat as a twig cracked in the undergrowth behind her.

What was that? She half turned towards the sound and thought she heard the thick grass rustle. Holy Mother, what was it – someone standing there watching her? She stood motionless, listening with every fibre of her being. Nothing. Just the chirping of the crickets. She turned back and something brushed her face making her cry out before common sense intervened. She put up her hand and caught at a horn-shaped carob pod a few inches from her cheek.

Her breath came out on a shuddering sigh. You are crazy, Tara Kelly. You have had too much champagne and your imagination is running riot. Time to go back to your quarters and try to get some sleep.

As she turned back to the clearing the foliage rustled

again. Her nerves screamed a warning – too late. Before she had time to react or even register, something all enveloping like a blanket or coat was thrown over her head and a body lunged at her. Tara screamed but the coat stifled the sound. Blindly she hit out, struggling and fighting, and for a moment she and her attacker swayed and stumbled together. Then Tara's foot caught, she lost her balance and fell heavily, her attacker on top of her. With a sickening crack the soft base of her skull smashed against the exposed root of a tree and Tara knew no more.

*

The clattering whirr of a fan interspersed with the insistent mewing cry of a baby awoke her. She came slowly through the layers of drug-induced sleep, opened her eyes to a blindingly sharp pain and quickly closed them again.

'Tara – are you awake?'

She squinted, trying to cut out as much light as possible. Sister Kate Harris was bending over her, her freckled face anxious.

'Yes,' Tara said. The effort made her mouth hurt – lips, gums, teeth, chin.

'How are you feeling?'

For a moment Tara did not answer. She lay still, assessing. There was not a square inch of her body which did not hurt. It had been like this every waking moment for the last three days, but without doubt it was the constant headache which was the worst.

'Terrible,' she said. 'And that fan – it makes such a racket. It's making my head throb. Can't you turn it off?'

'If I do you won't be able to stand the heat in here,' Kate said.

Tara moistened her lips. They were dry, so dry, but the spittle made them sting again. 'I can't win, can I?'

'No,' Kate said cheerfully. 'Now you know what it's like to be a patient.'

Tara rolled her head on the pillow. There was nothing to see but a wall of canvas. She was in a corner of the tent ward reserved for maternity cases but they had partitioned it off to give her a modicum of privacy.

'How long have I been asleep?' she asked.

'Hours. Captain Allingham has looked in at least three times to see you. And – not so pleasant – the officer investigating came again hoping to find you awake.'

'Oh.' Tara shuddered. She knew what that meant. More questions. And she knew none of the answers. They were all lost in that terrifying blackness between the struggle in the bushes and waking up for the first time to find herself in the tent ward. Somewhere between she had been raped and beaten. But she could remember nothing – only the vaguest of impressions. In some ways it was more disturbing than clear and painful memories would have been. To know she had been used and abused and to be able to recall nothing about it. 'Who was it? Who did this to you?' they had asked her when she first emerged from the blackness and she had only been able to whisper: 'I don't know. I don't know!'

At first they had not believed her. 'Don't shield him!' they had said. And later, when her denials became distracted, they had tried new avenues. What impressions had she gained? How tall was he? Did he speak? Had she smelled anything identifiable? Felt his hair, his face? Did he have a moustache or was he clean shaven.

'I don't know! Why won't you believe I don't remember anything?' she cried. But she knew they would not give up easily and in the half world where she drifted between sleeping and waking she tried to answer the questions.

In vain. Trying to remember simply made her head hurt and she could recall nothing. Again and again she returned to the moment when she had heard the bushes rustle, trying to fill in some other detail – a smell or sound – but there was nothing. And the moment when the coat had gone over her head was a jumble of impressions so confused as to be useless. How did she know it was a coat?

214

they had asked her. She had not even been able to answer that with any certainty. Because it was heavy material, perhaps, or because she had felt the buttons or smelled the rubberized fabric. Did she remember feeling the buttons? No. Then how did she know it was not a groundsheet, such as many of the audience had brought to sit on for the concert? That was more likely, surely; in the Dry no one would be wearing a rubberized ovecoat.

Wearily she agreed. But it did nothing to help identify her attacker and that was one of the nastiest aspects of the whole grim business. It could have been anyone.

Anyone, she thought, and there was a sick hollow sound even to the word itself. Anyone. It could have been a vagrant, of course, but most of those had been rounded up by the provosts. It could have been someone from one of the other camps in the area, someone who had been at the concert, perhaps, and been incited by her performance and their own sexual frustration. But why should anyone hang around in the clearing? Wasn't it more likely he was from 138 – someone who had been in the officers' mess, perhaps, and who had followed her back to her quarters? It was a sickening thought. Alibis would be checked out, she guessed, uniforms examined. But unless the culprit could be found Tara would spend the rest of her service looking at this man and that, wondering – Was it you? Could it have been *you*?

Tara moistened her lips again and Kate noticed.

'Would you like a drink?'

'Mm. Yes. Oh – I feel so thick . . .'

Kate bent over her, then straightened, a smile playing about her mouth. 'Oh-oh – here he is again!'

'Who? Not the provost . . . ?' Tara turned her head on the pillow, following Kate's line of vision. 'Oh – Richard!'

He came around the tent flap, bending his tall frame, and suddenly she was overcome with self-consciousness.

'She's awake now,' Kate said, and to Tara: 'I'll leave you for a while. But I won't be far away if you want anything.'

Richard sat down beside her bed leaning over to examine her face.

'I must look a fright,' she said.

One corner of his mouth lifted. 'A bit. But nothing that won't mend.' Then a shadow darkened his eyes. 'You still haven't remembered anything?'

'No! I keep telling them . . . have they asked you to ask me now?'

'Oh no. I'm the one who got most of the questions thrown at me.'

'You?'

'I was the last person to see you before . . .'

'But that is ridiculous!' She tried to lift herself but a sharp pain in her ribs made her fall back again. 'Surely they don't think . . .'

'I hope I have convinced them that I am not that sort of animal. It doesn't alter the fact that I feel responsible.'

'Responsible? Why?'

'I should have made sure you were safe. I can say I'm sorry, Tara, but it doesn't help now, does it?'

'You don't have to be sorry!' She struggled to form the words with lips that refused to work properly. 'I'm the one who should be sorry if they suspected you. I was the one who went wandering about in the middle of the night. If I'd gone straight in it would never have happened.'

'Don't!' He took her hand, stroking the scratched skin with his thumb. 'I know we have been trying to bring back the memory – we want to get the beast who did this to you. But the medical evidence is that you were probably unconscious from the moment your head struck the stone and it is my opinion that it's only distressing to you trying to remember. I think now that what you should do is try to forget.'

She laughed bitterly. 'That's not going to be easy. Especially when I hurt all over.'

'No, but it will get better – and quite quickly now. It's superficial damage only. That is not what concerns me.' He paused and Tara saw the anxious, faraway expression in his eyes as his mind raced over other, less tangible effects. 'I'll make it up to you, Tara, I promise,' he said.

You don't have to. She almost said it – the words were there, hovering on her lips. But the look in his eyes stopped her.

When had anyone ever looked at her like that before – with so much caring, so much compassion, so much *love*? Oh, she had seen desire often enough, and lust. But not tender concern – never that. Now his eyes were a fire at which she could warm herself, surrounding her with a glow which took away all her pain, made her forget every moment of shadowy horror.

I would go through anything – *anything* – to have him look at me like that, she thought.

The drugs were beginning to take a hold again, dragging her back into muzziness. But sleep held no terrors for her and the last thing she was aware of before drifting back into unconsciousness was his thumb, still stroking the back of her hand.

*

When she was fit enough to sit out for a few hours Colonel Adamson came to see Tara.

'Bad business, m'dear – shocked us all,' he said, compressing his large frame onto the economy size ward chair. 'And I'm afraid to say we are no closer to identifying the culprit. I'm of the opinion that we can safely lay the blame with one of the camps – so damned many around here – but every line of enquiry seems to draw a blank.'

Tara nodded. With her returning strength, she was beginning to be glad the enquiries had proved fruitless. It was disconcerting not to know who her attacker had been, of course, but an identification now would mean going over the whole ghastly episode again, more questioning – and worse. If there was a court martial she would be called to give evidence. Tara knew all about trials. The

217

defendant was not the only one to find himself in the dock, the victim was on trial too. And there was plenty in Tara's past which would not stand up to interrogation. Already there were those who, like Anastasia Bottomley, murmured that Tara Kelly had only got what she had asked for. Let a good defence counsel loose on her past life and she would be finished at 138 AGH.

'I'm afraid, m'dear, this sort of thing is one of the scourges of war,' the CO went on. 'When men think they may be about to die it can have an unfortunate effect on them. But let us not talk about that any more – let's talk about you. I expect you would like some leave when you are fit enough – go home and have a good rest.'

'Home?' Tara's look was puzzled, causing the Colonel to wonder what effect the rape had had on her state of mind.

'Yes, Sydney, isn't it?' he reminded her gently. 'I'm sure we could arrange some leave for you . . .'

'No!' Tara said quickly. 'I don't want any leave.'

'Oh.' He looked at her narrowly. 'You are not thinking of leaving us altogether, I hope. It would be a great pity. A tragedy. It won't be easy for you, I know, but we shall all be doing our utmost to help you adjust. And you will be working for me. You won't have to face hordes of people and you may depend on me to look after you.'

A knife edge of hatred for all men scythed through Tara. They were all the same when it came to the crunch, weren't they? Maybe she did not know who the bastard was who had raped her but he did not really differ in any way that mattered from all the others – Red, Dimitri, the renegade wharfies, the CO . . . Only one man is different, she thought. Richard. And if he knew the truth about me, he wouldn't want me.

Weak tears choked in her throat and ran down her cheeks. The CO rose, well meaning but embarrassed. 'Look, you're still not strong, m'dear. A thing like this can affect you in many ways. It may be that I should get Captain Kylie to have a chat with you.'

'No, thank you!' Tara said, horrified. Captain Kylie was the psychology expert, the doctor called in when men went 'troppo' – or worse. The very thought that she might need his attentions was enough to make her want to cry all the harder, but she controlled herself with an effort. 'No – I'll be all right.'

'Good. Good.' He patted her on the shoulder. 'We're all behind you, Tara.'

She nodded and wished that she could take some comfort in the sentiment. At times like this it looked like being a long road back.

Chapter Twelve

Richard Allingham pulled the ute into a clearing beneath the gums and switched off the engine. Then he turned to Tara who was sitting beside him, sliding his arm along the back of the seat and around her shoulders.

'Would you like to walk for a bit – or just sit?'

'Oh . . .' she hesitated, tossing it around in her mind. 'I'm bone lazy, really. For choice I'd sit and sit, especially since you were lucky enough to get the keys to the ute today. But I suppose we ought to stretch our legs.' She giggled and he thought it was one of the most heartening sounds he had ever heard.

Six weeks now had passed since the attack, six weeks when he had anxiously watched as the cuts and scratches healed on her face and body and wondered what would happen to the scars on her mind.

Oh, what wouldn't he like to do to the bastard responsible if ever he got his hands on him! But he had never been caught. For a time there had been the fear that the monster might strike again but so far at least that fear had proved unjustified. The nurses still walked from the wards to their quarters in twos – all except Anastasia Bottomley who boasted that any man who attacked her would soon wish he had never been born. But then Anastasia was not Tara. Anastasia was a formidable woman, more than capable of taking care of herself, whilst Tara . . .

Tara needed looking after. He was supposed to have been doing just that on the night of the concert and he had failed. He intended to make very certain he did not fail again.

The Dry had really taken hold now, the lush greenery becoming withered and yellow, and the dry earth spewed up in red clouds from the track. It was hot, but not so hot as to be unbearable, except sometimes between noon and two or three. When he took her out, Richard usually managed to split his duty so that they could get the benefit of the late afternoon. It was safer to drive on the Track during the day – in the dark there was always the danger of hitting a buffalo or kangaroo. But that was not his only reason for choosing to take her out during the hours of daylight – after what had happened he thought that perhaps Tara might be more comfortable in the company of a man whilst it was light. She was, after all, a young and innocent girl – heaven only knew how such a thing could affect her. He had seen for himself the way she shied away from the CO whenever he patted her hand or knee – and been surprised that Adamson had not noticed it himself. But then Adamson did seem to have a blind spot where Tara was concerned. Richard thought back to the night of the concert remembering how he had rescued Tara, and suffered another pang of guilt that he had not completed the duty.

'Are we going to walk then, or have you decided you can't be bothered?' Tara asked.

She was smiling at him, her eyes sparkling blue behind the dark fringe of lashes, and he thought she looked like an enchanting child. Something not quite chivalrous stirred within him. He moved abruptly, opening the door of the ute.

'We'll walk.'

She waited for him to come around and help her down, putting her hands on his shoulders and jumping down onto the track. Again he felt that tiny imp of desire, again he turned away too sharply – and failed to see the little frown that puckered between her eyebrows.

For a while they walked in silence. The sun was still high and hot, the trees giving little shade and most of nature seemed to be sleeping.

'I heard the girls say there's a water hole out here somewhere,' Tara said. 'If we brought bathing costumes we could swim.'

221

Richard did not answer. He was wondering how he could bear not to touch Tara if she was wearing a bathing costume.

'What's wrong?' she asked.

'Nothing. Perhaps we ought to be getting back.'

'Oh, do you think so?' Her voice was flat. 'We only just got here.'

'I know . . .' He glanced at his watch. 'We came farther out today. It will take us longer to get back.'

Still she said nothing. He found her silence unnerving. Tara was always such a chatterbox. Then suddenly, unexpectedly, she caught hold of his arm. He almost jumped at the touch of her fingers on his bare skin and turned to see her looking up at him, a challenge in her eyes.

For a long moment she held his gaze then she took her hand away and he saw the tears leap in her eyes. Tara, who had scarcely ever cried before that damned attack . . .

'I'm sorry,' she said abruptly. 'You can't bear to have me touch you, can you?'

He ran a hand through his thick fair hair. 'What do you mean?'

'You blame me for what happened. And you can't touch me because you keep remembering . . .'

'No!' he said sharply. 'No, of course I don't blame you. If I blame anyone I blame myself.'

'Maybe that's even worse. But whoever you blame, you don't like to touch me. You think I'm not clean.'

'That's nonsense. But it is going to take a very long time for you to get over what happened. A girl like you, young, inexperienced . . .' He saw the shadow flick across her face at his words and misread it. 'If it had been one of the older girls maybe it wouldn't have been so bad, but . . . No, I shouldn't say that, of course. Something like that shouldn't happen to any woman. But when it's an innocent girl like you . . .'

She turned her head away but not before he had seen the shadow darken.

222

'Tara . . .' Involuntarily, he put his hand on her shoulder and instantly she turned back, chin lifted, eyes full of . . . what? Her movement sent his hand sliding along her shoulder towards the nape of her neck; his thumb brushed the skin where it was warm and damp above the collar of her cesarine dress and below the line of her curls.

'Yes,' she said.

He wondered what she meant, but only for a moment. His mind was too full of the nearness of her. Her upturned face, lips parted; the brush of her breast against him; the whisper of her breath on his chin.

'Touch me. Please touch me,' she said.

He brought up his other hand, laying his fingertips on her cheek. It felt soft and rounded, velvety like a child's though as he stroked upwards he felt the cheekbone coming closer and closer to the surface as he moved towards her ear. Up past her eyes he let his fingers run, touching the edge of silky brow, and across her forehead to the bridge of her nose. It was small and straight, that nose. His fingers moving like the fingers of a blind man he explored it, down to her upper lip, then circled her mouth before moving in to touch her lips.

All the while she stood motionless, but as his fingers reached the centre of her lips she pouted them into a kiss, taking in just the very tip so that he was reminded of a sea anemone opening slightly in the gently moving tide.

'Thank you,' she said.

Emotion was thick in his throat, he thought he would choke with it. Gently, very gently, he drew her towards him, placing his lips where his fingers had been. He felt a shudder run through her, felt her breath coming out on a sigh and then he was kissing her, holding her, caressing her.

Oh Tara, Tara, all soft roundness. Oh Tara, perverse and funny, spirited and courageous, vulnerable yet resilient . . .

She pulled her head away, looking at him from beneath

those long thick lashes, and he felt his stomach contract.

'Perhaps we ought to be going back now,' she said. 'But we can come back here again, can't we? There will be other times?'

He touched his lips to her forehead again.

'Oh yes,' he said.

*

When she was adjudged fit enough to resume duties the CO came to see Tara. 'Well, m'dear, Bruce Callow seems to think it would do you good to take on some light duties. I explained you were coming to work for me and he agreed it was just the job for you.'

'No,' said Tara.

The CO swabbed at his face with a large khaki handkerchief. It was a hot day and the perspiration was trickling down towards his sandy moustache.

'I won't overwork you – give you my word on that. Make me a nice cup of Earl Grey, keep my desk tidy, generally help about the place and . . .'

'No,' Tara said again. 'I'm sorry, sir, but I really would prefer to go back to my old duties.'

'Nursing orderly?'

'Yes, sir.'

'Hmm!' He snorted, and wiped the droplets of perspiration out of his moustache. 'I thought you were quite agreeable to the change in duties.'

'That was before . . .' Tara broke off. 'I'd rather stay where I am.'

The CO folded his handkerchief and placed it in the pocket of his shorts. 'I could make it an order.' He looked up, noted the mutinous set of Tara's lips and continued hastily: 'But I won't. Perhaps when you are feeling quite fit again you will change your mind.'

'Perhaps,' Tara said. And the CO had no way of knowing the vow she had made in the weeks of her convalescence and was making again now as she looked him straight in the eye. Never, never again will I place myself in a man's power. No, no matter what it costs me.

*

The following week Tara went back to work on the wards. Her training was intensified now, she discovered, and she was treated less as a maid of all work and more as a student. Throughout September and October she moved from ward to ward and department to department gaining knowledge and experience.

Was it because of what had happened, she wondered? Or because of her status as Richard's girlfriend? Or merely because, with the war intensifying its stranglehold, more men were needed for the front line and more women had to be fully trained to take their places.

What a year it had been! In Europe, distant in miles but not in thoughts, England and Germany were bombing the hearts out of each other's cities. In the deserts of North Africa, the 'Rats of Tobruk' with many Australians amongst them were holed up defying the might and cunning of Rommel. But it was here in the Pacific, where the Japs were rampant, that the greatest danger to Australia lay. They had suffered defeats in May and June, it was true, in the battles of the Coral Sea and Midway, but the fighting that had followed, and was still continuing, was fierce and bloody – and oh so close to home shores!

As changes were made to gear up the medical services to meet the new challenges, there were movements amongst the staff of 138 and faces Tara had become familiar with disappeared from the scene as they were posted elsewhere – one officer to a special burns unit, a detachment of nurses to a fever isolation hospital in the south, and George Marshall, the dental officer who had compèred her concert, despatched to an AGH in Queensland where he was needed to help deal with casualties suffering fractured jaws as a result of battle injuries.

Kate Harris was seconded to Leaping Lena, the hospital train, an uncertain contraption comprised of converted cattle trucks which huffed, puffed and slithered twice-weekly from the Adelaide River to Katherine and back again. Tara missed her but thought it was probably good for her to be doing something completely different – it would help to keep her mind off the fact that she had still received no news of her fiancé in the hands of the Japs in Singapore.

What would I do if it were Richard? Tara wondered. I'd go crazy, so I would. Not to know whether he was wounded or sick, alive or even dead. She shivered and the shiver seemed to come from that cold place inside her that lay just beneath the surface, a lair where vague apprehensions and insidious fears lurked and the tiny voice of caution which niggled at her sometimes in the dead of night, warning her that loving a man as much as she loved Richard was an affront to a jealous God.

Not that their relationship had progressed quite as fast as Tara had hoped. They spent most of their spare time together, it was true, walking in the hills and driving out when Richard was able to get the keys of a ute to explore the countryside within reach from Pine Creek to Edith Falls, where freshwater crocs lived in the deep rock pools. Sometimes, they went for chop picnics with a dozen others, their appetites sharpened by the fresh air and satisfied by the freshly harvested fruit thoughtfully supplied by a local grower. Or they went to the picture shows and mess dances that were arranged by the surrounding camps. But whatever they did Richard remained slightly aloof, treating Tara with an old-world courtesy which was gratifying but also slightly frustrating. It was wonderful, of course, to be placed on a pedestal, to have her wishes considered, to be treated like a lady. But Tara also found it confusing and not a little disconcerting. When a man grabbed you at least you knew he found you attractive – in Tara's world men took what they wanted or at least tried to. If they did not try it probably meant they did not want.

But then of course Richard was not from her world. Richard was different.

Occasionally, he talked about his family and Tara listened with fascination and awe – and just a touch of discomfort. His father was an eminently successful Melbourne surgeon; his mother was the daughter of a family who could trace their ancestry back to government administrators in the days when Australia had been a penal colony; his sister was married to some high ranking official in the diplomatic corps.

When he asked about her own family she nervously concocted stories of a father who had been a merchant sea captain, drowned when she was a child, and a mother fallen on hard times.

'But sure we don't want to talk about me!' she would say, sliding the conversation back to the subject of which she never tired – his ranch-style home in the Melbourne hills with a stable of thoroughbred horses, a house filled with every conceivable luxury and a swimming pool of Olympic proportions.

'We had a swimming pool,' she said once, rashly, and then added quickly, 'when I was in Sydney that was. When I was staying with friends.'

He did not press it and she was relieved. Then later it worried her that he had not. If he was interested in her – really interested – surely he would be as eager to know about her background as she was to hear about his.

Except, of course, that it was not only love that made her avid for every detail but fascination for a world of which she knew nothing. Oh, Red had been powerful and wealthy, but Richard was something different again, and his heritage and lifestyle were as far removed from her own as the moon or Mars. What would he think if he knew the truth about her? She shuddered, a goose walking over her grave.

But he did not know and there was no need for him to

know. The only people who were aware of her past were far away and Dev, who had suspected, had not been seen since the night of the concert. She thought of him sometimes and wondered what had become of him and when she thought, it was with a pang of regret. The memory of the way she had felt when he kissed her still had the power to bring the colour to her cheeks and it was usually followed by a moment of guilt mixed with anxiety. She had not, she supposed, treated Dev very well. If she was honest with herself she had to admit she had used him – just as you often use men, a small voice of conscience whispered. 'Oh fiddle, I didn't do anything but get him to help me with the lights for the concert and that gave a lot of people a lot of pleasure,' she whispered back, but she knew it was more than that, and that when she had ignored him for Richard she had really hurt him. That was one explanation of why she had seen nothing of him since.

Another, of course, was that he had found some other way of getting rid of his anger and frustration – a way that had got him into trouble. She hoped that he had not done anything silly, like getting himself arrested and thrown into gaol. The provosts were everywhere and their tempers were known to be nasty if they were crossed. There was no state of marital law in the Northern Territory, but the provosts tried to run it that way and with a gun in their hands argument with them was pointless. Tara shivered, then gave herself a little shake. Sean Devlin was more than capable of looking after himself. Anyone who thought otherwise was fooling themselves.

And so the days slipped by, the halcyon days of the hot dry winter, when the Northern Territory wove its spell. There were, of course, sharp reminders of the war – a trainload of badly wounded men, news of the death of former patients and a doctor some of them had known – but mostly the conflict seemed very far away.

If only it could go on this way forever, Tara thought.

Not the war, of course, but 138 AGH cut off in a time warp. Never mind the others – she and Richard, the balmy climate and the lovely wild country. Just let her have him to herself for a little longer and she could break through his reserve – she knew she could. She was halfway to doing it already.

*

Towards the end of October Matron Swift sent for Tara.

'I don't know if you have heard the rumours about the formation of a new women's service,' she said directly.

'One or two,' Tara admitted.

'And what have you heard?'

'That if I want to go on working with 138 AGH I am going to have to join the army.'

'Hmm. Well that is one way of putting it, I suppose. The fact is that discussions have been underway at the highest level with a view to regularizing the position of all you VAs who are attached to military units on a full-time basis. There are plans to form a new force of enlisted medical aids – the Australian Army Medical Women's Service, I believe it is to be called. Naturally, as a serving VA you will be eligible for enlistment.'

Tara chewed her lip. She was not sure she was keen on the idea of formally enlisting. It sounded too regimented to be comfortable.

'Will I have to?'

'I think you probably will. The VA category is to return to being just that – part time voluntary workers – and I dare say you will find it to your advantage in many respects to enlist in the AAMWS.'

'I see.' Tara's mind was racing.

'Not that it's been formed yet,' Matron went on. 'But I don't think it will be very long before it is.' She tapped a sheet of printed paper lying on the desk in front of her. 'This is a directive stating that future VAs will be issued with khaki uniforms similar to those worn by the

Women's Army Service. It seems to me the writing is on the wall, Tara.'

Tara's hands flew protectively to her blue dress. 'Khaki!' Her tone reflected her horror. 'You mean I have got to . . . ?'

A flicker of impatience crossed Matron Swift's smooth face. Personally she was convinced that khaki would be a much more sensible colour. These blue dresses were all very well but when a VA was wearing a full uniform, navy blue and a white shirt with a starched collar, it was hardly the most suitable attire for long periods of duty or travelling in a sticky, steamy climate. But try telling a vain young girl that. Her only concern, no doubt, was whether khaki would make her complexion look sludge-coloured too.

'You will be permitted to continue wearing your blues as long as they are serviceable,' she said.

'Phew!' Tara whistled irreverently.

Matron glared. 'That is all I can tell you at the moment but I thought you should know what is being planned.' She picked up the directive and speared it onto a filing spike. It was a gesture of dismissal which not even Tara could misunderstand.

'Thank you, Matron,' she said. 'I'll think about it.'

*

The last week in October was a busy one. A young soldier from one of the US camps had been brought in suffering from a high temperature, head pains, sickness and a neck so stiff he was unable to touch his chest with his chin and meningitis was diagnosed. He had been moved at once into the isolation ward well away from the rest of the hospital but Richard, in whose care he was, still feared the worst.

'I hope to heaven we don't end up with an epidemic,' he said fervently.

Tara, who knew all about epidemics from her days in

230

the slums of Sydney, shivered. Nursing men with a variety of wounds was one thing but being forced into contact with those who could pass on serious illness through invisible bugs and microbes was quite another.

'Will he be all right?' she asked.

'He might, if it's the less serious strain. But meningitis is a killer, make no mistake about it. And if he lives it could leave him with serious brain damage of one sort or another.'

'Holy Mother.' Tara closed her eyes momentarily, crossing herself. She had not seen the young soldier but she could picture him all right – fresh-faced, gum-chewing, crew-cut, no doubt. Perhaps he had come to her concert, watched with eyes that might now be permanently blinded, listened with ears which might be stone deaf . . . And then again maybe he was the one who . . . Maybe this was his punishment . . . Tara shook herself mentally. For God's sake stop it! Don't even think such terrible thoughts! How can you go on nursing here when you do?

Richard reached for her hand and as his fingers curled round hers she knew why she would remain, in spite of the memories – or lack of them – in spite of the epidemics, in spite of the teeming torrential Wet which would soon return to the Territory, swamping them, covering their shoes and clothes with mildew, putrifying bites and sores, driving men mad. As long as Richard was here too she would endure anything – anything! – and still find it easy to smile.

'Take care you don't contract something yourself,' she said urgently. 'You're looking very tired.'

He smiled wanly. 'Am I? Let's not go any further then – let's sit down. Here's an old gum that managed to fall down in exactly the right spot.'

He lowered himself to the ground, easing his back against the fallen tree, and Tara sat down beside him. They were working a split shift today, both of them, and had snatched the opportunity to take a late afternoon walk along the river before going back on duty.

'The trouble is I didn't get much sleep last night,' he went on. 'If the crisis came I wanted to be there. I should be there now . . .'

'Hush!' Tara leaned over and silenced him with her lips. 'You can't be there all the time. Besides, he's not the only one who needs you. *I* need you too – and I've hardly seen you this past week.'

He did not answer but he slipped his arm around her shoulders, pulling her against him. She settled in, nestling her head into the hollow between his chin and shoulder and resting her head against his drawn up knee. Then after a moment she turned, nuzzling him and seeking his throat with her lips and teeth. His shirt was unbuttoned at the neck and the skin tasted salty. She kissed it, letting her tongue run in tiny darting circles then looking up at him along the jutting planes of his face. Their eyes met, blue holding blue, and he smiled faintly. Her fingers trailed from his knee to the long hard muscle in the front of his thigh and he moved suddenly, lifting her bodily across his lap. He kissed her as she straddled him, with a depth and intensity that almost took her breath and she strained towards him, her heart beating hard with happiness as it always did when he kissed her this way – he does love me! He does! He must!

His arms were around her, one hand exploring the length of her bare arm. She took it, moving it to her breast and squirming in ecstasy. Beneath the movement of his fingers and palm her nipple rose hard and erect; without moving his hand she unbuttoned the bodice of her dress and shivered with delight as his fingers slid inside. Now her nipple was rasping against his palm and it was as if a silver thread, so fine, so taut, ran from it to her very core. She moved her legs across his, wriggling and writhing as the hard cap of his knee inserted itself in the soft crooked underside of her own. Shivers ran up her hamstrings to join the silver cord attached to her tingling nipple.

Oh delight, delight! That such tiny touches could give such exquisite pleasure, start such powerful longings . . .

She put her lips to his again and felt her own longing echoed there. Tenderness became aggression, restraint was overcome by demand. Gently, he pressed her back so that she was no longer cushioned on his lap but lying on the scratchy turf and he was above her, blotting out the sun.

The breath came out of her on a sigh. At last – at last! She closed her eyes, waiting for the weight of his body, arching towards it, every nerve singing with longing. When it came it was brief, searingly brief, and she snapped open her eyes to see him sitting up again, running his hands up over his face and through the thick gold of his hair.

For a moment she could not speak. Hurt and dis-appointment were numbing her, freezing her vocal chords and thought and reason with them. Her body still tingled with desire, as a light bulb radiates a glow for a few moments after the current is switched off. Then she shook her head slowly, looking up at him with puzzled eyes.

'Why?'

His knuckles were pressed against his mouth now and he was staring over them unseeingly. The electric charge was still high in him too; she could feel it creating an aura all around him.

'Because it would not be fair to you,' he said.

'To me?' The words of surprise were forced from her.

'We have gone as far as we should. Probably further.'

'But *why*?'

He turned. His eyes were haunted.

'Tara, you have had a rough time. After what happened . . .'

'But I *love* you . . .' She was almost weeping with frustration.

Something flickered across his face. 'Hear me out, Tara. After what happened to you, you deserve to be treated with the highest regard. If I . . . make love to you now it would be because I was committed to you. And in war time it is just not possible to make that sort of commitment. I want you, darling, believe me, but that is not the way it should be.'

'I don't understand.'

He reached for her hand. Hurt, she jerked away. Again he reached for it. This time she let him take it, felt his fingers and thumb smoothing it as they had when she was lying battered in the hospital.

'Tara – I could be sent overseas at any time. Right into the field of battle. When I was in Tobruk we worked under fire most of the time. The hospital was bombed. Men were killed. I was hit myself . . .'

'Yes, I know.' Tara had heard before of the piece of shrapnel Richard had taken in his leg which had necessitated his being shipped back to Australia. 'But surely that's all the more reason for . . .'

'I don't think so.' The sun was catching the tiny fair hairs on his forearm, making them shine like burnished gold. 'When I commit myself I want to be sure of what I can offer. In time of war that is very uncertain. I could be wounded or crippled. I don't count that as a very good prospect for the woman I love. With things as they are she might even find herself a widow. I don't think it's fair to ask it.'

Tara's jaw had dropped slightly.

B'Jesus he was talking about *commitment* commitment – he was talking about marriage! The little tremble ran through her again and the whole of her skin felt like a pincushion.

'But you might not be sent overseas,' she said eagerly. 'I've heard furphies that if 138 AGH goes anywhere it will be to Queensland.'

'Yes, I've heard that rumour too. I think it's quite likely. But that's not to say I will be staying with it.'

The shiver turned chill.

'What do you mean?'

'138 was not my original unit. I left them behind in Tobruk. After Tobruk they went to the Holy Land. Now I believe they are in Columbo.'

'Columbo?' Tara's geography was sketchy. 'Where is that?'

'Ceylon. One of the places the Japs would like to get their hands on.'

'But you might not.'

'That's a chance I am prepared to take.' He stood up, holding out his hand to her. 'I think we ought to be getting back, Tara.'

Defeated for the moment she got up too. But she was thinking: if he is that serious then surely I can get around him! Not today maybe, but as long as we are together here I've got all the time in the world.

Above the withered trees the sky was deep, deep blue with hardly a fleck of cloud in sight – it was hard to imagine the deluge that would soon come, within the next month almost certainly. But the land was crying out for rain, the vegetation stretching hungry arms for it, the earth bone dry and cracking like a half demolished termites' mound. As they walked Tara's toe scuffed it and clouds of red dust flew up around her feet.

She pulled a face. 'Ugh – it's got between my toes now. It gets everywhere, this dust. Did you see Kate when she came back the other day? They had had problems with a derailment on the line and brought her back up the track in a truck. She was dickered – you would have thought she was a redhead!'

Richard laughed. Most of his tension had dissolved now. He was holding her hand loosely, fingers interlaced with hers; the warmth of them seemed to touch her heart.

'Speaking of redheads,' he said, 'do you remember Alys Peterson?'

The warmth became a sudden chill of warning.

'Of course I do.' How could she ever forget Alys? 'What about her?'

'I heard the other day that she may be coming back.' His tone had not altered nor had his step, it was still long and loping, but suddenly she found she had almost to run to keep up with him.

'Alys? Coming back?' The breath was tight in her throat – *that* was why she seemed to be almost running . . .

'Yes. Someone ran into her aunt – Sylvia Crawford, you know? She had had a letter from Alys. She is well on the way to recovery it seems and she is anxious to knuckle down and do her bit again as soon as she is able.

'She's coming back here?'

'Somewhere in the Northern Territory, I should think, since it's her Aunt Sylvia's domain. It will be good to see her again, won't it?'

Tara could not answer. She was picturing Alys as she had last seen her, lying in her hospital bed, face waxy but still incredibly beautiful, red-gold hair lying in a soft drift across the pillow. And Richard looking down at her with an unmistakable expression in his eyes . . .

A few moments ago she had been convinced that Richard could be hers. Now, suddenly, there was a shadow across the sun and that shadow had red-gold hair and aquamarine eyes. Not to mention a cut-glass accent and a look that said she was from Richard's world, the world of gentility and plenty, the world that she, Tara, had peeked into as a hungry child might peek into a shop window, nose pressed against the glass, but a world she had no place in.

If she comes back I have lost him, thought Tara. If she comes back he will look at her again as he looked at her then – he's doing it already. Just mentioning her name is making his eyes go all soft. And he has the nerve to talk to me about commitment! Who does he think he is kidding? These high ideals are all very well – how high would they be if *she* came back?

'We saved her life, Tara, you and I,' he said. 'It's a rather special feeling, isn't it?'

Each word was a barb in Tara's heart; each barb only increased her determination. She had thought she had all the time in the world to get Richard. Now she knew she did not. But days, weeks – whatever was left – would have to be enough. She would not let Miss Melbourne 1942

236

waltz back and take him away from her. Whatever she had to do she would do it. And when Alys Peterson came back she would discover that the situation was not quite the walkover she might have expected!

Chapter Thirteen

Alys Peterson swung her Alfa Romeo motor car through the gateway in the camphor laurel hedge of the Toorak mansion, jammed on the handbrake and sat for a moment looking down across the spires and rooftops to Hawthorn and Kew with their backdrop of the Dandenong Range a misty silhouette in the purple distance.

Beautiful. Beautiful like the house that had been built here to take full advantage of this view, all shuttered windows, white gables and arches beneath its red tiled roof. But no amount of beauty could prevent the restlessness that burned and bubbled in her veins – or compensate for the trapped feeling that encompassed her every waking moment. That was too deep-rooted, too much a part of the fabric of the place which her mother had moulded and transformed with her own special talent to a showpiece of taste and breeding. When it came to the house Frances had had it all her way – and when Frances had her way there was no more charming a woman in the whole of Melbourne, Alys thought wryly.

Today, for the first time since she had been brought home wounded and too weak to protest, Alys looked at the house and was not swamped by the feeling of being caught in a luxurious trap. Or, if she was still inside the cage, at least now the door was open.

Alys' lips curved and she stretched her back against the car seat luxuriating in the fact that now at last there was no more pain. She had known she was better, had hardly needed Dr Whitehorn to confirm it, but now he had and his words sang in her like heady wine.

'A marvellous recovery,' he had said, looking at her over the top of his spectacles which had, as usual, slipped down his nose. 'It never ceases to amaze me how resilient is the young human body. You're as good as new, Alys.'

She had not spoiled the moment by reminding him that it was not quite true. No point in dwelling on the permanent effects of the wound caused by a piece of flying metal. She had come to terms with that weeks – no, months – ago. All that mattered now was that Dr Whitehorn was telling her she was fit and that meant that at last she could go back to her beloved Northern Territory and do something useful once again.

Leaving the car on the drive, Alys got out and ran up the two stone steps to the front door. It opened at her touch and she went on in to the hall, spacious and vaulted, crowned with a cupola which ensured it never appeared dark or unwelcoming, and brightened with vases of fresh flowers.

'Mother, I'm home!' Alys called. Her voice echoed round the lofty hall. For a moment there was no reply and Alys was about to go upstairs to her room when Frances appeared in the doorway which led to the rear of the house, carrying a garden basket in which she had been collecting sprays of mimosa.

'Darling, do you have to shout?' Her eyes strayed to the front door still standing ajar. 'And don't tell me you've left that motor car of yours on the drive again! Daddy gets so annoyed if it's in the way when he comes home.'

'Morrie can move it,' Alys said unperturbed. 'You know he loves driving my car.'

Frances' lips tightened a shade. Sometimes she thought it would be better if Morrie drove the car all the time, with Alys in it. At least she would have some control over where her daughter went and what she did since it was she – or Daniel at any rate – who paid Morrie's wages.

'Where have you been anyway?' she asked now.

'To see Dr Whitehorn. He says I'm a hundred per cent.'

'Does he.' Frances' dry tone implied that she doubted the professional judgement.

'Yes. So there's nothing to stop me getting back into the thick of things. I'll write to Aunt Sylvia tonight.'

'Do you really think that is wise?'

'Why not? I've been sitting around here and stewing for long enough.'

'Well, I *don't* think it's wise, Alys. In your state of health . . .'

'Mother, I told you! Dr Whitehorn says I'm perfectly fit!'

'I can't see how that can be. You were brought home at death's door.'

'But I'm not at death's door now, Mother. I don't want to go on living like an invalid forever.'

'And I don't want you to go off again, Alys. Not while this dreadful war is going on, anyway.' She turned away dismissively, a short, stockily built woman in an expensively tailored shirt and tweed skirt, crossing the hall to the drawing room door. 'I'm just going to do the vases – why don't you help me?'

'Mother!' Exasperated, Alys followed her. 'You know I'm useless at flower arranging. And you can't change the subject just like that. I'm sorry if it worries you but when it comes to war it's up to everyone to do what they can.'

'You don't have to tell me that!' Frances said with an indignant upward thrust of her chin. 'No one has done more for the Red Cross than I have. The jumble sale I organized last week raised a lot of money and the series of whist drives has been most successful. If you would only interest yourself in it, Alys, you could be a great help to me.'

'But I'm not interested in it!' Alys picked up a sprig of mimosa which had fallen onto the polished surface of the sideboard and rolled it between her finges. 'I want to go back to driving my ambulance.'

'I should have thought after what happened you would be only too glad to stay out of harm's way.'

'Perhaps so, but I'm not.'

'Oh, I don't know!' Frances sighed heavily. 'I don't understand you, Alys. I just don't understand you at all. And another thing. Why did you find it necessary to visit

Donald Whitehorn in his consulting rooms when he always comes to see us here at home?'

'Because I felt so much better and he wasn't due to come until next week. And I wanted to talk to him quietly, without you fussing, Mother.'

Frances' eyes narrowed. Like Alys' own they were aquamarine, but much paler, like bits of greenish glass. 'I see. You preferred to go behind our backs.'

'Nothing of the kind!' Alys could feel the annoyance prickling her skin like heat-rash. 'It's simply that I'm twenty-two years old and if I want to see the doctor without your permission I shall do so.'

The colour came up in Frances' face also, a dark flush staining her cheeks and extending down her neck.

'You are a great worry to me, Alys.' Her voice had that angry edge to it which had struck terror to Alys' heart as a child. 'Why you can't be more like Beverley I'll never know. Find a nice young man and settle down – that's what I'd like to see you do. But you couldn't be content with that, could you?'

'Not if he was anything like Bev's Louis, no, I certainly couldn't! Look, Mother,' Alys deliberately softened her tone, 'I'm going back to Northern Territory and there is no point arguing about it. I'm sorry if you're not happy about it but you really must let me live my own life.'

Anger turned to hurt martyrdom. 'Have it your own way, Alys. You know whatever I say or do is because I am thinking of your good. That's all I have ever wanted. Unfortunately, caring so much about you when you behave so recklessly means you are a constant worry to me. And I can only hope with all my heart that you don't live to regret your folly.'

'I hope so too, Mother,' Alys said maintaining her level tone with a supreme effort. But as she marched up the stairs to her own room she could feel the blood pounding angrily behind her temples. It had always been the same – always! Warm cloying sweetness as long as she was doing exactly as her mother wanted. Icy disapproval at the first

241

signs of rebellion and if this failed to work then the trump card – moral blackmail. You worry me. You make me unhappy. You'll be the death of me. She shouldn't have had children – she should have had clay dolls, Alys thought bitterly. That way she could have moulded them the way she would like them to be – little extensions of herself. As it is . . .

I shall have to be very strong, Alys told herself. And I shall sit down and write to Aunt Sylvia immediately.

*

Alys laid a sheet of tissue paper on top of her favourite linen dress, smoothed it out and held it down with one hand while she closed the lid of the blue leather suitcase. Then she straightened up, brushing a strand of hair off her face and looking around the familiar room to see if she had left anything important out of her packing. Nothing obvious. Her china dolls, of course, sitting in a row on their shelf and watching her with their glass eyes blue and unwinking in the pale damask rose faces that Beverley had used to nag her to wash with milk and cotton wool. She couldn't take those. Nor the heavy cut glass perfume atomizer that stood on the dressing table. They were things that belonged here in her room in Toorak, they had always been here and they would still be here when she returned. She felt a swift ache of sadness as she looked at them, mementos from her childhood when she had been as innocent and happy as Robyn without any desire to be anywhere but in the home where she was loved and cherished. How long ago those days seemed – and yet in some ways how close, as if should she reach out she could almost touch that other self across the years.

She sighed, then as the door opened she turned towards it.

'Mummy!'

'What are you doing?' Frances asked. She was wearing a floral dress with a shirt top and skirt of unpressed pleats and in spite of the heat she looked as cool and elegant as ever.

'Packing,' Alys said. 'You know I'm going in the morning.'

'I can see you're packing.' There was an edge of sharp impatience in Frances' tone. 'Why didn't you ask Norma to do it? Heaven knows it's difficult enough to get maids these days and as for keeping them for more than a few months . . . While we have one you may as well make use of her.'

'I preferred to do it myself,' Alys said smoothly.

Frances did not answer. Her disapproval hung heavy and cold in the air and when Alys could stand the accusing silence no longer she said: 'Do you think I have time to wash my hair? What time is dinner?'

'The time it always is – and no doubt if you want to wash your hair you'll do so whatever I may say.' Again there was an uncomfortable silence. Alys caught herself from making an angry retort and felt another stab of that nostalgia which had ached in her just now. Impulsively, she turned to her mother.

'Please, Mummy, don't be like this! There's no need, you know. You just make it hard for both of us. I don't want to upset you, but . . .'

Frances jerked her hands away. Her eyes were hard, as hard as the glass eyes of the dolls on the shelf.

'I suppose there's a boy behind it.'

'A boy?'

'There usually is when you're so set on having your own way. I haven't forgotten . . .' She broke off, clamping her lips shut.

Suddenly Alys was trembling. The sadness was sharper now, a physical pain in her chest cutting off breath.

'Forgotten what?' The emotion was all there in her voice placing emphasis on each syllable of the question. She knew what Frances meant all right but she had to hear her confirm it before she could really believe her mother could bring it up after all this time.

For just a second Frances hesitated. Two high spots of colour had appeared in her cheeks so that it looked as if she was belatedly showing the effect of the heat.

'That rogue who tried to worm his way into your father's bank balance,' she said tartly. 'You were a fool for him and you'll be a fool again. My God, when I think of what a fool you were – and worse! All I hope is that you learned your lesson. I may as well warn you I couldn't stand for a repeat of that episode.'

And then the pain was very sharp in Alys, the past too real – and too bound up with the present.

'I loved him, Mother,' she said. 'You never understood that did you? Because you didn't approve you were so darned sure he was wrong for me.'

'He was.'

'How can you be so certain of everything? It's terrifying . . . Don't you realize that if you had taken a different attitude Race might be alive today?'

'Don't begin blaming me for that, Alys. There was no call for you to go to Bathurst that day – none at all.'

'But you were going to send me to Darwin without giving me the chance to see him or speak to him.'

'It was for your own good.'

'Rubbish! When did you ever think of *my* good? Your interpretation of it, perhaps. But always what *you* wanted for me, never what I wanted for myself. Oh, when I think of the things that are done because they are supposed to be for someone's good! It's frightening the way some people are so damned sure they know what's best for everyone else.'

'Don't you talk to me like that!' Frances' colour had risen still further so that her whole face and neck was now puce. 'I'm still your mother, remember.'

'How can I forget?' Alys asked bitterly. 'You still want to run my life, Mummy, just as you did then. Well, I'm sorry. It won't work. I make my own decisions now.'

'The trouble with you, Alys, is you're so stubborn! You won't admit that someone of my age and experience

244

knows best. Just take this Race business for a moment. We've never talked about it – you wouldn't see sense at the time and then you were in Darwin.' Frances' voice was rising. 'The point is you were so obsessed you couldn't see he was using you.'

'He wasn't.'

'Wasn't using you? Oh Alys, how can you continue to deceive yourself?'

'Will you please stop this? I don't want to hear any more. I shouldn't have listened to you then, either. I allowed you to spoil the loveliest thing that every happened to me. Oh, I don't blame you for Race's death – I blame myself. But you had a hand in it, Mummy, and for that I shall never forgive either of us.'

'My God,' Frances said.

For a long moment they stood quite still staring at each other. Then Alys turned away pressing her hands over her eyes as the pain inside doubled her up. Race, Race – how could it still hurt this much after so long? Oh Race, I loved you so. You did love me, didn't you? You did – I know you did . . .

Above the roaring in her ears she was aware of a dull thud but she remained bent double with her hands still covering her eyes as the painful memories unrolled as raw and fresh as ever. It was only as the dry sobs subsided that she realized something was wrong. She turned then gasped in shocked horror.

Frances was on the floor slumped into a half-sitting position against the tallboy. Her legs were folded awkwardly beneath her, her head lolled forward onto her chest like a broken puppet.

'Mummy!' Alys screamed. 'What's the matter? What are you doing?'

Frances made no reply. Alys took three quick steps towards her, then her trembling knees gave way and she half-fell to a crouching position beside Frances.

'Mummy, for goodness' sake . . .!' She took hold of her mother's shoulders lifting her up and as she did so the uncontrolled head rolled to one side. 'Oh God!' Alys cried. Her mother's eyes were open and staring, but one appeared to be wider and more staring than the other and one corner of her mouth was drawn. A thin stream of dribble had escaped from it and was trickling slowly down her chin towards the collar of the immaculate dress. Worst of all, her face seemed to have been frozen into a parody of that last accusing expression. Somehow, Alys staggered to her feet again and ran to the door.

'Norma!' she screamed. 'Morrie! for God's sake, somebody help me!'

And in the long moments before their footsteps came running Alys felt she aged a hundred years.

*

'Your mother has suffered a very severe stroke. No doubt you already realize that.' Donald Whitehorn, positioned in front of the marbled fireplace in the drawing room, rocked lightly back on his heels and looked from one sister to the other.

'Yes,' Beverley said. She was hunched in a nervous heap on the edge of the ruby velvet chaise while Alys slumped, head in hands, at the small escritoire. 'What we want to know is – will she get over it?'

'I'm afraid at the moment it is impossible to say.' Donald Whitehorn's tone was grave. 'The next hours and days will be crucial. The sooner there are any signs of a recovery, the better her chances. But I think I should warn you that at this stage there is no way of knowing how complete that recovery, if any, is going to be.'

Alys raised her head a fraction, looking at Dr Whitehorn over her splayed fingers. 'You mean she might be paralysed.'

Donald Whitehorn met her eyes levelly. 'To some degree, yes. She could have difficulty with speech – that is very common. And clearly the use of her left arm and leg – everything on the left side of her body, in fact – is going to

246

be impaired. But let us not cross our bridges before we come to them. She has not even regained consciousness yet. And then there is the danger that she may suffer a second stroke following on the heels of the first. If that were to happen . . .'

Beverley sobbed softly and Alys sunk her head into her hands once more.

'Can we come to practicalities?' Donald Whitehorn pressed them gently. 'Daniel – your father – is away on business, you say. How long is it going to be before he can get home?'

'He's in Perth and we haven't been able to reach him yet,' Beverley said. 'But we have left messages for him at his hotel and everywhere we could think of. He'll fly back the moment he gets to hear what has happened, but . . .'

'So you girls are going to have to make the decision. Shall I get your mother into the Cabrini Private Hospital?'

'Oh goodness . . .' Beverley hesitated. 'Do you think that would be best?'

'I do. That way she will be properly supervised when the crisis comes.'

'Well, then, in that case . . .'

'No!' Alys said. Her tone was sharp and they both turned to look at her. 'No, you can't have her taken off to hospital,' she said more quietly. 'You know how she hates hospitals. If she does regain consciousness and comes round to discover she is in one, she'll raise Cain. And if she doesn't . . . well, it doesn't seem right, going against what you know she would want when she can't speak for herself. I think she should stay here.'

Donald Whitehorn nodded. Since Alys had called him to the house she had scarcely spoken – she seemed in a state of shock. This was much more like her – having a firm opinion and expressing it forcibly.

'Are you in agreement with that, Beverley?' he asked.

'Well, yes, I suppose so . . .'

'It will mean getting a nurse in, of course. Two, in fact,

247

at the moment. One for the days and another for the nights.'

'Yes, do that please,' Alys said. 'If Daddy wants to change the arrangements when he comes home that's up to him. I don't think he will, but at least my conscience will be clear.'

Dr Whitehorn looked at her quizzically. What a strange turn of phrase to use at a time like this. Just what had been going on when Frances had had her stroke? he wondered. Strange, Frances being struck down like that. This was one of those cases he would simply never have predicted. Frances had appeared in good health and he would have been prepared to wager half his salary on her having at least another decade of trouble-free years. It just went to show you never could tell.

'Just one other thing,' he said, looking from one girl to the other. 'Be very careful what you say when you are in your mother's room. In spite of all appearances to the contrary she might be able to hear you without being able to respond in any way. So talk normally and don't make any comments about her condition. Now, if you will excuse me I'll get the wheels set in motion for the nursing staff you need.' He paused in the doorway looking back at them. 'If you need me any time, day or night, call me.'

He left the room and Alys got up to follow.

'Where are you going?' Beverley asked accusingly.

'To Mummy. One of us should stay with her until the nurse gets here. It's not fair to expect Norma to do it.

Beverley half rose, then sank back, 'It's a bit late now, isn't it, to start playing the concerned daughter.'

Alys swung round, her eyes narrowing. 'What do you mean by that?'

'You know very well what I mean!' Beverley was very pale, her trembling hands clenching and unclenching on a small lace handkerchief. 'You weren't concerned about upsetting Mummy before – it's a bit late to have an attack of conscience now!'

Alys opened her mouth then snapped it shut again. 'I'm not going to quarrel with you, Bev. Not now.'

'That will make a change as well!' Beverley retorted. 'You were ready enough to quarrel with Mummy, weren't you? And now see what you've done!'

'What *I've* done?' Alys repeated.

'Don't deny it!' Bev wept. 'Everyone in Toorak must have heard you. I heard you and I was in the nursery giving Robyn her tea.'

Alys, too, was shaking now. 'We were arguing, yes, it's true – but that isn't the reason she's . . .' She broke off, unable to frame the words. 'That's an awful thing to say, Bev.'

'Perhaps so, but it is true!' Beverley insisted. 'If you hadn't caused an upset, Alys, she wouldn't be lying up there now in a coma. And what is more, you know it's true. Otherwise you wouldn't suddenly be acting so concerned. "Someone has to stay with Mummy". Oh yes, if you had been willing to stay with Mummy in the first place none of this would have happened!'

For a moment, Alys stood choking back the angry words then she turned and ran from the room. Bad enough to have quarrelled with her mother, she did not want to quarrel with Beverley too. Up the broad staircase she fled, pausing only for a few seconds on the landing to compose herself before going into her mother's room.

As she pushed open the door the first thing that struck her was the quiet. Two people in that room and neither of them making a sound except, yes, when you really listened there was the soft even rattle of indrawn breath. Nervously, Alys took a step towards the bed. The curtains had been drawn to keep out the evening sun and the light coming through the rose pink silk cast a glow over the figure in the bed and disguised the pallor of the skin. From here the drawn side of Frances' face was hidden; she looked for all the world like a healthy pink sleeping child.

Alys crossed to the bed and Norma looked up, her eyes were full of tears. How tenderhearted she was, Alys thought in surprise. She had only been with them a month or so and Frances had not exactly treated her with loving kindness – in fact she had been more sharp than anything, tutting about the girl's incompetence. Alys gave her a small comforting smile which only caused the girl's tears to overflow.

'No change, is there, Norma?' she asked briskly.

'No, Miss Alys, none. She just lies there not moving at all. It's not natural – I'm glad you're here. I was afraid she might . . . well, die . . . while I was on my own with her . . .'

'Of course she's not going to die!' Alys said, making her tone falsely bright as she remembered the doctor's warning about loose talk in Frances' hearing. 'A day or two and she'll be fine again, you'll see.' But her eyes signalled to the maid that she was only playing a part and Norma pressed her hands to her mouth, choking back the sobs.

'Go on.' Alys tapped her hand. 'I expect Mrs Reilly would like you to go and help attend to Robyn. I'll stay with my mother for the time being.'

The maid got to her feet, obviously relieved and trying not to show it.

'Are you sure, Miss?'

'Quite. Off you go.'

In the doorway she paused, looking back. 'You won't be going off to Alice Springs tomorrow now then, I suppose.'

Alys looked down at the motionless form. She could see the twisted mouth now; lifted at the corner as it was it appeared as if Frances was smiling. A shudder ran through Alys and a swift involuntary thought, for which she was instantly and thoroughly ashamed.

You got your way again, Mummy.

She tore her eyes away from the face which it seemed had managed to dominate all her life.

'No, Norma,' she said. 'I won't be going now.'

*

Twenty-four hours later Frances came out of her coma

and the second stroke which Dr Whitehorn had warned of was uncharacteristically slight. Two weeks of dedicated nursing and Frances was able to sit out for short periods in the chair beside her bed, another week and she had graduated to whole days by the window. But although she gained daily in strength, there seemed to be no sign of her faculties returning to normal. Her face remained drawn, her speech slurred and uncertain, her arm and leg were still paralysed and she had trouble in swallowing, or indeed accepting food and drink into her mouth at all. The nurses fed her with devoted efficiency just as they washed and dealt with her every need and Daniel arranged for a lift to be installed on the staircase.

'You see – in no time at all you'll be downstairs again!' Alys said.

Frances merely stared at her. One eye was half-closed but the other, wide and shrewd, saying things that her lips could not, was disconcerting to face.

You are not going to leave me, are you? said that eye. I may have nurses to attend to my every need but that is not the same as having my daughter here. *I want you here.* And what Beverley said was true – it is your fault that I am as I am. I would never have had this stroke if you had not been so wilful and worried me into it. The least you can do now is remain here and do your duty . . .

Alys swallowed hard.

'Don't look at me like that, Mummy,' she begged. 'I'll stay here just as long as you need me, don't worry.'

'My . . . good . . . girl,' Frances managed, slowly and with great effort. But Alys saw the gleam of triumph in that glassy eye and the way the good side of her mouth curved upwards into a smile and cringed.

She could not go now. Her conscience would never allow it. But oh God, how long would she be here, trapped into submission by Frances' condition? Weeks – months – years – who could say? Only one thing was certain, Frances now had her in a strangle hold and as long as there was life in her body, she would not let her go.

Chapter Fourteen

Tara knew what she had to do. She had known from the moment Richard had said that Alys was coming back. She had pieced it all together with his ideals about commitment and his strictly honourable code and it pointed her in one sure direction.

Oh yes, Tara knew what she had to do – the difficulty was in finding the opportunity to do it.

The Wet had returned, hot and steamy – the dusty ground was already turning into a quagmire and the tropical vegetation was rioting all around. Why hadn't she pressed her advantage and tried to get things moving while the weather had been good? They couldn't go for walks now without wearing gumboots, and any drives in the ute, unless they remained on the bitumenized Track, were likely to end with their being very firmly stuck in the mud.

Tara gained a respite when Kate Harris told her she had received a letter from Alys saying that her mother had been taken ill and she would not be able to return to Northern Territory until there was some change in her condition, but Tara had no way of knowing how long that would be.

Then there was the problem of becoming an AMWAS. As Matron Swift had predicted, its formation was authorized on 1st December, 1942 and Tara knew she would soon be pressed into enlisting. But supposing when she did she was sent off to an army training camp to learn to drill? Worse – supposing she was posted elsewhere than back to 138 AGH – with another group of new AMWAS, perhaps? As an enlisted member of the armed forces she would have no leeway for protest. The thought of leaving a clear field for Alys Peterson was an agonizing one.

One steaming December day Tara was working in the dispensary. A new consignment of drugs and supplies was expected when the convoy could plough its way up the Track and the half-empty shelves made it an ideal opportunity to dust, clean and wipe away the little pocket of mildew that had already begun to collect in corners and grooves. Tara hated the work. The steam rising from the bowl of hot soapy water was making her uncomfortable and she had to stop every so often to wipe her hands and mop the little trickles of perspiration out of her eyes.

Never mind. Another half-hour and she was due off duty and she had nearly finished – praise be!

The door swung open and Kate Harris came in. The sister whose place she had taken on Leaping Lena was fully recovered from her bout of fever and Kate was now back with 138.

'How is it going?' she asked.

'Almost done.' Tara straightened, wringing out her cloth and giving the shelf one last sweep.

'I thought so. How do you fancy a trip out into the outback?'

'A trip?' Tara glanced out of the window. It was hardly the weather for trips, not actually raining at the moment but the sky looked laden and dark.

'Well, not a trip exactly. We've had a call from Bluey Freeman. It seems he is worried about Reg. His breathing is very bad and his temperature is high. Bluey has to go down to Pine Creek on urgent business but he doesn't want to leave Reg without getting somebody in to have a look at him. To be honest, it sounds to me as if he should have made the call a couple of days ago but Bluey says they've been very busy. You know what they are both like when it comes to that station of theirs – everything else takes second place, including their health.'

Tara flopped the cloth back into the bowl of water. 'I know.'

Bluey and Reg Freeman were fruit and vegetable growers who ran a market garden some twenty miles down the Track. They were two of the few civilians who had been allowed to remain in the Territory because they supplied the armed forces with fresh food. And very popular they were too. Besides sending in the extra special treats of bananas and pineapples, mangoes and tomatoes in season, they had opened their station to those on the nursing staff who were keen horsemen and women – Kate, herself raised on a Victorian farm, was amongst those who had been there to ride and take advantage of their easy-going hospitality. But, by the same token, the two men, bachelor brothers, were stubborn as mules about leaving their property – 'It would take a whole army of Japs to move them' was often said of them.

'Anyway, Richard Allingham is going,' Kate went on, automatically rearranging a row of bottles Tara had replaced on a shelf. 'He wants someone to go with him and suggested you. I know you are off duty in half-an-hour or so, but as Richard said, there is really no need for a fully qualified sister to go when they have so much to be doing here and he didn't think you would mind.'

Tara glanced at her and thought she caught the hint of a twinkle in Kate's eye, but before she could be sure it was gone again. Kate was not exactly overloaded with a sense of humour, she thought, but she was a very nice person.

'Of course I'll go,' she said.

Kate glanced at her wristwatch.

'Go and get your gumboots on then – ten minutes, Richard said. I'll finish putting these bottles back on the shelves.'

'Right – thanks.' Tara picked up the bowl of soapy water. In the doorway she glanced back. Kate was replacing the bottles with a precision that was almost unbelievable. Tara bit back a smile. She would be there all night at that rate!

Tara threw away the dirty water, went to look for her gumboots and the smile returned, full-blooded. A drive down the Track and back alone with Richard – thanks Reg Freeman! Once again you've turned out to be a sport!

254

The Freeman place was off the Track at the end of five miles or so of unmade-up road. In places it was only just wide enough for the ute and already the rain had made it heavy going. But not many vehicles passed this way – it had not been churned up as some parts of the Track were – and the four-wheeled drive ute held it easily.

'What do you think is wrong with Reg?' Tara asked.

'From what Bluey said he's got chest trouble – bronchitis probably.' Richard was concentrating on driving, looking out for potholes or dips in the track; his clear profile made Tara feel weak inside. 'He smokes too much, of course, they both do. But try telling them that!'

Tara said nothing. His words had brought her a picture crystal-clear, of Maggie, cigarette drooping from her lips, smoke curling up into her hennaed hair. Oh yes, Maggie, too, had smoked too much. And telling her so would have done no more good.

A small lump rose in her throat. Oh Maggie, Maggie, I still miss you so! Before you were always *there*. Now – now there is no one . . .

She sniffed sharply, tossing her head.

On either side of the track the foliage was thick and luscious. It was amazing how quickly it could grow once the Wet came. Fronds slapped the sides of the ute; looking past them Tara noticed the air was clear like a magnifying glass so that the distant trees looked to be within touching distance.

'There's going to be one hell of a storm when it breaks,' she said.

Richard steered around a hump in the road. 'Let's hope we can get back before it comes or we could get bogged down. These tracks pretty soon become impassable.'

A tiny imp of hope leaped deep within Tara. 'Marooned in the back of beyond with my favourite man!' she joked and her tone did not give away for one second the fact that she could imagine no nicer fate.

Another mile or so and the Freeman place loomed up – a sprawling bungalow which had once been white-painted but now, after thirty Dry seasons had spewed whirlwinds of dust at its rough-plaster walls, was nearly as red as its corrugated roof. To the front of it, across a broad yard, were the outbuildings – a shed which had once housed farm machinery and now provided cover for the Freeman brothers' battered ute, and a dome beneath which they nursed some of their plants and seedlings and grew the tomatoes. Behind the house was a paddock and stables and then the start of the nursery proper – plantations of banana and pineapple palms, mangoes and peach trees. Further out, the Freeman brothers had a small herd of beef cattle – they believed in having their own steak to precede the fruit sweets at table.

Often in the late afternoon one or other of the brothers could be seen sitting on the veranda which ran the length of the front of the bungalow, smoking and downing a cold beer. Today the house looked deserted. Bluey must have already left for Pine Creek. Richard drew the ute up to the foot of the veranda steps and reached into the back for his bag. Tara scrambled down onto the caked-mud yard and stood waiting for him. She felt oddly nervous.

I'd never make a real nurse, she thought. But as long as she could follow Richard in she supposed she would manage.

The door was ajar. 'Reg! Hullo-ah!' Richard called pushing it wide open. There was no reply. 'Hullo–ah!' Richard called again.

Tara hung back uncomfortably. The windows were open all along the veranda yet the room seemed airless somehow.

'He's in bed most probably,' Richard said.

Tara followed him across the narrow L-shaped kitchen. Dishes were piled in the sink, the remains of a meal heaped into a sheet of newspaper ready for disposal.

Plainly Bluey had forgotten to throw it in the bin before leaving, and now the flies were buzzing around it, jockeying for position and settling. There was a pair of gumboots abandoned in the middle of the floor and a trail of small clumps of dried red mud leading to them. Men! Tara thought impatiently. But considering that the women who 'did for' the Freemans had been evacuated south, the kitchen was remarkably tidy.

The bedrooms ran along the side of the bungalow but when he reached the doorway of the kitchen Richard needed no further guidance as to where to find Reg. The rasp of his breath carried across the passageway. Following him Tara saw a plainly furnished room with a bed, a washstand with a rose-sprinkled china jug and basin and a chest topped by a large glass-funnelled Tilly lamp.

Reg lay in the bed. He was flushed and not only his chest but his whole body rose and fell with every laboured breath. He was slumped against the pillows, his eyes half-closed; even the briefest greeting was too much effort for him.

'Well, Reg, you are a fine one!' Richard said. He had his medical bag open but Tara could fell from his expression that he had made a diagnosis already. Even she, with her scanty experience, was able to hazard a guess and she was not surprised when Richard straightened up removing the stethoscope from his ears and trading her a grave glance.

'How would you feel about us getting you into hospital Reg?'

Reg managed to recover enough breath to open his eyes wide. They were rheumy and distant, a faded watery blue. 'No,' he managed.

'I'm sorry, old sport, but I don't think you have any choice,' Richard told him. 'You're verging into pneumonia and you're going to have to be where we can look after you. When do you expect Bluey back?'

Again Reg summoned his breath with an effort. 'Tomorrow'.

'Well, you can't stay here alone. You are a lot worse since he left you, I expect. Now look, Reg, I'm going to have to use your wireless to call an ambulance. Where is it? In the kitchen?'

Reg confirmed with a nod. 'Pedal wireless,' he gasped.

'I know. I'll manage it,' Richard said. 'Stay with Reg, Tara.'

Tara sat down in a cane chair beside the bed thinking that if her life depended on it she would not know how to work a pedal wireless.

'Ugh – err . . .' Reg was trying to say something. Tara leaned closer, thinking how old he looked, his leathered face turned yellowish and those eyes watery and tormented.

'Is there anything you want, Reg? Can I get you anything?' she asked, lifting him a fraction and adjusting the pillow behind him.

'Horses,' he said.

'You're not to worry about your horses. They are fine,' Tara soothed.

'Water. Bluey forgets. They need water.'

'All right,' Tara said. 'I'm sure he didn't forget. But I'll make sure for you if you like.'

He nodded, satisfied. She went back into the kitchen. Richard, sitting on one of the cane chairs, was fiddling with the wireless. He glanced up questioningly as she came in.

'It's all right. He's just worried about the horses. Wants us to make sure they have got water.'

Richard fiddled with the wireless some more.

'You could do that, couldn't you? I'm having a problem with getting through. The static is really bad – it's the heavy weather I suppose.'

Tara hesitated. She was just a little afraid of horses.

'Oh, and you could bring in the respirator from the ute while you're about it. A whiff of oxygen might make Reg more comfortable,' Richard said without looking up from the crackling wireless.

Unwilling to admit to her nervousness, Tara had no option but to do as he asked her. As she went out the door the heavy atmosphere hit her, clogging her throat. No wonder Reg was so groggy, she thought. No wonder the static on the air waves was so bad. She crossed the yard to the stables. It was dim inside where the strange clear light could not reach and it smelled heavily of horses. Tara wrinkled her nose.

Missie, the mare Kate loved to ride, was in the end stall looking out. Her ears pricked questioningly. Tara spoke to her softly trying to move her away from the door by pushing her at arm's length. At first Missie tried to muzzle her, then, puzzled, side-stepped away. Tara opened the door and slipped inside, plunging her hand into the water bucket. Yes. Full. She hadn't thought Bluey would forget his beloved horses. She backed out of the stall and with the door closed after her again she was so filled with relief that she stopped to give Missie's nose a pat.

That left Barney, the gelding. Tara had never seen him but she had heard Kate talk about him – a mettlesome horse, highly strung, as likely as not to land a kick if you did not keep clear of his hind legs. Tara's heart came into her mouth.

Barney was in the next stall. A shaft of light coming in from the window behind Tara showed the rich chestnut gleam of his coat – and the flare of his nostrils. Tara went to open the stall and Barney came forward to meet her, not muzzlingly as Missie had done, but in a manner which struck Tara as threatening. She retreated hastily, sliding the bolt back into place.

I can't go in there! she thought. Surely if Missie has water, Barney has too!

But she couldn't be sure of that. She didn't like Barney but she didn't want to think of him going thirsty either. Again she tried to get into the stall, again Barney came between her and the water bucket rolling his eyes and curling his lip to reveal evil-looking teeth.

'Sure you've got the devil in you and no mistake!' Tara said to him.

She could not pass him, she simply could not. Never mind hind legs itching to kick out – she could not stand the way he was looking at her! She stood for a moment thinking. It wasn't that far to the water bucket – she could see it quite clearly from here. It was just that she could not see how much was in it. Well, there was one way . . .

She went back outside and searched for a smooth pebble, then another in case her aim was not good enough first time. Barney fortunately had retreated to the rear of the stall.

Stay there, Barney. I don't want to hit you, Tara thought.

She took careful aim and tossed the pebble towards the water bucket. A good shot. There was a satisfying plop as it hit the water and Tara saw spray fly. She smiled, feeling ridiculously triumphant. Beat you, Barney! And I haven't got to fill your bucket either – praise be!

Missie was back poking her nose over her own stall, curious to see what was going on. Tara touched it tentatively.

'Bye, Missie. That's a pat from Kate.'

As she left the stable she thought what a pity it was that she did not like horses. Richard rode she knew – he had told her about his stables at home in the hills outside Melbourne. For a brief moment, she had a vision of them riding together through the bush, laughing as they cantered, wind whipping their hair. Of course, it was only pleasurable viewed as a scene from a picture shown at Tom Harris's Star Cinema. Put her on a horse in reality and she would be terrified. But it was a pity, nonetheless. There were so few places she and Richard could go, especially now that the Wet had set in and the time they had together was so short. Take today – over so soon. She had come with Richard looking forward to being alone with him for the first time in a week and yet, as soon as the ambulance had collected Reg, they would be heading back to the hospital with Richard tearing along no doubt so that he could be the one to admit Reg and start his treatment. What it was to be so dedicated! It was always the same when he was working. Yet off duty he could be so different.

She smiled, imagining the way he would deal with the high-bred, high-spirited Barney. A firm sure touch that would say 'Don't think you can push me around, old sport.' And the horse would know that he had met his master and recognize that he was not the only blue-blood in the stable.

And I'll bet my bottom dollar I can think of someone else who could handle him, Tara mused. Alys Peterson. It was such an unwelcome thought that she pushed it quickly away but the aura of it lingered.

Alys Peterson. Why did I have to think of her?

She crossed the yard, stopping at the ute to pick up the respirator. As she leaned across the seat she noticed the keys were in the ignition. Unlike Richard to leave them there, even out here in the wilds. He was usually particular about making sure he had them in his pocket. Presently, when they came to leave he would be wondering where they were . . .

Tara stopped, a sudden smile hovering on her lips, then she leaned into the ute again, pulled the keys out of the ignition and pushed them down the back of the seat. Just far enough to be out of sight, not so far as to be lost forever. Then she picked up the respirator and, humming, went back to the house.

Richard was with Reg again now, making him as comfortable as possible for the journey. He asked Tara to find the things Reg would need – pyjamas, shaving tackle, tooth powder – and she did so, no longer minding the dark airlessness in the house. Then she made tea and they sat beside Reg's bed doing what they could for him while they waited for the ambulance.

At last it arrived. It had made good time down the Track and the driver, a cheery, chirpy corporal, had driven along the last five miles of unmade-up road with no respect for suspension.

'You riding in the back with the patient?' he asked Tara and her heart nearly stopped beating.

'That's your partner's job,' Richard reminded him and Tara breathed again, though the driver looked less pleased. Clearly he preferred to have company in the cab to yarn and smoke with as he did his imitation of a driver in the Monte Carlo rally.

The first sharp crack of thunder came as they were carrying Reg, on his stretcher, down the veranda steps. The edge of it seemed to split the sky and the echo rolled menacingly around the outbuildings. Tara drew back, hanging onto the veranda rail. She hated thunder – and feared it as much as she feared horses.

'Get in the ute, Tara,' Richard said over his shoulder.

'It's all right – I'll lock up the house.' She did not want to be there when he found the keys missing!

She made one last tour of the bungalow, checking that everything was safe. She heard the rain start as she returned to the kitchen – heard it come pattering onto the corrugated veranda roof with a sound like a volley of bullets. As she emerged the ambulance was just pulling away but the sound of its engine was unable to drown the rumble of thunder that announced there was not one storm but two and she saw a fork of lightning somewhere beyond the stables.

Richard had seen it too. 'Thank God for the rain – that's the sort of bolt that starts bush fires!' he said, running up the steps to help her lock the door. Already, within those few seconds, he was drenched, his shirt sticking to his back, his hair plastered to his head. 'Ready to make a run for it?'

'Yes, I guess so . . .'

He slapped his pockets and she saw the beginnings of a perplexed look.

'Did you see what I did with my keys?'

She looked at him; looked away.

262

'Perhaps you left them in the ute,' she said demurely.

He frowned. 'Perhaps I did. I didn't think . . . Wait here and I'll see.'

He ran down the veranda steps and she watched him go thinking; Don't let him find them *too* soon! Because of the rain he got right into the ute to check – sitting on them of course, she thought, amused.

After a few seconds he came running back.

'I can't see them, dammit. Perhaps I had them in my hand and put them down somewhere in the house.'

'I didn't see them anywhere when I locked up,' she said.

'They must be there somewhere. Have you got the door key?' She nodded, reached into the cooler beneath the veranda where she had hidden it and gave it to him. He unlocked the door and they went back into the house. Richard retraced all his steps, searching, and she followed, pretending to search too.

'They don't seem to be here – what the hell have I done with them?' he straightened, wiping away drips of rain that were running from his hair down his forehead. 'They *must* be in the ute – unless I dropped them on the path.'

He locked up again and Tara hung back under the veranda thinking furiously. She should have known, of course, that he would be too worried about losing the keys to think of making the most of their unexpected time together. Stupid really. Oh, for an opportunity, just a tiny opportunity . . .

Another fork of lightning split the sky followed by the thunder roll, loud enough to waken the dead. Tara caught at Richard's arm, pulling in close to make the most of her fear.

'Oh, I hate thunderstorms! I've always hated them.'

'It won't hurt you.' Richard sounded preoccupied.

'I know that really, but . . . I'll bet the horses don't like it either. That gelding is so highly strung. Couldn't we just go and see if he is calm? If he panics in his stall he could break a leg . . .'

263

'All right. Let me just have one more look for the keys in the ute.'

They were halfway across the yard when the heavens opened. Tara squealed and grabbed Richard's arm.

'Never mind the keys – let's get in the stable – shelter!'

She jerked his hand, veering off towards the stables, and to her relief he followed. Hand in hand they ran, while the rain lashed down with tropical fury all around them. A horse whinnied. 'It's all right, it's all right!' Tara soothed.

It was almost dark in the stable now that the thunder clouds had thickened the already heavy sky. Only the flickering lightning showed the looseboxes and the tack, the cobwebs – and the hay blocked up in the corner.

'Oh!' Tara was laughing and shuddering. She shook her head and the black curls sprayed water; her dress was soaked, her feet caked with red splattered mud. 'I'm drenched! And so are you!'

She put her hand on his chest where the taut wet material of his shirt clung like a second skin and ran her fingers up to his shoulders.

'Richard . . .' She turned her face up to his, sliding her other hand around his back, and felt his arms go around her. The thunder rolled again, directly overhead, and lightning illuminated the stable. 'Oh!' She pressed in close, burying her face in his chest. Her skirt was clinging to her legs; through it she felt the hard length of his body and thighs and the coolness of her plan became charged with the heat of desire.

She raised her face again without relinquishing the touch of a single square inch of his body and he bent and touched her forehead with his lips. 'It's all right, Tara.' A droplet of water ran from his hair and rolled down her nose. A shudder ran through her. 'It's all right!'

His mouth traced the line the droplet of water had made down her wet face to her mouth. Their lips touched, hovering for a moment, then clinging, parting, fusing. She moved against him, her breasts thrusting beneath the soaked cesarine, and heard the tiny suck and squelch as their bodies fused.

She could feel the desire mounting within her now, knew it was stronger than anything they had generated before. As she moved her hips against his he groaned softly into her hair and she felt the answering response shudder through her own body, darting a fine line of fire through the very core of her being, making her soft inner thighs prick and tremble. For a long unreal moment she felt as if she was floating – no, not floating but being lifted, very gently, on a column of water, up, up, with the happiness bursting in the sparkling droplets all around her and the love and desire drowning all thought, all reason and planning. She had wanted him to make love to her because she had thought it was the only certain way of making him hers, now suddenly she wanted him to make love to her only because nothing else in the world mattered. Not the thunderstorm, not the war, not the horses moving restlessly and curiously in their stalls. Nothing. Nothing. Except to be closer, closer . . .

Holding tightly to one another they stumbled towards the bales of hay. Tara felt them behind her knees and sank into them. The thunder rolled again but she scarcely heard it. Her wet dress peeled off like the skin of an over-ripe peach, the hay scratched her back and shoulders as well as her legs, but she scarcely noticed that either. There was only Richard, his body strong and white in the flickering lightning, only Richard taking her at last, making her his . . .

Love and triumph and a wave of passion so strong she thought she would drown in it overwhelmed her and she let herself be swept along – swept away – towards the inevitable white-water crescendo.

Afterwards, she opened her eyes to see Richard sitting up on the edge of a bale of hay. She put her hand on his thigh, trailing her fingers along the long muscle and feeling it still damp and sticky.

He turned and looked down at her. 'Tara, what can I say?'

She sat up too, touching his shoulder with her lips. 'Don't say anything.'

He looked at her; looked away. The haunted expression on his face was visible even in the half light; it touched her warmth with a chilly finger.

'No buts. Not now.'

He sat silently for a moment. She waited, wondering what he was thinking, wondering whether she should say something else or if it was better to say nothing at all. Then he moved, getting up, searching for his clothes.

'The storm is passing – and I still have to find my keys.'

'Richard . . .'

He looked back at her. The expression on his face tore at her heart.

'I'm sorry, Tara.'

'No, Richard, no!' She caught at his hand again. 'Don't be sorry, please. I wanted it too. If you're sorry I can't bear it!'

'I'm sorry . . . oh hell!'

He began to get dressed. There was nothing left for her to do but follow his lead. She found her own dress, getting into the wet clinging material with difficulty.

'The horses have their water all right, have they?' He seemed to be taking refuge in normality. Stop it! Talk about what happened – what we just shared! she wanted to say, but no words would come. All very well to scheme when your heart is not involved, but how different it is when you care so much, so very very much . . .

He moved to the stable door, stood waiting for just a moment, then went outside. She followed, her legs still trembling just a little. The rain had become a steady thick mist, the ground and the surrounding vegetation steamed into it. She could not understand how withdrawn he had become. They should be closer now, instead she had never felt more distant. He crossed to the ute, opening the door and searching about on the floor for his keys. She got in on

266

the passenger side, pretending to search also. Nothing for it now but to 'find' the keys and drive back. Back to the hospital. Back to reality. Back to hardly seeing him and worrying and wondering . . .

A tear ran down her nose. He did not see it. She felt inside the crack of her seat then leaned across and pushed her hand down the back of his, pulling out the keys.

'Oh – they're here!' To her own ears it sounded flat and false – surely he must know what she had done, she thought. But he did not appear to.

'Thank God for that! How did they get down there? I must have dropped them . . .'

'Yes,' she said. 'You must.'

He started the engine and drove in silence. The unmade-up road was awash with mud and it needed all his concentration to negotiate it. Once they were back on the bitumenized Track she thought he might say something, but he did not and the set of his face made the muscles of her stomach tighten.

The journey seemed endless, yet when the hospital buildings came in sight she felt the last twist of desperation. He parked the ute, leaned over and for a brief second she thought he was going to take her into his arms again. Instead, he pulled a strand of hay from her hair.

'Richard . . .' Her distress was all there in the one word. His expression softened momentarily, then closed in again.

'Don't worry, Tara,' he said. 'I'm not going anywhere. You know how I feel about committing myself while this damned war is on but if anything . . . if anything happens as a result of this afternoon, you know I'm here. We'll get married.'

'But . . .'

'I'd just have to forget my misgivings about wartime marriages, wouldn't I?' He leaned across, kissing her, and the tenderness of the kiss warmed her again, breathing new hope into her.

'You don't think I would abandon you – or let a child of

mine be born fatherless, do you?' he said. 'What do you take me for, eh?'

She reached for him, burying her face in his shoulder, clinging again.

'I love you,' she whispered.

But her words were soft and muffled and he did not hear her.

Chapter Fifteen

Alys Peterson put her foot hard down on the accelerator of her Alfa Romeo and kept it there.

In front of her the road shone, sticky with heat; above the sky was endless blue. The sun, directly overhead, beat down mercilessly and as the car followed the kinks in the road it caught the wing and central mirrors, sending bright shards of light into Alys' eyes. A bend loomed up ahead and Alys took it the way Race had once taught her – braking slightly before it yet keeping up the revs with her heel overlapping the accelerator then driving round it fast, fast! Even on these sticky roads she felt the weight of the car holding it steady and smiled with satisfaction. Oh, there was nothing like driving for helping to put your problems behind you for a little while. With the powerful engine roaring and the wheel between her hands she could forget that she was trapped in the mansion in Toorak, forget that her mother had once more become her gaoler. The faint odour of petrol on the fresh country air replaced the smell of the sickroom in her nostrils, a smell which seemed to cling to Frances Peterson even now she was able to come downstairs for a good part of each day. She would ride down in the special invalid's lift Daniel had had installed for her – a chair which hummed up and down its runners at the side of the broad stairway – dressed in a flowing caftan which hid the uselessness of one arm and leg, and with her head turned slightly to one side so that the twisted mouth and eye were not visible, she looked for all the world like a queen on her throne. But the smell came with her all the same, disguised by clouds of perfume yet still clinging to her, defiantly, inexplicably, immutably part of her.

Something materialized on the road ahead of Alys – a

big black American Buick, shimmering in the bright heat. Alys eased up slightly to pass it. Unusual to meet much in the way of traffic out here on a scorching summer afternoon. Sometimes it was possible to drive out and see nothing at all. Then she depressed the accelerator again and the Alfa Romeo surged forward, eating up the road.

Oh, bliss – bliss! If only she could keep her foot flat down and drive forever. But she could not. A few hours' respite was all she could allow herself and Frances would be asking for her again, not because she needed anything that the servants could not do for her but because she liked to know that Alys was not far away; that the gossamer threads of her web held her as strongly as ever.

And they did. Alys had only to look at the drawn mouth, hear her mother struggle to form the words that had once come acid-sharp from her lips, to feel the familiar rush of guilt. And when the good eye looked at her with that 'you wronged me but I forgive you because I am your mother and I love you' expression, any thoughts of escape were instantly quashed.

'How long will she be like this?' she had asked Dr Whitehorn one afternoon when he had called in to see Frances.

He had shaken his head. 'Impossible to say. In cases like these progress is very, very slow. But your mother has done well. She is regaining her speech; she should soon be able to walk a little on the flat, provided you are there to support her. Yes, all things considered, with a stroke as serious as the one she suffered, her progress has been little short of miraculous. You are very lucky to have her, I don't mind telling you.'

Alys had hastily averted her eyes, ashamed of the small ironic voice in her head which had echoed 'lucky?', but placed a quite different emphasis on the word. She only hoped Donald Whitehorn had not seen her think it. But when he continued: 'And, of course, you must be prepared for the fact that she could suffer another stroke at any time,' she felt that he might be reproving her.

That had been the end of any thoughts of escape and she had resigned herself once more to playing the role of dutiful daughter. Only sometimes she thought if she could not get out for just a few hours she would go quite crazy.

She was in flat open country now – the vast rich pasturelands where the Victorian cattle barons held sway. Not the small- to medium-sized farms of the north and north-west here, the family properties worked by a father and one or two of his sons with a plough pulled by a six-team, a few cattle, sheep and chickens. These were the properties and stations of the squattocracy, the wealthy families whose forefathers had established their claims when the land was there for the taking. As far as the eye could see it stretched, broken only by lonely clumps of gums and wattle or stands of box or the occasional creek and as the pasture stretched out, so did the distances between the lane entrances, guarded by the obligatory mailbox drums, marked with the name of the property which was way, way back out of sight of the road. Occasionally, there were the signs that a bush fire had passed this way – the blackened stumps of burned out gums, the scorched scrubby look of the land – and Alys suppressed a shiver. The thought of bush fires terrified her and always had done. The nightmare of being trapped in a hell of bright orange flame and choking black smoke, with the terror of the animals caught in its path in the wind and the sure knowledge that however fast you could run the fire could run faster, outpacing the swiftest horse, perhaps the Alfa Romeo even, leaping roads and firebreaks with ease, setting the next clump of withered gums alight with only the slightest touch of its hot breath. And the land was so ripe for a bush fire now – there had been no rain to speak of since 1936.

1936. How long ago it seemed! So many things had happened since then. Falling in love with Race. Getting pregnant by him. Seeing him die. The war. The bombing. Frances' stroke . . . all that and more, but no rain.

I have gone far enough, Alys decided. Time to be getting back.

She slowed the Alfa Romeo, executed a neat turn, and headed back the way she had come, but although she still drove fast it was not as fast as she had driven on her way out. Much as she still loved the sensation of speed, it had a little less attraction when it was taking her back to Toorak and Frances.

Some way back and she saw a dark shape on the road in front of her. At first, the distance was too great to see what it was or which way it was going, then as she came nearer she recognized it as the black Buick which had passed her earlier on her way out. Closer still and she saw that it was stationary, the bonnet up, emitting a cloud of steam. She slowed. A breakdown on a lonely road such as this meant trouble.

At the sound of her engine a man emerged from beneath the bonnet of the Buick, straightening and wiping his hands on a dark blue handkerchief.

'Having trouble?' she called.

He came towards her, a tall well-made man of about fifty. His face was leathered from exposure to the sun, his hair still thick though iron-grey and his eyes were grey also, sharp and piercing in that dark-tanned face.

'Hi. You could say that.'

Alys eyed the Buick hungrily. Not a car she knew – and a new car was as attractive to her as a fresh clump of untouched honeysuckle to a bee. She pulled into the side of the road in front of the Buick and got out.

Careful, now! she was warning herself. Don't upset him. Men could be so funny about a woman knowing something about what went on under the bonnet of a car. Casually she ambled back. He did not look the sort to be easily annoyed. A strong face, too strong to feel threatened by a woman, no matter what her talents.

'Can I look? I'm terribly interested in cars.'

He cast a glance at the Alfa Romeo. 'I can see that,' he said dryly.

She leaned over the engine marvelling at the condition it was in.

'You keep it beautifully!'

His mouth quirked humorously. 'I can't take the credit for that, I'm afraid.'

'Oh, it's not yours then?' She was still bending over the engine and when he did not answer she wondered briefly whether perhaps the car was stolen, then dismissed the thought. If ever a man looked like a car thief, it was not this one.

'Hmm. One of your hoses has gone, hasn't it? Looks like it's a job for the garage.'

She looked up to see him watching her with an amused expression.

'I'd come to that conclusion myself,' he said wryly. 'The damn nuisance of it is there's no garage for at least twenty miles and I'm due in Melbourne for an appointment. I'm late already.'

'Well, that's no problem,' Alys said. 'I'm going back to Melbourne. I can give you a ride.'

Again his mouth quirked.

'Are you sure about that? Don't you know it could be dangerous, picking up strangers on lonely roads?'

Alys laughed. 'If you had wanted to attack me you've had plenty of opportunity already. Besides, you look perfectly respectable. I'll take the risk.'

'In that case – thanks!' He locked up the Buick, then followed her to the Alfa Romeo. 'This is some motor you have here.'

She flushed slightly, remembering his borrowed Buick.

'Yes, it's my pride and joy. And my salvation. I have an invalid mother to look after. If I couldn't get out and blow away the cobwebs once in a while I'd go crazy.'

'You don't get out much then.'

'Hardly at all. Oh, I have a married sister I visit sometimes but we don't really see eye to eye.' She broke off, her flush deepening. She did not usually open up like this to a perfect stranger. Yet somehow she felt totally at

273

ease with him. 'You don't live in Melbourne, do you?' she said, changing the subject.

He smiled, deep crinkles appearing in the dark tanned skin around his eyes.

'How do you know that? Here am I, all dressed up in my best city-going bib and tucker . . .'

She smiled again, noting the smart lightweight suit. 'Oh, it has nothing to do with your clothes. But no one from the city would be as brown as you are. My guess is you're a farmer – am I right?'

'Close.'

'What do you mean, close? Are you a farmer or not?'

He relaxed against the leather upholstery. Concentrating on the road she did not notice the small smile that quirked his mouth again as he answered. 'Yep. Got me in one.'

'I knew it. But whose is the Buick if it's not yours?'

'Like it, do you?' he asked.

'I certainly do. I haven't seen one like it before.'

'Look – I'll tell you what. If you are still looking for escape when it's repaired – and that shouldn't take more than a few days at most, even in these sleepy parts – you are welcome to come out to my place and have a look at it. Drive it if you like.'

She eased off the accelerator, looking sideways at him in surprise.

'But you said . . . I didn't think it belonged to you.'

'Well, it does. It's just that I don't have the time to look after it myself. I have to let someone else do that. Trouble is now he's gone off to join the AIF . . .' The grey eyes sharpened suddenly.

'Your son?' Alys asked.

A muscle tightened in his cheek. 'Yep.' There was a moment's silence, then he grinned. 'What else can you expect anyway? When there's a war to fight they don't stop to think of the old man. I guess if I was twenty years younger I'd do the same thing. Trouble is I'll be running the bloody place on my own soon.'

Though there was no self-pity in his tone Alys felt a rush of sympathy. It couldn't be easy shouldering a lot of extra work when your boys went off to fight, even if you were as fit as this man looked. And the drought was making things difficult for farmers, too, she knew.

A cluster of buildings materialized on the horizon – the first signs of a small town. However few houses, there would be a garage on the roadside, a garage reminiscent of Jeff Holder's place where Race used to take her. A nerve tightened in her stomach. Oh God, it could still hurt, even after so long . . .

'Do you want to stop off here and get someone to go back for your car?' she asked, reducing speed as the white blur of the buildings took shape and separated.

'Yes. And if they can hire me one while mine is being repaired, that's what I'll do.'

'It's no trouble for me to take you into Melbourne.'

'I know, but I still have to get back.'

She pulled into the side of the road. An old man in a pair of trousers that had once been part of a suit was sitting just inside the garage resting upon the back legs of his chair. His shirt was collarless, rucked up by the uneven pull of his braces, a greasy looking hat was jammed onto his head. He appeared in no hurry to attend to his customers.

'Perhaps you had better check up that they can do what you want before I drive off and leave you,' Alys said.

'Perhaps I had.' He got out and went over to talk to the man. Again Alys was struck by the fluid ease with which he moved, the breadth of his shoulders, the narrowness of his hips. He was as old as her own father, perhaps older, but he looked twice as fit. Daniel was beginning to show the effects of days spent sitting behind a desk – and too many business lunches, Alys thought.

A few moments later he was back. 'It's all right, they have a ute they can loan me.'

'Are you sure?' She was oddly disappointed; she had enjoyed his company.

'Quite. Thanks for your help. I'm sorry, I don't know your name.

'Alys. Alys Peterson.'

'Well thanks, Alys.' He fumbled in his pocket, pulled out a small embossed card and handed it to her. 'Don't forget, the offer is still open for you to drive the Buick. This is where you can find me.'

She glanced at the card. John Hicks. Buchlyvie.

'I'll be pleased to see you any time,' he said.

She nodded. 'I'll probably take you up on that.'

'I hope you do. And remember, don't go picking up any more strange men. Right?'

'Right,' she said, laughing.

She glanced in her rear view mirror as she drove away and was surprised to notice that he stood there watching until she was out of sight.

*

'Alys – I have to tell you that you were seen in town the other day with a man driving a Buick.' Beverley Reilly's eyes were small and sharp, concentrating suspiciously on her sister's face.

'That is probably because I *was* with a man driving a Buick.' Alys smiled and the smile seemed to infuriate Beverley all the more.

'Who is he?' she demanded.

Alys' smile died. 'Just a friend,' she said cagily.

'But who do you know with a Buick? We don't know anyone with a Buick! And that is not all.' Beverley paused for a moment. 'It seems he was quite an *old* man.'

Alys felt her irritation rise another notch.

'John is not old,' she said coolly.

'That's not what I heard.' Beverley leaned across to rearrange the wafer-thin bread and butter Alys had set out on a plate for Frances' afternoon tea. 'Old enough to be your father was what I heard. You want to be careful, Alys.'

Alys snatched up the bread and butter plate. 'I'm quite capable of taking care of myself, thank you. Bev.'

'But are you?' Beverley persisted. 'I'm not so sure that you are. You've never been a very wise chooser when it came to men.'

'I've never had much opportunity to be a wise chooser or a foolish one.' Alys said, deadly calm. 'Excuse me, please, Beverley. Mummy is waiting for her tea.'

'But who is he, Alys?' Beverley followed her to the doorway but Alys moved on, steadfastly ignoring her. The small smile was back on her lips. Let Beverley stew. She was getting to be just as bad as Frances had been, trying to run other people's lives for them.

She could see, of course, how it would look to someone who did not know the truth about her friendship – it was perfectly true that John was old enough to be her father. But what business was that of Beverley's or anyone else's, if it came to that? Except, of course, John's wife, Anne. And she was in a hospital as sick in her own way as Frances – worse actually. She was mentally ill and had been since the birth of her son – and John's – twenty-three years ago.

Perhaps it was that which had drawn them together, the fact that each of them was tied in their own way to a sick relative. Yet even as she thought about it she knew it was more than that. She and John had simply hit if off. If they had not she would never have taken him up on his invitation to go out and drive the Buick, however fascinated she was by the big American car.

Carrying Frances' tea tray to the drawing room, she remembered the first time she had driven out to Buchlyvie, and smiled. She had had no idea, honestly no idea, of the size of the place, no idea that John Hicks was one of the squattocracy, with a property covering, as she put in disbelief, half of Victoria, and a fortune that was double and treble her father's not inconsiderable wealth.

It had been a week after her first meeting with him and whilst she had been keen to take up his offer she had also been a little hesitant. Perhaps he had not meant it – perhaps he had just said it for something to say. Yet oddly, she was quite sure he had meant it.

The scorching weather seemed to have settled in over Melbourne and that afternoon the house seemed more oppressive than ever. Alys took Frances iced coffee and fingers of fudge cake, but her mind was busy with her plans. No use to go out to Buchlyvie too early – if John had practically to run the farm on his own the chances were he would be still at work – but leave it too late and she might interrupt the family's evening meal. And if not his evening meal, then Frances'. Her mother insisted on gathering the family together each evening for dinner just as she always had done, except that Daniel seemed to be working late more and more often and Alys, in addition to being present like the dutiful and loving daughter Frances demanded, also had to feed her.

Alys glanced at her watch, working out the timing of the exercise.

'Mummy, I thought I'd go out for a few hours. Is that all right? she asked, holding the glass to Frances' lips.

Frances' head came up sharply so that coffee ran in a small dribbling stream down her chin, and questioned Alys with her eyes.

'Just for a drive,' Alys said.

Frances raised her good hand, pressing it to her chest. 'I . . . would . . . like . . .'

'No, it's too hot for you this afternoon,' Alys said hastily. She broke off a piece of fudge cake and offered it to Frances. 'Norma will sit with you for a while. And I shall be back for dinner.'

She offered the cake again and Frances snatched it from her in a gesture of impotent fury. If you can't be bothered to take me with you don't bother feeding me either, that gesture seemed to say. She put the fudge cake to her own mouth, biting into it, and as her lip failed to control it properly crumbs tumbled down onto her caftan.

Controlling her impatience with difficulty, Alys wiped

Frances's mouth with a napkin, brushed away the crumbs and straightened up.

'I have to go out sometimes, Mummy.'

Frances' eyes followed her. 'You . . . want to go . . . all the time . . .'

I shan't answer that, Alys thought. If I do I might just end up telling her a few home truths and then I shall hate myself for it.

She was still simmering as she drove the Alfa Romeo along the fast straight road which she imagined must lead to John's farm, Buchlyvie, and not even the freedom of the open air could quite dispel her feeling of oppression. Because she was a little uncertain that she should be doing this, she supposed.

Each time she saw the mail drum that marked a driveway looming up she slowed, reading the name painted on it, but none of these early farms was Buchlyvie. The private roads grew farther and farther apart, the land opened out to the vaster pastures and still she had not come to it. Then, just when she thought she must have missed it she saw another track, overhung with wilga gums and marked not by the customary oil-drum mail box but a grand white-painted structure built in the shape of a house and below it the legend 'Buchlyvie'.

She screeched to a stop, reversed and turned in between the gums. The track seemed to go on forever, beyond the fences the pasture land spread as far as the eye could see. No one had escaped the drought but it looked as though Buchlyvie was weathering it as well as anyone. The cattle she saw looked sleek and fat and in the white picket-fenced paddocks close to the house half-a-dozen thoroughbred horses flicked their tails against the flies.

The house itself was vast – white-painted with a roof of cool green corrugated and the walls covered with deep red climbing roses and brilliantly blue morning glories. The place appeared deserted but when Alys got out of the car to look around an old woman, part-aborigine, came out of the house wiping her hands on her apron.

'I'm looking for John Hicks,' Alys said, slightly self-conscious.

'Boss man out mending fences. You want him?'

'Yes.' Alys scoured the horizon. 'Is it too far for me to walk?'

'Could be.'

'Oh,' Alys experienced the falling away of disappointment. On a property as big as this one appeared to be there would be no way of reaching the boundaries except on horseback. It looked as though she was going to have to give up and go home without driving the Buick – and without seeing John. She turned back to the aborigine woman.

'Will you tell him Alys Peterson was here,' she began.

'You wait! You lucky!' The woman pointed.

Far out, too far yet to be distinguishable, a man was riding in. Alys waited. At last he was close enough for her to be able to recognize him – and see his surprised expression.

He cantered into the yard and reined in the horse. 'Well, hullo!'

'Hullo.' She was looking at him and thinking that, although tiredness seemed to have etched the lines on his leathery face deeper, at the same time he somehow looked years younger sitting astride that horse, hat pulled down to cover his iron grey hair, tight-fitting shirt and breeches showing that his body was still hard and trim. 'I took you at your word and came out to have another look at your car.'

'I'm afraid you're out of luck. I haven't got it back yet. I thought while it was in the garage I might as well get them to give it the works.' He hitched up the reins and dismounted.

'Oh well, never mind – it was a nice drive out anyway.' Alys half turned and he stopped her.

'Don't rush off – it's good to see you. I'm just going to have a cold beer. Why not join me?'

'That sounds like a nice idea,' Alys said gratefully. 'If

280

you're sure I'm not keeping you from what you should be doing, that is.'

'No worries. I was due for a break. Come on, we'll go on the veranda.'

It was cool on the veranda. John fetched the beer, bitingly cold from the ice box, and they sat in cane chairs to drink it.

'You've got a large place here,' Alys said.

He tipped back his chair, stretching long muscled legs. 'A lot of hard work. I've lost half-a-dozen hands to the AIF. Not to mention my son. If the war goes on much longer I'm not sure I can keep going. I've put my word in and the government have promised me some land girls. Land girls! I ask you, what bloody use will they be?'

'Hey, steady on, I shall take exception to that remark on behalf of my sex,' Alys said.

He looked at her, amused. 'You think you could be a stockman then?'

Alys took a sip of her beer. 'I'd have a darned good shot at it.'

He laughed. The crinkles bit deeper into the skin around his eyes. 'I bet you could at that. And if you learned as much about it as you have about cars you'd be bloody good, I reckon.'

Pleased, she laughed with him. 'So tell me about the Buick. It was a hose that had gone, was it?'

'Just as you said.' He looked at her over his beer, his eyes flinty sharp. 'Where did you learn so much about mechanics? Be fair now, most girls haven't a clue what goes on under any bonnet but their own.'

'I had a boyfriend once who was a racing driver.' Her voice was determinedly light.

Those sharp eyes narrowed a fraction. 'Anyone I would have heard of?'

'No, he was killed.' Her tone still gave nothing away, though if she had been looking she might have noticed his gleam of understanding. 'You know, I thought I'd missed this place,' she went on, changing the subject. 'I had very

281

nearly given up looking when I saw the drive. And the mailbox. Very impressive, that mailbox.'

'Do you think so?' he asked dryly.

'I do indeed.' She glanced at him quizzically. 'It doesn't sound as if you like it much.'

'I don't. A fancy thing like that isn't to my taste at all. Give me an oil drum, honest to goodness weatherproof, like everybody else.'

'So why have you got a mailbox?'

A small shadow darkened his eyes. Momentarily, the lines around them bit deeper.

'Anne always wanted one. My wife. I had it made for her.'

'Oh yes, your wife . . .' Alys glanced around embarrassed suddenly. Stupid of her, she hadn't thought of John's wife. Suppose she took exception to the sudden appearance of a young lady met at the roadside?

'She's not here,' John said and Alys recognized the same tone she had used a few minutes ago to refer to Race – deliberately matter-of-fact.

'Oh, I'm sorry, you mean she's . . . ?'

'Anne is sick,' he said. 'She's in hospital.'

'What's wrong with her?' Alys asked sympathetically, saw the tiny muscle tighten in John's cheek, and wished she had not.

'She never recovered from Stuart's birth,' he said in the same matter-of-fact tone. 'She had a hard time – it unhinged her. It happens to some women I'm told. I must confess I never knew another it happened to, but then I don't suppose I've known many women. First there was the Great War running off with my youth and then the farm . . . Anyway, giving birth to Stuart did something to Anne's mind, God knows what, but it did. I tried every damned whitsway I could to avoid having her put away but the time came when I couldn't put if off any longer.' His voice tailed away as if he was remembering some incident too private and distressing to mention. Then he took a long gulp of beer and wiped his mouth with the back of his lean sunburned hand. 'I had to have a nurse raise Stuart. She became more of a mother to him than Anne ever was. When she died last winter it was the first time I'd ever seen him shed a tear. Even when he was a youngster he never cried – certainly not when his mother went away.'

'And she has been in hospital all these years!' Alys said, thinking. Dear God, more years than I have been alive, probably.

'Oh, we've had her home at times over the years, trying to get her back to normal. Sometimes, she'd be quite good for weeks at a stretch but it always caught up with her again.' His eyes narrowed reflectively. 'It was when she was home once that I had the mailbox made for her. She fancied it. God knows why. But she'd got this idea in her head that she wanted a mailbox different from any others hereabouts.'

'Did it please her?' Alys asked.

'I suppose so, for a bit. Yeah, I can remember her running down the road like a kid to look at it, see if there was anything in it. But you could never please Anne for long. No, whatever makes a woman happy and content, well it had just got shut down in her somehow. She'd start criticizing everything, every damn little thing, and then down she'd go into this black depression.' He looked at Alys. 'Ever seen a horse caught in a bog? Not a pretty sight. But that's what it was like watching Anne. She'd flounder and we'd try to help, but she'd still go in deeper and deeper until she ended up a danger to herself and everyone else . . .'

Alys was silent.

John drained his beer. 'Well, I don't suppose you came all the way out here to listen to my troubles,' he said, the corners of his mouth creasing into a smile.

'I'm really sorry,' Alys said.

'Don't be. I'm used to it. If you feel sorry for anyone, feel sorry for Anne. She's missed so bloody much.' He stood up. 'Hey, I'm going to get another beer. D'you want one?'

'No, it's all right. I've got enough. But don't let me stop you.'

He went back into the house and Alys sat, staring down the track and thinking of the woman who had run like a child to see her mailbox.

When he came back the mood had changed. They sat drinking their beer and chatting but the conversation was at a superficial level now. The time for confidences had passed. At last Alys rose.

'I think I had better be getting back. But thanks for the beer and your company. I've enjoyed it.'

He stood up, too, and she thought that for all his troubles there was no stoop to his shoulders. He looked tall and straight and strong.

'My pleasure. I hope you'll come again. With any luck the Buick will be back. If not we can still crack a beer, can't we?'

She laughed. 'We certainly can. Yes, I'll be back, John.'

She had gone back. Again, there had been the easy communication, the pleasure in each other's company. This time he had drawn her out and she had found herself telling him about Frances in much the same way that he had told her about his wife, frankly, without embarrassment, but leaving out the details that were too private to mention to someone she had met only three times – even if she did feel she had known him for years.

He listened sympathetically. 'You must be champing at the bit.'

'I've resigned myself to staying as long as I'm needed. Ninety per cent of the time I feel I could be making myself much more useful working for the war effort and releasing another man to go overseas, but the doctor told me straight out that if I did anything to upset Mummy it could bring on another stroke. I couldn't have that on my conscience.'

'Hmm. You're in a tight spot, aren't you?'

'You could say that. Never mind, I expect I'll survive.'

His mouth twisted into that 'S' that she was beginning

to know – and feel affection for. 'I'm sure you will. You are a survivor, Alys.'

Two days later he telephoned. Alys was in the garden cutting roses for Frances' room when Norma called her.

'A Mr Hicks for you.' Her eyes were curious – not many men telephoned Alys. Alys bit back her amusement at the maid's expression and took the call.

'John – how did you know where to find me?'

'There is only one Daniel Peterson in Toorak – only one in the whole of Melbourne probably.' His wry tone told her he had realized who her father was. Still, to John Hicks that would be of no importance. Wealthy though her father was, John could probably buy and sell him several times over.

'It's nice to hear from you, anyway,' she said.

'Good. Look, Alys, I'm picking up the Buick this afternoon – it's ready at last. It wouldn't take me long to come on into Melbourne and pick you up. I know you're keen to take her for a spin.'

'Oh super! But don't come here. I know this will sound odd to you but I learned a long time ago it's better to keep my personal life and my family life separate. I'll meet you in town – say beside the fountain in Parliament Place.'

'That's insane. I'm coming to Toorak or not at all.'

'Not to the house, please. You'll only upset Mummy. If you insist on coming to Toorak, I'll walk up to St John's Church. I'll be on the corner.'

He did not argue any more but later, while she was trying to enjoy the glories of the Buick, he raised the subject again.

'I don't honestly understand why I had to meet you away from your house. You're quite sure you haven't got a husband at home?'

She laughed. 'Chance would be a fine thing! No, as I told you on the telephone, I learned the hard way that my family feel they have the right to vet my choice of companion. And if they don't approve they do all they can to make things unpleasant.'

'And what makes you think they would disapprove of me?'

'Oh, I don't know,' Alys said irritably. 'Let's leave it. I thought the idea of this trip was to drive the car. So why don't we drive it?'

For the next hour Alys was able to lose herself in the intricacies of the Buick but though John did as she asked, dropping her off where he had picked her up, there was a slight tension between them that had not been there before and Alys hoped she had not offended him by her insistence that he should stay away from the house. But she could not bring herself to explain to him the way she tightened up inside at the thought of Frances' reaction – the questions, the ill-disguised surprise that Mr Hicks was so much older than Alys, the refusal to believe that it was a friendly, platonic relationship and nothing more. Frances, with her insinuations and innuendos was expert at spoiling things – whatever her stroke had done it had not robbed her of her talents in that direction, Alys was sure.

'What a choice! she thought. Have John think I'm crazy – paranoid – or maybe that I really do have something to hide, or give Mummy and Beverley the ammunition to wound me all over again.

Well, *that* had been decided now, Alys thought, as she carried the teatray to the drawing room where Frances was waiting. She had been seen with John and Beverley was now in full cry. Yet it had not worried her much. I think I handled it pretty well, Alys thought, smiling to herself. I didn't lose my cool at all. Perhaps I'm growing up – at last!

She pushed open the drawing room door. Frances was sitting in the wing chair which Alys had set by the window so that she could look out at the garden, but she was not admiring the view. Her head was half turned and cocked to one side; the expression on the good side of her face told Alys she had been listening. Alys' heart sank. Ridiculous how that look from her mother could turn her into a child again.

'What . . . was that?' Frances demanded haltingly.

'Nothing, Mummy.'

Frances eyed her malevolently.

'Don't . . . lie, Alys. A man is it?'

If you heard why are you asking? Alys thought. Aloud she said: 'Yes.'

The good corner of Frances' mouth tightened so that it almost matched the pulled side.

'No!' Her tone was violent. 'No! Don't want you to . . .'

Alys had begun to tremble. How the hell was it her mother could do this to her? With an effort she attempted to reconstruct the cool attitude she had adopted when speaking to Beverley.

'He is just a friend, Mummy, that's all. I have to have friends.'

'No!'

'You're getting worked up about nothing.'

'No! You . . . and men . . .' her mouth worked for a long moment. 'Miserable!' she finished triumphantly though Alys felt sure it was not quite the word she had been searching for. 'I . . . worry 'bout you.'

Oh yes, thought Alys. Same old story. Do as I want or you will worry me. Same old blackmail. I am your mother. Don't cause me unhappiness.

'Look, Mummy, I have stayed here to look after you and I am doing the best I can, but I have to have some life of my own.' Alys' voice was rising though she had meant to keep her temper. 'You can't expect me to do nothing but stay in all the time.'

'You don't want to . . .' Frances' voice, too, was rising tremulously and there were tears in her eyes. 'I'm as . . . I am . . . and you . . . begrudge me . . . You're hard, Alys . . .'

'Oh, for heaven's sake!' Alys exploded.

'Alys!' It was Beverley, standing in the doorway looking shocked and angry. 'I thought you had come in here to upset Mummy!'

'I did no such thing!' Alys retorted. 'I never intended . . .'

'Well, for someone with no intentions you have made a pretty good job of it!' Beverley stormed. 'You should be ashamed of yourself. Just look at her, Alys! Look what you've done!'

Alys looked. Frances was without doubt in a state of agitation. Her colour was high, her mouth worked, a tic pulled jerkily at the one good eye.

'You'll bring on another stroke before you've finished,' Beverley hissed, adding under her breath: 'It's probably what you want to do!' She crossed to Frances, going on her knees beside her and taking the lifeless hand in her own.

'It's all right, Mummy.' Her voice was loud and patient as if to a deaf child. 'Alys doesn't think, that's all. She won't worry you any more, will you, Alys?'

Alys could not find the strength to answer. She turned away, sick at heart. How did one cope with moral blackmail of this kind? She simply did not know. All very well to refuse to be blackmailed, all very well to try calmly to enforce one's own point of view. But supposing Frances *did* have another stroke? It was quite possible. Even Dr Whitehorn had said so.

Oh God, where will it end? Alys wondered helplessly. How much tighter does she want to weave her web? He's only a friend, for goodness' sake, but he gave me something to look forward to. Surely she can't intend to have even that ounce of flesh?

She glanced back at Beverley on her knees and Frances slowly calming under her soothing words.

If this little scene was anything to go by it certainly looked as if she intended to try.

Chapter Sixteen

Tara tidied her hair with her fingers, straightened the skirt of her uniform dress and went into the hut where Richard had just finished taking his morning surgery.

'Richard – I have to talk to you. Please!'

He looked up from finishing his notes, a small frown puckering between his eyes. He had just seen almost twenty men, spread right across the board from the malingerers looking for an excuse to get out of an honest day's work, to those who had tried too long to avoid bringing their condition to the attention of a Medical Officer – including one married man with advanced VD and an alcoholic who had bruised his ribs badly in an inebriated fall – and his mind was still busy with their problems.

'Please, Richard!' she begged. 'I know you're working but I never seem to see you these days.'

The urgency of her tone seemed to get through to him. He put down his pen, straightening up and looking at her anxiously. 'What is it?'

'I – I don't know how to tell you.'

Oh my God, he thought. Aloud he said: 'You're pregnant.'

'I think so. I've missed a period. And I never miss periods. I'm very regular.'

He picked up his pen again, scribbling calculations on the edge of his blotter. 'Let me see, when was it we . . . ? It's too early yet to be sure.'

'Oh, for goodness' sake, stop being a doctor!' she snapped. 'It's my body, isn't it? I ought to know, shouldn't I?'

'Not necessarily. You could be late for all kinds of reasons.'

'Oh, I see! So you're trying to get out of it now, are you? Here am I, worried sick, and you talk about "all kinds of reasons". I might have known you didn't mean what you said about marrying me. Well, all right. I'll have the baby alone. But I shall make certain everyone knows who the father is! And . . .'

'Calm down, Tara, for goodness' sake!' He got up, crossing the room to her and taking her by the shoulders. 'I said I'd marry you and I meant it. I'm only saying it's far too early yet to be sure if you're pregnant or not.'

She shook free. 'Oh yes, and by the time we wait to be sure, anything could happen. You could be posted abroad – I could be sent to AAMWS Training Camp – anything. At the very least everyone will be able to do sums and know that we – that I – was, well, you know, before we were married . . .'

The tired lines of his face softened.

'Oh Tara.' He turned away, paced to the window and back, his fingertips pressed to his lips, eyes distant and thoughtful. Tara waited, shoulders drooping, eyes downcast, and felt as if her chest would compress and collapse beneath the weight of her own breath. When she could bear it no longer she sobbed softly.

'I'm sorry. Oh Richard, I'm sorry. But I'm just so worried . . .'

'I know.' He dug his hands deep into the pockets of his medical coat, leaning back against his desk. Then he sighed and raised his eyes to hers. 'Don't worry any more, Tara. I'll fix everything up.'

He missed the quick gleam of fear. 'You mean . . . ?'

'I mean I'll arrange for a special licence. I don't know if we can be married here or if we have to go into one of the towns. I'll find out.'

'Oh yes!' The fear was gone now, replaced by something quite different. 'I really am sorry, Richard.'

'You are not the one who should be sorry.'

She ran to him, burying her face in his chest.

'It will be all right, you'll see. All the things that worry you about committing yourself in wartime – none of them will happen. We'll be happy, Richard, really happy, I know we will.'

'Yes.' He touched her forehead lightly with his lips. 'Now, I have a lot of work to get through, Tara.'

'You're not angry?'

'Of course I'm not angry.' He kissed her lips as lightly as he had her forehead. 'Keep smiling. It doesn't suit you to look so glum.'

She nodded. 'I'm all right now. Everything is all right now.'

As she left she looked back. He smiled briefly but by the time she closed the door the smile had gone. Richard went back around his desk and sat down but the stack of notes ceased to hold his attention now. There was a new problem to add to those of the married man with VD and the alcoholic who had finally decided to admit to his weakness.

This time it was his own.

*

Tara's feet flew her back across the camp to her own hut. At this time of day it was empty – all the girls she shared with were at work, none sleeping off a spell of night duty, thank goodness. She let herself in, closed the door and leaned against it, sighing with relief. She had done it. He had accepted her word for it. They were going to be married.

Oh thank you, Holy Mary, thank you! she whispered and realized she was trembling from head to toe. Had ever anything been as important to her as this? She couldn't remember that it had been, not even when she had been fighting so desperately for a job in the clubs of Sydney. Then, it had always been at the back of her mind that there were other clubs, other places, other cities the world over. But there was only one Richard. She had gambled everything on this one throw – the prospect if she had lost just did not bear thinking about. But she had not lost. She had won. Richard's strong sense of responsibility had carried the day. He was going to marry her.

If nothing went wrong now.

Oh, don't let it take too long for him to arrange the wedding! Tara prayed. If it takes too long he might come the heavy doctor again and discover there really is no reason for him to rush into marrying me – well, no reason that he would count good enough, anyway.

She walked the length of the hut to her bed and lay down, glad to remove the responsibility of balance from her shaking legs.

Oh, the nights she had lain awake here since that day at Reg and Bluey's farm, praying that she really would be pregnant and there would be no need to deceive. There were enough girls, goodness only knew, who had 'got into trouble' with just one deviation from the straight and narrow. Why shouldn't it happen to her? But it did not happen. The day before her period was due the warning niggles began deep in her stomach and there it was, not only on time, but – insult to injury – early! Tara had leaned against the wall of the toilet tent with the frogs croaking and multiplying in the quagmire beside her and wept.

That was it, then. She wouldn't get another chance – Richard would make sure of that. He would make quite certain they did not get into a situation where a repeat performance of the ecstatic ten minutes in the stable was possible – he had even been avoiding her since it happened, she suspected. Oh, the hospital had been very busy it was true, but then it always was and he had managed to find time to see her before.

Not only that, she sensed a reserve about him when she was with him and it was a barrier she was unable to break through, however hard she tried. It was as if having been taken unawares once and overcome by emotions he had been confident he could control, he no longer trusted himself under any but the most unpromising circum-

292

stances. His attitude not only dismayed but infuriated Tara. If this was what being a gentleman entailed, then to hell with it!

But even as she poured mental scorn on his attitude she knew her own weakness – it was because Richard was as he was that she loved him; his total variance to anyone she had ever known before was the very thing which attracted her.

So – that was it. Or was it? When the plan had suggested itself to her it had momentarily shocked even her. She was not pregnant, but if she could make him believe that she was . . . The sense of shock subsided, leaving her mind very clear and sharply alert like a live wire brought to humming activity by a surge of electricity. She turned the idea over, looking carefully at each facet. It was possible. She could do it. And afterwards she could explain it all away as a mistake – or worse.

Just so long as he did not say 'wait and see'. If he did it would not only be the end of her plan, it would also mean he did not really care. She would have lost him. Her stomach contracted at the thought.

But he had not said it. Well, not absolutely. It was all right. They were going to be married.

I can make him happy, I know I can, Tara thought. I love him so much. If he only loves me half as much we shall be all right.

The door of the hut opened and Kate came in.

'Tara! What are you doing here? Are you okay?' she asked.

'Sure, I'm fine,' Tara said, wondering whether she should tell Kate the news here and now, then deciding against it. Better to wait until Richard had made some plans and everything was a little more definite. They would know, all of them, soon enough. And how surprised they would be!

*

Colonel Adamson straightened himself to an upright position in his chair, easing his damp shirt away from his sweating back with fingers that were beginning to turn yellow from tobacco stains. Before the war he had almost managed to give up smoking, now, dammit, the strain of duty in the tropical conditions of the Northern Territory had undone all the work his will power had done for him. Cursing himself he reached for the packet lying open on the desk, took one and lit it before remembering Richard, sitting opposite him.

'Sorry, Allingham – do you want one?' Richard shook his head and Colonel Adamson felt a stirring of bad-tempered dislike. Bloody self-righteous young sod! 'Now what was it you were saying? You have a request to make? Well, no need to be so formal. Just spit it out.'

'Very well, sir.' Richard hesitated only briefly. 'I want to get married.'

The words caught the Colonel at the moment of inhaling; he spluttered slightly and the smoke came out in a cloud temporarily obscuring his vision.

'Married. Married, eh! Well, well, you do surprise me, Allingham. I didn't realize you had a serious young lady. Someone at home in Melbourne, is it?'

'No, sir. She will need your permission to marry too. It's Tara. Tara Kelly.'

'Good God.' The words were out before he could stop them; he looked at Richard with a mixture of admiration and disbelief. 'I knew you'd been seeing her, of course, but I never dreamed . . . Good God!'

Richard's face showed no hint of emotion. 'As we are both on active service, sir, I realize we shall need not only your permission and Matron's, but also that of the General Officer Commanding. But naturally I am speaking to you first before putting it in writing.'

'I see.'

'The thing is, sir, we would like to make it as soon as possible.'

'Yes. I see.' The first numbness of the shock was passing

294

a little; Colonal Adamson's eyes narrowed shrewdly. 'Everything is all right and above board, is it?' he asked and thought he saw a slight shadow pass over Richard's handsome features, but it was only momentary.

'Of course.'

'Yes. Well. It's a good thing we have the church here at the hospital then, isn't it? A fine job that church. I must say I am proud of it.'

Since 138 AGH had moved to the Adelaide River some of the men had used their spare time erecting a building of bamboo which could be used as a church by all the denominations on the site, and the sisters had put their talents to making kneelers, altar cloths and screens.

'Yes, we should like to be married in the hospital church,' Richard said.

'Hmm.' Adamson drew on his cigarette, his fingers trembling slightly. That little minx! he was thinking. No wonder she turned down the offer of working for me – she had other fish to fry and her sights set on something a little more permanent! 'Well,' he said aloud, 'you will have no objection from me, of course. And I don't foresee any stumbling blocks being placed in your way by higher authority, either. There is just one small problem, though. You'll be looking for some leave, no doubt, to have a honeymoon.'

Again, he saw that small flickering shadow and wondered about it.

'Well, yes – though of course we quite understand . . .'

'The point, Allingham, is this. I've received another piece of news today and under the circumstances I'll tell you about it, though I'll be grateful if you will keep it under your bonnet for the moment. We are on the move again.'

'We are?'

'Yes. 138 is being posted to Queensland. There is a lot of activity there. As you know the war in New Guinea has hotted up considerably and quite apart from all the units in the area, it's a first staging post for wounded men being brought back from the field hospitals across the water. I can't see that you could be granted leave until we've settled in there. All hands will be needed to help make the move go as efficiently as possible.'

'And when do you expect the move to be?' Richard asked.

'More or less immediately after Christmas.' He stubbed out his cigarette, looking at Richard steadily. 'I would say this, however, I expect we can work something out so that you and Tara,' his tongue slid smoothly over her name, 'so that you and Tara could have a day or two at least away somewhere in the vicinity.'

'That's very kind of you, sir,' Richard said.

'Right.' The CO moved abruptly. 'I expect when this gets out there will be great excitement in the camp.' He rose and when Richard followed suit he extended his hand. 'All that remains is for me to offer you my congratulations and wish you well. You are a lucky man, Allingham.'

'Thank you, sir.'

When Richard had left the CO sat staring into space for a few minutes.

Yes, you are a lucky man, he repeated softly. Though marrying her – I'm not so sure about that . . .

The perspiration began to trickle down his back again and the feel of it annoyed him even more than usual. Damn bloody place. He'd be glad to get to Queensland – though by all accounts that was just as bad.

Colonel Adamson snorted irritably and stretched out his hand for another cigarette.

*

'For heaven's sake, Tara, will you keep still for just a minute!' Kate, on her knees in the middle of the sisters' dormitory block, spoke in half-amusement, half-exasperation, through a mouthful of pins.

'Sorry – I'm just trying to see what I look like, that's all!'

Tara, standing on a chair at her elbow, pulled a demure face and froze, still as a statue. 'How's that – better?'

'Uh-huh!' Kate grunted. She worked quietly for a moment, then sat back on her heels, taking the remaining pins out of her mouth and dropping them into the lozenge tin beside her. 'You can get down and have a look at yourself now – just as long as you're careful. But if you burst a seam or pull that hem down again, I'll cheerfully murder you!'

June Day got up from the bed where she had been sitting to watch proceedings, took Tara's hand and helped her down from the chair.

'Stay there, I'll bring the mirror to you,' she offered. 'The light is better over here.'

Tara stood quite still, almost afraid to move. Each time she did a pin dug sharply into her waist and besides this, in spite of her excited wriggling a moment ago, she was terrified of spoiling Kate's handiwork. June lugged the long mirror down the aisle between the beds and Tara almost gasped as she caught sight of her reflection.

Was it really her, standing there in a fairytale creation of white lace? Yes, that was unmistakably her face above the cutaway 'sweetheart' neckline – and her sensible lace-up shoes peeping from beneath the full crinoline of the skirt.

As if following her gaze Kate frowned. 'We shall have to do something about your shoes. They spoil the effect completely. You haven't got any, you say?'

Tara shook her head and a pin dug into the base of her neck. 'No. My one and only civilian pair went mildewed months ago.'

'The way most things do in the Wet.' Kate sounded thoughtful. 'And the pair Mrs King sent to go with the dress are too big on you.'

'To be honest, I think Mrs King would make two of me,' Tara said, then added hastily, 'not that I'm complaining, mind you. I think it was fantastic of her to offer to loan me the dress. If it belonged to me I don't think I'd ever let it out of my sight.'

'You would. You'd do just the same, Tara,' June said. 'We all would. A wedding is just what we need to cheer us up, isn't it, Kate?'

Kate did not reply. Her small freckled face was as serious as ever and momentarily Tara wondered if she was thinking of her fiancé and whether her own wedding would ever take place. But she had been marvellous, they all had, rallying round and enjoying the preparations from the moment they heard the news. It was the first time in the short history of 138 AGH that there had been a wedding in the hospital and everyone had wanted to be a part of the preparations.

Tara knew – though it was supposed to be a secret – that three Christmas cakes of varying sizes had been donated by their owners to be formed into a wedding cake, the hospital cook was busy fixing them into tiers by using the cardboard cylinders from the centre of Elastoplast rolls as supports, icing them over and decorating them with loving care. When he had come to visit Reg – now thankfully almost recovered – Bluey had been asked if he could spare flowers to decorate the church and assured the deputation that they could have free rein to take whatever was needed, and arrangements had been made for a unit band to play for the evening celebrations which would follow the ceremony. But most exciting of all had been the arrival of the dress.

Tara had quite resigned herself to being married in uniform, but one evening Grace had returned from a duty south on Leaping Lena and burst into the mess where the sisters were eating dinner bearing a huge cardboard box.

'Just wait till you see what I've got, girls!' she announced.

They had downed knives and forks and crowded round, venturing guesses at what the box contained. But when Grace proudly opened it to reveal yards of white satin and lace the gasps that greeted it were more enthusiastic than ever she could have hoped for.

'A wedding dress!'

298

'Where did you get that?'

'It's beautiful!'

It was. It was also far too large for the petite Tara. Elsie King, a grower's wife, and one of the few women who had been allowed to remain in the Territory, had heard of the wedding and insisted Grace should take it back to Tara to wear for her great day. She was a large-boned woman of the outback and at first when she tried it on Tara could have wept with disappointment. Six inches too long and several sizes too big around. But Elsie had generously agreed that any necessary alterations could be made.

'I shan't be wearing it again,' she had said with a laugh. 'Do whatever you have to to make it fit her – no worries. Just as long as I have it back again to show my grandchildren. If it comes to that I'll be able to kid them along that I used to be as little as that, won't I?'

Kate was the best seamstress at 138 and so she had been delegated to make the necessary alterations. Now, just a few days before the wedding, she was putting the finishing touches to her work – watched by half-a-dozen pairs of envious eyes.

'You'll be a beautiful bride, Tara,' June told her, holding the mirror steady. 'Turn around now and have a look at the back view.'

Tara twirled, the lace skirt swished over the board floor and the watching girls clapped. Kate sat back on her heels, surveying her handiwork with pride.

'We haven't decided what you're going to do about those shoes, Tara.'

Tara surveyed her feet and wrinkled up her nose thoughtfully. 'I suppose I could stuff paper into the toes of Mrs King's. The trouble is I might fall over my own feet.'

'We can't risk that. Hasn't anybody here with feet your size got a pair of party-going shoes?'

Silence. Most of the girls had travelled around Australia on slow and uncomfortable troop trains carrying their own kit. Party-going shoes were an unthought-of luxury – even if they could have been squeezed in without the knowledge of the authorities.

Claire Dober, a pretty dark-haired sister, sat up on her bed, swinging her feet up beneath her. 'I've got friends in the Alice. There are still civilian women there. Maybe if I sent an SOS we could get a pair sent up on the convoy.'

There was a general murmur of agreement.

'We'll leave that with you then, Claire,' Grace said. As provider of the dress she was naturally taking charge of making sure it was shown to its best advantage. 'Now let's see you in the veil as well, Tara. We want to make sure we can fix the head-dress properly.

Out of the box came the veil, another froth of white lace, and the head-dress, a simple circlet of orange blossom. Tara stood quite still this time as Kate placed it over her curls, easing it into place and evening out the spread of lace around her shoulders. This time there was a hush. Tara looked so like a fairytale bride that it took the breath away.

'Well, Tara,' June said at last, 'I think we can safely say you'll do.' Her voice sounded slightly choked and her eyes were suspiciously bright.

Entranced as they were by the picture Tara made, none of them noticed the voices as two people approached the hut. The first any of them knew of it was the dragging creak as the door, warped by the wet and the heat, opened and a girl's voice said: 'She's here, I'm sure. You'd better come inside before you drown . . .'

Six pairs of eyes switched from Tara to the door. Six girls' breath came out on a concerted gasp of horror. Hearing them, Tara swung around and her heart seemed to stop beating.

'Richard!'

He was standing in the doorway behind Marje Curry, the masseuse who had invited him in. Rain was dripping out of his hair and running down his face but he made no move to wipe it away. He might, Tara thought, have been turned to stone – so might they all as they stared at him, frozen by horror. Then June was on her feet, diving towards the door.

'Get out! Go on – get out of here! Don't you know it's unlucky to see the bride in her dress before the day?'

'Oh I'm sorry! I didn't know she was . . .' He backed out and Grace slammed the door behind him, turning angrily on Marje.

'What the hell were you thinking of, bringing him here?'

'How was I to know she was trying on her dress?' Marje defended herself. 'He was looking for her and it's bloody wet outside.'

'Well you've done it now, haven't you?' June stormed. 'Of all the bloody silly idiotic dills!' She turned. 'Tara, are you all right?'

Tara had not moved. She stood as immobile as Richard had done, fingers pressed to her mouth, eyes wide.

'Don't let it worry you.' That was Kate, always quietly matter-of-fact.

'But – he saw me.' Tara's voice was shocked.

'Yes. It's a darned shame but there it is. What's done can't be undone.'

'He saw me! He shouldn't have seen me!'

'No, but as Kate says it's no use crying over what can't be altered. And all that other stuff is just superstition. I mean, I know I said it's unlucky, but that's just an old wives' tale to keep your dress a secret. It doesn't mean anything,' June comforted.

Tara could not answer. A dread she could not explain was welling up inside her. Partly, perhaps, it had to do with the superstition. Old wives' tale or not, Tara's Irish blood made her less sceptical than some when it came to superstitions. But it was not only that. It also had to do with the look on Richard's face as he had seen her standing there.

He hadn't just been surprised. He had been shocked. Shocked to his upright moral core because she was wearing viginal white, perhaps. And shocked because he had suddenly been brought face to face with the reality of what was happening.

In a dream Tara raised her hands to her head,

301

removing the circlet of orange blossom and the cloud of white lace. And as she laid it down in its box she found herself wishing that she would never have to put it on again.

*

Richard and Tara walked down the track just out of sight of the hospital. The rain had stopped but the vegetation and the ground still steamed, filling the air with suffocating mist. Tara reached for a bloodwood leaf, pulling it down as she walked, and moisture sprayed from it, splashing her face with a damp film.

'There's something I have to tell you,' she said. 'I'm not going to have a baby.'

For a moment there was no sound but the chirping of crickets and grasshoppers and the croak of the frogs.

'So you see you don't have to marry me after all, if you don't want to,' she said.

It was the night before the wedding and all day she had been nerving herself up for this moment. She had known really the moment she saw his face on the previous evening that she had to do it – she could not go through with this, could not go ahead and trick him into marrying her. Much as she wanted to be his wife, certain as she was she could make him happy, she simply could not do it. She looked at him now and thought she saw a shadow lift from his eyes.

'I see,' he said quietly.

She felt numbed as if all emotions were muffled, but somewhere deep within she could feel her heart beating uncomfortably fast and when she spoke there was a tremble in her voice.

'I made a mistake. I don't know why it happened. I'm always so regular I was sure . . .'

'Maybe it was because you were anxious,' he suggested. 'Emotional disturbances can upset the cycle.'

'Maybe that's what it was.' She couldn't look at him

now. 'Anyway, if you want to call it off I shall understand.'

He stopped walking, caught her hands and turned her to face him. 'Do you want to call it off?'

She still could not meet his eyes. 'I don't want to feel I've forced you.'

'You haven't answered my question. Do you want to call it off?'

The tears were there behind her eyes. All day they had been threatening, now she felt them prick more urgently.

'No, of course I don't want to call it off.'

'Well, in that case . . .' he paused. 'In that case I think we should go ahead with the wedding as planned.'

'But you don't *have* to.'

'Tara, I never *had* to. Oh, I know what I said about my responsibilities and everything and I meant it. But I always had my doubts that you were pregnant. It was much too soon to know for sure – so many things, as I say, can play havoc with your cycle.'

'Then why . . . ?'

'It was possible, for goodness' sake. I wanted to play safe. Better to go ahead and plan the wedding than leave it until it would be obvious to everyone. But, by the same token, I can hardly go to the CO now and say we're calling it off – we only asked permission to marry because we thought Tara was going to have a baby.'

'Oh.' Her voice was small and mortified. 'And that's the only reason you don't want to call it off?'

'Tara!' He held both her hands in one of his and with his free hand stroked the curls away from her forehead. 'Of course it's not the only reason. What the hell sort of a marriage would that be? No – you know what my feelings were about taking on responsibilities while this damned war lasts but I suppose I've come to terms with that now. Other men do it – what's so special about me? Or rather, what's wrong with me that I can't cope with that kind of situation. You can cope, I'm certain of that. You're strong, Tara.'

'Sometimes I don't feel very strong.'

'Maybe not, but you are. Where did it come from, that strength? Your Irish blood maybe. Or . . .'

'Yes, well, maybe you're right,' Tara said hastily. 'But I just couldn't live with thinking you only married me because you thought it was the right thing to do.'

'Believe me, it's not just that.'

'You mean – you do love me?'

Rain began to patter onto the branches again.

'Yes.'

'Oh Richard! Oh . . . Richard . . .'

Those threatening tears overflowed and began to run down her cheeks, mingling with the rain. But they were happy tears. Oh thank you, Holy Mother, thank you, thank you! I don't deserve it, I don't, I'm so wicked. But thank you, thank you!

'We had better get back,' Richard said.

He took her hand and they ran together between the dripping trees. At the door of the hut he kissed her again quickly and lightly.

'I'll see you in church tomorrow.'

'Yes.'

She stood in the doorway and watched until the mist had swallowed him up. And it was only then that she realized he had only replied 'Yes' when she had asked her last question. He had not said: 'Yes – I love you.'

*

The tiny bamboo church was packed to overflowing and those who could not get in stood outside waiting expectantly. As she crossed the clearing, holding her dress well up to prevent it from trailing in the mud, Tara saw them through a haze.

'Lucky the rain has held off for you, m'dear,' Colonel Adamson said, ushering her between them. He was his usual bluff self this afternoon, putting his private feelings under lock and key in his determination to make a good job of his key role – giving the bride away.

'Yes,' Tara said. She felt breathless, just as she did before going on stage for a performance. And this was just what this was, of course – the performance of her life.

As they went in through the doors the perfume of the flowers wafted out to meet them – flowers that had been banked in every available nook and cranny, roses, wild orchids and lilies in the window ledges and against the pillars, and a great pitcher of bouganvillaea beside the altar rail. The padre met them at the door, a nod from him and Grace Dunwoody began thumping out the Bridal March on the upright piano which had come down the track from Darwin after the evacuation.

Tara looked at the tightly packed rows of chairs and saw only a sea of faces turned towards her. Only one was clear – the face of Richard as he stood at the altar rail waiting for her. She bit her lip, emotion welling, but as she reached his side he smiled, his gentle warm smile, and she smiled back.

'Dearly beloved . . .' The padre's voice filled the tiny church and the congregation was hushed. Somewhere near the rear a sister blew her nose loudly but Tara did not hear it and those who did were too choked emotionally themselves to blame her. The service seemed to be going by so fast yet the familiar words took on fresh and important meaning for all those who heard them. Richard spoke his vows slowly and clearly; Tara, for all her stage experience, found herself whispering hers. Then the ring was on her finger – the ring which had arrived just in time, on the same convoy as the pair of shoes Tara was wearing – and the congregation were joining in with the final stirring hymn.

> Grant them the joy which brightens earthly sorrow,
> Grant them the peace which calms all earthly strife;
> And to life's day the glorious unknown morrow
> That dawns upon eternal love and life.

They turned to walk back down the aisle between the rows of chairs and Richard's arm felt very strong and steady beneath her hand. Glancing at him proudly she thought how very handsome he looked in his freshly pressed uniform. Then they were out of the church again, with the warm damp air clinging to their faces like a sponge, and into a barrage of confetti thrown by those waiting outside. This was one preparation they had managed to keep a secret from Tara – and no one was prepared to admit just how much toilet paper had had to be painstakingly cut into tiny squares to produce this hail of celebration. Someone was taking photographs – Tara laughed for the camera, all her pent up emotion released now into a blaze of happiness.

'Come on, hurry up with those photos,' someone shouted. 'The rain is not going to hold off much longer!'

Tara looked up at Richard and smiled. She hardly needed a photograph to remind her. This was a day that would remain etched clearly in her memory to the end of her days.

And it was not over yet. There was still the reception in the officers' mess, with mounds of sandwiches and that beautifully decorated cake, and then the dance – they would have to put in an appearance, at least.

Then and only then could they slip away to the isolated bush camp which had been placed at their disposal for two nights. It was all very special, very wonderful.

Oh I'll never forget, thought Tara, smiling, sparkly-eyed, for the camera one more time. Never, never. No, I'll never forget.

Chapter Seventeen

Two weeks after Tara and Richard were married 138 AGH moved to Queensland but, as Colonel Adamson remarked tetchily to Matron Swift, it looked as if they had arrived two months too early!

A new hospital was under construction and no doubt when it was completed it would be marvellously cool, efficient and convenient. But when the advance party from 138 trundled in the timber huts had barely begun to rise above the stumps that would support them Queensland style, and when the rest of the hospital arrived they found themselves still nursing in tent wards and quartered in a commandeered school building infested with huge dark brown cockroaches.

But at least the weather was a relief, especially to the long-suffering Colonel. Hot it still was, scorchingly blisteringly hot, but without the constant rain of the Adelaide River that was bearable – pleasant, almost!

When she knew the hospital was moving to Queensland, Tara had hopes that their honeymoon leave might be spent on the beaches of the Gold Coast or exploring the Great Barrier Reef. But Richard had other ideas. He had told her about them in their quiet hideaway bush camp back in the Northern Territory.

'If we get a ten day pass we could easily make it home to Melbourne.'

Tara's heart had sunk at the thought.

'Could we?'

'Certainly. Two or three days there and the same back – we would still have plenty of time. Don't look like that, Tara – it's almost two years since I was at home. And I know my family are longing to meet you, too.'

Tara's heart sank lower still.

'I don't think my mother will ever get used to the idea that I have married a girl she has never even seen, or that she couldn't be there to have a little weep into a lace hanky when we said "I do".'

'She'll probably hold it against me,' Tara said morosely.

'Of course she won't. She'll be tickled to death to have a daughter-in-law once she has got used to the idea. And knowing you, you'll have her eating out of your hand in no time at all.'

Tara had smiled wanly, reaching out to run a teasing finger down Richard's bare arm in the hope of bringing about a change of subject. But he merely caught her hand and held it, smoothing it with his fingers in the manner she was coming to know.

'It's a fairly easy journey from where we'll be,' he went on. 'Brisbane to Sydney, Sydney to Albury, then onto the Victorian train and home. You see, I have it all worked out!'

Tara pulled her hand away and rolled over onto her side. Sydney. Holy Mary! She had tried to get as far away from Sydney as she could and he was taking her back.

Misunderstanding her gesture he put a hand on her neck beneath the damp tumbled curls.

'I'm sorry, I almost forgot you have a home too. We could always spend a couple of days in Sydney if you would like to.'

'No!' The fear was clear in Tara's eyes but her back was towards him and he could not see it. 'No, there's no one I want to see in Sydney any more and that's what counts, isn't it – people, not places.'

'I expect you're right,' he said thoughtfully. 'Though there are some places too I'd give the world to see again. And not only the ones you might expect. Sometimes there will be a place and you'll have forgotten all about it, but it's there all the same, tucked away in your memory, and when something happens to trigger it, it all comes back as clear as if it were yesterday.'

Tara said nothing. When her memories were triggered it was all too often an uncomfortable experience.

'There was a place I used to know when I was a boy,' Richard went on. 'We used to ride out to it, my sister and I. Not a very special place, you might think, just a clump of gums and willows with a creek running through. But it was the spot where it was – with the hills folding round so that you felt enclosed, and the trees would hide you too. It could be anything to me that place, anything I wanted it to be. I used to lie on my back under those trees and pretend . . . oh, all kinds of things. That I was a ship's captain – that was one of my favourites – and the trees were the masts – it was a sailing ship. Or that I was a settler trying to find a way over the Flinders Range – anything but a doctor, like my father! I liked it best when I was out there alone. Eve, my sister, didn't like pretending on her own. She always wanted me to join in her games and she spoiled things.' He stretched and sighed. 'Funny, isn't it – I haven't thought about that place for years but somehow being out here at the bush camp has reminded me of it. It's got the same sort of feel to it – oh, I'm not very good at describing it but you know what I mean.'

'And I suppose I'm in the way like your sister,' Tara teased. 'Coming between you and your dreams.'

He ran his hand down her shoulder, cupping her breast, and felt the nipple rise at his touch. He curved his body around hers and without turning towards him she nestled in so that they fitted from shoulder to knees like two curved joints. Her curls tickled his chin, her rounded bottom filled the angle between his stomach and thighs. Slowly, with the luxury of a desire that has been satisfied many times in the last twenty-four hours, he ran his hands down her body, exploring every hillock and curve, loving the warmth and the giving which had brought him so much pleasure.

'Not you, Tara,' he said softly. 'You are a part of my dreams.'

She turned towards him, melting inside.

'That is the nicest thing you have ever said to me.'

For a while then there had been no time left for talking but that night, while he slept, she had lain awake thinking about the ordeal ahead of her. What would they be like, Richard's family? And, more importantly, what would they think of her?

In his sleep Richard had stirred, pulling her into his arms, and pleasure and love drove out the fear. She had married the man, not his family, for goodness' sake. And if she couldn't act and put up a good pretence, well, she had no business ever wanting to go on the stage. It wouldn't be for long, after all, just a few days . . .

Back with the AGH, their short break over, there had been little time for worryng about the coming leave in the upheaval of the move to Queensland. But the apprehension began again, a small uncomfortable niggle, as the date of their leave approached and the days fell over themselves to bring it closer. Not the least of her worries was the thought of passing through Sydney. Supposing she should see someone from the old days, someone who would recognize her and rush up to greet her? Worse, pass on to Red the news that she was back, back from wherever it was she had disappeared to. All very well for Richard to talk of half-remembered dreams of his home, for Tara it was the nightmare of the revenge Red would take on her which recurred too often for comfort to disturb her quiet moments.

No use worrying, Tara told herself repeatedly. But one fear, more than all the others, refused to go away. If somehow Red should discover her whereabouts again it might not only be her life that would be in danger. All too clear in her memory was the sight of his men gunning down Jack – Jack, who had committed no crime against Red but be the friend of her own dear Maggie. Ludicrous to suppose Red could carry his jealousy this far, but if he did – might he not also exact revenge upon Richard?

Stop it! Stop it! she told herself. Red is in gaol. He is not going to find you. You are Mrs Richard Allingham now –

all you have to do is to concentrate on being a good wife –
when the army gives you the chance.

And that includes every single one of the next ten days!

*

'Well, this is it, Tara. Almost there.'

As the taxi sped along the straight country road that cut
through the expanse of rolling green Victorian countryside Richard reached for her hand and smiled at the
pleasure written all over her face. 'Now you can see why I
was so anxious to come home.'

'It's gorgeous,' Tara said, looking out at the rolling
hills, dotted with boulders, the clumps of trees and the
dells and hollows between. They passed a creek running
down a broad valley to meet the road and beneath the
trees the cattle stood, ankle deep in the little water that the
drought had left in it, idly swishing their tails against the
constant bombardment of flies. Above the hills the sky
was clear unbroken blue; behind them, when she turned
to look out of the rear window of the car, the high distant
ranges also looked blue, but a shade of misty purple that
might almost have been described as violet. Lovely,
lovely, a reflection, really, of Richard himself. Yes, it was
easy here to picture him as a small boy, riding his horse
and dreaming his dreams, easy to see how he had grown
into the man he now was, all moderation and the perfect
gentleman. And impossible, almost, to understand the
fears that had plagued her on the journey.

They had proved to be groundless in any case, hadn't
they? The train had been packed with service personnel,
so had the great domed building that was Sydney's central
railway station. The faces above the uniforms had been
anonymous, all of them, and Tara had taken comfort in
the fact that she and Richard must look anonymous too.
Who would think of looking for Tara Kelly in AAMWS
khaki? Certainly not Red Maloney! As tiredness brought
on by the long hot journey ate into her bones Tara found

311

the idea more and more ludicrous. Red was nothing. The only worry of any importance was when she would be able to get some sleep.

Now, however, the clear Victorian air seemed to have given her a second wind. She leaned her shoulder against Richard's, drinking it in with delight. A few miles further and he leaned forward, giving the driver instructions.

'Turn off the road here – that's it – and about another five miles.'

The driver swung the wheel without answering. Tara guessed he was offended that Richard was travelling in the back with her, not up in front where the two men could have a good discussion about the war, but she did not care. It was too good to feel like a couple with Richard, too good to feel the line of his body beside hers and to have eye contact when she turned to look at him, eye contact so close and intimate that it started little shivers deep in the pit of her stomach.

'That's it there,' Richard said.

The house looked golden in the bright sunshine, roses and virginia creeper covered the walls, the shutters, half-closed against the afternoon sun, looked like sleepy brown eyes. Two kelpies had been sunning themselves at the foot of the veranda steps, now they came running towards the car and their colouring seemed to match that of the house – brownish – brownish-tan coats, creamy paws and chests.

Richard paid the driver and they got out, walking down between the white picket that edged the paddocks and the flower beds, bright with roses and geraniums, to the broad expanse of green which fronted the house. Closer, and Tara thought she saw a shadow on the veranda; a nerve tightened in her throat. Closer still, and the shadow materialized – a tall slender figure in a floral silk dress of blues and mauves.

'Mother,' Richard said. There was pleasure in his voice but no excitement. Tara had half expected him to run to her, swinging her up in his arms. But that was not his way –

nor apparently hers. She came down the steps quickly but not urgently, smiling and holding out her hands to them. The sun glinted on hair as fair as Richard's, though now faded slightly and streaked with silver, and Tara's first thought was how like his mother he was – the clear clean lines of his face were obviously inherited from her.

'Richard, darling. And this must be Tara.'

Cool hands took Tara's hot ones and she bent forward, kissing her once on each cheek. 'How lovely to meet you.'

'And you,' Tara said. She felt awkward.

'You must be exhausted. We didn't know when to expect you.' Mrs Allingham extended her cheek to Richard also and Tara recognized her feeling of discomfort. *This* was what she couldn't get used to in Richard – this restraint. Clearly inherited from his mother along with his looks. Momentarily, Tara found herself comparing it with the welcome Maggie would have given them – all hugs and happy tears.

'Oh Mother, it's good to be here. You don't know!' Richard said.

'How long has it taken you? Two days? Three?' She glanced at the kit bag Richard was carrying. 'Is that all the luggage you have?'

'Yes, we travelled light. The army marches on its stomach,' Richard joked.

'Let's go into the house.' Mrs Allingham took Tara's arm, linking it through hers. They walked towards the veranda, the kelpies at their heels. 'We'll have a lovely cool drink. Unless you want a bath first. I expect you can't wait to change.'

'You still have enough water for baths, have you?' Richard asked.

'Yes – thanks to the tanks. Your father always said they would last us ten years. Let's just hope we don't have to put that to the test.'

It was cool in the house, cool and gracious. A maid served lemonade poured into tall glasses over chunks of ice. Richard and his mother chatted, the kind of slightly stilted conversation which comes from having so much ground to cover that it is impossible to know where to begin, and Tara sat quietly on the green velvet chaise, taking in the opulence of her surroundings. This was what she had married into, this genteel world of plenty, so different to her own. It was wonderful, better than she had imagined it even, and yet . . . Oh, for just a little of the spontaneity that had abounded with Maggie . . .

You can't have everything, Tara scolded herself silently.

She drained her glass and set it down on a leather-topped octagonal table.

'Well, Richard – are you going to show Tara to your room?' Mrs Allingham asked.

Richard rose, Tara followed suit.

'Yes, we'll have that bath, I think, and then perhaps Tara would like a rest before dinner. We've had to sit and stand the entire way.'

'Of course.' Mrs Allingham rose too, crossing and taking Tara by the hands once more.

'We'll have a lovely long talk later and get to know one another properly, won't we?' she said. 'I am sure we are going to be great friends. Welcome, my dear daugher.'

But the smile did not quite reach her eyes and Tara knew that what Richard had said was true.

It would be a long time before his mother felt truly able to accept her.

*

'Tara – are you going to stay in that bath all night?' Richard's voice from the other side of the door was amused and just a little impatient.

Tara stretched out luxuriously in the warm scented water and felt a clutch of bubbles tickle up her back.

'You can come in if you want to. The door is not locked.'

He pushed it open and she slid down deeper so that the bubbles reached her chin.

'Tara Allingham, I am beginning to think you married that bath, not me,' he teased. 'The number of times you've used it since we have been here you'll be getting through my father's ten years' supply of water in a week!'

'I know. But it is such heaven!' Tara said happily. 'I'd almost forgotten just what heaven a bath can be.'

He removed her underclothing from the wicker chair, laid it down on the carpeted floor, and sat down.

'I know. Return to civilization. You've enjoyed it, haven't you?'

'Oh yes, I have. It's been marvellous. The best week of my life.'

And that at least, she thought, was no exaggeration. From the somewhat unpromising start things had just got better and better, the closest thing to heaven on earth that she had ever experienced.

To begin with there was the house. After the spartan conditions of 138 AGH the luxurious Allingham home was like paradise itself – the large, light living rooms, furnished for elegance as well as comfort, the veranda where they sat each evening to enjoy the sunsets, the fresh flowers everywhere bringing the scent of the garden into the house. Richard's room, which was now hers also, offered the kind of comfort and privacy she thought had gone forever, with its big feather bed, mirrored furniture – and this en suite bathroom which was theirs alone. At first glance it had appeared luxurious but impersonal, a room kept tidy for its occupant who had not lived in it for almost two years, but then she had seen the mementoes – the trophies, team photographs and the cricketing cap on a shelf above the dressing table, the small plastic battleship tucked away behind the bottles in the bathroom cabinet – and had felt close to the boy and young man Richard had once been.

Then there was the food. Months of stew and meat puddings in the mess had dulled Tara's palate – she had almost forgotten the near sensual pleasure which good food imaginatively prepared could be. The Allinghams'

315

cook-housekeeper was a genius, meeting the problems of shortages as a challenge; the smells that wafted from her kitchen made the mouth water and her sweets were enough to tempt even the most figure-conscious to indulge in an orgy of eating – feather-light sponge cakes with passion fruit icing, chocolate-soaked lamingtons rolled in coconut, pavlova crisp on the outside yet melt-in-the-mouth inside and dripping with raspberries and cream. Tara asked no questions as to where it had come from, she simply enjoyed every mouthful and in doing so made a friend of the woman who, after years of working for the Allinghams and watching Richard grow up, had been determined to disapprove of his choice of wife.

Even Richard's parents Tara had found less daunting than she had expected. Mrs Allingham was hard to adjust to, it was true, with her reserved manner and practised niceties, and after almost a week Tara felt no closer to her. But she had formed an instant rapport with Richard's father even though, with a full work load at his Melbourne hospital, he was able to spend little time at home. A big bluff man with gentle hands he made her feel instantly welcome – there were no awkward questions, no attempts to impress, and she thought fondly that perhaps as he grew older Richard would come to resemble him more closely. His sister, Eve, she quite liked too; though she embodied some of her mother's reserve, there was also her father's warmth. She had come one day to visit and they had all spent a pleasant afternoon lazing by the pool, drinking iced lemonade and swimming – thank heavens Red had taught her to do a passable crawl.

But, best of all had been the luxury of time to spare with Richard, to be alone together and enjoy the closeness which had come with a wedding ring upon her finger. To have him there beside her holding her hand as they watched the sunset, to see his eyes smiling at her across the table at dinner, to lie beside him in the big feather bed and watch him sleep. And to close the door behind them and know that the expression of their love could be private and legal, passionate as well as warm, absolutely, perfectly, marvellously right.

She smiled at him now as she lay there in the bubbles in the bath tub and held out her hand. 'Why not come on in – the water is lovely!'

'An invitation like that might be difficult to refuse.'

'Why refuse it then? I'll make room for you.' She sat up. Her body was rosy from the water; bubbles still clung to her nipples and across the line of her shoulders.

'Tara Allingham you are a minx. I have no intention of taking another bath tonight.' But she could see the way he was looking at her and she stood up, reaching for the towel and stepping out onto the soft carpet.

'Come here,' he said.

She wrapped the towel around her, teasing him.

'Oh no, you had your chance.'

'Come here, I said.'

He reached for her; she sidestepped. 'No!'

He stood up and came towards her; she danced away, laughing. 'You'll have to catch me.'

'Oh, I'll do that all right!'

She skipped into the bedroom and he followed, cornering her by the door.

'Now where are you going?'

'I don't know.' Her face was flushed, her curls clustered around it damply. He tugged at the towel; she held on to it. He scooped her up in his arms then, carrying her bodily to the bed and dumping her there unceremoniously. She was still laughing. Then, as she watched him shed his clothes, the laughter died and the surge of familiar desire began. She reached up for him pulling him down on top of her. Her fingers clawed his back and she arched towards him sobbing deep in her throat as he entered her.

When it was over she still held him tight between her thighs, reluctant to relinquish the closeness.

'Are you glad you married me?'

'Of course I am.'

'And you do love me?'

'Why do you keep asking that?'

'Because I like to hear you say so. You do, don't you?'

'Yes.' He rolled away. 'I hope you didn't pull the plug out of the bath because now you need another before dinner – and so do I. Come on, Mother will wonder what we've been up to if we're late.'

'She'll guess, surely,' she said mischievously. 'We are newly-weds.'

'There's no need to advertise the fact.' He moved to the connecting door to the bathroom. She lay for a moment watching him, loving the long clean lines of his body, then she rose herself and followed him into the bathroom. The water was still warm though most of the bubbles had dispersed. They took opposite ends of the tub, washing quickly this time.

Back in the bedroom Tara slipped into clean dimity underwear and one of the dresses Richard had bought her on a trip into Melbourne – oh, what luxury it was after her uniform and regulation issue bloomers!

'I've been thinking.' Richard was buttoning his shirt as he spoke. 'There's something we really should do while we are here.'

'What's that?' She leaned towards the dressing table mirror, applying lipstick.

'Look up Alys Peterson. She lives in Melbourne, doesn't she?'

Tara froze. In the mirror she could see Richard reflected; he was tucking his shirt into linen slacks, seemingly unaware of the turmoil he had begun in her.

'You think so?' Her voice was breathy and uneven.

'It would be nice to know how she is getting on. She had a pretty rough deal, that girl, what with one thing and another. And while we're so close, why not?'

Tara could not answer. A dozen reasons why not were flapping around inside her but they were all nebulous and she could not put them into words. I don't like the way you look at her, would sound childish. You must have hundreds of friends here – you haven't suggested looking

318

any of them up so why her? would sound churlish. And the
other objections were all allied, all more connected with
gut feeling than with reason.

'I'll give her a call, shall I?' Richard asked. 'Perhaps we
could meet her for dinner or something.'

'Wouldn't that offend your mother?' Tara ventured.
'We only have a few days left after all.'

He reached past her for the tortoiseshell-backed brush
which lay on the dressing table and smoothed his hair into
place.

'Mother isn't the possessive type – that's one thing she
is not. Now, are you nearly ready? It's past seven . . .'

Tara screwed the top back onto her lipstick, dashed it
down onto the dressing table and stood up, lifting her chin
with a characteristic movement.

'Yes,' she said and had he noticed it the defiance was
there in her voice as well. 'Yes, I'm ready.'

*

She could not follow him when he went to telephone – she
wanted to but could not. His mother was regaling her with
the story of an old friend who, in spite of living in the city,
was having problems having groceries delivered.

'The poor dear lives alone with no servants and no car
and she is having to carry her shopping home herself in a
string bag. A string bag, imagine it! But at least the bag is
light and no weight to carry on the way to the store. And
she says with all the shortages it's quite often light coming
home as well! What is the world coming to?'

The door clicked open and Tara glanced up quickly.

'That's it then,' Richard said.

She experienced profound relief. 'You couldn't get her.'

'Couldn't get who?' Mrs Allingham enquired.

'A young Melbourne woman we knew in Darwin,'
Richard explained. 'And yes, I did get her. She was
delighted to hear from us. Mother, you won't mind if we
eat out tomorrow evening, will you?'

'Of course not, dear. You and Tara should be having some fun. Goodness knows you'll be back to grim reality soon enough.'

'That's all right, then. I expect you'll be pleased to see her again, Tara. She sounded thrilled at the prospect of seeing you.'

'Yes, of course,' Tara said falsely. 'It really does sound like the most incredible evening.'

And that, she thought, was the most accurate way she could think of to describe it.

Chapter Eighteen

Alys Peterson put down the telephone and stood looking at it for a moment as if she still could not believe she was not dreaming.

Richard Allingham here in Melbourne. And Tara Kelly. No – not Tara Kelly any more, Tara Allingham. They were married. One of those facts alone would have been surprising enough. Taken together, Alys found them almost stupefying.

When Norma had called her to the telephone saying a Mr Allingham wanted her, she could not at first think who she had meant. Then when she heard his voice, low and cultured, she had known. *Richard* Allingham. It had been a shock but a pleasant one.

'Richard! What on earth . . . ?'

And then he had told her. And suggested they should all meet.

'Yes. Yes, of course. Can I bring someone? I have a friend . . . we could make it a foursome.'

There had been just a fractional pause and Richard had agreed. A foursome would be splendid.

Alys reached for the phone again thinking, Thank heavens for John! It would be lovely to see Richard and Tara again but she would have felt very much the odd one out with them on their honeymoon. In fact, thank heavens for John full stop. Having him around had made all the difference these past weeks between feeling lonely and frustrated and enjoying life again in a way she had thought impossible while she was still trapped here in Toorak. As she dialled his number Alys remembered the moment when things had begun to brighten.

It had been two days after the altercation with her mother when Frances had tried, yet again, to tighten the screw of emotional blackmail. Alys had spent them in an abyss of depression, unusual for her, but after the glimpse of sunshine when she had spent a few enjoyable hours with John, the prospect of being returned to the prison of loneliness had been almost too much to bear. How long did she have to go on paying Alys she had wondered bitterly. Yet she had not dared to risk upsetting Frances, ridiculous as her objection to Alys' friendship was.

She had been in the bathroom washing her hair when she heard the front doorbell jangle its musical chime. She wound a towel around her head and went to the top of the stairs as Norma opened the door. She could not see the caller but the voice was that of a man. She held onto the banister, craning forward and unwilling to believe what her ears were telling her – it sounded like John.

'Just a moment,' she heard Norma say.

She dived across the landing and into her room, looking out of the window, and her heart came into her mouth as she saw the Buick drawn up on the drive. It was John! She reached for her wrap and slipped it on, twisted the towel more tightly round her head and hurried down the stairs. She had to get him away from here before Frances became upset again!

As she ran down the stairs he came into view bit by bit. First his boots, then his well-tailored lightweight slacks, then . . .

He was carrying an enormous bouquet of flowers. Roses, orchids, something fine and feathery which spread out like a mist behind the bright summer colours. She checked, startled, then ran on. Flowers or no she had to get rid of him. She had reached the hall before the thought struck her – where was Norma? Why had she left John standing there yet not come to call Alys?

'John!'

'Well, hullo there!' He smiled, that twisting 'S' of a smile, but made no attempt to hand her the bouquet. From along the hall, Alys heard Norma say: 'Yes, she will see you now, Mr Hicks.'

322

John touched Alys' arm. 'I thought perhaps I should make your mother's acquaintance,' he said easily. 'Maybe I'll see you afterwards.'

He followed Norma to the drawing room and Alys was left gaping. She heard Norma announce him and then the door closed and there was only the murmur of voices beyond. For a moment she hesitated, then ran back upstairs. No time to dry her hair but at least she could get dressed.

It was ten minutes later when the drawing room door opened again. John emerged and smiled at her.

'Sorry, I can't stay to be sociable now as I have an appointment with my accountant,' he said. 'That will take about an hour. Afterwards, I'd like to buy you lunch – if you'd like it, that is.'

'Thank you, but . . .'

'Don't worry.' His smile broadened and he nudged his head in the direction of the drawing room. 'I've got your mother's permission.'

'Oh!'

'About an hour then?'

She watched him go then hurried into the drawing room. In spite of what John had said she was still afraid of what she might find. But Frances was seated serenely in her chair, the bouquet lying across her knees. As Alys approached her diffidently she raised her eyes from her lap. They looked very bright and shrewd.

'Charming man,' she managed. 'Lovely flowers.'

Alys felt the beginnings of a smile tugging at her own lips.

'I'm glad you think so, Mummy. Shall I put them in water for you?'

Frances nodded and Alys experienced a pang of sympathy. Once Frances had been so talented at flower arranging.

'Hope . . . we may see . . . something . . . of him.' It was as long a speech as Frances had made since the stroke. She looked thoughtful but pleased, like a cat that has got the cream, Alys thought.

Whatever John had said he had worked a miracle.

She had asked him later over lunch in a small but exclusive restaurant, 'What did you say to her? She's absolutely charmed by you.'

He had smiled, crinkling the sun-dried skin at the corners of his eyes.

'I haven't reached the grand old age of fifty-two without learning a little diplomacy.'

'Well, whatever it was, you have done her a world of good – and me! She is actually saying she hopes to see something of you. I hope you realize what you have let yourself in for!'

For answer he had merely refilled her glass from the bottle standing in the ice bucket on the table.

'Maybe I've done for her what you have done for me, Alys. If so, it's a fair exchange. Do you think if I pay her another visit she'll approve of me taking you out sometimes?'

The bubbles tickled Alys' nose and she laughed.

'Oh, I do hope so!'

In the weeks that followed John and Alys had become companions. John was a busy man, under great pressure to run his farm with a reduced labour force, so Alys often drove out to Buchlyvie, riding the paddocks and turning her hand to whatever jobs she could. But, when he was able to come to Melbourne to take her out, he always stopped off to spend a little time with Frances.

'He would make . . . a good husband,' Frances said. Her speech, though stilted, had improved rapidly – suspiciously so, Alys sometimes thought. 'He's too old for you . . . but . . .'

Alys wondered if she should tell her mother that John already had a wife – and thought better of it.

'We are just friends, Mummy,' she assured her. 'We just happen to like one another's company.'

That was no more or less than the truth. Close though they were there was no hint of anything other than friendship between them. They discovered they shared the same sense of humour and they joked and laughed, enjoying the easy communication of humour both had been missing from their lives for too long. They talked about their mutual interests – cars and horses and, inevitably, the war. And sometimes they dropped their guard and revealed a little more of the deeper, secret side of themselves.

'Have you ever been in love, Alys?' John asked her one afternoon.

She was bending over the engine of the Buick, her hair hanging down across her face, and wearing her oldest shirt and shorts. The question was totally unexpected; it stopped something within her momentarily. Yet it did not occur to her that John might be asking because of his own romantic interest. The affinity between them was too warm and platonic for that.

'I'm in love with motor cars, or hadn't you noticed?' she said lightly.

He stood wiping his hands on a rag and looking at her; she had no idea of the picture she made which had prompted the question.

'Yes, I have noticed,' he said. 'I'd have to be blind not to see the way your face lights up when you look at a car. But it should light up like that for a man, too. Hasn't there been anyone?'

She adjusted a tappet, not looking up. 'There was someone once. But that was a long time ago. I don't want to talk about it, John.'

He respected her desire for privacy and did not ask again, and Alys loved him for it, in a way which had nothing to do with romanticism or sexual attraction, the love between two very dear friends.

Christmas had been one of the best she could ever remember. John had had to go to the hospital to spend some time with Anne but had accepted an invitation to eat the main meal of the day with the Petersons. He had arrived during the afternoon and the tired sad look of him told Alys that the visit had been a difficult and trying one.

But after sitting in the garden for a while, relaxing in the warm sunshine, the tension began to fall away and she was glad. What sort of Christmas would it have been for him if he had had to return alone to Buchlyvie where he could do nothing but brood? And what kind of a Christmas would it have been for her without him?

John had brought presents for all the family. There was a handsome leather hip flask for her father, a crystal rose bowl for her mother, a huge Mama doll for Robyn and handmade chocolates for Beverley. But when Alys opened her own present she had to laugh with delight – a gold pendant shaped like a Buick motor car!

'Oh John, how clever! How did you manage to find it?' she asked.

And he had to admit he had had it made especially for her. After that her own present for him, cuff links and tie pin, seemed very ordinary, but he expressed his pleasure and the seal of perfection was set on the day.

Yes, it was good, so good, to have someone to whom she could turn for support and company. Good to have someone who enjoyed *her* company without imposing any restrictions. Good to have someone she could ask along to make up a foursome with Tara and Richard, knowing that he would help cover any slight awkwardness and help make the reunion a success even though he had never met either of them before.

He answered the telephone now himself and she explained the situation.

'Can you make it, John? I know you're busy, but . . .'

'Of course I can make it. It'll be good for you to see old friends.'

'I'm looking forward to it,' she said. But as she replaced the receiver she wondered. *Was* she looking forward to it? Really, she was still so startled by the news she honestly was not sure.

*

Tara was nervous. She had been nervous from the moment she awoke, wondering at first what it was that seemed to be hovering somewhere between her throat and solar plexus like a plate of oysters eaten too late at night. Then she remembered. Tonight she and Richard were going to dine with Alys.

The nervousness remained all day and it was not helped by the fact that Richard, too, seemed tense and a trifle abstracted. Perhaps it was her imagination – or a reflection of her own tension. But somehow she did not think so.

When it was time to get ready Tara took special care over her toilet. Thank heavens for the dress that Richard had bought her! She would have felt so terribly conspicuous meeting Alys and her friend in uniform – though almost everyone seemed to be in uniform these days. She put the dress on and surveyed herself in the mirror – cornflower blue to match her eyes, with a pretty sweetheart neckline and a small peplum that exaggerated the neatness of her waist. Yes, she looked nice – if only she could feel as confident as she appeared.

They drove to Melbourne in one of the family cars. A nerve was catching in Tara's throat as they were ushered into the lounge bar of the restaurant and her eyes skeetered round the couples and groups already there. Oh, but they all looked so grand! Again, Tara thanked heaven for her dress, which on the surface at least, made her one of them.

'It doesn't look as though they are here yet.' Richard checked his watch. 'We're a bit early.'

Tara thought uneasily it might be another sign of Richard's eagerness. But he always liked to be punctual, she comforted herself.

They ordered drinks and sat sipping them, watching the door. After ten minutes or so Richard checked his watch again.

'Perhaps they are not going to come,' Tara said hopefully.

'I'm sure they will – ah! Here they are now!'

Tara looked up. A couple were coming in through the doorway, a young woman with auburn hair falling gracefully to her shoulders, dressed in soft green – unmistakably Alys, though she bore little resemblance to the pale girl close to death whom Tara remembered – and a man in a light-coloured suit. As she took in the silver hair and the weathered face Tara realized with a slight shock that he was considerably older than Alys.

Richard rose and Tara followed suit, setting her glass down on the low table. The nerve was jumping in her throat again. Oh Holy Mary, she was beautiful! There was no other word to describe her. That smile. It seemed to light up her face, making it glow like a stained glass window when the sun shines through.

'Tara! How lovely to see you! Tara – Richard – this is John. Tara saved my life you know.' She took Tara's hands, kissing her on the cheek. 'You are looking marvellous, Tara. Marriage obviously suits you. When I heard the news I simply could not believe it! But I'm very happy for you.'

'You are looking marvellous yourself,' Richard said, and Tara heard and hated the admiration in his voice. 'When I last saw you you were at death's door.' He held out his hand. 'Good to meet you, John. Now, will you have a drink before we go in for dinner? What will it be? Alys?'

But beneath the easy manner Tara sensed something else and felt sick with apprehension.

Over their drinks they chatted, the kind of small talk that people make when they have not seen one another for a very long while, when there is so much to tell but no recent base of intimacy. Tara said little. For once she could think of nothing to say.

When they were shown to their table she panicked again to see the array of silver laid out on the crisp white tablecloth.

Holy Mary, so many knives and forks! She had never seen so many! The menus came, huge leather-bound tomes hung with silk tassels, and when the waiter handed one, ready opened to her, Tara gazed at it in horror. It was all in a foreign language – French she guessed – and not a word of it made any sense to her.

The waiter hovered. 'Yes, madam?'

'Oh, I don't know, it all sounds so nice,' she stalled.

'Well I am having *Consommé Andaluz* followed by the *boeuf en croûte*,' Alys said and Tara leaped in quickly.

'I'll have the same.'

'Thank you. What vegetables madam?'

'*Petit pois* and *champignons*. And perhaps some *haricots verts*.'

'Certainly. And you, Madam?'

'Yes – the same.'

The waiter completed the order and, to Tara's relief, some of the array of cutlery was whisked away. And, by having the same as Alys, she had not only saved herself from having to pronounce the unpronounceable, but she would also be able to see which knives and forks she used.

The soup arrived. Tara crumbled her roll feeling slightly smug. She had learned not to cut it by watching the Allingham family. And the soup spoon at least was clearly recognizable. Thank heavens Alys had chosen soup and not that peculiar looking thing Richard was eating – what was it, artichoke? She spooned some soup towards her, remembered that was incorrect and spooned it away.

By the time they had reached their main course Tara was feeling no more comfortable. How was it they all managed to converse so easily and eat at the same time, whereas she seemed to have her mouth full whenever a question was addressed to her? Trying to get rid of the food and answer without the silence between becoming embarrassing was almost choking her, and she had managed to bite a portion of her inner lip which was already swelling and making her taste blood.

But the other three seemed to be getting along famously, Tara thought, wishing she could feel as much at ease as they did. She tried to spear a pea and it hopped from her plate onto the clean white tablecloth. Mortified she managed to roll it under her plate.

'Tell us about the wedding – I'm longing to hear the details!' Alys said and Tara managed to swallow a mouthful and answer.

By the time dessert was finished and coffee had arrived, accompanied by a plate of tiny delicious petit-fours, the conversation had inevitably turned to the war.

'So you are an AAMWS now, Tara?' Alys asked.

Tara drained the tiny bone china cup. 'Yes. I'm expecting to have to go off on a training course and learn to march and salute and everything. I can't say I'm looking forward to it much.'

Alys laughed. 'I don't suppose you are. We're really showing them, though, aren't we? I don't believe they thought we girls could be of much use in the war, but they are having to revise their opinions!'

'I heard you were thinking of coming back to the Territory, Alys,' Richard said.

Alys popped a crumb of marzipan into her mouth. 'I'd like to get involved again. I feel a fraud, stuck here away from it all, but as things are . . .'

John took a pack of slim cigars from the breast pocket of his suit and offered them to Richard. 'You know what I think you should do, Alys? You should join the AWAS. They are desperate for drivers and someone who knows engines as well as you do would be a tremendous asset.'

'John!' Alys joked. 'I believe you are trying to get rid of me!'

'You know that is the last thing I would want to do. I just think for your own sake you should put yourself first for once.' John turned to Richard. 'It was a lucky day for me when she picked me up beside my broken down Buick – and not just because I was stranded in the back of beyond. She is a great girl.'

'We are certainly aware of that,' Richard agreed – a little too readily, Tara thought.

'I'd have thought that after what you went through you would want to stay as far away from the war as possible,' she said.

John drew on his cigar. 'Just watch out for the convoys. One of these days you might see Alys driving a ten-ton truck.'

'Oh John!' she laughed. 'There's not much danger of that. You know how Mummy would react if I wanted to do something like that!'

'You handle your mother all wrong,' he chided her. 'One of these days I shall speak to her about it – even if it does mean I am cutting my own throat.'

'You'll do nothing of the sort!' Alys reached for his wrist, turning it over so that she could see the face of his watch. 'And sorry as I am to say it, I really think I am going to have to break up this party. Mummy won't go to sleep until she knows I'm home and she does need her rest.'

'Of course.' Richard raised his hand to call for the bill. 'It's been a very pleasant evening. We've enjoyed it, haven't we, Tara?'

'Very much,' Tara lied.

Outside the restaurant they said their goodbyes, Richard shaking John by the hand and repeating how good it had been to meet him.

'And we shall be watching out for the convoys, Alys,' he said, smiling. 'Remember, if you ever get to be an AWAS and find yourself in the vicinity of 138, let us know. It'll be a good long while before we are back in Melbourne, I'm afraid.'

As she slid into the passenger seat of the car beside Richard, Tara heaved a sigh of relief.

'Nice bloke,' Richard said as he pulled out into the stream of traffic. 'Much too old for her though.'

Tara glanced sideways at him but the shadows cast by the passing lights obscured his face and she could not tell what he was thinking.

Perhaps you are wrong, she told herself. Perhaps he

331

doesn't have any thoughts about her beyond that he knew her in Darwin and saved her life. But certain little barbs still niggled at her, joining the one fact that she had known all along and which had been brought home to her more sharply than ever this evening.

Richard and Alys came from the same world. The same self-assured world of plenty and charm and grace.

Act her heart out though she might, Tara was uncomfortably sure she would never really be a part of it.

Chapter Nineteen

On a cold June afternoon Alys drove out to Buchlyvie. She found John in one of the sheds behind the main house trying to repair some farm machinery.

'Goddam war and shortages,' he said, straightening up and aiming a kick at the offending contraption. 'It's busted now beyond repair if you ask me, but I suppose I've got no chance of getting hold of another.'

'Goddam war and petrol rationing!' Alys rejoined. 'Do you know I've been riding around on a bike to save enough petrol to come out and visit you?'

He laughed, wiping his hands on a rag.

'That I would like to have seen. Still, I guess two wheels are better than no wheels at all.'

'And half a farrow will be better than none.'

'You said it.' He tossed the rag into the corner of the shed. 'Come on, let's go in and find something to drink. A nice hot cup of tea would hit the spot.'

'I came to see if I could help, not interrupt you.'

'Rubbish. Besides I won't need your help soon. It looks as if I shall be getting my Land Army girls.'

'Good for you.' She followed him across the yard where the wind blew the dust in small cold flurries and into the house. John looked into the kitchen where Flora, the cook-house-keeper, was preparing the evening meal and asked her to make a pot of tea.

In the living room he subsided into a chair, propping his feet up on an ottoman. Dried mud kicked out from beneath the flat heels of his ankle high boots and fell onto the soft leather cover in a small avalanche and Alys smiled wryly.

This was a man's room, right enough. It was so many years now since a woman had lived in it that it had lost any leaning it might ever have had towards femininity. The furniture was square and functional with no frills and furbelows, the rugs, though clean, bore the scars of being walked over too many times in booted feet, the ornaments and pictures had been reduced to a bare minimum.

Two photographs only dominated the room, standing in their leather frames on the oak sideboard – one studio portrait of an attractive yet slightly drawn-looking woman with a small boy, the other of a young man in uniform. Beneath his slouch hat the young man's face shone with pride; the angles of the nose and chin, the mouth with its half-humorous twist, might almost have been those of a young John.

Seeing her looking at it he smiled faintly.

'He's a good bloke, Stuart.'

'Good looking too,' Alys said. 'Like his father.'

'Aa-ah. Better looking than his old man ever was.'

'I don't believe that.'

'With any luck you'll meet him one day. He's in the thick of it at the moment, though, in the Mubo area. Goddam war.' He was silent for a moment and with the ease of close friends Alys read his thoughts. A few minutes ago he had been complaining about the inconveniences of an unserviceable piece of machinery, whilst the reality of other, irreplaceable, losses lurked so threateningly close to home.

Flora brought the tea on a cane-edged tray and Alys poured. As she handed him his cup she felt John's eyes on her.

'You remember I asked you once if you had ever been in love?'

'Yes, I remember.'

'That doctor we had dinner with in Melbourne – Richard Allingham. Was he the one?'

She experienced a slight sense of shock. It was more than four months since they had had dinner with Richard and Tara – how strange that John should hark back to it now. Besides which . . . Throughout that meal she had

334

been aware of Richard, aware of the same attraction she had felt for him back in Darwin, but she had tried not even to think about it and had been quite confident she had been successful in concealing it. Now she felt a qualm of concern. Had she been that transparent?

John was looking at her steadily; she could feel his eyes on her face, repeating the question – was Richard the one she had been in love with? Alys shook her head, relieved that in all honesty she could say he was not. Though perhaps in other circumstances he might have been . . .

'No, it was much longer ago than that. The man I was in love with was a racing driver.'

'Ah – now I remember! The one who taught you to drive.'

'That's right. He was killed. His name was Race Gratton.' The words flowed smoothly; to her surprise she found she could mention his name without pain.

'That must have been bad for you.'

'It was. I was there. And there was more.' Suddenly, she found herself wanting to tell him about it. 'I was pregnant. I had told him about it just before the race. I blame myself because I can't help feeling his mind was not completely on his driving. I still think – if only I had kept it to myself a little longer he might be alive today.'

'It's no use thinking on those lines. We can all look back at events and think – if only this, if only that!' He drained his cup and set it down, looking at her steadily. 'What happened to the baby?'

'I lost it. They had sent me to Darwin to friends and I stayed there. I didn't want to come back here, ever.' She laughed lightly. 'Yet you see – here I am!'

He reached over, taking her hand, and they sat for a few moments without speaking.

'Life goes on I suppose,' she said. 'I'm glad you weren't shocked, John.'

'It takes a great deal more than that to shock me,' he said with a wry smile. 'And yep, life goes on. One day, Alys, there will be someone else.' His eyes strayed to the

335

photograph and she found herself reading his mind again with the ease that was almost disconcerting. He was hoping that maybe one day she and his son . . .

She stirred, setting down her own cup.

'I'd better be getting back. This was only supposed to be a fleeting visit.'

He stretched. 'And I suppose I'd better have another look at that damned plough. I'm glad you told me, Alys.'

'Yes,' she said. 'So am I.'

On the drive back to Melbourne she felt curiously light-headed, and she knew it was partly because of sharing with John a part of her life which she had kept so very much to herself. But only partly. In a strange way it seemed suddenly that life had opened up again. Nothing had changed. There was still no one to fill the gap Race had left behind in her heart – no one she had any right even to think about in that way. Yet she could see the truth in what John had said. The wound was healing. One day there would be someone else.

She swung the Alfa Romeo through the gates of her home and realized with a slight shock that the drive was crowded. Beverley's car was there – no great surprise. Beverley often drove over in the afternoons. But what was Daddy's car doing home? And that grey Austin – Dr Whitehorn's car . . .

Alys manoeuvred between them quickly and skilfully. Then she braked to a halt and leaped out. Her legs seemed to have turned to jelly. In spite of the wintry weather the front door was not properly closed. Alys pushed it open and ran in.

The first sound she heard was Beverley's weeping and the jelly-like sensation spread from her legs to the whole of her body. The awful sound was coming from the drawing room. She ran towards it, then froze in the doorway at the tableau within – Donald Whitehorn standing as he always seemed to, back to the fireplace; Beverley hunched in a chair; her father in front of the window, staring unseeingly into space.

336

And on the chaise, Frances. A Frances who lay motionless without any of the twitches and jerks that had characterized her last months. A Frances whose face was waxy already, yellowish white apart from a livid discolouration around the forehead and eyes.

Alys stood, holding on to the doorpost for support. She tried to form the words to ask what had happened but her lips refused to obey. Donald Whitehorn looked around as if giving the family the chance to speak first and in the silence Beverley appeared to become aware of Alys' presence.

Her head came up with a jerk, her eyes, washed out with tears, blazed at Alys. Then, the lower half of her face contorted with grief and anger, making her uglier than Alys would ever have believed possible.

'Oh – so you've come home then.' She spat the words out of her wobbling lips. 'You've deigned to come back. But you're too late, aren't you? Too late!'

Again, Alys tried to speak and this time her voice obeyed her. But it was such a tiny voice it seemed scarcely to belong to her.

'What happened?'

'Alys . . .' her father began but Beverley broke in hysterically.

'You may well ask what happened! After you abandoned her, Mummy must have got herself to the lift to go upstairs. And it must have got stuck halfway – it's there now. There was no one to help her, no one. Norma was out and so were you. Poor Mummy must have tried to climb out of the lift and get back downstairs. But she couldn't manage it. She fell. Fell, Alys. All the way down the stairs. I came over to visit. I found her . . .' She disintegrated once more into noisy sobs.

Alys' horrified eyes moved from one to another. When they reached her father he nodded slowly.

'It's true, Alys. Beverley phoned for Dr Whitehorn and for me but there was nothing we could do. By the time we got here . . .' He spread his hands expressively.

337

'Oh no!' Alys pressed trembling fingers to her mouth. 'But where was Norma?'

'This is Wednesday, isn't it? Her afternoon off.'

'Wednesday?' Alys repeated vaguely. The shock seemed to have removed her ability to think coherently. 'Yes, but her afternoon was changed to a Thursday several weeks ago. No, she should have been here.'

'When she does turn up she will be given a moment's notice!' snapped Daniel.

'Oh Daddy, you can't do that!' Alys protested. 'Norma has been wonderful all through Mummy's illness. I'm sure she must have a very good reason . . .'

'Such as you told her she could go!' Beverley's voice was harsh with tears and they all turned to look at her. 'You probably set the whole thing up, Alys!'

Shocked and horrified, Alys could do nothing but stare at her sister.

'What the hell are you saying, Beverley?' Daniel demanded.

'She's been waiting for something like this to happen!' Beverley cried. 'She's never cared about Mummy. I've been here. I've seen. She knew if Mummy died she would be free to go off with her sugar daddy.'

'Beverley!' Daniel thundered.

'It's true!' Beverley insisted. 'You don't know the half of it. Ask her where she's been this afternoon. Ask her!'

'Beverley, please! Have a little respect! That is your mother lying there.'

'Because of her!' Beverley rose, pointing with a melodramatic finger. 'My sister – her own daughter. Well, you got what you wanted, Alys. I only hope it makes you happy.'

She rushed to the door, pushing past Alys in a paroxym of weeping.

Alys stood motionless, her eyes wide and staring.

'Take no notice of her, Alys. She's upset. Naturally we all are . . .' Daniel crossed the room, placing a hand on

338

Alys' shoulder. 'She doesn't mean it. She'll regret it tomorrow.'

Alys nodded without speaking although she knew better than her father ever could that Beverley, so ready to blame and accuse, meant every word.

And as she looked at her mother, lifeless now after suffering that could indeed have been avoided had she been here, Alys felt the weight of guilt constrict her heart like another notch turned in an instrument of medieval torture.

*

'Jesus said, I am the resurrection and the life; he who believes in me, though he die, yet shall he live . . .' The Minister's words rose clearly, reaching every corner of the packed church.

The funeral was to have been a quiet family affair, a Memorial Service for all the many friends and acquaintances of the Peterson family would follow later. But word had spread quickly and many had come along, impatient to pay their last respects.

Alys had seen the full pews as she came into church, the sea of faces, the frill of white lace handkerchiefs. And through the numbness which had seemed to blunt her every emotion these last days one thought penetrated: did they think as Beverley did that it was all her fault? Would their heads nod together as they watched her pass by, following the simple oak coffin? Would they whisper: 'She left her mother alone you know. Imagine – leaving a woman in her condition!'

Alys bowed her head. She had experienced none of Beverley's genuine grief – love for her mother had died too long ago and it was then that she had mourned her. Now there was nothing to buffer the torments of her guilt.

'I should have known – I should have been there!' she had wept over the phone to John when she rang, still shocked, to tell him what had happened.

'Alys, stop torturing yourself. You couldn't be there every minute of the day. Nobody expected it.'

'Beverley expected it.'

'Then why wasn't Beverley there?'

'She has her own family. Louis and Robyn.'

'And because you haven't she thinks you should dedicate the whole of your life to looking after your mother. That is neither fair nor reasonable. You have to have a life of your own – go out sometimes, have friends.'

'But I should have made sure Norma knew I was going out. I shouldn't have taken it for granted she would be there. I shouldn't . . .'

'Alys!' he had interrupted her sharply. 'You have done all you could possibly do. A great deal more than most girls would ever contemplate doing. If you don't stop this foolish talk I shall have to come to Melbourne, put you across my knee and spank you!'

'No, you mustn't come here . . .' She broke off. 'You could come to the funeral, though. That would mean a lot to me and I think Mummy would have liked it too. She was actually very fond of you.'

'Of course I'll come,' he said.

She glanced at him now, immaculate in his dark suit, white shirt and black tie, and found herself wishing briefly that there could be more than just friendship between them. But it was not possible and anything more intimate might even spoil the quality of their relationship. Maybe one day she would meet Stuart, his son, as John so clearly hoped she would. Perhaps she could find with him not only the warmth and companionship she had found with John, but something more – that indefinable something which would eclipse the shadow of a face which haunted her no matter how often she tried to put it out of her mind – a handsome face with a good strong bone structure, with fair hair that receded slightly and blue eyes which had met hers and said . . .

May God forgive you, you wicked girl! Thinking thoughts like that at your own mother's funeral!

She folded her hands, listening to the words of the Minister and watching the pale winter sun slanting in through the windows and turning the pale arum lilies which decked the coffin to warm gold. If only her feelings could be transmuted in the same way. If only the regret could become real grief, not just for what might have been, but for her mother too; if only the self-recrimination could be tempered with some sort of understanding, not only from John, who loved her, but from the others, who had also loved her mother.

But it would not be. Her eyes slid from the coffin along the row of principal mourners. There was her father, his head bowed, but his shoulders straight. He had no time for her – nor for any of them. He would always plead the pressures of business as an excuse to keep his distance and pressures undoubtedly there were – but they were his life. He loved them. Then Beverley. Any pretence of closeness between the sisters had gone now, shattered by Beverley's vindictive and shrewish attitude. We were always quarrelling, even as children, Alys thought – but one does not expect to quarrel in the same way in adult life. Yet why not? Personalities are there, already more than partially formed, it is only later we learn to conceal our feelings behind a veneer that is expected of us. Louis, Bev's husband. He was nothing to Alys. She had never liked him. Perhaps even Bev had become disappointed in him and that was the reason she had become so exceptionally bitter and emotional. Robyn . . . Alys was fond of Robyn, but she would be just another battleground for fighting Beverley on if Alys saw much of her – she could not stand the way Bev mollycoddled the child and tried to take away her individuality and squash her spirit.

No, of all of them, the only one who would keep her here now was John, and he would not do so. Hadn't he already told her she should do what she wanted to do – go off and do her bit to help the war effort.

She glanced at him again now and felt his quiet strength lift her. The Minister spoke the final words and the family fell into line to follow the coffin down the aisle between the pews.

For the first time Alys felt warm tears on her cheeks. This was the end, really the end. Not just for her mother, but for the family as well. They would go their own ways now that Frances had gone. Perhaps they would never come together again in quite the same way. Whatever her failings, she had been the lynch pin.

Through the door, onto the pavement, following those lilies turned golden by the sun. But there was no warmth in it. The chill made Alys shiver and the cold breeze dried the tears on her cheek.

*

Two weeks later she drove out to the farm to say goodbye to John.

'You're really going then,' he said.

She nodded. 'Yep. They actually decided I might be of some use.'

'What did I tell you?'

She smiled, ignoring the teasing remark. 'I'm off to training camp first, to learn how to be a soldier. And they think they need to teach me a thing or two about engines before I become an AWAS driver.'

It was his turn to laugh. 'You'll teach them a thing or two!'

Her face grew serious; she patted the bonnet of the Alfa Romeo. 'Would you do something for me?'

'What?'

'Give my car a good home while I'm gone.'

'Of course I will, if you want me to.'

'I do. I can't imagine anyone else bothering to take care of it.' She smiled. 'You can even drive it – if you can get hold of the petrol.'

'I am honoured!'

They looked at one another for a moment, then she laid her head against his chest.

'Oh John, I'll miss you.'

'No, you won't. There won't be time even to think of me. You'll be too busy with all your new experiences.'

'Oh, I don't know about that.'

'Well I do. If anyone does any missing, it will be me. Left here all alone.'

'Not all alone,' she teased. 'You'll have your Land Army girls.'

'So I will! So off you go and enjoy yourself.'

'You make it sound like a holiday.'

'For you, Alys, after what you have put up with, that is just what it will be.'

A shadow crossed her face. 'Don't say that, please. I did what I had to do. But I was a terrible daughter. I was nothing but a disappointment to her. And what I did I did grudgingly. She must have known that.'

'That was her choice, Alys. She could have chosen to keep your respect and love. Instead she chose to keep you.'

The shadow came fully into her eyes. 'It's so sad. When I was a little girl she was a good mother really.'

'Because then she knew she could make you do what she wanted. There are people like that, Alys. Just as long as life – and everyone in their vicinity – conforms to their pattern they can be wonderful. Step outside their wishes and they become tyrants.'

She took his hands. 'Oh John, I wish I could be as wise and calm about things as you are.'

He smiled his sideways smile. 'When things can't be changed there's no point wasting energy worrying about them.' He kissed her lightly on the forehead. 'Goodbye, Alys. Take care of yourself.'

'And you. I'll write and let you know the news.'

'You'd better. But you probably won't have time. All your free moments will be spent cavorting with handsome young officers.'

'I doubt it.' She laughed and once more thought of one handsome young officer with whom she would very much have liked to 'cavort'.

But he had married someone else.

And that, thought, Alys, was very much that.

Chapter Twenty

Richard Allingham carried the two beers from the mess bar to the chairs in the corner of the veranda where Tara was sitting.

She took one from him with hands that shook slightly and drank. 'Ah – I need that!'

Richard set his own drink down on the floor beside his chair, leaning forward urgently. 'Right. Now tell me again what the CO said.'

'I told you already. There's nothing else to say. They are sending me to New Guinea.'

Richard swore softly. 'But why for God's sake? You're doing fine here. You're a good medical orderly and we need you. Why send you to New Guinea?'

Tara laughed nervously. 'Why does the army do anything? They are a law unto themselves. And I'm in the army now, remember.'

'But it doesn't make sense.'

'To them it does. The whole unit I trained with is going. I should have thought of what might happen before I agreed to sign on. I did think of it. But I assumed that . . .'

'That because we were married they would have more consideration,' Richard finished for her. 'Yes, I'd have thought so too. Perhaps, if I have a word with the CO . . .'

'It won't do any good,' Tara said. 'He's under orders like the rest of us.'

'But maybe he could put in a word.'

'No. It wouldn't do any good,' Tara repeated stubbornly.

She did not add that she had suspected she had seen a gleam of triumph in Colonel Adamson's eyes when he had told her the news, nor that she was fairly certain he had never forgiven her for rebuffing him and then marrying

Richard. Jealousy seemed too petty a motive to attribute to a senior officer – and there was a hint of conceit in suggesting it. She had never told Richard of the CO's approaches to her; now did not seem the right time to bring it up.

'It's no good. I'll just have to go and hope it won't be for too long,' she said.

'Well, they had better look after you,' he said vehemently. 'It does seem as though we have got the Nips on the run at last, but I don't like it. New Guinea is no place for a woman. It's a hell of a climate for one thing and too damn close to the action for another.'

'I expect I'll be all right,' Tara retorted a shade indignantly. Having Richard anxious about her was very nice but she was irrationally proud of the toughness which was her only heritage. 'They say they put atebrin tablets on the dinner table with the salt to stop us from getting malaria, and since Guadalcanal the Japs have really got their tails between their legs.'

'A wounded dog can be dangerous,' Richard said, sipping his beer. 'Oh, I'll be glad when this damned war is over and we can get back to normality. Go back to Melbourne, have a home of our own, and just get on with our lives. We've been married more than six months, Tara, and how much of that time have we been able to spend alone together? Precious little. But that will all be different when we get home and that's a promise.'

Tara nodded but said nothing.

She did not want to go to New Guinea it was true. But the thought of returning to Melbourne with Richard was a daunting one, too. Remembering her evening of discomfort with Alys and her friend, John, she shuddered. Life back in Melbourne could be a series of such evenings, every one of them spent with people with whom she was totally out of her depth.

But she was in no immediate danger of that.

She sighed, raised her glass and smiled at Richard over the beer foam.

'Papua New Guinea – watch out. Here I come!'

*

From the very outset Tara disliked New Guinea. She had not, she supposed, made a very auspicious beginning, for even the journey to Port Moresby had been fraught with discomforts. First there had been the 'trooper' – the train taking her and the other AAMWS from Brisbane to Townsville – hot, packed tight with perspiring bodies, and laid up so often in sidings for hours on end that the journey took three times as long as Tara had expected. Then there was Townsville, crowded to suffocation point with service personnel, and the long stumbling walk in the blackout to the waiting ship. Tara had staggered along under the load of her heavy kitbag, with all the items of equipment that would not fit into it draped around her neck. Fortunately, some of her issue of tropical kit had been stowed away in a tin trunk and was not her concern for the moment, for there was no way she could have managed such items as the beekeeper's head net and the heavy boots, and the smart new khaki trousers and safari jacket which had been issued to her would have been rags if they had had to be stuffed into the kitbag along with her pyjamas.

The troopship on which they sailed had once been a luxury liner but now had none of the trappings of those balmy days. The bunks cramped into the 'brown-out' below decks were stained and without sheets; the blankets which eventually arrived to cover them – one grey woollen army issue per bunk – were scratchy and uncomfortably hot, but at least they were clean. In spite of the stabilizers which had been fitted to the ship in her cruising days, Tara began to feel queasy the moment the swell began to lift it and by the time they put to sea she was violently seasick. Lying miserably on her hard narrow bunk, Tara remembered that other voyage when she and Mammy had sailed halfway round the world and the nightmare of it was suddenly all too real, as if it had been yesterday instead of almost two decades ago.

The cabin hummed with the conversation of the other girls and the thuds, bumps and metallic clunks as they scrubbed and cleaned in an effort to make it habitable, but Tara heard it all as if it were a dream. More real was the musical lilt of Mammy's voice somewhere inside her head as she sang softly 'Too-ra-loo-ra-loorah! Too-ra-loo-ra-lay!', and the smell in her nostrils was not the hot water and disinfectant smell but that indefinable mix of cheap perfume and whisky fumes which always evoked for her the essence of Mammy.

Six days after leaving Townsville they had landed at Port Moresby. Struggling along the jetty, laden once more, Tara was still weak and shaky but the nausea was passing and by the time she was ensconced in one of the waiting jeeps her usual perkiness had begun to return. Driving along the gravel roads where the dust flew in choking clouds from the wheels of the jeep, she made a special effort to take in her surroundings and listen to the friendly patter of the driver as he pointed out the sights – Fairfax Harbour, bathed in morning sunshine, the small houses which had been built on stilts over the water – and the landmarks the war had left, a ship sunk by enemy action, looking now like a great pathetic beached whale, a paddock where a fuel dump had gone up sky high, bomb craters resulting from the frequent air raids. Brought face to face with destruction of the kind she had witnessed at first hand in Darwin Tara shuddered but made mental notes all the same. She had to have something more interesting than an account of her seasickness to put in her letters to Richard, though on reflection she supposed the censor would chop most of it to pieces in any case.

When they had staged at a well-established AGH Tara's spirits had lifted a little. In the hot sunshine the mess was an oasis of beauty, thatched with sago palm leaves, surrounded by thick tropical ferns and shrubs and neat gardens bright with flowers of every hue. There were cool showers to wash away the sticky heat of travel and ice-cold beer finally settled her queasy stomach. But the hospital for which she was bound was no nearer completion than the one in Queensland had been – and less comfortable.

Bulldozers were still carving out terraces for tent lines and showers on the hillsides and scooping out pits for latrines, sudden storms of torrential rain turned the earth into a sea of mud and dripped through every weakness in the tents where the girls slept, lived and worked, even though the Wet was a full two months away, and between the storms the mosquitos descended in thick clouds to nip and irritate. The girls slept six to a tent, their clothes stowed in cupboards made from wooden boxes laid on their sides with a curtain to replace the lids – which were then utilized as bedside floormats.

For the first time in her life, almost, Tara was aware of a creeping sense of lack of purpose. It wasn't that there was not enough to keep her busy – there certainly was. But most of the AAMWS in Tara's draft had received formal training as medical orderlies and it was they who were assigned the nursing jobs, while Tara found herself ordered to do the menial tasks which fell to those on 'general duties'. She began to dread the morning parade and roll call when the day's work was allocated. Someone, she supposed, had to sweep and tidy the sisters' tents, empty the rubbish bins and clean the covering of fine dust from the lantern shades; someone had to scrub the wooden seats of the latrines and make sure they were as hygienic as possible under these conditions. But why did it have to be her?

'Oh, couldn't we have a swop around for once?' she asked one morning when Sister detailed her yet again to the hated tasks, and the chilling glance she received by way of reply only deepened her resentment.

'We are fighting a war, Allingham. I'm afraid there is no room for adhering to the niceties you may be used to in civilian life,' Sister told her crisply.

349

Had she not been so wretched Tara might have smiled at the irony of it. But she was in no mood for smiling. As she washed and scrubbed, and pegged out endless lines of bandages with hands puffy from immersion in hot harshly-treated water, Tara remembered the days when she had worked for Dimitri Savalis. But even then, she thought, she had been driven by motives which had somehow kept her going – her determination to find a way back to a better life, her fear of Red and her anger at what he had done to Jack, her grief, still raw, at the loss of her beloved Maggie. Now, it seemed she had gained everything she had ever dreamed of only to lose it again. She was here for the duration, caught frustratingly in a trap of her own making from which there would be no escape until the war ended – whenever that might be.

The separation from Richard ached in her like a nagging tooth which sometimes, in the quiet of the night, flared into raging pain. Was he missing her as much as she missed him? His letters told her he was, but always in the same carefully modified language that was a hallmark of his well-bred nature – not for him phrases of undying love for the censor to gloat over. When she had been there with him Tara had been confident of her own ability to hold his attention and affection. Now, with the distance between them, she wondered uncomfortably just how much he remembered her. Might he not forget the warmth of her touch and the delights they had shared and remember instead the small awkwardnesses? Might he have time to think about the manner of their marriage – and wonder? Lying sleepless beneath her mosquito net, listening to the hum of insect life and the scuttle of something she feared might be rats, Tara fretted, and when she slept her dreams were all too often highly coloured, nightmarish affairs. Sometimes she dreamed that she came upon Richard holding another woman in his arms, but her face was hidden and Tara always woke before discovering who her rival was. Sometimes she dreamed of the bombing and saw Richard killed before her eyes the way the wharfie had been. Sometimes she dreamed of Jack's murder, only when she turned Jack over to comfort him it was Richard's face which stared up at her, lifeless from the cobbles. She woke from these dreams in a cold sweat with tears pouring down her cheeks; once she believed she was being stifled and fought through the layers of sleep to find a hand pressed over her mouth. Panic made her fight wildly to escape, then the fog cleared a little and she realized it was only Jill Whitton from the neighbouring bed.

'Sorry, but I had to do it,' she whispered to Tara. 'You were screaming out loud. You would have woken the whole ward!'

One horror at least was missing from her nightmares, however. The rape never came back to haunt her – at least not while she slept, though she did sometimes feel a chill run up her spine when the bushes rattled behind her, and once in a while she found herself remembering and wondering who her attacker had been. Investigations by the Provost had long since been abandoned, she guessed, and her file 'lost' beneath a pile of more pressing ones. But it seemed strange the culprit had not been apprehended. Thousands of men in the area there might have been, but surely whoever was responsible must have taken away with him some evidence of what he had done, even if it was only dust and leaf mould on his uniform. Surely, in some billet somewhere, someone must have looked at the man in the neighbouring bunk and wondered. But nothing had ever come to light – and Tara was glad. Much as she would have liked to see him brought to justice, the facts about her past life which would have come to light under cross-examination at a court martial would certainly have ended any hope she might have had of becoming Mrs Richard Allingham.

Throughout the months of early spring the AGH worked at full stretch. The battles of the notorious Kokoda Trail had been fought and won, but many of the victims were still here, too ill to be shipped home to Australia, often delirious, always emaciated, their bodies

351

covered with a honeycomb of weeping sores. Add to them the constant stream of casualties from the skirmishes which still continued as the Allied forces drove the Japs back and attempted to cut them off from their command at Salamaua, and there were enough patients to occupy every available bed in the tent lines and keep the operating theatre busy.

Here in New Guinea the fighting was always at close quarters, conducted with machine guns and rifles. Though bayonets were fixed in place all the time and the distances between the enemies was often more suited to hand-to-hand fighting, quite often it was the guns that were used, firing at one another at point blank range. There was sniper fire to contend with and the Japs were notorious for the way they could creep up swiftly and silently and take a man, or a battalion by surprise.

As if the wounds and the burns inflicted by battle were not enough, the climate, too, took its toll in casualties. Dysentery was rife, malaria still reared its head in spite of the prescribed atebrin tablets, and mild beri beri was not uncommon. Sometimes, even, a man was admitted suffering from the dreaded scrub typhus, contracted in the mangrove and sago swamps around Buna and Gona and in the suffocatingly hot areas of tall kunai grass, further inland.

Nor was it only the Allied forces who required medical treatment. There was a POW ward at the hospital too – a ward to which the sisters and AAMWS orderlies went only under the protection of an armed guard. It was a place which aroused Tara's interest and sparked her imagination, but she never had cause to go there.

Week in, week out her duties remained the same. On one occasion she managed to whittle down her 'lat' cleaning rota by one – by placing an 'Out of Order. Dangerous!' notice on the door of the furthest little hut. But that ruse lasted only a day or two before a stony-faced corporal marched up, took a good look round, and marched back again – bringing the notice with him.

When a new consignment of ward equipment was delivered and Tara was allocated the duty of cleaning it where it stood, at the edge of the dusty gravel track, she was glad. It was hot and dirty work – black dirt and mud caked everything – and for hours, as the heat of the day gathered, Tara worked with a scrubbing brush and a fire bucket full of water, cleaning until her arms ached and the sweat ran in rivulets through the powdering of fine black dust which covered her face and neck. But at least she felt she was doing something to help the sick and wounded fighting men and not simply skivvying for the other women, who were better qualified than she was. And when she saw the beds and cupboards carried away into the ward by a couple of perspiring orderlies, she experienced far greater satisfaction than she ever could from a polished toilet seat or a freshly-swept tent.

'You did quite a good job on those, Allingham,' Sister said and Tara recognized her far-from-effusive comment as praise indeed.

'Sure wouldn't I like to have another go at them when they are all in place,' she said craftily – thinking that perhaps a job well done might prove her passport into the wards – and the much more rewarding task of ward orderly. To her delight Sister nodded.

'More dust probably will shake out of the wood when we carry them into their places. Heaven knows it gets everywhere! All right, Allingham, you can spend some time on that tomorrow – just as soon as you finish the lats.'

By next morning, however, the job had attained top priority in Sister's eyes. A new plane load of casualties had arrived, flown in from 'over the Owen Stanleys' – the mountain range that bisected the island – and were now occupying the tent wards to which the new equipment had been allocated.

'Leave everything else and make sure the equipment is pristine clean!' she instructed. 'Some of the new patients have some very nasty wounds and one or two are

353

threatening gangrene. I don't want any MO saying they got infected through dirty equipment in my wards!'

Tara smiled, her old irrepressible spirit returning. And when she went into the ward, the comments and soft wolf whistles from the patients fit enough to appreciate the sight of a pretty girl lifted her spirits still further.

It seemed so long since she had been in the company of men! The girls were all very well, but Tara had never had close girlfriends. Her looks – and the fact that she was popular with men – too often made her the object of cattiness and, sometimes, outright jealousy. Oh yes, give her a man any time! Even if he did have to be kept in his place . . .

She bantered with them as she scrubbed the tables yet again, removing any last lingering traces of the thick black dust, passing amused comments about their incapacity to carry out their good-humoured threats and teasing them about the state of their feet – a subject too tender really to be a joke, since many of them had skin and flesh between their toes rotting away from the enforced encasement in boots and shoes day after endless days in wet and steamy conditions.

'You know what the army advises you,' she told one of them pertly. 'A change of socks every day and you would have nothing to worry about.'

'Turn it in, love!' he rejoined. 'I wasn't going to be caught by any Jap with my boots off! I'd as soon be caught with my trousers down!'

At the end of the ward lay the more seriously sick – a man whose arm had been amputated at the elbow, another with a part of his shoulder shot away. Tara became quieter as she approached them, recognizing the need for them to rest quietly. In the very end bed and set aside a little from the others lay a still figure, his head turned away from her as he dozed fitfully. Tara moved towards him quietly, her soft-soled shoes making no sound. She set down her bucket and wrung out her cleaning cloth in the water, avoiding the crust of dirt which floated on it. Then she leaned across to the table – and froze.

There was something oddly familiar about the shape of the head, the dark thickly springing hair. She let the cleaning cloth fall back into the bucket and walked around the bed. Her breath was coming quick and shallow, and even now she was telling herself she must be wrong. But when she saw his face, pale and drawn though it was, with the skin stretched too tight across the cheekbones, dark smudges beneath the eyes and a growth of stubble around his mouth and chin, she knew she was not mistaken. Heavy lids lifted with an effort but the eyes that met hers, though dulled by drugs, were unmistakably hazel streaked with dangerous looking green. His mouth moved, the lips too thickened by the drugs he had been given to be able to form the words he wanted to say, but the small curve of a smile was there all the same to prove that he had recognized her too.

She stood motionless for a moment, her eyes wide. Then she dropped to her haunches beside the bed.

'Sean Devlin – what are you doing here?' she said.

*

When Dev first opened his eyes and saw her there, he was convinced he was hallucinating. Damn the stuff they were pumping into him! The quack had said it would do him good and he had thought it was beginning to – but when he started seeing things, well, he wasn't so sure, even if what he was seeing was a very pleasant sight. Tara Kelly! Dammit, he'd thought he had got her out of his system when he had left her at the Adelaide River more than a year and a half ago. He *had* got her out of his system – and done it the hard way. So why the hell should he be imagining she was here now, standing beside his bed and looking as pretty as she had ever looked – a bloody sight prettier than any girl had a right to look?

His eyelids drooped; with an effort he forced them open

again. It was not a hallucination – or at least if it was, it was a lot more vivid than any of the other figments his fevered imagination had been conjuring up. She was flesh and blood, he could have sworn it – and dressed in tropical kit too. He could see from her expression that she was as shocked as he was. And when she spoke her voice was unmistakable – that Irish lilt was very real despite the ringing in his ears.

'Sean Devlin, what are you doing here?'

With an effort he forced his lips to move.

'It's a long story, darling.' His voice sounded thick; there was no way he could make the effort to tell her, though it was all there. Fragmented but real all the same, in spite of the long harrowing months since the night he had left her to that bloody upper crust medico Richard Allingham.

Once again he forced his lips to form words.

'Well, it wasn't the bastard Japs who got me,' he said.

Then the effort – and the drugs – became too much for him and his eyelids drooped once more.

*

It must be malaria, Tara decided. The look of him and the details on the chart at the end of his bed made it almost certain, and his remark about the Japs seemed to confirm it. There had been a number of cases lately, Tara knew, in spite of the atebrin tablets with which every man was issued, and she had heard the doctor speculating that a new strain, resistant to the drug, was rearing its head. Nasty. Malaria was not something to wish upon anyone. Even given that you survived the first bout it could go on recurring for years and years. No, good as it was to see Dev again, she could have wished it had been under different circumstances.

But when she sought out the AANS sister in charge of the ward to confirm her suspicions, Tara was in for another shock of quite a different kind.

356

'You're talking about Lieutenant Devlin are you?' she said coolly.

Tara almost dropped the mop she was still carrying.

'Lieutenant? How did he get to be a lieutenant?'

The AANS sister gave her a strange look. 'He's quite a hero by all accounts. Acquitted himself very well on the Kakoda Trail and earned himself a commission by his exploits. And yes, you're right, he has come down with malaria. Very unfortunate. He was due to be going home – then the day before he should have sailed this had to happen.'

'What a shame!' Tara said, but her head was spinning. Dev – an officer! She'd never have believed it. Surprise enough to find him in the army at all. How had he managed that?

Later, he was to tell her how with his business in Darwin non-existent, he had volunteered for the AIF and been accepted, how he had done a spell at the Jungle Training Camp at Conungra and then been posted to New Guinea, and how he had fought long and hard on the notorious Kakoda Trail. What he would not tell her was that she had had a great deal to do with his decision to enlist. That last night after the concert he had finally conceded defeat and it had been the most painful thing he had ever had to do. He would not admit that, any more than he would boast of the courage and good humour, grit and perseverance and qualities of leadership that had made him a legend on the Kakoda Trail and led to his commission – and a decoration for valour. It was not in his nature to wear his heart on his sleeve and so there were things that Tara had no inkling of that day as she left the ward, surprised and oddly cheered to find a familiar face here in New Guinea, even if he was a patient – and a rather sick one at that.

I'll come and see him whenever I can, Tara decided. For after all, shouldn't old friends stick together?

Chapter Twenty-One

The intravenous quinine injections did their work. Gradually, during the weeks of spring, Dev began to recover, emerging from that strange cloudy land somewhere between coma and dozing to lie, weak but more rational, staring at the canvas tent walls and wondering how the hell a damn silly thing like malaria had managed to put him in hospital where the Japs had failed. For someone as fit as he had always been, it was a blow to his pride, and he snapped irritably when the medic questioned him closely as to whether he had been taking his atebrin tablets and hinted he might be one of those who avoided them because of the rumoured risks to manhood.

'Where the bloody hell have you been sitting out this war? We haven't seen a woman for months on end. Not being able to get it up would be the least of our worries. Christ, some of you HQ wallahs seem to think we have had nothing to do but cavort about on the beaches with dusky lovelies. Well, let me tell you, sport, it has been nothing like that!'

'All right, there's no need to lose your temper,' the HQ wallah murmured petulantly and in spite of his own annoyance – and his weakness – Dev had to smile. It was about time they sent some of these cossetted clerks out into the battle lines and taught them to be real men. Not that he personally would want one of them standing shoulder to shoulder with *him* when the chips were down – on second thoughts perhaps it was better to leave them where they were after all. At least this way they could only irritate a bloke, not get him killed.

The HQ wallah's lips tightened as he noticed the grin.

'It really is not funny,' he said primly. 'We can't afford to lose men unless it is absolutely necessary.'

That caused Dev to roar with laughter, but moments later the laughter had turned into a fit of convulsive shivering. They still came regularly, these bouts when every hair on his head – and body – seemed to stand on end and his teeth chattered uncontrollably. He hunched himself over, ignoring the medic as he tried to gain extra warmth from the blankets, and when at last the spasm passed the man had gone – crept away rather than face the reality of malaria, no doubt, Dev thought scornfully.

He lay for a moment with the blanket still wrapped around him, cursing his luck once again. It was so bloody frustrating, being laid up – even now when he was still too weak almost to walk down the ward unaided it was getting to him. What it would be like as he began improving he dreaded to think.

There was one bright spot, of course, Tara. Since the day when she had discovered he was in the hospital she had come to visit whenever she could. Just to see her sitting there beside his bed was as good as a tonic. And the envy of the other men had done his heart good too. But now that he was getting better and his brain was functioning more normally he found that seeing Tara was just another frustration. It would have been bad enough knowing, as he had done in Northern Territory, that she regarded him as an old friend and nothing more, but Dev was not used to being a loser and he thought that he might have looked on this encounter as one more chance to try to get through to her. But things were different now. She was someone else's wife. Not a nice thought at all – and that was putting it mildly.

He had tried, God knew, to be pleased for her. He had known, after all, how badly she had wanted Richard Allingham. But self-sacrifice had never been one of Dev's strengths, he had always laughed at nobility and scorned submissiveness. Now, the best he could do was pretend indifference and so salve his pride.

'Well, well, Tara, so you married the man! Congratulations!' he had drawled when she had shown him her wedding ring. 'I never thought you'd make it, but . . .'

'Why not?' Her eyes had snapped blue fire.

'Oh, come on now, Tara, it wouldn't be chivalrous of me to spell it out. And chivalry is something you prize very highly, isn't it? It must be or you wouldn't have fallen in love with Richard.'

She looked at him sharply, suspecting that he was mocking her yet not able to put her finger on exactly how he was doing it.

'If you are going to be rude, Sean Devlin, I shall not come in to see you any more. I'm not a ward orderly here, you know, I'm a maid of all work. And I am visiting you out of the goodness of my heart in my own time.'

'Sorry – sorry!' He raised his hands in mock surrender, a ghost of his old smile creasing his face.

He had no idea of the way his appearance had shocked Tara – 'He was such a fine, upstanding man, now he looks like a scarecrow!' she had confided to Jill Whitton. She kept her shock well hidden, however. It would not do for him to know what she was thinking every time she looked at his emaciated frame and sunken cheeks.

'And it's sorry you should be!' she said tartly. 'Just thank your lucky stars they brought you here. At least you had a friendly face when you came around. You weren't surrounded by strangers.' She leaned closer. 'I think if I'd been as ill as you were and I woke up to find myself surrounded by the natives, I'd die.'

Dev's lips twitched. Marriage had not changed her one scrap.

'Those natives have not been christened the Fuzzy Wuzzy Angels for nothing. We'd never have done what we did without them. And they always seem to be cheerful. Always smiling, never mind the fact that every tooth in their head may be gone and the gums turned red from chewing betel nuts.'

'Well, I think they look fierce,' Tara said.

Dev was silent for a moment, remembering the native New Guinea islanders upon whom they had relied in the mountains – men whose dark curly hair receded from high veined foreheads, who went bare-chested but often knotted a scarf around their necks or adorned themselves with all the bracelets and rings they could find. Perhaps it was the thick eyebrows, set low over their eyes, which gave them their fierce appearance; perhaps it was just that to Tara they were an unknown quantity. But he knew them better than that; knew the way they could unerringly find paths through the rain forests, their bare feet sure as a mountain goat's despite the slippery mud and rippling tapestry of tree roots; knew that as stretcher bearers they were dedicated to getting every wounded man to medical aid.

'I hear we have to call you "sir" now,' Tara said, changing the subject. 'A commission! My, my!'

'That's right. I shall expect a little more respect from you in future.'

'Respect – hah!' She was laughing. 'The best you can hope for is that if you behave yourself I shall come and see you again.'

'Quite an honour, I agree,' he said, heavily sarcastic, and to his surprise saw the colour flame in her cheeks. Tara embarrassed? Never!

She leaned over, dropping a quick kiss on his cheek. The touch of her lips made the tiny pinpricks tingle over his skin as if he were about to start another shivering fit. He reached out and caught her around the wrist. In his haggard fevered face his eyes were very sharp.

'Is this a bonus I get now that you are a married lady? If so – it was almost worth losing you. Especially as your husband is a good long way away.'

She looked at him in confusion and he shook his head sadly.

'He has never known how to look after you, that bloke.'

'What do you mean?'

'It's obvious isn't it? If you were my wife I would never let you be posted so far away.'

'And how could you prevent it?'

'Oh, I'd find a way.'

'Well, I am not your wife.' She snatched her hand away. 'And I'll be much obliged if you would remember that.'

Suddenly, he felt very tired. Strange how it could creep up on him so suddenly that one minute he could be feeling he was well on the way to recovery, the next as if he was being dragged down into that morass of muddled dreams which had stretched end to end through the early days of the illness.

'Tara.' He controlled the movement of his lips with difficulty. 'Tara – did I ever tell you you are beautiful?'

Then, before he could hear her reply, before he could see the expression on her face when he said it even, he was asleep.

*

Tara stood in front of the notice board gazing longingly at the announcements and invitations. A picnic to Fisherman's Island – a visit to a native village – a sailing trip on a lak-a-toi – a dance in the mess at Base. The visit to the native village did not interest her, nor the sailing trip – just the thought of it made her feel seasick all over again. But the picnic and the dance – oh, it would be so good to put on a pretty dress and enjoy herself for a little while!

Teeth holding her lip in the effort of concentration, Tara calculated on a mental calendar. No. The picnic was out. Definitely not one of her days off. But the dance – she was almost sure that was a day off – and even if it was not she should be through with her duties in time to go.

Tara scrabbled around in her bag, found a stub of pencil and added her name to the list. Four names up already and with any luck there would soon be two more. Six girls to be interested in any invitation before it could be accepted was the rule, and six escorts to go with them.

A shadow fell across her shoulder and Tara turned to see Jill Whitton standing behind her.

'What's on then?' she asked.

'There's a dance,' Tara pressed hopefully. 'Shall I put your name down?'

'Well – yeah, all right, go on,' Jill agreed. 'I expect I can wangle it even if it means swopping duties with that dill Edna Royston. How did she ever come to be an AAMWS, I'd like to know?'

'She's mustard keen, she's efficient, she does twice as much work as anyone else in half the time.' Tara added Jill's name to the list and turned to grin at her. 'She's a gem. I've heard Sister say so.'

Jill snorted. 'She is also the biggest crashing bore I've ever met. She is so earnest, Tara. And the clothes she wears when we get out of uniform for an hour or two! I wouldn't put my grandmother in them!'

'It's one less to compete with then, isn't it?' Tara teased.

The girls fell into step heading back towards their tent.

'If there's one thing I like about this war it's the men!' Jill said with a laugh. 'So many to choose from! Not that there's much chance to misbehave. Back home they seem to think we are all fallen women. They don't seem to realize we're too tired most of the time for carryings on, even if we did have the opportunity. Not that it bothers you much, I suppose, as a married lady.'

Tara pulled a face. 'A ring on your finger doesn't change you that much. I still long to have a bit of fun.'

'Well, now's your chance. There are a lot of Yanks about – and I've heard they can get you all kinds of things our lads can't. Silk stockings, perfume, even pretty underwear, if you play your cards right. And ciggies and chocolate and cookies . . .' Jill broke off, laughing. 'All I hope is if we get to go to this dance that my escort doesn't turn out to be a killjoy. They can be, can't they? They tend to get carried away with the responsibility of making sure your honour is preserved and act as if they own you!'

'Hmm, I think I might just take my own escort,' Tara said.

'Your own? Oh, you mean that officer with malaria who you're always trotting in to see.'

'Yes. He's so much better now I think I'll ask him.'

'I can see you were right – marriage certainly doesn't seem to have changed *you*!' Jill remarked and Tara failed to notice the sprinkling of spite in her tone.

'Yes, I'll have to get clearance from the MO first to say he's fit enough and then I'll ask him,' she said

*

The Aussie army truck ploughed its way along the muddy road and each time the wheels slithered and spun, the six girls piled in the back held their breath. As it was after sundown they were dressed in their safari jackets and trousers – civilian dress was restricted to the hours of daylight even on special occasions – but no one wanted to arrive at a dance covered in mud after having to push a truck which had become bogged down.

'You'd never think there could be so much water up there would you?' Dorren Callis, one of the AAMWS remarked, peering up into the thick haze which almost obscured the tops of the trees. 'You'd think the whole sky was going to fall down.'

'Yeah, it reminds me of when I was in sugar country up in Queensland . . .' one of the men began, but Tara was not listening.

The storm and the truck jolting over the boggy track had brought back memories of her own, though she had no intention of sharing them. That night when she and Richard had gone down to the Freeman brothers' farm was too private – and too precious – for that.

Oh Richard, so damned far away! Tara thought, and in spite of the crowded company in the truck she felt lonely. She had told Jill marriage had not changed her much and probably that was true. But falling in love most certainly had.

A cheer of relief went up when the driver ground to a

halt outside the base camp recreation hut where the dance was being held. They all piled out and headed in the direction of the music – popular tunes being played by the unit band.

The hall, scarcely big enough to contain all those who wanted to let their hair down, was already crowded. A thick haze of cigarette smoke floated just below ceiling height. Dev managed to fight his way through the crowd at the bar to fetch a drink for himself and Tara, then they stood squeezed into a corner sipping them. As the crush increased Tara glanced at him anxiously. He still looked far from well, though perhaps it would be less obvious to someone who had not known him before. He was thin and wiry now where before he had been strongly muscled, his skin an unhealthy yellow instead of his normal deep tan. As if reading her thoughts he grinned at her over the rim of his glass.

'Stop worrying, love. I'm not about to pass out on you.'

'I hope not!'

'No way am I going to miss out on the chance of a dance with you. After all, it might be my last.'

'Your last? Whatever do you mean?'

'If they think I'm fit enough to be allowed out on escort duty for an evening, they must think I'm damned near fit enough to be discharged.'

Tara ran a finger around her mouth wiping away a tiny fine line of beer foam. 'But the thing with malaria is it can keep coming and going, surely.'

'Yep. For years. They can't keep me that long. Especially when I'm taking up a bed that could be needed urgently.'

'But yours is a particularly nasty sort of malaria. I thought they wanted to study your case.'

He laughed. 'Tara Kelly – Allingham! – I don't believe you want me to go!'

'Hah!' she snorted, but the thought passed through her mind – no, I don't believe I do.

Dev took the glass from her hand, putting it down with his on a table.

365

'Come on, let's have that dance while we can. Before long the floor is going to be so crowded not even a flea would be able to do a hop on it. Now, hang on to my jacket and we'll see if we can get through without losing one another in the crush.'

He ploughed off in the direction of the dance floor and Tara followed. A breathless romp to 'The Boogie Woogie Bugle Boy from Company B' was just coming to an end – just as well, thought Tara. She really did not think Dev would have been up to leaping about to that. No, the tune the band had just begun to play was much more suitable – the slow, haunting 'String of Pearls'.

'Right then, Madam, may I have the pleasure?'

He executed a small theatrical bow and she giggled.

'How could I refuse?'

His arm went around her waist, his hand held hers, firmly and steadily. No hint of the 'shakes' now. For a moment she moved unselfconsciously in his arms, enjoying the lift she always got from being at one with music, feeling it flow through her veins, touch and sensitize every muscle, every nerve ending. Her head was thrown back, lip caught between her teeth, eyes half-closed as she lived each throbbing beat. He was watching her though she did not know it; as she brought her head forward their eyes met.

And suddenly it was not just the music that was singing in her. It was more, much more, and it had to do with Dev and the way he was looking at her. Deep within, she felt something lurch and then it was as if every bit of her was being drawn towards him, as if his eyes were magnetizing her just as they had that day back in Darwin when he had been helping her prepare for her show. Only then she had been able to escape.

Today, she was on a crowded dance floor, hemmed in by a mass of perspiring bodies. And she was not so sure, anyway, that she wanted to escape . . .

'Dev . . .' she said. Her voice was small and breathy and almost lost in the haunting music.

A muscle moved in his cheek. Abruptly he swung her round so that she was at his side instead of facing him. He still had hold of her hand but now his fingers bit into her sinews. He turned, forcing his way between the dancing couples and dragging her after him. Startled, she offered no protest.

The night air was thick and moist, still retaining the heat of the day. Across the packed mud yard from the club room was a clutch of single storey buildings. The moon glanced palely off the white wood supports on which the corrugated roofs rested but the windows were unlit. Were they store rooms of some kind, or offices? Dev and Tara neither knew nor cared. As they rounded the corner there was nothing but a line of palm trees in front of them and Dev moved into the shadow of the huts, leaning back against the wall beneath the overhang of the roof and pulling Tara with him.

The whiplash catapulted her against him; she felt her breasts flatten against his hard chest.

'What are you doing?' she tried to say but his mouth was on hers, muffling all speech. For a moment, she let the tide of ecstasy that had begun with the dance carry her along; her lips moved and responded beneath his while desire ran flickering through her veins like a line of fire along a fuse. His body was hard against hers, his arms held her in a vice-like grip and she could think of nothing, nothing, but melting into him.

Then, somewhere out in the wild jungle beyond the fringing palm trees a night bird called, its cry a jagged screech against the background of music which was carrying softly from the club room. The sound jarred Tara to reality. She jerked her lips away from his, pushing at his chest with her hands to free herself, but he held her fast.

'Dev – let me go! What are you thinking of?'

'I'll give you three guesses, Tara my lovely.' His voice was low.

'Let me go!' She was amazed at how strong he was. She had thought he was still weak from the malaria.

'Supposing I don't let you go, huh? What are you going to do about it?'

'Dev . . . !'

'I think I'll keep you here. Make sure that you don't go back to that husband of yours. Ever.' There was an undertone in his voice now which frightened her. All humour had gone and violence was there, raw and unchecked. 'Do you know what it does to me, Tara, thinking of you with him? Christ, I think I would rather kill you than have his hands on you . . .'

As he spoke he slid one hand up around her neck. The span of it from thumb to finger was enough to circle her throat from ear to ear. He began to press gently, then held steady as he brought his lips towards hers again. She stood mesmerized but unresponsive while he tried to kiss her back to awareness. After a moment, he lifted his head a few inches leaving his fingers still splayed around her throat.

'I could do it, you know.' His voice was still low and dangerous. 'I could do it and you wouldn't even get the chance to cry out. But I'd rather hang on in there and show you what you're missing. You and I, Tara . . .'

Just when she began to panic she was never afterwards certain. One minute she had been alive with an electric desire more potent than anything she had ever experienced before, the next the hysteria was welling up from some hidden place deep within her and she was shaking violently as she fought to free herself from his grasp, sobs gurgling from her restricted windpipe.

'Tara!' He let go of her throat, sliding his hand up to cover her mouth and cut off the sobs. 'For Chrissakes, cut it out! I won't hurt you!'

After a moment her sobs subsided, though she still trembled and her eyes were huge, wide and staring, above his hand. He kissed her forehead lightly and eased his hand away.

'All right now? Take it easy, darlin' . . .'

She put her own hand protectively around her throat. It

hurt from the pressure of his fingers and when she spoke her voice was slightly hoarse.

'Don't ever do that again!'

'I didn't mean to frighten you. God Knows, the last thing I want to do is . . .' He broke off then swore. 'Oh hell, Tara, I'm sorry. I guess you're nervous after what happened to you.'

There was a small silence. Into it she said, puzzled: 'What do you mean?'

'The night of the show. When you were attacked. No wonder you're easily scared.'

The world seemed to be standing still. There was only the distant throb of the music, muffled by the moisture in the atmosphere, and the pounding of her own heart.

'How did you know about that? You'd left, hadn't you? You left straight after the show. When I . . .'

'When you were spirited away by the good doctor. Yes. But news travels. You can't keep a thing like that quiet.'

'No, but . . .'

'You see, is it any wonder I don't trust him to look after you? You were with him that night, yet someone managed to . . .'

She pulled away. 'I don't want to talk about it.'

'No, I guess you don't. And you don't want to stay out here any longer with me. Oh, don't protest that you do. There's no need to worry about my feelings. Come on, I'm supposed to be your escort. Let me escort you back inside.'

She went with him, still shaking. The band had moved on to some popular wartime numbers – the strains of 'Yours' came floating out.

'I'm surprised you haven't asked the band if you can sing with them,' Dev said.

'What?' It was as if she was coming back from a long way off.

'Sing. What you can do best.'

'Oh yes.' For the first time in her life singing was almost unimportant. She could not forget the thought that had occurred to her out there in the dark with his hand around her throat.

Could it have been *Dev* who had raped her? He was strong enough. And he had wanted her. But had he wanted her enough to wait under the trees, crazy with jealousy because she had left with Richard? Could it be the reason no serviceman had ever been turned in by his mates was because it had not been a serviceman who had raped her, but a man everyone thought had left the camp hours before? Could it be . . . ? There was a hollowness inside her now that was worse than the fear had been. Oh Holy Mary, not Dev. Please, please don't let it have been Dev. Don't let me even think it, not even for a moment. He has always been like a rock to me. I get annoyed with him, I know, but oh, if I can't trust him, who can I ever trust?

'Come on, I'll have a word with the band leader,' Dev said and she nodded.

Singing might remind her of that other night, but it would also mean she had no time to think. Feel, yes, but not think. As Dev had said it was what she did best. So come on, Tara, entertain the troops, show 'em what you're made of . . .

She summoned her brightest smile, the one which switched on naturally now when the spotlight was on her, and followed him towards the stage.

*

A week later Dev was discharged from the hospital and put on a plane for Townsville. Tara went to see him before he left but there was an edge of strain between them now that had not been there before. Neither of them mentioned what had happened the night of the dance, but it was there between them all the same.

'Goodbye then, Dev. Look after yourself,' she said.

He shrugged. 'I'll be all right. But the same goes for you. You take care, right?'

He was still looking yellow and much too thin. His

uniform, hanging on him, clearly showed the weight he had lost. Remembering how strong and muscular he had been before she suffered a pang or two and was immediately struck once more by the terrible nagging suspicion. If he was still strong enough to overpower her how simple it would have been for him to take her that night . . . She pushed the thought away. She did not want to think it. In truth, she did not. So why did it keep rearing up like this, giving her this nasty uncomfortable feeling?

'If you happen to see Richard make sure he's behaving himself,' she said, and saw the hard edge embitter his smile.

'I'm sure you need have no worries on that score. The good doctor could never do anything else.'

She moved a trifle impatiently. 'Why do you have to be so nasty about him? What has he ever done to you?'

The hard line around his mouth cemented. 'I won't answer that. Now, it's time I went. Keep smiling.'

'Of course!'

But it was not always easy. With Dev gone she felt oddly bereft though she honestly could not understand why – when he was there he was such a constant irritant.

She was missing Richard badly, too. With all the movement out to the islands she had lived in hopes that 138 might be posted there, but it seemed that was not to be. Heaven knows when I'll see him again, she thought, and the loneliness and the wanting grew in her until it was a physical ache.

The Wet began early and working conditions were worse than ever. Tara ploughed her way through thick mud to clean the latrines and gulped and shuddered at the multitudes of frogs who lived and bred there. Drips and leaks developed, the neat flower gardens which the sisters had planted were threatened with suffocation by jungle vegetation which sprang up between the blooms as fast as they could be weeded out. Drying the washing was a problem – it was bad enough coping with army-style bloomers, but often Tara had hospital linen and bandages

371

to deal with as well and it was a question of pegging it out between storms and then keeping a sharp eye on the sky to get it in again before it received another, unscheduled, rinse.

The hospital was overflowing with casualties who were flown in from the fighting on the other side of the Owen Stanley Range, but Tara got to see few of them. Her tasks were so mundane, so utterly frustrating, that she thought she would go mad.

There was one bright spot, however. Plans were underway to build a special club for the AAMWS and the nursing sisters. The girls talked about it over their meals in the mess tent and it was good to have something to take their minds off the appetite-depressing 'iron rations' which appeared on the table with monotonous regularity – corned beef and biscuits, dried apricots and custard made from powdered milk.

'They say it's going to be just for us,' Edna Royston said. 'Not even a General will be able to go there without an invitation.'

'Well, let's hope to goodness somebody invites one!' Jill Witton remarked, spearing a piece of corned beef without much enthusiasm. 'A General or two would liven things up!'

Edna glowered. 'I honestly believe some of you never think of anything but men. It's no wonder we have such a bad name with the folks back home. Personally, I think it will be a treat to have somewhere we can go and be comfortable without soldiers leering at us.'

'It's not you they're leering at, Edna,' Jill said spitefully. 'It's that needlepoint you do that turns them on.'

'Come on, girls, no quarrelling!' Doreen Callis, always the peacemaker urged. 'If the club is as good as they say it's going to be, there will be plenty of room for everybody to do their own thing.'

It was certainly true that the club looked like being a splendid asset. It was taking shape fast as gangs of natives worked under the supervision of an HQ team and, in addition to the handsome new building, an area had been designated as an outdoor picnic area and tennis courts were being laid out and a swimming pool sunk.

One afternoon late in November, Tara had just completed her laundry duties when a young AAMWS runner came puffing in out of the rain.

'There you are, Tara! Thank goodness I've found you.'

Tara rolled a bandage irritably. It had been a bad drying day and the bandages were still slightly damp; she hoped they would be used again fairly quickly before mildew formed on them and she was hauled in for yet another roasting from matron.

'You shouldn't have had too much trouble. Look for me in the lats – if I'm not there then I'm bound to be in this damned wash house. What do you want me for, anyway?'

'It's not me that wants you. It's top brass.'

'Oh Lord, what have I done now?' Faced with the probability of immediate discipline, Tara thought better of trying to get away with the still-damp bandage, unrolled it again and festooned it along a makeshift indoor line. It probably would not dry there but at least it wouldn't go mildewed either – at least not today. 'Who is it that wants me?'

'Major Rice.'

'Oh Lord!'

Major Rice was an AAMWS officer known for her sharp tongue and iron discipline where 'her girls' were concerned. Tara dried her hands, tidied her hair and took her mackintosh down from its hook. Then she ran out into the rain, squelching across to the office block.

'Ah, come in. Tara Allingham, is it?' Major Rice was sitting sideways on a corner of her desk flicking through a pile of papers and she straightened as Tara entered. 'Close the door, will you?'

'You wanted to see me, ma'am,' Tara said with less trepidation. She felt that if this was to be a wigging Major Rice would be seated more formerly.

'Yes.' The Major rose and crossed to her chair. She was

a short stout woman, her dark hair already flecked with grey, tied back into a sensible bun. 'Sit down, will you? Now, I'll come straight to the point. You have no doubt heard that a club is being built for use by the AAMWS and AANS.'

'Yes.' Tara perched herself on the edge of the chair, her wet mackintosh dripping water down her legs. 'We are all looking forward to it.'

'I am sure. It will be very good for morale.' Major Rice reached for a pencil, twirling it between her fingers. 'Now the thing is, we want someone to run it and your name has been put forward, Tara.'

'Oh!'

Major Rice's eyes narrowed. 'You sound surprised, Tara.'

'Yes, well, I am surprised!' It was an understatement; whatever she had expected it was not this. 'Why me?'

'I asked the same question. I was told you are not inexperienced in the world of entertainment.'

'Yes, but – I don't know anything about organizing things. I'm a singer.'

'I was told you made an excellent job of running a concert back in Adelaide River.'

'Yes, but that was just one thing. This would be . . .' She broke off, her mind boggling at what running a club might entail.

Major Rice sat back in her chair, the pencil balanced between her index fingers.

'So you don't want to take it on.'

'Oh I didn't say that.' The shock was wearing off a little and Tara realized she was on the point of talking herself out of a job that would mean an end to cleaning latrines and washing bandages. 'It's just that I never expected . . .'

'No, I don't suppose you did.' Major Rice sounded amused. 'Well, what do you think? Will you have a go at running it for us?

Tara took a deep breath.

'Yes. Yes, I think I'd like to.'

'Good. We shall promote you, of course. You will become a corporal with immediate effect, and if you make a success of things you should be a sergeant before long.' She snapped the pen back down on the desk. 'That is all for the moment then, Tara. I'll arrange for you to liaise with Captain Greenaway regarding the details. And may I take this opportunity of wishing you every success in your new post.'

'Thank you, ma'am.'

Still in a daze, Tara left the office. She had gone in expecting a rocket and emerged a corporal. With a job that would be as fascinating as it was demanding. Already the enthusiasm was beginning to bubble in her, a return of her old effervescent spirit.

If this works out I shall be quite satisfied to remain here until the end of the war, Tara thought.

And for the first time since she had met him there was no shadow of Richard in her plans.

*

The letter came with a bunch of mail which was delivered just after Christmas.

The intervening weeks had sped by for Tara. Relieved of her menial duties she had been able to throw herself headlong into the plans for the club, which was scheduled for opening somewhere in the middle of January, and she had enjoyed every minute of it. She had experienced a certain coolness from the other girls, it was true – Jill in particular had been a little spiteful about her appointment – but Tara was determined not to let that spoil her pleasure.

Jill would get over it. When she got used to the idea that it was Tara, not she, who had been promoted; when she was able to come to the club and enjoy the various activities Tara had planned, then perhaps she would mellow. If not . . . It will be her loss, Tara thought. Why should I care?

For the most part the new job revitalized her life. There was no longer time for fretting, no time even for missing Richard. At Christmas, it was true, she had experienced a terrible longing for him, especially when her present had arrived – a lovely little coral brooch and matching earrings – with a loving note promising her more, much more when eventually they were together once again. But Tara had organized a carol concert and directed a nativity play and they had occupied her so fully both physically and mentally that she had soon put the momentary ache and loneliness behind her.

A letter from Richard was always something to be excited over, however, and when the mail was delivered that December day she took the letter into her tent, sitting down comfortably on the bed before tearing open the envelope and taking out the sheets of paper closely covered with Richard's neatly artistic writing.

He was working hard; the hospital was busier than ever. There had been some staff changes, some promotions, a new operating theatre. Tara read every word, trying to absorb the essence of Richard from the unadorned items of news. Then, as she came to a new paragraph, she felt her stomach falling away in a kind of dreadful anticipation even before she had had the time to read beyond the first bald statement.

'You'll never guess who is here in Queensland, Tara. Alys Peterson. She has joined the AWAS now. Do you remember when we met her in Melbourne she said she was going to? Well, she has done it. She is a driver, and she has been sent here as a chauffeur to the CO. She asked after you and wanted me to send you her love.'

Tara sat staring at the page, now shaking slightly in her unsteady hand. Alys in Queensland. Alys, at whom Richard looked with such admiration in his eyes. Alys who came from his world while she, Tara, did not. She could hardly believe it, yet somehow it was as if she had always known that she had not seen the last of the girl whose life she and Richard had saved.

'Bloody, bloody hell! said Tara.

But vehement as they were, the words did nothing to dispel the foreboding in her heart.

Chapter Twenty-two

Alys swung the staff car smoothly out of the camp entrance and onto the road. It was a cold night in early July with no moon; though the lights of the car cut a swathe through the darkness they only illuminated the road – the rich pastoral land which stretched from its perimeters was hidden from view by the blackness of the night.

'Step on it, honey. Let's burn some gas and get back to Base so that I can have a good stiff drink before bed.' The voice from the rear seat of the staff car was weary but vibrant – and unmistakably American.

'Yes, sir!' Alys' response was sharp but humorous, a parody of the parade ground obedience of a new recruit for a sergeant-major, and her lips curved in a smile as she put her foot down hard on the accelerator and concentrated her gaze into the sharp white path of the headlights.

She was enjoying her new role. What heaven it was to be able to drive a powerful motor car and not have to worry about petrol rationing! What bliss to have her freedom at last and to be able to use it doing what she loved best! After the restrictions of caring for Frances and the sense of guilt which had plagued her every second when she was away from her, the rigours of army life seemed like a holiday. The long hours, divided enjoyably between driving and tinkering under the bonnet of her car, slipped by so fast that there was never a moment for boredom or regrets from the time she rose, before dawn, splashing cold water onto her sleepy face, to the time when she could fall exhausted into bed at night, feeling sleep rushing in to claim her even before she had settled herself comfortably in her hard campo bed and closed her eyes. It was exhilarating, this life, as working for the Red Cross in

Darwin had been, providing just enough of a sense of purpose to keep her from feeling guilty that in a world where there was so much hardship and suffering she should be so ridiculously, chronically happy!

She flicked her eyes up to the interior mirror in the staff car, checking the road behind her for following lights, and caught a glimpse of her rear-seat passenger – US Army General's cap covering a thatch of dark, grey-flecked hair, thin face clean-shaven and lined with a tiredness which was never allowed to impinge on his forceful manner.

Greg Burton had command of the Allied forces in Queensland and every facet of his appearance and personality endorsed the responsibility of his position. Ruthless and decisive, endowed with unflagging energy and an unexpected sense of humour, he was the very epitome of a man who could change the course of history with a bold stroke, order a necessary withdrawal without any apparent loss of confidence, and bounce back to take the initiative the moment the opportunity presented itself. His reputation as a commander was flawless – he was hero-worshipped by the men who were proud to boast they served under him. The stories of his conquests of women, too, were legion – but Alys happened to know that his wallet contained snapshots not only of his wife, but also his grandchildren. He had shown them to her over a quiet drink at HQ after one of their long and exhausting schedules, and their relationship had taken on a new and unexpected intimacy.

'Well, how do you like driving the old man?' he had asked, lighting one of the small cigars he indulged in during his rare moments of relaxation, and she had smiled, musing briefly that he was a little like a brasher, more forceful version of John.

'I like it – though I must confess I had a few doubts to begin with.'

'Why?' He asked direct questions as John did, not bothering to wrap them up in niceties.

'I'm English by birth, Australian by upbringing. I wasn't sure I wanted to be seconded to a Yank.'

He laughed, amused by her responding frankness.

'You resent us.'

'A little. I thought you would want to come in and take us over. And I'd heard that you didn't like the girls to interfere with things like the maintenance of a vehicle. We are trained to look after them ourselves – we don't like it when mere males are brought in to do our mechanical jobs for us.'

'I guess that's because we like to see our girls looking fresh and sweet, not covered with engine oil and grease.'

'No, it's not – it's because you think we're not capable.'

He had drawn on his cigar, blowing a thin stream of pungent smoke into the already hazy atmosphere.

'Knowing you, Alys, I am quite sure you are capable of rectifying any fault an awkward engine can throw at you. In any case, I don't see how you can accuse us Yanks of sex discrimination when your own authorities refuse to allow your girls to serve overseas.'

'True.'

It was a decision which rankled with the girls – to be denied the chance to serve outside Australia. The British forces and the Americans were backing up everywhere with girls, but the Australian authorities remained adamant – they were to remain within the home shores.

Alys had wondered if the newfound rapport would disappear once more with the resumption of daily duty. It had not. She liked the General, liked his forthrightness and lack of cant – provided things were done as he wanted them he did not stand on ceremony. She liked the feeling of controlled energy he radiated, liked the fact that whatever his private doubts they were never allowed to diminish his publicly exhibited confidence. They were qualities which in a way mirrored her own so that she had soon become more than simply his chauffeuse, rather a small part of a highly charged team.

Now, driving the staff car on the deserted stretch of road

heading back to HQ Base she was aware once more of the sense of satisfaction which pervaded her days. She was tired, yes, but tired physically, not weighed down by the mental exhaustion which had plagued her during the months of caring for Frances. This was a tiredness she could cope with – even if it did mean that sometimes she wished for a couple of matchsticks to keep her eyes open!

Once again she glanced up at the mirror and registered twin pinpricks of brightness far behind her on the road. She gave her head a small shake. Funny how some sixth sense could tell her when there was another vehicle coming even before it was close enough to be seen. She did not understand it, yet that gut feeling was almost infallible.

Greg Burton fumbled for his cigars and lit one; the pungent smoke wafted past Alys' nose. He said nothing and Alys respected his desire for a few moments' quiet thought. But glancing in the mirror again, mostly to check on how tired he was looking, she noticed that the lights of the following vehicle were much closer.

Good grief, what sort of speed was it notching up? She checked her own needle and saw that it stood at a steady seventy. Given the rate at which the following car was catching her it must be doing close on a hundred.

The small warning bells which belonged to the same sixth sense system jangled against her nerve endings. It was going too fast – clear though the road may be it was not wise to drive at that speed in the dark. This was no race track for heaven's sake . . .

Race track. The phrase hit her like a double-take and momentarily she was back on the road side at Bathurst, waiting to see the Nippy pass by again and fighting the dawning realization that it was not going to. Nervously, she checked her mirror again and as she did so the headlamps caught her staff car for the first time, bathing the interior in sharp, jolting light. Then she heard the roar of an over-worked engine and a dark shape shot past, making the staff car sway slightly with the force of its velocity.

'What the hell . . . ?' General Burton, shaken out of his reverie, shot forward in his seat.

Alys had automatically eased her foot off the accelerator, now she depressed it again, shooting forward in the wake of the overtaking vehicle's tail lights.

'Just some crazy fool,' she said.

'It had better not be one of my men. Did you see who . . .' the General broke off in mid-sentence. Up ahead the lights spun suddenly, shooting an arc in the darkness first one way, then the other. In the quiet of the night there was a sickening thud and silence, apart from the purring engine of the staff car.

'Christ!'

Shock sent tingling waves to each of Alys' muscles and her voice came tense yet strangely soft. 'He's lost it!'

'Not surprising! Bloody idiot!' Greg Burton sounded more angry than shaken.

Alys reduced her speed, her foot shaking slightly as she eased off the accelerator. The lights of the crashed car were still working; now they made a tunnel of brightness across the width of the road. Beyond it her own lights picked up the dark slewed shape. Closer and she could see it was on its roof, wheels spinning. She braked in behind it, switched off her engine and opened the door. Greg Burton was out of the car as quickly as she was, striding towards the wreck, cigar still clamped between his teeth.

'Sir – you had better put that out. There may be petrol.'

He swore, backed off to a safe distance and ground his cigar out into the road with the heel of his shoe.

The crashed car had hit a tree at the edge of the road, upended and flipped onto its roof. The bonnet had folded concertina-like into the body and there was indeed a sickening stench of petrol. Alys approached it. The tremble of her foot seemed to have transferred itself to her stomach. She did not want to look into the car, did not want to be a first-hand witness to what she might find there, but she ignored her apprehension, bending down to

peer through the smashed window, preparing herself for
. . . what?

The lights of her own car were illuminating the wreck;
as the General approached again she straightened,
puzzled.

'There's nobody there!'

The General crouched down beside her, reaching
through the broken window, feeling into the condensed
space between dashboard and driver's seat.

'He must have been thrown out.'

'Thrown out! But . . .' She saw the shattered windscreen, a gaping hole where before there had been a sheet
of glass and nodded, comprehending.

'We had better look for him.'

For seemingly endless minutes they searched in the
darkness then Greg Burton called: 'Over here!'

The broken body of the young driver lay yards back into
the undergrowth. Barely recognizable. Barely alive. Alys
bent over him, feeling for a pulse. When she found it, it
was weak and irregular and her fingers became sticky with
blood.

'He's in a bad way.'

'What the hell would you expect!'

'We'll have to get him immediate medical attention or
there's no chance. Oh, if only I had my ambulance!'

'We'll use the car.'

'But maybe he shouldn't be moved.'

'We'll have to chance that. By the time we get a doctor
to him he could be dead. There's a groundsheet in the car.
We'll use that.'

Alys returned to the staff car, found the groundsheet
and took it back to where General Burton was bending
over the inert body. Gently, they lifted the boy onto it,
then Greg Burton took two corners and she took the
others, terrified she might not be strong enough to support
his weight, but she found it much easier than she
expected. Manhandling Frances in and out of her chair
had been better training than she had realized, she

thought ruefully. At the car there was another problem –
how to get him in. Greg Burton took the boy's shoulders
and together they managed to lay him across the back
seat. Then he installed himself in the front passenger seat
alongside Alys and reached for the telephone he used to
communicate with HQ.

Alys started the car while he carried on a brief staccato
conversation and when he had finished she was ready and
waiting to go.

'Where are we taking him?'

The General's voice was as cool and unruffled as ever.
He might be divorced now from front line action, but this
incident had proved him as capable of dealing with an
immediate crisis as deploying men for copybook actions.

'It seems we are closest to 138 AGH,' he said. 'They will
be ready and waiting for him, Alys, if we take him there.'

*

Alys took a long drink of strong sweet tea, set the mug
down on the scrubbed wood table in front of her and
bowed her head into her hands, smoothing the lines of
tiredness out of her forehead with her fingers.

How much longer would it be before General Burton
finished his conversation with the CO and was ready to be
driven back to Base? Exhaustion was catching up with her
now; all she could think of was how wonderful it would be
to fall into her bed, close her eyes and snatch a few hours,
blissful oblivion before it was time to be up and working
again. But General Burton was tireless. Just when she
thought he had reached the same sort of low ebb she was
experiencing he seemed to discover a new fount of energy;
the man existed – no thrived – on no more than three or
four hours' sleep a night. All very well when he extended
his day at Base when she was no longer needed, not so
good when she had to try to remain alert enough to be able
to drive him again the moment he was ready.

Alys turned her wrist over to look at her watch and even

that small movement was an effort. Half-past-two – and still no sign of the General. But tomorrow he would be up with the dawn and ready to go again – and expecting Alys to be ready, too.

She sighed, almost wishing she had taken a different route home tonight and not been driving on the road where the accident had occurred. But that was not only futile it was selfish too. If they had not come upon him the young man could have lain injured and undiscovered for hours and would almost certainly have been dead by now. As it was . . .

The last Alys had seen of him was when he was whisked away on a trolley surrounded by concerned hospital staff. The General had gone off to talk to old friends he had not expected to see and she had been shown into the rest room to wait. That had been well over an hour ago and since then she had seen no one but a couple of night duty sisters who had come in for a brief break and a cigarette and an orderly who had brought her a mug of tea.

Footsteps sounded in the corridor and Alys looked up expectantly as the door opened. Then her eyes widened and her lips curved in a smile of surprised greeting.

'Richard!'

'Hello, Alys. I heard you were here.'

He looked as tired as she felt, his face rumpled as if he had been dragged from sleep, his hair still slightly tousled.

'I didn't expect to see you!'

It was true, she had not expected to see him. It had crossed her mind when she had been on her way to 138, but during the last hour the probability had faded. Now, her tiredness dropped away as pleasure sent a fresh supply of adrenalin coursing through her veins.

'If you will bring in these casualties in the middle of the night . . .'

'Yes.' She lifted her mug and sipped the now luke-warm tea. 'How is he?'

'Your young man? Not very well I'm afraid. I don't think he'll make it.'

'I didn't think he would. He was going like a bat out of hell.' She was silent for a moment, remembering the broken body and the tragic memories it had rekindled for her. 'We still don't know who he is, do we?'

'An American serviceman. He had papers in his pocket.'

'American. Oh Lord.' Greg Burton would not be too pleased about that.

'He has just come out of the operating theatre. We've done what we can but I don't think it will be enough. He had massive internal injuries.' Richard sat down, stretching his tall frame wearily. 'I was got out of bed to assist.'

'Oh . . . sorry.'

'That's what we are here for. Anyway, it's always a pleasure to see you, Alys. How are you getting on?'

'Fine. General Burton is a hon.' She used the General's own expression unselfconsciously. 'How about you?'

'Fine. Life at an AGH doesn't change much. The problems are much the same wherever you are. And at least conditions here are pretty good since we got our new buildings.'

'And Tara. How is Tara?'

She saw the faintest shadow flicker across his face.

'Still in New Guinea. You know she is managing an AAMWS club there?'

'I knew she was going to. How does she like it?'

'Very much, if her letters are anything to go by.' Again there was the slight hesitancy in his voice. Something about that is not pleasing him, she thought. Aloud she said: 'It must be very hard, being separated so soon after your marriage. You have had very little time together.'

'Very little. I have some leave coming up and I have the problem of deciding what to do with it. Try to get over to New Guinea by hook or by crook to Tara, or travel down to Melbourne to see my parents.'

A slight puzzled frown creased her eyes, 'Is that a problem?'

'As it happens, yes. I know Tara is expecting me to at

386

least try to hitch a lift over to the islands, but my father has been very poorly and I feel I ought to try to get home and see him. I don't think he has much time left.'

'Oh dear. What is the matter?'

'He had a heart attack a few months back. Now the winter has come and he has bronchial problems too. I'm afraid the combination might prove too much for him.'

Alys twirled the mug on the table between her hands.

'It's no business of mine, but if he is that poorly I think I would go to see your father. I mean – I know you want to see Tara, of course you do, she's your wife, but I know from experience how guilty it's possible to feel about neglecting your parents.'

'You!' He raised an eyebrow. 'You could hardly be accused of neglecting your mother, Alys.'

She pulled a face. 'You would be surprised. Anyway, the point I'm making is, hopefully you and Tara will have the rest of your lives, while if your father dies and you haven't been to see him . . .'

He nodded. 'I must confess I think I'd almost decided that way. For one thing, it's not even certain I could get to New Guinea, for another – yes, you are right, I'd never forgive myself if the old man died and I hadn't got to see him one last time. It's strange, isn't it? You take your parents so much for granted, don't even realize they are getting older, and then suddenly one day you turn around and . . .'

'I know. I haven't been home since it happened. I'm due for some leave too, but I've been putting off taking it.' Alys gave a small nervous laugh. She did not want him to know about the compulsion which drove her constantly towards going home to try to mend fences with the family she had left so acrimoniously, or the tightening of her stomach which she experienced every time the possibility looked even remotely like becoming reality.

'I'll tell you what.' Richard stretched again, thrusting his hands into the pockets of his white coat, pulled hastily on over pyjamas. 'You take your leave and I'll take mine. We could travel down together.'

'Oh! She felt the small surprised tightening deep inside once again. Was it the prospect of going home that caused it this time – or something else?'

'It's a long journey to do alone,' he went on, seemingly oblivious to her hesitation. 'We could keep one another company.'

'Yes, I suppose we could.'

He smiled, half-teasing. 'Never mind your family. I'll bet that farmer friend of yours – John – would be pleased to see you.'

She experienced a moment's poignancy that he could mention John so easily. But there was no reason why he should not be able to. Then, as she thought about what he had said, warmth came flooding in. Yes, John would be pleased to see her – and she would be pleased to see him.

'All right,' she said. 'If the General will let me go I'll take you up on that offer.'

*

Richard stopped the car beside the white house-shaped mailbox bearing the legend Buchlyvie but left the engine running.

'Are you sure you don't want me to drive you down to the house, Alys? It's one hell of a way to walk.'

'No, I want to surprise John and if he hears the car it will spoil it.' Alys opened the passenger door and swung her legs out.

'Well, if you are sure. I'll pick you up again in what – say two hours? Unless, of course, you want to drive your own car back to Melbourne.'

'Better not – not today. I asked John to look after it for me while I was away but I want him to know I came to see him today, not my car.'

'As you like. Give John my regards, won't you?'

'Of course.' She waved as the car pulled away, then turned and began walking up the drive, smiling a little as she imagined John's surprise when he saw her.

She should have let him know she was coming, she supposed. But the dates of her leave had not been confirmed until the last moment and when she had arrived in Melbourne she had not liked to phone immediately. To have done so would have been hurtful to her father.

It was ironic, Alys thought, that having persuaded Richard to come home because of *his* father's health, she should have found such a change in her own. She had always thought of him as a giant of a man, a little unapproachable perhaps, more concerned with his business interests than his family, but a powerhouse it was impossible not to admire nonetheless. Now, he seemed to have grown old overnight. Could her mother's death have had something to do with that? she wondered. They had never struck her as a particularly close couple, but even after her stroke Frances had still been there, a part of the old regime – and a magnet for the loyal Beverley. Now she came to visit less often and there was an air of desolation about the house which had once seemed to be the hub of the family. It was still cared for by the staff, of course, but it no longer felt like a home, just an elegant, half-empty shell.

Her father shared a little of her own guilt, too, Alys believed. Over dinner on her first night he had said as much.

'I should have spent more time with her, I suppose,' he had said, picking at the food which once he would have wolfed down. 'But there you are, I was always too busy making money. Now, I look at myself and wonder what it was all for.'

'Oh Daddy, you couldn't have done anything else. The business has been your life. You'd never have been happy in some nine to five job or working for someone else,' Alys had tried to soothe.

He had hardly seemed to hear her.

'I won't be able to keep it up forever though, will I? And what else is there left to me? No family life, nothing but an empty house to come home to. I don't even seem to know my own children. Beverley was her mother's girl – she hardly comes here any more. Not that we'd have anything to talk about if she did. She hasn't a brain in her head – never had. Can't understand it. You – you are the sharp one. But you aren't here either.'

Alys had felt the familiar tightening in her chest. Oh no, she thought. Not Daddy too . . .

'I'm sorry,' she said. 'There's nothing I can do about it. I'm a member of the AIF now.'

'I should have taken you into the business.' He was staring straight ahead, his dinner going cold on the plate in front of him. 'I think you would have done well. Your mother would never have heard of it, of course. Not the life for a girl, she would have said. But look at the jobs you girls are doing now! The world is changing. When this war is over nothing will be the same again. They're out in the market place now, doing all the jobs a man used to do – and doing them well. They'll never be satisfied with just being wives and mothers again.'

'Beverley will be.'

'Beverley!' Alys was shocked by the underlying scorn in his voice. 'Beverley hasn't the wit to want anything different. But you . . .' He looked at her directly, his eyes very sharp in his unhealthily blotched face. 'You could have been the son I never had.'

'Could I?' She was embarrassed now by the way he was talking to her – the dose of frankness coming after all the years of non-communication was disconcerting.

'I wanted a son when you were born. Still hoped for one afterwards. But your mother didn't want any more children. Said two was enough. I could never understand that. Dammit, she had nothing else to do, did she?'

'Oh I don't know, she was always busy with her committees,' Alys said.

He snorted. 'Committees! They were all she ever cared about. Still, I miss her. Yes, I do. After thirty years, you get to take someone for granted.'

390

Alys said nothing. She was thinking of John, who had never had the chance to take his wife for granted.

She had wanted to phone him then, wanted desperately to hear his soft drawl and feel the easy understanding that was so real it was almost tangible and worlds removed from the awkward confidences being thrust upon her by her father. But she had known this was not the moment.

That night, lying sleepless in her old room she had thought of him again, longing to talk to him. Everything seemed so simple when she was with John. It was a knack he had, taking one problem at a time so that it dissolved in common sense, dispelling depression with his easy going attitude.

Now, walking up the drive, she quickened her step, anxious to be with him without any more delay. Unless he was still burdened down by farm work he would be at home.

The front door of the house was closed against the cold August wind. Alys rang the bell and heard it jangle somewhere within. Silence. She rang again, then tried the door. It opened.

'Anyone at home?' she called.

A shadow materialized – Flora, the old aborigine housekeeper. Alys beamed at her.

'Hello, I've come to see John. Is he in?'

The dark weathered face was set in the same uncompromising give-nothing-away expression Alys remembered so well.

'Boss man in sitting room.'

'Oh good. May I come in?' Alys closed the door behind her, glad to shut out the biting edge of wind. 'Don't tell him I'm here, I want to surprise him.'

'But Miss Alys . . .' Flora was following her across the kitchen, wiping her hands on her apron.

'It's all right, Flora.' Alys had always found the woman's presence slightly oppressive; she did not want her behind her shoulder when she greeted John.

She crossed quickly to the sitting room, slightly

surprised John had not heard her voice and come to meet her. Perhaps he had had an early morning and was asleep. She pushed open the door.

'Hello! Surprise!'

He was sitting at the big old bureau in the corner with his back towards her. Papers and books were spread out before him but Alys had the odd impression he had not been looking at them even before the interruption. At the sound of her voice he turned, then rose quickly.

'Alys!'

She froze, the smile of greeting fading to shock as she took in the look of him, hair turned from iron-grey to white standing straight up from his forehead where he had been pushing his fingers through it, lines etched more deeply around his eyes and mouth, the flesh falling into small pouches between. He seemed to have aged ten years since she had last seen him.

'Hello, John,' she faltered. 'I got some leave – I thought I would . . .'

'Good. It's good to see you.' His voice was heavy like his face and no welcoming smile lifted the weight of those lines. 'Come in – sit down. Would you like some tea?'

'Well –yes . . .'

Flora was still hovering. He spoke to her. 'Make us a pot of tea, would you, Flora?'

Tentatively, Alys crossed to the chair and sat down. She could not tear her eyes away from John's haggard face, couldn't get over the change in him. As if reading her thoughts he smiled, but it was a parody of his old quirky smile.

'I'm sorry. This isn't much of a welcome for you after all this time.'

'Don't be silly. I . . .'

'I might as well tell you right away. I had some very bad news yesterday.'

She felt the falling away inside; knew what he was going to say before he said it.

'Oh John. Not . . .?'

392

'Yes, I'm afraid so. Stuart. He has been killed.'

'Oh no! Impulsively, she jumped up and ran to him, taking hold of his arm. 'When? How?'

'I don't know any details yet, except that he was in the islands. Killed in action, they said. Whatever that may mean. I suppose I shall get to hear more eventually. Not that it will change anything.'

'Oh, I'm so sorry. I don't know what to say. I had no idea . . .'

'Well, of course you wouldn't have.' He was matter-of-fact now. Only that flatness of tone revealed his emotions – and from time to time his eyes strayed to the framed photograph of the handsome young man.

Flora brought the tea. The kettle must be permanently on the boil for her to be able to do it so quickly, Alys thought irrelevantly. John acknowledged it but made no move; he looked oddly drained of energy, like a man in a dream. Alys dropped to her knees beside the low table, milking the cups and adding two large spoonfuls of sugar to John's.

'Here.' She pushed it into his hand. 'Drink this. You look as though you could do with it.'

He gulped at the scalding liquid then set the cup down.

'God, it tastes awful.'

She sipped her own tea. Nothing wrong with it.

'Drink it. It will do you good.'

'No thanks.'

'Drink it!' She pushed him down in to the chair and put the cup in his hands. He sat holding the cup but not drinking and after a moment the tears began to run down his cheeks. She dropped to her knees, taking his hands, and he laid his head against her, his body shaking with silent sobs.

'Oh John . . .' She held him, knowing that nothing she could say would ease his agony, helpless in the face of his grief.

After a while he raised his head. 'I'm sorry. I'm sorry – I just can't – oh Christ!'

Again, she was overwhelmed by helplessness. It was terrible to see him this way – such a strong man, a rock of strength with his own foundations crumbled beneath him.

'Don't be sorry. I'm just glad I'm here. I wish there was something I could do or say. But there's nothing, is there?'

'He was a good boy. Young and headstrong, of course, but weren't we all? I thought when this war was over and he came home he could start taking over the running of the farm. He'd find a girl, get married, there would even be children in the house again. I thought . . . you know, I even thought maybe he and you . . . Stupid, really. Told myself it was just wishful thinking, but you would have liked him, I know you would.' He was talking now more than he ever talked, letting his innermost thoughts pour out. 'It's funny but it keeps you going, somehow, knowing there's someone to hand things on to. You don't think about it that much but it's there all the same at the back of your mind. Then one telegram. One damned telegram, just a few short words, and there's nothing left. I keep thinking of him when he was a boy, you know. The things he used to do – the things we did together. I taught him to shoot. He liked that. Used to take his guns out and bag a few bunnies. Then he'd come back, proud as you like, and say – "There's a few less to eat your grass, Dad." Now he's gone. No more life in him than in one of those bunnies.' A shudder ran through him. 'Why him, Alys? That's what I keep asking myself. Damned stupid, really. He's only one of thousands and yet I still keep asking – why him?'

'I know.' She had seen some of the dead and maimed, all some father's sons, their pride and their hope for the future. Yet she too felt the unfairness. Why John's son? He was all he had.

'His mother – does she know?' she asked.

He shook his head. 'I went out to see her this morning. I couldn't face it yesterday when the telegram came, but today I thought – well, it's got to be done. I've got to tell her. But when I got there, there was no way. She's like a child. She wouldn't understand. I think she has forgotten she ever had a son. She didn't even know me. I had to come away and leave her. For the first time in all those years I just couldn't take it.'

She nodded, understanding.

They sat for a while longer, silent sometimes, talking sometimes. There was nothing really to say, yet Alys hoped that just by being there she might be some small comfort to the man who had been such a comfort to her.

It was only when the mantle clock chimed the half-hour that she remembered Richard would be waiting for her.

'John, I'm going to have to go.' She got up reluctantly, not wanting to leave him.

He looked at her, half-puzzled, as if it had only just occurred to him to wonder how she had got out to Buchlyvie.

'Richard Allingham ran me out,' she explained. 'You remember him? We had dinner with him and his wife.'

'Oh – yes. Give him my regards.' John was in full control of himself again; his ravaged face was now the only outward sign of his grief.'

'I will,' Alys said, afraid suddenly that if she was late at the gates Richard might come up to the house looking for her. She did not want John to have the added strain of having to face Richard. 'And I'll be out to see you again. Tomorrow, perhaps?'

He stood up. She noticed the slight stoop now to his straight shoulders.

'You don't have to, Alys. I shall be all right. You don't want to spend your precious leave like this. I'm not going to be much company, I'm afraid.'

'You're insulting me now,' Alys said briskly. 'Suggesting I'm a fair weather friend. I shall come because I want to – if you'll let me of course.'

He smiled wanly, his mouth moving but his eyes remaining darkly shadowed.

'Woe betide anybody who tried to stop you doing what you want to do, Alys.'

'That's more like it.' She reached up and kissed his

cheek. It felt slightly grizzled as if he had not been able to find it in himself to bother shaving properly that morning. 'Bear up, John. I'll be seeing you.'

He went with her to the door and she could feel his eyes following her as she started down the drive. She turned and waved but he did not wave back, just stood, immovable as an old-established gum, framed in the doorway.

There was a great weight round her heart and she knew it was because she was sharing his grief. God, but life could be cruel! The cold blustery wind whipped her hair and roared in her ears and she wished that she too could cry because tears would be the only relief to the pressure of sadness within her.

At the end of the drive beside the white-painted mailbox she saw a flash of gleaming black. Richard was waiting for her. She glanced over her shoulder, saw the indistinct figure of John still watching her, and checked the desire to run.

Richard was leaning against the bonnet of the car. He looked somehow young and strong and invincible. As she approached he turned and smiled at her. And she could no longer keep her feet from running.

'All right?' he greeted her.

At first, no words would come for she found her lips were trembling.

She saw his face change. 'What's wrong?'

And still she could find no coherent way to begin.

'Oh Richard,' she said, and began to cry.

*

When at last her sobs began to ease she realized his arms were around her. Somehow she had told him and the sharing was beginning to lessen the weight inside her. She hoped she had done the same for John, knew she had not, and began to cry again.

Why, why, why? There was no answer. But here was

396

comfort in the broad strength of Richard's shoulder beneath the smooth twill of his jacket. She clung to him while the words poured from her in an unthinking torrent.

'It's not fair. It's just not fair! He's a good man – a really good man. For this to happen to him . . .'

'Don't, Alys. Come on, I'll take you home.'

Home. Home to her father. Another oddly pitiful figure in this world which seemed suddenly to contain nothing but suffering and pain.

'Oh Richard.' She pulled away, shading her eyes with her hand. 'Don't you sometimes wish you had never been born?'

He looked at her, saw a girl who had been raised with all the trappings which could have made her utterly spoiled and selfish but who had lost none of her capacity for compassion, a girl who could endure her own suffering yet cry for the grief of others. And felt something deep and powerful stir within him.

'No, Alys,' he said truthfully. 'Life may sometimes be hard. But no, I never have wished that.'

'Then perhaps you are lucky,' she said.

He turned on the engine, battling suddenly with a surge of desire so strong it threatened to sweep away all reason.

'Perhaps I am,' he said roughly.

Chapter Twenty-three

The silence in the tent was broken only by the even breathing of five of the six occupants. Quietly, Tara set down her bunch of clubhouse keys on top of the wooden box which served as her wardrobe, picked up her kitbag and crept between the beds where the other girls lay sleeping. Then she slipped out, fastened the tent flap behind her and stood for a moment breathing deeply to steady the racing of her pulse.

The night was balmy, the stars very bright in the soft velvet tropical sky. Beyond the tent lines the breeze stirred gently in the palms, reminding her briefly of another night when the undergrowth had whispered, disturbed not only by the forces of nature but by a human intruder. She shivered, then hoisted her kitbag onto her shoulder, pushing the thought away. If she dwelled on it she would run straight back to the safety of the tent and that certainly did not fit in with her plans.

The shiver became a tremor of excitement. She left the tent lines, walking quickly across the open patch of ground which separated them from the clubhouse. Dotted with tables and chairs which during the hot days and warm evenings were crowded with relaxing service personnel it was deserted now, the light of the moon showing it in soft relief. Tara glanced about her, ears cocked for the distinctive engine hum of an approaching ute. There was no sound but the everlasting chirping of the grasshoppers and crickets and she was aware of a twinge of misgiving.

Perhaps they would not come for her. Perhaps something unexpected had cropped up to prevent them. Perhaps the whole thing had been a joke from start to finish – a practical joke played by bored US air crew and they had never had the slightest intention of doing what they had promised. It was after all, a crazy idea, hopping over to Queensland to see Richard without telling anyone what she was doing, without permission from her superiors, without anything but the clothes she stood up in and what she could carry in her kitbag. But when she had got talking to the crew of the US transport plane in the club that evening and heard they were flying out, empty, in a few hours, it had seemed like the answer to a prayer.

She had to see Richard. Whatever the consequences. It might mean the end of her career as manager of the AAMWS club – it probably would. But if she could not get to Australia soon to see him she was terribly afraid it would be the end of her marriage. And when it came to weighing one against the other there was scarcely a decision to be made.

Why, of all possible postings, had Alys Peterson had to be sent to Queensland? Tara wondered, quickening her step to take her across the stretch of open ground. When she had joined the AWAS the authorities could have chosen to send her anywhere in the whole wide continent of Australia. But by some quirk of fate she had been sent to the very place where she was in contact with Richard. And not only in contact with him but very friendly from the tone of his letters. Tara had registered alarm bells the moment she had heard about it, back in the New Year. She did not like the way Richard looked at Alys, liked even less the fact that they had so much in common, which she and Richard did not. And when he had written to say that he and Alys were taking leave together to go to Melbourne it had been the last straw.

How could he do it? It was so long since they had been together and her own requests for leave had been constantly parried. But what was there to have stopped Richard hitching a lift to New Guinea to see her if he had really wanted to? Instead, he had chosen to go to Melbourne – with *her* (Tara could scarcely bring herself to think of Alys's name, let alone speak it aloud) – travelling

399

all that way, and seeing as much as he could of her while they were there, no doubt. Oh, keeping it all very proper, knowing him, but being with her, talking about things that she, Tara, would never understand, carrying her bag for her, solicitously making certain she was comfortable – and admiring, maybe even desiring, her. Jealousy so strong it outweighed every other emotion had coursed through her and for the first time Tara felt something akin to understanding for Red. I'd kill *her* if I could, Tara thought. I'd like nothing better than to stick a knife in her and twist and twist. But there was no danger of that. Alys was too far away on the other side of the Torres Strait. With Richard.

Alongside the jealousy helplessness had burned. There was nothing she could do – nothing. She was stuck here in New Guinea, unable to fight Alys for her husband, tied hand and foot by a job which had at first seemed like a godsend. She had enjoyed every moment of running the club and thought she had done it well, but her very success had created the ties which kept her here.

If I was still cleaning latrines and washing bandages I'll bet they would have authorized my leave, Tara thought, surprised by her own bitterness. As it is I have to sit here, organizing recreation for a lot of other women, while *she* steals my husband from under my nose!

And then, this evening, the US air crew had come out to the club.

'Can I sign them in, Tara?' Jill Whitton had asked. 'They are only here for a few hours – they brought a load of troops this afternoon and they are due to fly out again during the night. They could do with a drink and a bit of relaxation.'

Tara had smiled. 'Don't give me that. It's not their relaxation you are thinking of, it's all the spare dollars they have to spend on you!'

Jill pulled a face. 'Well, that too. How about it – can I bring them in?'

'As far as I'm concerned, yes. Just as long as they don't

overindulge on the drinks. I should hate them to give their passengers a bumpy ride home.'

'They haven't got any passengers on the way back. They're empty.'

Tara snorted. 'What a waste! When there are so many people on this island just dying to get back to Oz – me included!'

But still the idea of actually begging a lift had not occurred to her. That came later as she looked at the happy-go-lucky group gathered around a clubhouse table, laughing as they peeled dollar bills from a wad of notes to pay for their drinks, muddying the air with the smoke of dozens of cheap issue cigarettes, looking as if they had not a care in the world. They took things so casually, the Yanks. Of course, it wasn't really their war. That made a difference, she supposed, for the Jap attack on Pearl Harbor was the closest the enemy had ever got to 'home'. But their whole attitude was devil-may-care, as if rules and regulations were there to be flouted.

They look like fun, Tara thought. I'll have a word with them later. Maybe they'll cheer me up a little bit.

Towards the end of the evening Tara always entertained with a song or two. Tonight the applause from the Yanks' table was raucous and on her way back from the stage Tara stopped at their table.

'Enjoying yourselves, boys?'

'You bet!' One of the Yanks, a tall lanky young man with a short-cropped crew cut, rocked his chair onto its back legs, eyeing her appreciatively. 'How about letting us buy you a drink, baby? Singing is thirsty work.'

Tara cast a look at the crowd around the bar. Busy. But her girls seemed to be coping well.

'Sure an' why not?' she said, sitting down on the chair that one of them pulled out for her.

The Yanks were good company. She stayed with them for a while, laughing at their jokes and enjoying the attention they were paying her.

'I hear you are flying out tonight,' she said. 'Where are you headed?'

The Yank with the crew cut drained his glass. 'Townsville.'

'Oh, Queensland.' Tara felt the familiar lump in her throat. 'I only wish I could come with you.'

The Yank, busy collecting glasses to shout another round, glanced round at her. 'Why don't you then?'

'What?'

'Come with us. We've got plenty of room to spare. We'll give her a lift, won't we, guys?'

'I can't do that,' Tara said, and stopped. A lift to Queensland. She was being offered a lift to Queensland – and she was turning it down!

'Why not?'

'Because . . .' Because I have no leave pass. Because if I go with you I shall probably be court martialled. Because what in the world is going to happen to the club – *my* club – if I do? The reasons raced through her mind and became unimportant. Richard was in Queensland. Richard and Alys. If she could only get to see him, hold him, love him, remind him of what it was they shared, perhaps she could drive out the spectre of Alys.

Oh Richard! The longing was so fierce in her it drowned out all other considerations. Tara had never been a one to waste time weighing odds. She had always acted on impulse – and she acted on impulse now.

'Would you really take me? she asked.

'Sure – as long as you keep quiet about it.'

'Where are you going from?'

'The airstrip, 0200 hours.'

'I couldn't get out there.'

'We could pick her up, couldn't we, Hank?'

'Sure – why not?'

'All right!' Tara was trembling now with eagerness. 'I'll do it.'

'O.K. We'll pick you up at, say, 0100, somewhere about here. You won't chicken out now, baby, will you?

Wouldn't want to make the trip out here for nothing.'

'No, I won't chicken out,' Tara said.

The rest of the evening she was on a high, buzzing with nervous tension and suppressed excitement. She must be mad! No – she would be mad *not* to do it. When the Yanks left they merely waved to her from the doorway and she thought they were being discreet.

Now, however, waiting on the deserted roadway, she began to wonder if perhaps they had only been teasing, stringing her along. Or not taking her seriously. She glanced at her watch. Five past one. A sense of depression settled in the pit of her stomach. What was Richard doing now? In bed and asleep? Working on some patient, using all his talents to mend a broken body? Or sharing a coffee and a chat with Alys? The depression deepened. She looked at her watch again. Ten past. They weren't coming. She was not going to be able to get back to see him after all. She would have to go back to her tent, unpack her kitbag, pocket the club keys before anyone found them and wondered why she had left them out on her cupboard, and settle back for more countless weeks or months knowing that he . . .

A bright path of light cut through the darkness. She drew upright, every nerve tingling, straining her eyes towards the lights. Closer, closer – and the engine sound of a ute drowning the chirping of the crickets . . .'

Tara hoisted her kitbag onto her shoulder and ran towards the ute.

The crew cut Yank was driving; he leaned over and opened the door for her. 'Ready then, gorgeous? You still wanna go?'

'Well, of course I do!' Tara said and climbed in.

*

In the grey dawn Tara walked towards 138 AGH. After a night without sleep her legs felt heavy, her mouth tasted stale and the excitement tingling within her was tinged with nervousness.

All very well to do something utterly crazy like this, but what was Richard going to say when he saw her? He would be shocked, of course – but would he be pleased? Suddenly, even that didn't seem in the least likely. After all, he had gone to Melbourne instead of hopping over to New Guinea when he had his leave.

The cluster of huts which comprised 138 loomed up, slightly forbidding now she was this close to them. After the swift flight in the transport plane she had managed to hitch another lift to take her south; she shivered, the cold morning air seeming to dissolve every stitch of her tropical kit clothing and striking deeply chill against skin accustomed to twenty-four-hour heat.

The sound of a vehicle on the path behind her made her turn and she saw an ambulance approaching. Instantly she thought of Alys. She did not want to meet her before seeing Richard – she would not know what to say to her. And besides, she did not want Alys to be the one to tell Richard she was here. 'I have a surprise for you – guess who's here?' she could imagine that cultured voice saying. And she would be the one to see the expression on his face when she said it and know whether it registered pleasure – or dismay.

The ambulance passed and Tara remembered that Alys was no longer working for the Red Cross but driving a US Army General. Typical. Typical of her to be assigned to top brass.

She walked on, praying there would be no provost at the entrance to the hospital. If she was asked for a pass the cat would be well and truly out of the bag. But when she approached the hospital buildings there was no sign of life. The ambulance was parked at the door of the admissions block, empty now. She hesitated for just a moment then gave herself a mental shake. Look tentative and someone would wonder what business she had being here. Tara had never been one to let her nervousness show. Life was an act, wasn't it – so . . . act!

She pushed open the door and walked into the admissions room.

'Could you tell me where I could find Richard Allingham?' she said.

*

It seemed she had been waiting forever when she heard his voice in the corridor outside.

She jumped up, passing the astonished AAMWS clerk, and ran into the corridor. He had just passed through the door leading from the treatment room and she thought her heart would burst with happiness just looking at him, standing there with hands thrust into the pockets of his white coat, hair slightly rumpled as if he had just taken off a sterile cap.

'Richard!' Her voice was small and breathy. All the time she had been waiting while he was attending to the patient who had come in on the ambulance, she had been planning the million and one things she wanted to say to him; now she was face to face with him and every single one of them deserted her.

'Tara?' He said it questioningly, as if he simply could not believe his eyes.

'Yes – it's me!' And then she was running to him, unable to restrain herself for another moment. 'Oh Richard – Richard!'

She was in his arms, feeling the hardness of his chest beneath her cheek, the long sinews of his back with her outstretched hands, oblivious to the AAMWS clerk, oblivious to everything but that she was with Richard once more after the long months of separation.

After a moment he held her away. 'What are you doing here?'

She looked up at him, seeing his beloved face through a mist of tears, and felt a small knot of panic tighten her throat. She couldn't tell him the truth. Not here.

'Oh, I got a three-day pass and hitched a lift with a US transport.' The panic dissolved into longing and she hugged him tight once more, wanting nothing but to hold him and never let him go.

'Tara . . .' He took hold of her arms, pushing her away. 'Not here!'

Hurt, puzzled, she looked up at him and saw his expression – embarrassment verging on distaste.

'Come on, we'll go outside for a few minutes.' His hand slid to her elbow, turning her, urging her back along the corridor. 'I won't be far away if you need me,' he said to the AAMWS clerk.

The morning was brightening now towards full daylight, the hospital was beginning to come to life. A couple of sisters walked chatting between the buildings, an orderly trundled a trolley of linen. Tara did not recognize any of them – the hospital staff must have changed considerably in the time she had been away.

'You should have let me know you were coming,' Richard said.

Again the panic knotted her throat threatening to cut off speech. This was the moment to confess she had no business being here at all – but she knew now she was not going to tell him. He would be shocked – furious with her, probably – and everything would be spoiled. Knowing him, he might even insist she return immediately before the provosts came looking for her.

'There was no time,' she said. 'I didn't know myself until yesterday. I got the chance – and I just came!'

They were around the corner of the building now and she turned to him again, as desperate for reassurance as for his touch.

'Oh Richard, I've missed you so!'

This time he did not push her away. She felt the response in his body and the hungry pressure of his lips on hers and for a few moments she let the avalanche of delight sweep away all her doubts and worries. She loved him – and if she had to spend the rest of the war scrubbing latrines and washing bandages to pay for her few stolen days it would have been worth it. Then, gradually, she felt

406

the tide of his passion ebb, his back stiffening into rigid lines, his arms slightly tentative around her and she could almost imagine his eyes, alert and watchful, looking over her shoulder to see if anyone was coming.

The pain of rejection destroyed her own mood of loving and longing. How could he be like this, so cool, so unmoved?

'Aren't you pleased to see me?' she asked in a small voice.

'Of course I am!'

'You don't seem very pleased.'

'Oh Tara, it's not that. But this is a hospital. I'm a doctor.'

'You are also my husband and I haven't seen you for months and months.'

'There are some things you just don't want to do when all the world is looking on.'

She stiffened. She should have known that Richard would never show his emotions in public. It was not his style. But surely after such a prolonged parting it was not unreasonable to expect him to display just a little pleasure – a little desire for her? But then passion was not Richard's strong suit – even in private.

'I just wish I'd known you were coming,' he said again. 'If I had known maybe I could have arranged some leave myself.'

The imp of disappointment and rejection twisted within her to something close to anger.

'I thought you used up all your leave going to Melbourne.'

'Yes – well . . .' His eyes slid away from hers. 'I'm sorry about that but as I explained when I wrote to you my father has been very poorly. I felt I ought to get down to see him in case he didn't make it through the winter.'

'But he has,' she said. Her voice sounded hard to her own ears and she thought: I must not be this way. Richard can't help the way he is. It's how he has been brought up – all cold politeness and family commitment, but no real warmth. If I go on like this I shall spoil everything.

'In any case,' he continued, 'I have got a day off duty tomorrow. We can spend that together. Maybe we could get right away – down to the Gold Coast. Or even take a launch out to one of the islands. Right now though I ought to get back to the hospital. The bloke who was brought in was in quite a bad way – motorcycle accident. I may be needed.'

'Yes,' she said dully.

'You look shattered. Did you get any sleep last night?'

'No, not really. I only dozed' She had not felt tired before, adrenalin had buoyed her up. Now, she realized her eyes were heavy and a dazed sensation was beginning to deaden her senses and thought processes.

'We'll see if we can find you somewhere to have a rest then. And by tomorrow you should be fit for a really nice day out.'

'Yes,' she said again.

And hoped that tomorrow would not be too late.

Chapter Twenty-four

Tara pushed her half-eaten chicken piece back into the picnic box, tossed the remains of her bread to the hovering seagulls and rolled over on the sand, resting her forehead against her arm.

Richard, a beer in his hand, looked down at her with a faintly anxious expression.

'What's wrong, Tara?'

'Nothing.' Her voice was muffled.

He reached across, putting a hand on her sunwarmed shoulder. 'Come on, something is. You can't fool me. You're not yourself. You haven't been yourself ever since you came. What is it?'

She sighed. The sand was gritty beneath her cheek. She shifted her head a little farther up onto her arm, hating herself for the mood which she knew was spoiling this precious stolen day, yet quite unable to shake herself out of it. She was on edge and she knew it. All day yesterday the tension had been there, stretching her nerves tight, so that it was an effort to speak naturally to anyone without revealing her fear of discovery. And though that fear had lessened today when he had brought her out to the island, blown away by the stiff breeze as the launch he had commissioned had skimmed them across the waves, there had been a new anxiety ready to creep in – the awful sick fear that Richard had not wanted to see her as much as she had wanted to see him, the growing certainty that something was not as it should be in their marriage.

It had begun, she supposed, with his cool greeting, yet that could have been explained by his natural reserve. But it was more than that – even when they were alone together there was an awkwardness that made her feel distant from him, as if they were strangers.

She had wanted him to make love to her the moment they landed on the island; if he had swept her off her feet and carried her into the funny little beach house on stilts, straddling the island's only river, where he had arranged for them to spend the night, it would have been all right. She could have broken through that reserve, demolished it stone by stone with the warmth and passion and love that flowed through her in great dizzying waves. But he had not. He had been content to talk and swim – and her sense of frustration had thickened until it began to choke her. She had never much liked swimming and talking seemed such a waste of precious time! As for lunch – the food had stuck in her throat, catching on the thickening knot of tension.

Now, as the touch of his hand on her shoulder stirred her senses once more and rekindled her desire, she turned over again, sitting up and leaning against him with only the dusting of fine gritty sand separating the skin of her back from his bare chest.

He slid his arm around her, holding her there, and for a moment they sat in silence looking down the deserted beach to where the sea ran in ripples of blue, broad bands of colour which sparkled almost cornflower where they touched the land, until further out they became deep rich aquamarine, blotched in places by dark patches of weed.

On the far side of the island the huge Pacific rollers pounded in, rollers which a surfer could ride in a dizzying heart-stopping sweep, but here on the landward side they were gentle and rhythmic and the roar and suck as they reached the beach was almost hypnotic in its regularity.

'Have you missed me?' she asked.

She almost felt the surprise stiffen the sinews of his arm.

'What a peculiar thing to say! Of course I've missed you!'

'No, I mean really missed me. I've missed you so much! I've lain awake at night thinking what you might be doing and wanting – oh, just wanting you to be near me! Have you felt like that?'

410

'Tara!' He turned his head and kissed her face; the touch of his lips on the sensitive jut of her cheek bone sent a tremor of longing coursing through her once more. But still he made no move to go beyond that single chaste kiss and she felt the tears sting her eyes and begin to run in silent rivers down her cheeks.

'Tara!' he said again and the concern in his voice only made her tears run faster. 'What is it? Tell me, please.'

Still she could not speak. There was nothing she could say for she knew now it went much deeper than just the tensions between them since she had arrived, knew her unhappiness was rooted in her fears that she was not, could never be, the wife he wanted. I tricked him into marrying me, she thought, and this is my punishment. Never to be sure that he really wanted me, except for a fleeting physical attraction. And even that seemed to have faded now. She had thought that given the chance she could build on that attraction, believed that her love was strong enough to envelope both of them. But it had not worked out like that and with the loss of that one area of common ground, it seemed that everything else was slipping away, too, and turning them into two strangers.

Please tell me I am wrong, she wanted to say. Please tell me you do love me and you don't care that I am not sophisticated and cultured and elegant – like Alys..But she could not bring herself to put it into words. Drawing attention to the differences between them could only make things worse.

'It's nothing,' she said. 'Just me being silly.'

He twisted her round and pulled her close.

'It's been hard on you, hasn't it? New Guinea hasn't been any picnic I know.'

She laid her face against his chest and after a while her sobs subsided. He held her until the tiny pinpricks of chemistry began to stir in them, bringing first one area to awareness then another. His hands moved over her bare sandy back and she sat quite still feeling the desire begin

411

to flow in her once more, yet unwilling to make any move. This time it had to come from him.

'Oh Tara.' His lips were in her hair where it tangled, sticky with salt and sand, on her forehead and involuntarily she lifted her face. But it was his mouth which took hers, kissing her with an intensity which seemed to have erupted from the very soul of him so that he was now the aggressor and she was drowning in him.

Almost without knowing how she got there she was lying on the sand. The pressure of his body on hers seemed to release the weight of her heart and senses and she could no longer hold back from the mounting compulsion to respond to him, open like a sea anemone, have him within her. Doubts and anxieties and heartaches were forgotten as the age-old magic transformed her and she could think of nothing but his nearness and her need.

Afterwards, as they lay still damply entwined hearing the pull and rush of the sea and the calling of the seabirds, the doubts began to return but she pushed them away. Don't let that mood descend again; don't spoil everything.

The day and night which followed became a dream, something stolen, unreal almost, in the midst of the continuing frenzy of the war. Now that the barriers had come down they talked and laughed and made love more easily, and Tara found that her appetite had returned so that she was ravenously hungry for the tropical fruit and fresh fish that the island could provide.

Only the next morning when the launch arrived for them on the wooden jetty did the ache of sadness and anxiety begin to return. It was over. They had to return to the real world.

On the way back to the mainland she sat close beside Richard, holding tightly to his hand and willing this closeness to go on forever, to transcend whatever was to come.

Should she tell him now what she had done? Try to explain? But she could not bring herself to do it – it might be unnecessary, she tried to persuade herself. If she left immediately and attempted to find a way back to New Guinea before she was apprehended or even gave herself up to the authorities, perhaps there would be no need for him to know.

The launch returned them to Brisbane, the car Richard had arranged for was waiting to take them back to the AGH. Tara's depression deepened but this time she fought to hide it.

'Chin up,' Richard said, taking her hand. 'This war can't last much longer now. It'll soon be over, you'll see.'

She nodded, looking up at him and memorising every line of his face to take with her into whatever lay ahead.

'I love you, Richard.'

'And I love you. Don't forget it.'

The moment they drew up outside the AGH and she saw the military police vehicle waiting she knew what it meant. A provost stood beside it and there would be others, she guessed, inside the hospital, asking the questions which would mean the end of her brief freedom.

'You go on in, Richard,' she said. Her heart was beating very hard, her stomach seemed to have fallen away within her.

It was over. She knew it with the certainty that she knew the sun would rise tomorrow and that the hot Australian summer would soon follow the spring which had already begun. But she did not want him to be there to see the moment when it ended.

He glanced at her questioningly.

'There is something I have to do,' she said.

He bent and kissed her lightly and she watched him walk away towards the hospital buildings. What would he think when he knew what she had done? She did not know. But he had said he loved her. Pray that he loved her enough to forgive – and understand. With a characteristic lift of her head, Tara crossed to the military vehicle and the waiting provost.

'I am Tara Allingham,' she said and there was no hint

413

of nervousness in her voice. 'Are you by any chance looking for me?'

*

'What on earth were you thinking of, Allingham?'

Major Rice, seated behind her desk, glared angrily at Tara.

'I'm sorry, ma'am.' Tara fidgeted uncomfortably beneath her gaze.

'Keep still, can't you?' the AAMWS officer snapped and Tara came smartly to attention, her rigid stance hiding her quaking heart.

She had been right in thinking the provosts at 138 were looking for her. They had arrested her and brought her back and their stony treatment of her had been every bit as bad as Tara had expected it would be. But one thing had been worse. As long as she lived she did not think she would forget Richard's face when they drove away with her. His bewilderment and distress would live with her in nightmares for many weeks to come, his disbelief that his wife could flout the regulations of her service would rankle for even longer.

'I am very disappointed in you, Allingham,' the Major continued. 'A great deal of trust was placed in you and you have let us down. Badly. I am waiting to hear your explanation for your behaviour.'

Tara hesitated, trying to sum up Major Rice's mood so as to present her case in the most advantageous manner. The Major's gaze was frosty and uncompromising and Tara decided upon frankness – and a touch of pathos.

'I wanted to see my husband, ma'am. I hadn't seen him for nearly a year.'

'There is a war on, Allingham. In times such as these separations are inevitable.'

'I know. I'm sorry. It was wrong of me. But we have only spent two weeks together since we were married. I just had to see him. I'm sorry. I won't ever do it again.'

414

She glanced up under her lashes trying to gauge Major Rice's reaction, then snapped them quickly down again as she saw the mouth tighten beneath the fine line of hair which might almost be the beginnings of a moustache.

'Indeed you will not! Or at least if you do you may expect to be dealt with extremely severely!' Her words heartened Tara as her expression had not. She rifled through the papers on her desk and drew out a sheet covered with handwriting which Tara recognized as Richard's. 'I have a letter here from your husband setting out what he thought we might consider mitigating circumstances, but I wanted to hear what you had to say for yourself by way of explanation.' A pause. 'Do you realize the seriousness of what you did? Absenting yourself without leave, taking an unauthorized passage on an Allied transport – you could be court martialled for this, you know.'

'Yes, ma'am,' Tara said meekly.

The Major looked up. 'Well, on this occasion I am going to deal with you leniently. I have decided not to take that course of action, justified as it may well be. I am of the opinion it will be sufficient punishment if you are relieved of your responsibilities at the club. Additionally, you will be stripped of your rank and you will return to your former duties as an orderly. And I assure you that should you ever again behave in such a stupidly irresponsible manner you will be dealt with with the utmost severity. That will be all, Allingham.'

Tara snapped to attention once more. 'Yes. Thank you, ma'am.'

Outside the office she relaxed, letting her breath out on a long sigh. It could have been worse. She had been lucky, she knew. But lucky to be going back to cleaning latrines and washing bandages . . . ?

With a slightly impatient movement Tara lifted her chin. Richard had said the war would soon be over. For goodness' sake, in this at least, pray that he was right!

Tara emerged from the latrine, set down her bucket and leaned against the wooden door, pressing her fist against her mouth. The faint smell of disinfectant on her fingers tickled up her nose and seeped down into her stomach, bringing a fresh wave of nausea. She removed her hand hastily, tipping back her head and taking great gulps of fresh air.

Holy Mother but she felt sick! It was not like her. It was never ill – well, almost never. But these last few days she had begun to wonder whether she might be going down with one of the tropical diseases. Hardly surprising, really, when you took into account the conditions she had to work under. But what was it? Dysentery? No, not likely. The other unmistakable symptoms of dysentery were missing. Scrub typhus? God forbid! Or malaria . . . ?

She laid her hand against her forehead. It felt sticky and hot. The weather . . . or a temperature?

Perhaps I ought to report to the MO, Tara thought. Whatever it is, the sooner they start treating me the better. And at the very least it may mean I can get a few days off from this horrible grind.

She glanced at her watch. Too late now – the clinic would be closed for the day, except for emergencies. But if she felt no better when it was time to turn out tomorrow morning she would be the first in line at the MO's door.

With the prospect of a few days' rest before her the nausea began to pass and Tara felt decidedly more cheerful. If she could swing it, it would almost be worth being ill! As long as she was not too groggy to enjoy it!

Tara picked up her bucket once more and humming softly to herself started back down the hill.

*

The MO straightened, thrust his hands back into his

pockets and stood with his head slightly to one side like a bird, looking down at Tara.

'Well?' From her position lying on the couch she had a strangely distorted view of the MO – he was a much older man than Richard, dark hair flecked grey, and from this angle the jowly skin beneath his skin looked looser and baggier than when seen straight on. 'Well – have you decided what is wrong with me?'

'Yes.' He was looking at her oddly, she thought.

'Well, what is it?' she asked impatiently. 'Is it serious?'

His face did not alter by so much as a single muscle.

'Nothing that nine months won't take care of.'

For a moment she stared back, uncomprehending. Then, as light dawned, she wriggled up into a sitting position.

'You don't mean . . . ?'

'You're pregnant.'

'I am!'

'You seem surprised. Hadn't it occurred to you that you might be?'

'No.' It had not – not for one moment!'

'You went to visit your husband a few weeks ago, did you not?' She could hear the faint undertones of amusement in his voice now, but it was still barely registering. 'I should have thought your condition was a very natural result of that, wouldn't you?'

'I suppose so, but . . .' Oh, the irony of it! When she had desperately wanted to be pregnant nothing had happened. Now . . . 'Are you sure?' she asked.

He turned away, crossing to the basin and beginning to wash his hands.

'As certain as I can be at this early stage. Yes, I would say almost without a doubt that you are going to have a baby. May I be the first to offer my congratulations?'

'Thank you,' she said. She was still dazed. 'What do I do now?'

He turned back, drying his hands on a towel.

'Medically – nothing. As far as I can make out you are a

perfeclty fit and healthy young woman. Just make sure you go for regular check-ups when you get back to Australia and there is no reason why you should not present your husband with a bonny baby next Autumn.' He reached for a pen, doing a quick calculation on his desk pad. 'Next May, I would say.'

'Australia!' I sound like a dummy, she thought. But her mind was still refusing to function.

'Of course.' He put down his pen and for the first time during the entire consultation a grin spread across his slightly raddled features. 'I am afraid you will have to tell your CO she is going to have to find somebody else to clean the latrines!'

*

The wheels were set in motion quickly now; the last thing the CO wanted was a pregnant AAMWS who would be, in her judgement, not only a liability but also an embarrassment. When Tara's waist began to spread the bulge beneath her uniform would be far more readily noticeable than the rings on her fingers and charges against the morals of the service girls, unfair as they were for the most part, were a thorn in the flesh of authority.

Tara wrote to tell Richard the news but even before he had time to reply she had received her discharge papers and she took them with a mixture of relief and regret – a summing up, really, of her feelings about her condition. I'll never make a mother! Tara thought in panic. I'm not sure that I want a baby at all – I just won't know what to do with it!

But it was too late now to wish she had given some thought to such an eventuality. The baby was a reality growing inside her.

At least it will get me out of New Guinea, Tara thought, trying to look on the bright side. And it will be a bond between me and Richard. He'll think twice about dumping me if there is a baby to consider.

This time when she arrived back in Queensland Richard was there to meet her. And it was plain from the outset that while she had her private doubts about the prospect of becoming a mother, Richard was delighted.

'Are you all right?' he asked, fussing around her with all the solicitude of the father to be. 'The journey didn't upset you?'

'No – no, I'm fine. I just feel a bit sick in the mornings, that's all,' she said, enjoying his concern.

He nodded. 'I could give you something for that but I'd rather not. The less medication you take now the better for the baby. We don't want to do anything that might put it at risk, do we?'

Tara said nothing. She hated the constant nausea and felt that she might have been prepared to take a slight risk in order to get rid of it. But she did not want to invite Richard's disapproval. It was so lovely having him fussing over her.

'Anyway, once you get to Melbourne Mother will take care of you,' he went on.

She looked at him sharply. 'Melbourne?'

'Where else? You can't stay here, Tara. This is still a battle zone. And besides . . .' His face softened into a smile. 'The Allinghams have been born in Melbourne for generations. I'd like my son – our son – to follow that tradition.'

'You would?' Why don't I come right out and tell him I don't want to go to Melbourne? Tara wondered. It was so unlike her to give in so easily. But then where Richard was concerned she wanted nothing more than to please.

'I have telephoned Mother and she is delighted,' he continued. 'It's just what she needs to take her mind off my father's poor health. I know she isn't an outgoing person, Tara, but she is very fond of you and she has promised me to make sure you are well looked after.'

'Good,' Tara said in a small voice.

'If you ask me your biggest problem will be preventing her from spoiling the baby when it arrives,' he said. 'She is delighted at the prospect of a grandchild. And so am I. You have made me very happy, Tara.'

He held her close and with her face buried in his chest Tara, for the first time, felt truly happy herself about the coming event.

Chapter Twenty-five

At last it seemed the end of the war was in sight. In May 1945, Prime Minister Churchill and President Truman proclaimed Victory in Europe and there only remained the final Japanese resistance to overcome.

In June, Alys Peterson was granted two weeks' leave and her first thought was to go home to Melbourne to see John.

Since she had last seen him they had corresponded regularly and his letters had given no hint of his personal heartache. But there had been one piece of sombre news – Anne, his wife, had died suddenly – and knowing him as she did Alys guessed that coming on top of the death of his son, John would be more deeply affected than he would ever show, and she was anxious to see him and offer what comfort she could.

A day or two before she was due to leave for Victoria she was in the vicinity of 138 and she sought out Richard.

'I am going home the day after tomorrow. I wondered if you might want me to act as carrier pigeon.'

'That's kind of you, Alys!' He was looking extremely cheerful, she thought. A moment later she discovered the reason. 'One thing you will be able to do that I haven't yet been able to do – see my new daughter.'

'Your daughter! Oh Richard – Tara has had the baby then?'

'Three weeks ago.' He beamed, every inch the proud father. 'We are calling her Margaret.'

'That's a pretty name. After Princess Margaret Rose?'

'I don't know about that. It was Tara's choice.'

'And they are well?'

'Both doing fine. I spoke to Tara on the telephone yesterday. She says the baby has a lusty pair of lungs – but what else would you expect? She gets them from Tara, too, I expect.' He smiled and she felt a stab of envy tinged with sadness. Once she might have given birth to a baby with a pair of lusty lungs. Once . . .

'They are living with my parents at present,' he went on, unaware of her moment's grief for a baby conceived and lost again so swiftly. 'As soon as this war is over and things get back to normal we shall be able to set up a home of our own, but for the moment they are better off under my mother's wing. I wouldn't want Tara on her own with a young baby to take care of.'

'A new baby must be a tremendous responsibility,' Alys said. 'I expect your parents dote on her.'

'I'm sure they do! Anyway, Alys, if you do have time to look them up, I know Tara would be delighted to see you. And you can pass on my love – and give me a full report when you get back.'

'I will,' she promised.

This time, travelling alone, the journey seemed much longer and for the first time for months she had time to think. In Queensland, driving the General, every moment was occupied. Now, as the train surged endlessly along she gazed out at the rolling vista of New South Wales and gave free rein to her thoughts.

The war seemed to have been going on forever. It was difficult almost to remember that there had been a life before it began. But it would soon be over now – the end was definitely in sight, everyone said so. Germany had collapsed and it was only a matter of time before Japan went the same way – thank God. The Allies had recaptured Rangoon, the USAF had devastated Tokyo in a night bombing raid. It could not be long now before the last defiant resistance crumbled and peace was declared in the Pacific, as it already had been in Europe.

And when the war was over – what then? The POWs would be released – briefly, Alys thought of Kate Harris' boyfriend and the thousands like him who had spent the last years in captivity under God-only-knew what conditions. The boys would come home. And gradually the armed forces would be demobilized. Men who had grown accustomed to service life and boys who had never known any other regime would return to a world where the women had taken over their traditional jobs. They would have to adjust, all of them.

And she – Alys – what would she do? Terrible as it had been the war had given her a purpose in life, a niche where she could make use of her talents. What use would they be in the brave new world? She could never go back to living the life of a lady of leisure, that much she knew. But what was the alternative?

The knowledge that she personally was dreading the inevitable limbo weighed heavily on her. How could any sane normal person actually wish that this hell would continue? But she did. She did.

I'll think of something, Alys promised herself. I'll have to. But the question of what was blurred into an impenetrable fog by the constant movement of the train and the racketing wheels threw back no answer.

*

The nursery was decorated in lemon. Lemon curtains, paler lemon walls, a blanket and quilt edged with frilling to match the curtains on the clear varnished drop-sided wooden cot.

The baby was not using the cot yet, though it was ready for her – she was still far too small. She lay in a wicker cradle, draped with a froth of lemon lace – a small pink scrap with perfect shell-like ears, a button nose and a mass of soft dark hair.

As Alys bent over the cradle the baby looked up at her with unwinking blue eyes, eyes that at less than a month old were sharp and focussed. Alys touched her small fist and tiny perfectly formed fingers closed over hers.

'She is adorable,' Alys said.

'You wouldn't think that if you heard her yelling in the

423

wee small hours,' Tara returned with grim humour.

Somehow, she looked oddly out of place in this room – in the whole house, really. The thought had occurred to Alys the moment she had been shown into the cool luxury of Richard's parents' home and Tara had come downstairs to greet her – a Tara who was still a little plumper than she remembered her, wearing a green dress which had somehow been acquired to fit her new shape in spite of clothes rationing and shortages; a Tara who, for all the broken nights, looked rested and normal yet somehow, at the same time, slightly ill at ease.

There was a nanny to look after little Margaret, of course. That was the reason Tara managed to look rested in spite of the nights when the baby cried. But perhaps it was also the reason for her air of discomfort. She was Margaret's mother, yet there was always someone there who apparently knew better than she did what the baby did, or did not, need.

Now, as they peered over the edge of the crib, the nanny hovered, a middle-aged woman picked by Richard's mother for her capability.

'Would you like to hold her for a minute?' Tara asked and the nanny stepped forward.

'I wouldn't pick her up, Mrs. Allingham.' Her tone was intimidating. 'Babies need to get used to a routine.'

'I am sure it won't hurt her!' Tara snapped, turning back the covers and lifting out little Margaret.

'You'll spoil her!' the nanny clucked.

Tara ignored her, placing Margaret in Alys' arms, but the frost in the atmosphere was apparent.

'Well, what do you think of her?' Tara asked.

Alys held the small round bundle with slight awkwardness. The baby's hair was silky against her bare arm and the smell of oil and powder tickled in her nose. A sense of wonder suffused her and with it a sharp stab of sadness for her own lost baby – and for the babies she would never now have. When Dr Whitehorn had told her that the wounds she had sustained in the Darwin bombings would mean she would be unable to bear a child it had hardly seemed important. Becoming pregant again had been the last thing on her mind – all that had mattered was that she was alive.

Now, however, holding Tara's baby in her arms, she was aware of a rush of choking primeval emotion.

'She is beautiful,' she said and the words caught like small pebbles in her throat. 'You must be very proud of her, Tara.'

'Yes.' Again there was an expression of uncertainty on Tara's face but this time Alys did not notice it. Carefully, she handed the baby back, relinquishing her warm softness with reluctance.

'I shall tell Richard he has the most gorgeous daughter imaginable,' she said. 'It's a shame he can't see her like this. They grow so quickly, don't they? I hope you are taking plenty of photographs.'

'Mrs Allingham has arranged for a professional to come in and take some studio style ones next week.' There was a hard note in Tara's voice. For the moment Alys wondered if it was directed at her, then as Tara went on: 'Nanny doesn't think it's good for Margaret to have too many flashbulbs popping', she relaxed. No, it was probably the nanny arousing Tara's venom. This suspicion was reinforced when Tara replaced the baby in the cradle and the nanny immediately swooped to rearrange her position and re-tuck the covers in her own fashion.

Poor Tara! Alys thought, then smiled ruefully. Tara was more than capable of holding her own with an overbearing old woman. And what a small price it was to pay for all she had! Not only a man like Richard in love with her, but also his baby.

Not poor Tara – lucky, lucky Tara!

It was only as she left the house that the moment's insight flashed briefly once more. She turned to wave and was struck by an impression of utter loneliness surrounding the girl in the doorway.

Loneliness! Oh ridiculous! She dismissed the thought and instead repeated her earlier mental comment.

Lucky, lucky Tara!

*

'You are very quiet, Alys,' John said.

They were in the big rambling kitchen at Buchlyvie. It was Flora's day off and Alys had cooked them a meal – steaks and fried potatoes, followed by tinned passion fruit. Haute cuisine was not one of Alys' talents but she had wanted to do it and had managed well enough. The steak, from John's own beef cattle, was too tender for even a novice cook to spoil and the potatoes, luckily, tasted better when burned a little around the edges. Now they were lingering over their coffee, hot, sweet and freshly brewed so that the kitchen was full of the aroma.

She glanced up at him, smiling briefly. 'Sorry. Am I being dreadful company? I didn't mean to be.'

He stretched his legs. 'You couldn't be dreadful company if you tried. You're just not yourself, that's all.'

'I know. I came to cheer you up and here I am behaving like the original wet blanket.'

He smiled. He was looking better, she thought, much better than when she had last seen him, better than she had expected. Except, of course, that the underlying sadness was there, waiting to be uncovered in unsuspecting moments. 'You don't have to make an effort to cheer me up, Alys. You do that just by being here. More coffee?'

'Mm, yes please.'

He stood up and crossed to fetch the coffee pot from the range.

'This damned war has gone on for too long, that's the trouble.'

She was silent, remembering her thoughts on the journey.

'Too long for most people. Certainly too long for you. But me . . .'

426

He turned, coffee pot in hand, looking at her questioningly.

'I don't know what I'm going to do when it's over,' she confessed. 'I've been thinking about it for a while now. I shall be like a fish out of water.'

'You'll find something.' He refilled her cup and handed it to her. 'Something will turn up. It always does.'

She nodded. 'I suppose so. The trouble is I don't really fit in anywhere any more. I went to see Tara yesterday. You remember Tara – Richard's wife. She has a baby now, a lovely little thing. For a bit I almost envied her, especially since having a baby of my own is something I'll never be able to do. And then I thought . . . would I really want to be her anyway? All the things she has are the things I tried to escape from – luxury living, everything done for you so that you feel totally useless, even a nanny to take care of the baby. So what do I want? A challenge, I suppose so, but . . .' She broke off, sipping her coffee. 'It's funny, last time I was home my father said something that made me think. He said he wished he had taken me into the business, treated me like the son he never had. And you know I think I would have liked that. But it's too late now, of course. No, I'm not looking forward to the war ending, John. It's a terrible thing to say, I know. I'm being utterly selfish. But I simply don't know what I shall do.'

For a moment he said nothing. The silence in the kitchen was broken only by the comfortable burping of the coffee pot and the regular tick of the mantle clock. He sat down, propping his feet on a low table and easing his back to the lines of his chair.

'I could make a suggestion,' he said. 'But I don't suppose it would appeal to you.'

'I'm open to any suggestions. Try me.'

'You could always marry me,' he said.

She froze, her cup halfway to her mouth. 'Marry you?'

'You see, I told you the idea wouldn't appeal to you.'

'It's not that. But you must admit it's a bit sudden.'

'It is, isn't it? And selfish of me too. I'm a selfish old man, Alys.'

'Don't be silly,' she said. 'You are not selfish and you are certainly not old. It's just that – well, it had never occurred to me. I thought we were just friends.'

'Just friends.' He nodded. 'That's what makes me say I'm old, Alys. To me, at my age, it seems that is the best possible basis for marriage. To get on really well together. To enjoy one another's company. And I'm selfish because to you, at your age, it's quite plain you want – need – more than that.'

'Oh John!'

'It's true. I know that. You want to be swept off your feet. I'll never do that – we've gone past that, you and I. And I'm too damned old to play games, anyway.'

'Will you stop saying you are old!'

He ignored her. 'Do you know that once I had this crazy idea that perhaps you and Stuart . . . ? Don't know where I got it from – I'd have been jealous as hell if it had happened! But that's all in the past. Foolish dreams – all broken now. I've lost my son. I don't want to lose you too, Alys.'

'You'll never lose me!' she said vehemently. 'I enjoy being here with you too much for that.'

'Of course I'll lose you. It's inevitable. When you make a new life for yourself you'll have less and less time for me. There you are. Now you can see how selfish I am! But I do have a few things to offer you. If you married me you certainly would not have a life of luxury as you call it. This is a working house – a very busy one. You could help me run the farm; take over the business side of it, perhaps. We could work out the details. And, of course, there's always my car . . .'

'Your car!' she laughed. 'Do you really think I would marry you for your car?'

'Well, I have to be able to offer you some inducement.'

'You underestimate yourself. What makes you think I would need inducement?' She hesitated. 'You know I can't have children?'

428

'At my age I'm not at all certain I would want to start again anyway.' He drained his cup. 'If you had wanted children, I might have thought twice about what I'm suggesting. As it is . . . well, think about it anyway. You don't have to give me an answer in a hurry. I shall still be here waiting when the war ends and you are demobilized. And don't think I shall tell you never to darken my door again if the answer is no. I hope we can still be friends.'

'Oh John, of course!' She crossed to him, taking his hands. 'I'm very flattered that you should ask me. And I will think about it. But I can't give an answer now. You've taken me too much by surprise.'

'Take your time.' He smiled at her. 'But I can't pretend you wouldn't make me a very happy man if your answer was to be yes.'

*

She thought about it all the way home, she thought about it while sharing a bedtime drink with her father, she thought about it most of the night, getting up when she finally accepted that sleep was impossible and sitting in her dressing gown at her bedroom window looking down over the sleeping city of Melbourne.

Her mind had been set awhirl by the suddenness of it, yet at the same time she was aware of a soft glow of something very like peace suffusing the core of her.

This was not the way she had imagined it would be when a man proposed marriage to her – there were no wild bells of joy, no heady currents of excitement coursing through her veins and setting up whirlpools of anticipation in the deepest parts of her. But then her relationship with John had never been like that.

Briefly, she found herself remembering the way it had been with Race – dizzying desire, crazy all-consuming longing – and uncertainty and heartache, pain and despair. Maybe she would never reach the heights with John, but there was no danger of falling into the depths either. Did she really want to risk that kind of total misery ever again? For a while, foolishly, she had thought she might – that perhaps Richard Allingham could have tempted her to take that risk. But Richard had married Tara and she had glimpsed – just glimpsed, no more – the bitter truth that she could still be hurt.

But John . . . John was different. John would never hurt her as Race had done. Partly because he was John – and partly because she would never give him the emotional weapons. She loved him, yes she *did*, but in a different way. This was a quiet love, enduring, a love born of friendship and respect, nourished by caring and sharing.

But marriage. It had never occurred to her – now she wondered why not. They would be good for one another, that much was certain. The easy warmth of their relationship would extend far beyond the marriage bed. And she liked the idea of living at Buchlyvie, being mistress of the house and learning to deal with the business side of the farm. And, of course, giving John some of the comforts of home he had been missing all these years.

As dawn began to lighten the sky behind the roofs and spires of Hawthorn, Alys knew she had decided.

*

Buchlyvie's paddocks were withered and yellow from the continuing drought and the hooves of the sleek bay kicked up a fine haze of dust as he cantered towards the ridge where a clump of gums stood in sharp relief against the deep blue of the sky.

From the ridge John saw him coming and though he was still half a mile away knew who the rider would be. The bay had a wicked reputation so that none of the Land Army girls would go near him and the only other person to ride him with that reckless skill was dead in the islands. John untied his own horse from the wilga gum where he was tethered, mounted and rode down the slope towards the cantering bay.

430

As he drew nearer he was able to make out the figure of the rider and knew he had been right. She was wearing well-tailored breeches and shirt, but her hat had slipped back down her head to rest against her shoulders and her hair had come loose to stream in the wind. She reined in the horse and he obeyed her, slowing to a trot and then a walk with a slight contemptuous toss of his head that seemed to say: I did what you wanted but only because I thought I would!

'Alys! What are you doing here?' he greeted her.

She was straight in the saddle holding the reins firmly yet tranquilly with one hand while the other caught the loose strands of hair, tucking them behind her ear.

'I thought I ought to find out if you have changed your mind about that brainstorm you had yesterday – when you asked me to marry you, remember?'

He tipped his own hat further down to shade his face.

'Yes, I remember – and no, of course I haven't changed my mind.'

'Just as well!' She smiled, using both hands now to hold the restless horse steady. 'You see, once this war is over – well, I've decided to take you up on your offer.'

Chapter Twenty-six

Alys sat back in the mess chair crossing her long legs and looking at Richard from beneath the sweep of her eyelashes.

'Well, there you are. I did your visiting for you and I am glad to report you have a fine and healthy daughter, every bit as beautiful as I had been led to believe. She is a sweetie, Richard. No bald head, dry red patches or pressure marks on your Margaret. She would be a perfect advertisement for baby oil or shampoo – or anything!'

Richard smiled broadly making no attempt to conceal his pride.

'I wish I could get to see her. She'll probably be toddling before I make it. Still, they are getting some photographs done of her, you say. That will be something. But it won't help her to get to know me. She'll scream her head off no doubt when I do finally put in an appearance, wondering who in the world is this strange man.

'I'm sure your bedside manner will soon win her over,' Alys said impishly.

'You have to be joking' Any bedside manner I ever had got left behind in the Holy Land. Since then I have discovered bluntness is the best policy when dealing with servicemen. When I eventually get back to civilian life I am going to have to completely relearn my 'bedside manner' as you call it. And find out how to deal with a daughter into the bargain!'

'Deal with a daughter – I don't know that I care for the sound of that!'

'I never imagined I'd have a little girl! A son and heir – that's what I wanted. The funny thing is that now I've got her I can't imagine anything nicer than having a daughter. A little girl in frilly petticoats holding onto my hand and looking up at me as if I was the greatest bloke in Australia.'

'Hmm.' Alys pulled a face. 'That sounds like a typical man's view to me. Just don't forget she is a person in her own right. She might not fit your image of what she should be at all.'

Richard held up a placating hand. 'All right. Point taken.'

'I hope so. She might be like me and prefer motor cars to dolls.'

His eyes met hers. 'If she was to turn out like you, Alys, I should be very pleased.'

Colour flooded her cheeks at the unexpected compliment. Then she said quickly: 'I have some news of my own for you. John has asked me to marry him.'

She was looking directly at him and she saw his face change. The momentary surprise – and something else. Dismay? Surely not! Why should he be dismayed that she was going to marry John? Then it was gone.

'I take it you have accepted.' His voice was even yet she could have sworn for a moment that same quality which she had glimpsed in his expression was reflected in it.

'Yes. Oh, it won't be until the war is over, of course, but . . .'

'That shouldn't be long now. Well, Alys, I am very pleased for you if that is what you want.'

Again, that slight reservation. It communicated itself to her and suddenly she was thinking. Is it? Is it what I want? I don't know. I'd be happy with him. I could make him happy. But the way I feel about him – is it enough? With a conscious effort she collected herself.

'You are the first to know. And I promise you that when we do decide upon a date you and Tara will be top of our guest list.' She hesitated, aware of the slight uncertainty in her own voice, then laughed. 'If the war lasts much longer, Margaret might be old enough to be a bridesmaid!'

He laughed too and the awkwardness passed – almost, but not quite.

433

'I certainly hope it won't be that long! Thanks for coming to see me, Alys, and passing on all the news.'

She stood up. 'I'd better be getting back to my base.'

He rose also, following her to the door. 'Take care, Alys. Come and see me again if you are nearby.'

'I will.' She smiled at him, their eyes met. Then, because something very odd was happening in the pit of her stomach, she turned and walked quickly away into the night.

Richard stood watching her go, watching her slender figure, trim in her uniform, silhouetted against the lights of an approaching ambulance. He passed a hand through his hair. He felt tired suddenly, yet strangely awake. Alert in every nerve, every brain cell. And there was a knife edge of emotion driving into him too – something halfway between anger and despair.

He swung on his heel and went back into the mess room. What the hell was wrong with him? A few minutes earlier and his mind had been full of Tara and the baby, his feelings pure and simple – pride in being a father. Now, suddenly, he could think of nothing but that Alys was going to marry John.

But why should that fact stir up such a hornet's nest of emotion? Why shouldn't she marry him? They were obviously close – and it was only natural that a girl like Alys should want to marry.

But – not him! He's too old for her, he thought and felt a stab of anger again, not white hot, because white hot anger was something Richard was incapable of, but a dull ache painful in its intensity. He is too old for her – old enough to be her father. She's young, beautiful, strong – and yet at the same time somehow very vulnerable. A picture of her lying in the hospital bed after the bombing of Darwin, face chalk-white, hair fanned out on the pillow and gleaming like burnished copper, came into his mind and he was remembering how he had felt then – angry at the waste of all that youth and beauty and moved by a twist of emotion which had been close to desire. He had

434

quickly squashed the impulse as unprofessional and she had been shipped south passing out of his life as quickly as she had entered it. But if she had not been shipped south who knew what would have developed? She had not known John then and he had not been involved with Tara. There would have been nothing to come between them.

The same indefinable sense of regret sunk a bore hole to the pit of his stomach again and he moved abruptly, leaving the mess and pulling the door closed behind him. The night was dark, no ambulance lights illuminating the drive now, only the tiny pinpricks of brightness creeping between the 'brown-out' at the mess windows and in the darkness another picture crept before his eyes – Alys in Melbourne; coming into the restaurant with John, radiantly beautiful in her green dress. He had experienced another emotion then – jealousy. At the time he had scarcely recognized it, so foreign was it to his nature. But he recognized it now with a suddenness that shocked him to the core. She had stood there holding onto John's arm and he had experienced a moment's blinding hurt – just as he had when she had revealed that John had asked her to marry him. And in truth it had nothing to do with John's age – nothing at all. Whoever the man at her side had been it would have been the same.

Dear God, I'm in love with her! he thought and the shock waves ran through him in ever-widening circles. I'm in love with her and I never realized it until now. How blind and stupid could I be?

The darkness swallowed him and he walked with no inkling of where he was going, while the newfound realization opened doors in his mind. In the bushes beside the path the crickets chirped and a breeze stirred in the leaves drawing from them a soft whispering rustle which seemed to give tangible voice to his thoughts.

How had it happened? Life had always seemed so simple to him, even in moments of crisis. Now suddenly all was confusion. In love with one woman and married to another. But how – how? Useless to blame the war and tell himself that in time of peace such a thing could never have happened. He suspected that Tara could have bewitched him under any circumstances. She had been a madness with him and he had desired her as he had never desired any other woman. But in all honesty he thought he had known almost from the moment of marrying her that it could never work. She was uneasy in his world, he was uneasy with her uninhibited philosophy of life. Being apart had been almost a relief and only the fact of her pregnancy had brought him down to earth, made him realize his responsibilities and actually enjoy the prospect of being a father.

Until Alys had walked into the mess and told him she was to marry John. And there was suddenly nowhere to hide from the knowledge of his feelings for her.

The path petered out into bush, the leaves of an overhanging gum whipped his cheek and he stopped abruptly. It was too late now to harbour thoughts of Alys – almost three years too late. You are a husband and a father now – she will soon be a wife. Might as well resign yourself to the fact.

But as he turned, walking back towards the lights of the hospital, his step was slow, his shoulders had the stoop of an old man and there was no escape from the weight within him.

*

Tara set down her coffee cup, folded her napkin and pushed back the Chippendale dining chair. At once conversation around the dinner table ceased and five pairs of eyes turned to her questioningly.

'Excuse me, I just want to make sure Margaret is all right,' she said quickly.

'My dear, I am sure there is no need for that,' Mrs Allingham said. There was a hint of ice beneath the pleasantly modulated tones which was not lost on Tara. 'Nanny is with her is she not?'

436

'Yes, but . . .'

'Tara wants to see for herself. That is a mother's prerogative.' Charles Allingham smiled, his eyes, so like an older version of Richard's, twinkling at her. 'Go on, Tara, take no notice. If you want to look in on your baby I am sure nobody here will mind.'

'Thank you,' Tara said gratefully. She crossed the room, aware of the swift resumption of conversation behind her and the chink of glasses as the port and liqueurs were passed yet again – and aware, too, of Mrs Allingham's disapproving eyes following her.

She closed the door behind her and let her breath out on a sharp sigh. Blessed escape! She had offended Richard's mother again, of course, but that could not be helped. She had the feeling that nothing she did or did not do would ever meet with Mrs Allingham's complete approval. It was a fact of life that she was disappointed in her son's choice of wife and, however well her breeding led her to disguise it, Tara could see through the veneer. So, upsetting Richard's mother was a daily hazard and in this case infinitely preferable to remaining at the dinner table with her and her snobbish guests a moment longer.

Through the closed door Tara heard the tinkle of their rather forced laughter and cringed. How she hated these dinner parties – hated the polite conversation and the stiff propriety, hated the tiny portions of food which were picked at rather than consumed, hated the vast quantities of different drinks, all of which had to be taken in the correct glasses. Damn stupid, she thought. She liked a drink as much as anyone but these people simply used it as yet another excuse for one-upmanship, discussing the wines knowledgeably, comparing vintages and origins – and spending on a single bottle a sum of money which would keep a poor Sydney family in food for a week. It was the one thing amongst all the luxury which truly grated on her, though in calmer moments she told herself she was being irrational – Red had never spared any expense when it came to his champagne and his whisky. But that had

437

been different somehow. How she could not quite explain. But different for all that.

I'll never fit in with these people, Tara thought, not if I live to be ninety-four – and was immediately struck by a shaft of self-doubt.

Just where did she belong? As a child in Sydney she had wanted nothing more than to break away from the squalor – longed for a little luxury. In the army, she had disliked the rigours and the discipline and the hard living. Now, she had a life of wealth and opulence beyond her wildest dreams and she was still not satisfied. She loved Richard, of course, but Richard was not here. She had married him and found herself all alone in an environment which was totally foreign to her.

I was probably happiest when I was with Red, she thought, climbing the sweeping staircase. Not because I loved him but because at least I had the comforts I enjoy and the company of people I felt at home with. And I still had contact with the world of entertainment. He didn't let me sing, but I always thought that one day he might.

And that, of course, was the knub of the matter. She was never happier than when she was performing. Apart from Richard it was the one great passion of her life – the one thing that could make her feel she had something to give. For a moment, with the chandeliers casting their glittering light upon her as she climbed the stairs, she imagined she was back in the glare of a spotlight, hearing the murmuring anticipation of an audience and the roll of drums, seeing the smoke of countless cigars and cigarettes dancing in the shaft of light, experiencing the twist of excitement and fear and the power which would hold them in her spell. Oh, how she loved it! Loved everything about it, the glamour and the glitter, the surging adrenalin and the high on which it left her. But she had left it behind her now, left it for a husband she loved dearly and a child born of that love. Useless to hanker after it.

She pushed open the door to Margaret's room. A shaded nightlight showed the dim outlines of the cot and the crib, the tall chest of drawers, the low nursing chair. The connecting door to the nanny's room was ajar, a band of bright light showing that Nanny was still up, probably reading or knitting. Tara crossed to the crib, leaned over and peeped inside.

In the shadows she could see the silky soft hair dark against the lemon pillow, the curve of cheek and nose. She reached inside, turning back the sheet and trailing her finger against the baby's cheek. It was smooth like a peach, Tara thought, but even softer. A moment's love welled in her. She was not a maternal type. When Margaret had been born and the nurse had asked if she wanted to hold her she had shaken her head.

'I'll just look at her.'

The nurse's disapproval had been as obvious as Mrs Allingham's but Tara had not cared. She was exhausted and the baby had looked unpleasantly sticky, a small pink scrap that had nothing whatever to do with her. Even afterwards, when Margaret had been washed and dressed in her soft wincyette nightgown, she had felt strangely detached. No rush of maternal love. Nothing really beyond a mild interest and a certain amount of pride. These emotions had been extended to include incredulity when the visitors began to arrive. What did people see in a baby to go so completely overboard about them? She was a nice little thing of course and very pretty – Tara did not think she could have borne it if Margaret had been fat, bald or marred in some way. But to coo and visibly melt . . . she simply could not understand it. She herself was vaguely disconcerted by the baby's wide blue stare and damp nether regions. And when she yelled long and lustily Tara was only too glad to hand her over to Nanny, in spite of her almost equal irritation with the woman's cold superiority and obvious impatience with Tara's half-hearted efforts to quieten her.

Now, however, leaning over the crib she was aware of the first stirrings of real tenderness. Margaret looked like a little cherub sleeping there with the tiny soft toy dangling

439

beside her. Nanny had not wanted the toy in the crib, saying that for the sake of hygiene it was best to have nothing near the baby which could not be sterilized or at the very least thoroughly washed, but Tara had insisted, as much to assert her authority as Margaret's mother as for any other reason, and so the teddy was there, dangling on its lemon ribbon a few inches from the small button nose.

'Margaret!' Tara said softly, liking the sound of the name and thinking how pleased Maggie would be if she knew the baby had been called after her.'

'Mrs Allingham – please!' The sharp hiss from behind her made Tara jump, her fingernail scagged Margaret's cheek and she began to squirm. Tara spun round to see Nanny standing threateningly in the doorway. Her uniform had been abandoned now. She was wearing an enormous 'sensible' dressing gown but this in no way detracted from her awesome appearance.

'Do you have to creep up on me like that, Nanny?' Tara demanded.

Margaret's squirms became convulsive and she emitted the first warning wail.

'Now see what you have done!' Nanny bustled towards the crib. 'She was asleep. Now you've woken her – and she is not due to be fed for another hour.'

'She's woken up because you made me jump,' Tara objected.

Nanny practically elbowed Tara aside, turning Margaret over and rocking the crib, but the crying only grew louder.

'Seeing she's awake she might as well be fed now,' Tara said.

'Certainly not!' Nanny snapped. 'Babies have to learn a routine.'

'But if she's hungry . . .'

'Allow me to know my job please, Mrs Allingham.'

'Oh, for heaven's sake!' Tara said angrily. 'She is my baby!'

440

Nanny's cold back was her only reply and Tara turned away overcome with a feeling of helplessness. Under any other circumstances she would have flared back, asserting herself without hesitation. But since she had been here in the Allinghams' house her self-confidence had deserted her.

Well, what now? Stay here and admit she had no say in the routine of her own child, or go back downstairs and be intimidated by Mrs Allingham and shamed by her smart friends? Tara felt her lip tremble. If only Richard were here! If Richard were here she could put up with anything!

I'll telephone him! she thought suddenly. It's late but he'll still be up, relaxing in the mess. Richard was not one to retire early.

Eager to hear his voice she hurried along to her own room and lifted the extension telephone to place the call. Crackles, clicks, and operators' monotonous tones charted its progress along the miles of telephone lines. And then at last the AAMWS clerk at 138 AGH.

'Captain Allingham? I'll try to find him for you.'

Another wait. With every crackle Tara wondered if the line would be lost. She sat in the basket chair beside the bed, one foot drawn up beneath her, picturing his surprise. She hardly ever called him. It was not exactly forbidden but it was frowned upon. But surely just once in a while no one could object?

'Hello?' It was Richard, his voice slightly distorted by the distance.

'Hello, it's me, Tara.'

'Tara! What's wrong?'

'Nothing. I just wanted to speak to you.'

'Oh. You're all right then, are you?'

'Yes. Your mother is having a dinner party and the baby is crying but apart from that we're all fine. How about you?'

'Tara, this is a hospital line. You shouldn't ring me on it for no reason.'

'Richard – I miss you . . .'

'And I miss you. But we can't talk about it now. I'll write to you. Goodnight now.'

'Good . . .' she began obediently, but before she could even finish the word a click and a buzz indicated the line gone dead. '. . . night,' she said and it echoed hollowly back in her own ears.

I ought to understand, Tara thought. Perhaps I do. Perhaps I understand too well.

And for a long while she sat there in the half-light with the telephone still cradled to her chest.

*

'Richard, do you think you could do something for me?' Alys put her head around the door of the treatment room where he had just finished seeing his last patient.

'Alys! What are you doing here? Come in!' Pen in hand he looked up from completing a notes sheet.

'My boss is seeing your boss and I'm taking this opportunity to ask if you could have a quick look at my thumb for me. I think I've got a bit of glass in it – it's giving me hell but I can't see anything. I know it sounds idiotic but every time I grab the gear stick I'm yelling and it's driving the General mad.'

He smiled. 'A mad General in this neck of the woods we can do without. Just give me a second to finish this and I'll have a look at it.'

'Thanks.' She pulled up a canvas-seated chair and relaxed into it, watching him work. After a few minutes he put down his pen, boxed the record cards and stacked them on top of his filing cabinet.

'My clerk can put these away. Now, tell me about this thumb of yours.'

'There's nothing to tell really. One of the girls broke a glass in the mess and I helped to clear it up. I felt it prick at the time and thought no more about it. But now . . .'

'That will teach you to let people clear up their own messes. Let's have a look.'

She gave him her hand and he prodded the ball of her thumb where a single spot in the broken skin showed angry red. She winced. 'Ow!'

He was holding her hand, dabbing at her thumb with antiseptic-soaked cotton wool. She looked up at him and as their eyes met something sharp as the glass had been yet strangely sweet stirred in the pit of her stomach.

He felt it too. His hands stilled, his whole body seemed to freeze. Only within the frame of utter calm he was aware of the inner turmoil which was sweeping away the barriers of propriety. He looked at her and felt the values of a lifetime lose their importance, looked at her and desired her more than he had ever desired anyone, even Tara, because the desire he felt for Tara was a physical thing and this was much much more. The physical was there, in the touch of their hands and the vibrant chords which sprang from that touch. But it was mental too, the reaching out of two minds, and also spiritual. The wholeness of it was dizzying, reducing thought to a single level – Alys sweeping away any consideration beyond her.

She moved slowly, like a dreamer, one fluid movement and she was on her feet and in his arms. Her hair brushed softly against his cheek and then their lips were touching, drawing, clinging. For one long timeless moment they remained rendered helpless by the suppressed desire of the years suddenly became reality. Then she twisted away, pressing her hand to her mouth as if physically to remove the touch of his lips.

'No!' Above her hand her eyes revealed her conflicting emotions – shock and longing, fear and love. 'Richard – no! We mustn't!'

Why not? he wanted to say. But already sanity was returning. He knew why not and so did she. No point in making things worse by putting into words things which were best left unsaid.

'Alys . . .'

'I think I had better go,' she said. Her voice was taut

443

and breathy, adding to the awkwardness between them. He nodded, unable even now to wish she had not come.

Only when the door had closed behind her and he was alone did the thought occur. And even then it had nothing to do with the fact that he regretted the moment of truth and love which they had shared. Only that he knew with a feeling of great sadness that nothing in his life could ever be simple and straightforward again.

Chapter Twenty-seven

Tara sat in the basket chair in her bedroom reading and rereading the letter with a mixture of dawning horror and disbelief. The war was virtually over. After the Allies had bombed Hiroshima and Nagasaki the Japs had agreed to lay down their arms – it was not only a matter of the official surrender being signed. But Richard was not coming home. He was going to Singapore to help set up a hospital to care for the Australians who had survived the Japanese prison camps.

'They are going to be in a bad way after being in Japanese hands for three years,' he had written. 'They will be suffering from all the tropical diseases that you know only too well and they are probably half-starved into the bargain. We have to be ready to do all we can to help them.'

The words blurred before her eyes in a red mist. Oh yes, I'm sure we do, she thought. Poor sods, I don't begrudge them anything we can do for them. Send food. Send medical supplies. Send every able-bodied doctor and nurse we can spare. But not Richard. Oh no, not Richard.

She riffled the pages together and stood up, crossing to the window. Darkness had fallen, the soft dark of a late August evening, but it was too early yet for stars. She jerked the curtain across, shutting out the night, but some of it seemed to have crept inside making a small dark place at the pit of her stomach.

It had been a good day, one of the best since she had come to Victoria. She and Nanny had taken Margaret into Melbourne to shop for baby clothes – first-size dresses and matinée jackets – with spring and summer just around the corner Tara wanted to have first choice of what little there would be in the shops. Nanny for once had been in a good mood, pushing the lightweight pram which stowed away conveniently in the Daimler when a journey was involved (trips within walking distance were made with Margaret riding in the regal navy blue coach built perambulator whose handlebars reached halfway up Tara's chest), and Tara had walked happily alongside enjoying the appreciative glances which Margaret attracted.

Oh, she was a beautiful child, everyone said so – except, of course, when she was crying. But today she had not cried. She had been a model baby, sleeping peacefully during the journey, cooing at the assistant at the baby-wear counter in the Department Store and not depositing a single damp patch on Tara's skirt or shoulder when she cuddled her. In spite of the shortages they had been quite lucky with their shopping – Tara had chosen half-a-dozen dresses, three smocked, three lace-trimmed, and a little jacket with a rabbit-fur collar. The jacket was an extravagance, she knew – with the warmer weather just around the corner there would hardly be the opportunity for Margaret to wear it – but Tara fell in love with it and Margaret looked so adorable with her small face peeping above the snow-white fur. She had managed, however, to resist Nanny's urgings to buy two or three bonnets – it was such a shame to cover Margaret's lovely hair! – and she placated the older woman by tracking down a good supply of baby wool as Nanny had expressed a desire to do some knitting for Margaret in the long hours when she sat alone in her room with only her wireless for company.

Yes, all in all it had been a good day, marred only by the knowledge that she had to sit through one of Mrs Allingham's dinner parties this evening. But, as they drove home through the failing afternoon light, she had felt she could cope with even her mother-in-law's snobbish friends.

And then this. She had been so excited to find a letter from Richard awaiting her – when she recognized his handwriting on the envelope lying on the silver salver in the hall she had snatched it up eagerly, escaping as soon as possible to read it in privacy. She had curled up in the wicker chair, wanting to extend anticipation yet unable to resist tearing open the envelope immediately. And then her pleasure had turned to dismay as she read what he had to say.

Why Richard? she asked herself, distraught at the prospect of the long months before she would see him again. Of all the doctors who could have been sent, why Richard? Surely there must be enough single men who would have been only too happy to take the opportunity to see another country before settling back to civilian life. So why send a man who had a career to resume, and a wife and baby waiting for him?

She glanced at the brass carriage clock which stood on the mantelpiece. Ten past six – an hour and more yet before she would be expected to put in an appearance for dinner. She had planned to look in on Margaret's evening feed and perhaps insist on giving her her bottle. From time to time she experienced feelings of guilt that she had been unable to produce enough milk to feed Margaret herself – though she was also relieved at how quickly her figure had returned to normal. But now all domestic thoughts were far from her mind. She could think of nothing but that Richard was not coming home.

I suppose I ought to go down and tell his mother before the guests arrive, she thought. Richard had asked her to do this. 'I'll write to my mother myself in the next few days but perhaps you would prepare her,' he had put it. Well, it would not be fair to spring it on her in front of her guests. And little as she liked Mrs Allingham it would be a relief to talk about it to anyone – even her.

She found Richard's mother in the dining room making last minute adjustments to the table settings. As usual they were immaculate – snow-white tablecloth with the napkins folded into white water lilies, crystal glassware and silver cutlery reflecting each tiny facet of light from the overhead chandeliers, and a perfectly arranged

447

centrepiece of Christmas roses and anemones low enough not to interfere with the guests' view of one another across the table. As she entered the room Mrs Allingham looked up, surprised.

'Tara! I thought you would be resting after your tiring day.'

Normally, Tara would have been irritated by the suggestion that an afternoon's shopping could have been too much for her. This evening her mind was too full of Richard to allow room for any other thought.

'Richard is going to Singapore,' she said.

One of Mrs Allingham's eyebrows arched slightly. 'I beg your pardon?'

'I had a letter from Richard. He's not coming home – not yet anyway. He says doctors are needed to take care of the POWs and he is going to be one of them. He's sailing any day now. He didn't give a date of course – I suppose the censor would have cut it out if he had – but reading between the lines he could have left already.'

'Oh, I see.' Mrs Allingham's voice was expressionless. Only the slight tremble of her hand on the flower arrangement betrayed any emotion. 'Singapore – good heavens. I thought he'd finished with overseas service.'

'So did I!' Tara's usual reserve with her mother-in-law was forgotten now in her distress. 'Oh, why couldn't they have sent someone without any ties? I thought now the war is nearly over he'd be coming home.'

'Hmm.' Mrs Allingham was silent for a moment. 'I suppose he must have volunteered.'

'Volunteered?'

'Wouldn't you think so?' Her voice was ice cool now, her eyes hard and bright. 'Now I wonder why he would do something like that?'

In spite of the spareness of her words her meaning was crystal clear.

Tara reacted violently. 'How dare you! How dare you suggest he doesn't want to come home to me!'

Mrs Allingham assumed an expression of distate. 'Don't be ridiculous, Tara.'

'Sure I know you don't like me,' Tara ran on. 'I know you think I'm not good enough for him. But suggesting he'd rather go to Singapore than come home to me – well! And there's Margaret too. He's never even seen her. Oh, he wouldn't do it – I know he wouldn't!'

Mrs Allingham turned away, moving a crystal goblet a mere fraction of an inch. The set of her shoulders was stiff.

'You are becoming hysterial, Tara. You are upset, I expect. I am upset to think I shall not be seeing my son again for a while. But that is no excuse for such wild talk. I think the best thing would be for you to retire and compose yourself. I wouldn't want our guests to see you like this.'

Tears blurred Tara's eyes – tears which seemed to come too readily since Margaret's birth. 'Don't worry, I won't disgrace you. I'll be the model daughter-in-law this evening – as far as I'm capable, anyway.'

She turned and ran from the room back up the stairs but there was no escape from the hurtful implication behind Mrs Allingham's words. Had Richard volunteered to go to Singapore? Didn't he want to come home to her? It was a terrible thought, worse even than the prospect of more months in this prison without the comfort of his presence, worse than the knowledge that she could never be the daughter-in-law Mrs Allingham wanted. She couldn't believe it – wouldn't believe it – and yet . . .

Too clearly she was remembering the lack of warmth in his greeting when she had surprised him by hopping over from New Guinea. Reserve where there should only have been joy, coolness instead of ecstasy. The look on his face when the provosts had come for her. The way he had cut her off when she tried to telephone him . . .

I forced him to marry me, she thought. Oh yes I did. I know I told him the night before the wedding that there was no need, but Richard is a gentleman. It wouldn't have been in his nature to pull out then. He hates scenes. He avoids unpleasantness. Perhaps he is delaying coming home because when he does he will have to face the most unpleasant fact of all – that he is married to me, Tara Kelly, immigrant Irish, raised in the slums of Sydney.

No, no, it's not true! her heart cried. He loves me! But the uncertainty was eating into her, and the knowledge that by now Richard was probably too far away to offer her any reassurance was the final acrimonious truth.

*

The eight people around the dinner table had almost reached the end of their meal. Another of Mrs Allingham's perfect dinner parties. Lobster bisque had been followed by a crown roast of lamb, decorated with cutlet frills and garnished with petit pois and glazed carrots; then liqueured peaches had been served with mountains of whipped cream and toasted almonds. The cheeseboard had been passed and the Allinghams' maid had served coffee in the tiny bone china cups which had been in the family for generations.

Tara sipped the sweet dark liquid gratefully, glad that she did not have to force another single mouthful of food down her resisting throat. Throughout the meal she had spoken hardly a word but it had not mattered. The Allinghams steered the conversation with the fluid social grace which was typical of them, and their guests had all been carefully chosen to complement one another – an eminent lawyer and his wife, a high-ranking local government officer and his wife, and the obligatory solo male to make up numbers. Tonight it was Andrew Sperring, owner of a chain of highly profitable hardware stores, who occupied his spare time by playing at politics and fancied himself as a small time philanthropist. His main qualification for being invited to make up the party, however, was that whilst he had been widowed for a dozen years he was, in Mrs Allingham's opinion, much too old to cause tongues to wag with the suggestion that he was being paired off with Tara.

Of all the guests Tara thought she liked him the best. The lawyer was too fond of the sound of his own voice, the local government officer was pompous and stuffy and their wives were mere shadows, reduced over the years to little more than appendages of their husbands. Any personality they might have once possessed had long since been suffocated by effusive politeness. But Andrew Sperring was cast in a different mould. Big, bluff and cheerful, he had built his business empire by taking risks and now he enjoyed his reputation for generosity with both his time and the profits of his success. He could be by turns funny, entertaining and kind and Tara was glad that tonight of all nights it was his rather florid but definitely good-humoured face which was facing her across the oval dining table.

He was speaking now, punctuating his words with short encouraging puffs on a Churchillian cigar; the pleasant scent of Havana leaf floated across the table mingling with the aroma of freshly brewed coffee.

'Good thing this war is over, that's what I say.'

'It's not over though, is it?' Mrs Allingham interjected. There was a slight edge to her voice and Tara glanced at her in surprise. Usually her mother-in-law's prime objective was total harmony at her dinner parties; that she should inject a sour note, no matter how slight, was proof that she had been more upset by the news of Richard than she would admit.

'Surely it is only a matter of days before Japan signs the surrender.' That was the lawyer. He was sitting well back in his chair, surveying the company over the top of a pair of half-spectacles which were perched on the very tip of his nose.

The women murmured their agreement. Did they have a single opinion of their own? Tara wondered.

'I am sure you're right,' Mrs Allingham said. 'But in my opinion the war won't be over until every one of our boys is home again.'

A small respectful silence followed her words and into it she said: 'I heard today that my son is going to Singapore.'

'Oh Ria, you mean he won't be coming home yet?'

'Oh how disappointed you must be! What it is to be a mother!'

The sympathy flowed towards her and Tara began to feel annoyed. He's *my* husband she wanted to say – how do you think I feel?

'Why is he going to Singapore, Ria?' the lawyer's wife enquired.

'To help the POWs, of course!' Mrs Allingham touched the corners of her mouth delicately with her napkin. 'I keep telling myself that, disappointed as I am, I simply must not be selfish. At least my boy has come through all this unscathed – well, physically, anyway. And if he can do anything to help those less fortunate than himself then he must do it. Not that Richard needs me to tell him that, of course . . .'

'They will be in a bad way,' Charles Allingham said. (Trying to stop her effusive flow, Tara thought wryly.) 'The tropics can play hell with a man's health and strength even when he's properly looked after. The devil alone knows the sort of conditions our lads have been kept under. They'll be malnourished, that much is certain, and they may have been put to work on some wild Jap scheme like the Burma railroad, or marched from place to place. Even the natives would go down in a set-up like that. Those who have survived will bear the scars for the rest of their lives, just as so many men from the First War never got over being gassed and shelled in the trenches in France or mowed down at Gallipoli.'

They were silent, remembering the scandalous way those who had returned had been treated twenty years earlier. They had given their health and strength for freedom and liberty and had died, many of them, forgotten men, trying to piece together lives which had been shattered forever by their sacrifice.

'I think we should start a fund,' Andrew Sperring said. 'I would be more than willing to organize it. We could at

452

least make some money available to help with the rehabilitation of local men.'

There was a general murmur of agreement.

'Could you draw up some kind of framework, Hubert, to take care of the legal side?'

'Hmm. Yes. I see no reason why not.'

'Good.' Andrew Sperring was in full flow now, thoroughly enjoying himself. 'Now, we shall need some sort of spectacular social event to launch the scheme. A charity ball, perhaps, or a concert. Yes a concert. That's it. I'll hire the Town Hall. We may be able to persuade them to let us have it for free. If not, I'll foot the bill for it myself. And we shall have to put out feelers in the entertainment world for anyone who will give their services to a worthy cause. Any suggestions?'

'I believe I might be able to get Robert Holroyd, the tenor. I advised him once over some nasty domestic problems,' said the lawyer.

'And the ballet would help us out I'm sure,' Mrs Allingham suggested.

'We'll need more, of course. Now, who else . . .'

'I'll do it,' Tara said.

They all looked at her and she felt a quick flush of amusement at their startled expressions.

'You, Tara?'

'Why not? It's a singer I am.' She was trembling with excitement. She had been from the moment a concert was mentioned. 'I'm very good,' she added immodestly.

'I didn't know that!' The lawyer's wife was torn between shock and admiration; she had never before met anyone who admitted to theatrical experience, in spite of her husband's professional association with the tenor.

'Well, well!' the administrator's wife murmured.

'I don't think it would be in keeping, Tara,' Mrs Allingham said sharply.

The silence this time was tinged with awkwardness. Tara felt her cheeks begin to burn with dull anger.

'I would have thought you'd have been pleased I can do

something to help our gallent returned servicemen, Mother,' she said sweetly.

'Yes, but . . .'

'I don't see why she shouldn't do it!' Richard's father said. 'It's a very sweet thought, Tara.'

'Yes, why not?' Andrew Sperring beamed at her across the table. He felt rather sorry for Richard's wife who was so clearly out of her depth in gatherings of this sort. She was a pretty little thing and looked as if she might be fun under different circumstances. 'If you can sing why shouldn't you take part? I shall put you down as my first artiste!'

'Thank you,' Tara said demurely – and cast a quick triumphant look at Mrs Allingham.

I'll teach her, she thought. Since she already thinks I'm a trollop I might as well behave like one. I'll show her she can't insinuate Richard doesn't want to come home to me and get away with it.

And oh, I shall enjoy myself doing it!

*

The Town Hall was ablaze with light. The war was finally over. 'Brown out' was a thing of the past and the organizing committee of the Grand Charity Concert were determined to make the most of it. Outside the glitter of a thousand celebratory bulbs studded the night, turning the façade of the hall into a fairyland palace; inside the corridors and reception rooms were illuminated by the huge crystal chandeliers, in full use for the first time since the outbreak of war had plunged Australia into darkness. Here in the main hall, however, the light was dim. Only the rosy glow of a few obligatory safety lamps lit the auditorium and the stage too was in pitch blackness apart from the one central pool of bright white light where the three strategically placed spots mixed and merged.

In the wings Tara stood taut with nerves. A comic was on stage now – Russell Bennett had become a household name with his radio broadcasts during the war and the organizing committee had been lucky to get him. He was linking the acts and doing it well – Tara could hear the ripple of laughter at each cleverly worded punchline – and she wondered for a brief terrified moment how she would fare. Suppose she couldn't do it? Suppose she forgot her words or muffed the intro? They had rehearsed it often enough, but still . . .

Two and a half bars and *in* . . . She counted them in her head, drowning out the comic's droll voice. Of course, you can do it. Of course you can! But it had been so long since she was on a proper stage. This was no AAMWS club where any kind of entertainment provided welcome relief. This was Melbourne Town Hall and the well-heeled audience had paid small fortunes for their tickets. She had to be good. She had to be. Oh Holy Mary, please let me get it right. Let me get it right and I'll never do anything wicked again. I'll say a rosary every single day and I'll go to Mass regularly and . . .

'Ladies and gentlemen, we have a special treat for you this evening.' The comic's word hit her like small bullets of ice. 'A young lady all the way from the Emerald Isle with a voice that I promise will go on haunting you long after you get home tonight. I give you – Tara Kelly!'

She took one last steadying gulp of air, feeling the oxygen run a trickle of tingling calm to her tense muscles, and stepped onto the stage. The spotlight blinded her, the warm murmuring expectancy swept up from the auditorium to envelop her. She could hear the organ, positioned just below her in the centre of the orchestra pit, see the white moonface of the organist looking up at her expectantly. And then she was singing, her voice rising sweet yet full-bodied, passing through the microphone and coming back at her from the amplifiers and she had forgotten everything but the thrill of performing, of giving herself over to the music and channelling her talent at that warm living mass of humanity beyond the footlights.

She finished her first number and the roar of applause

rose louder than she could ever remember it, louder even than the stamping cheering servicemen when she had performed at the camp concert, for here it was in an enclosed space and the roof and walls caught the sound and ricocheted it back into the swelling whole. Time for another song.

'Yours – till the stars lose their glory . . . Yours till the birds fail to sing . . .' She was loving it and they were loving her. She was singing and it was all she had ever wanted to do. Richard, little Margaret, stiff-faced Mrs Allingham, beautiful sweetly threatening Alys Peterson, all belonged to another life. They had nothing to do with Tara Kelly, singer, performer, star. Her spirits soared with her voice and she was giving, giving – and getting back.

When she finished the wave of adulation was so potent it made her dizzy. Somehow she remained upright, smiling, blowing kisses, moving to the side of the stage until the spotlight no longer held her. Then, in the dark, she crumpled, physically exhausted yet so elated she was close to tears. She felt something trickle down her neck, raised her hand to wipe it away and discovered it was perspiration.

'Wonderful! Well done!' the stage crew congratulated her.

She made her way back to the dressing-room, not wanting to go and leave the atmosphere up here close to the audience but enough of a professional to know there was no excuse for cluttering up the wings. There were three other girls in the dressing-room; the large mirror surrounded by light bulbs caught their reflection and doubled the number. They looked up expectantly, two dancers and a soubrette, one wearing nothing but bra and tights, one with a cardigan pulled on over her stage costume.

'How was it?'

'Fine . . . fine . . .'

She collapsed against the counter, ran her hands

through her hair, straightened again, paced, the adrenalin still flowing too fast to allow her to rest. The mirror threw back her image now, glowing face, shining mop of curls, skin gleaming with the film of perspiration. Oh wonderful – it was wonderful! And over so soon! But think about that tomorrow. Tonight just revel in how wonderful it was!

There was a tap at the dressing-room door. The dancer wearing the cardigan answered it, keeping the door pulled almost closed behind her to protect her half-naked friend. Then she came back in.

'Someone to see you, Tara. A man.'

'A man? To see me? Who . . . ? She crossed to the door and opened it. A man was leaning against the wall opposite. As she appeared in the doorway he straightened and came towards her.

'Dev!' Surprise almost robbed her of her voice.

'Hello, Tara.'

'What are you doing here?'

'I might ask you the same.'

From inside the dressing-room one of the girls shouted to her to close the door. She did so and in the half light his bulk seemed to fill the corridor.

'Dev, I don't believe it!' But her brain was beginning to function again. 'I can't take you into the dressing-room. I have to share. But there's another little room just along here . . .'

She led the way. In keeping with the rest of the building the lights were on in the small room next door. It was empty except for a table and an overflowing ashtray and the air was heavy with the aroma of perfume – someone connected with the show must have been using it. She went in and perched herself on the edge of the table.

'How are you, Dev? Last time I saw you you were . . . Oh, you're looking fine. Back to normal!'

He laughed, his teeth showing white in his swarthy face.

'I'm glad you think I look fine when I'm normal.'

'You do. But what are you doing here?'

'I'm here because of you, of course. I saw the show advertised, starring Tara Kelly.'

'Hardly starring!'

'Tell your audience that! Radio comics might top the bill but they have no doubt who the star is! Anyway, when I saw the poster, I thought – Tara Kelly! There can't be more than one of them. So here I am.'

'Oh Dev!' she scolded. 'But that doesn't explain what you are doing in Melbourne.'

'I'll fill you in on that later. It's you I'm interested in. What have you been doing? I left you in New Guinea, remember.'

'Oh, there's so much to tell . . .' She did not know where to begin.

'How is Richard?' he asked conversationally.

'Fine – I think. I haven't seen him for ages. He's in Singapore.'

'Still married to him are you?'

'Of course . . .' she broke off. 'What do you mean?'

'When I saw you were using your maiden name – I wondered.'

'It seemed more tactful. Richard's mother didn't approve of me disgracing the family by flaunting myself on the boards – and besides Tara Allingham is a bit of a mouthful, isn't it?'

'Yes. It certainly is hard to swallow,' he said dryly.

'So I thought – Tara Kelly. I've always been Tara Kelly and I suppose I always will be. Now, tell me about you.'

He thrust his hands into his pockets looking sheepish. 'Oh, I've diversified.'

'Don't throw the dictionary at me, Sean Devlin. Just tell me what you mean in plain English.'

'All right. I have an interest in the theatre.'

'*You?*'

'Yes, me. Doing that show with you whetted my appetite.' He threw her a wicked look and when she did not react he went on, 'As you know I was pretty groggy in New Guinea, groggy enough for the powers that be to

458

decide I wouldn't be any further use to them as a fighting man. When I recovered sufficiently they dumped me. So there I was, no business left in Darwin, no army paycheck – meagre as it was it kept the wolf from the door – just my few little talents and that was it. Then, quite by chance, I met up with someone else from the theatre world. Stephen Craigie.'

Craigie?' Her eyes went big. 'Not one of *the* Craigies?'

'The very same. Duke Craigie is his father.'

'Phew!' Tara's lips pursed into a soft whistle of surprise. Duke Craigie was probably the biggest impresario in Australia – even people not even remotely connected with the theatre knew his name. A larger-than-life figure with all the trappings of success and some of the scandal that accompanied it too. But throughout it all Duke Craigie had ensured that Craigie Enterprises remained very much a family concern. He had held the reins, supported by his three sons, until . . .

'Wasn't one of them killed in an air crash?' Tara asked.

'Yep. That was Marcus. His plane went missing over the Pacific two years ago – he'd been off arranging concert parties for the troops. That left Phillip and Stephen. Phillip is more concerned with a new project – a string of hotels. But Stephen works closely with his father.'

'How on earth did you meet him? Tara asked.

He pulled out a pack of cigarettes. His lighter she noticed was chunky gold – a far cry from the cheap one he had used before.

'It's a long story. Suffice it to say we passed one very long night together stranded in a dry pub in the back of beyond. Naturally we had plenty of time to talk and by the time the ninth cavalry had arrived in the shape of one of his fleet of chauffeur driven cars we were mates. I'd told him some of the ideas I'd mulled over since we did that show about the ways lighting could be used to create special effects and he was very interested. To cut a long story short, he offered me a job.'

He drew on his cigarette and as his cuff fell away from his wrist Tara noticed that his watch, too, was gold.

'And a hefty salary to go with it, I imagine,' she said pertly.

'Oh Tara, marrying into the aristocracy hasn't changed you one bit, has it?' he chided. 'You're just as mercenary as ever.'

'I am not mercenary!'

'Oh yes you are. And you've still got your eye on the main chance, too. Which is why I risked getting the length of your tongue in coming to see you. I thought I might stand a chance now I have something to offer you. It seems I was wrong.'

'What do you mean – something to offer me?'

One corner of his mouth lifted. 'Well, what you always hankered for, of course. A career in the theatre. But of course, since you are still married to the good doctor . . .'

The adrenalin had begun to tingle in her again.

'Explain yourself.'

'If you were back in business as Tara Kelly, singer, I could make you a star.'

'Oh!' she said.

'Tara! Where are you? Everyone on stage – final curtain!' Footsteps in the corridor and a voice calling urgently. She sprang into action.

'I'll have to go.'

He pushed a card into her hand. 'Think about it. Here's where you can contact me if you are interested.'

'Right. Thanks, Dev.'

When she came off stage again he had gone but she still had his card. In the bright light thrown by the bulbs around the dressing-room mirror she looked at it. Sean Devlin. Craigie Enterprises. Melbourne – Adelaide – Sydney. The knub of excitement deep in the pit of her stomach welled up into a fountain.

A star, he had said. I could make you a star.

Oh, Tara thought. If only I could!

Her fingers closed over the card again. It was one

460

tangible thing in the glory that had been this evening. She did not intend to let it go lightly.

Chapter Twenty-eight

Tara lay on top of the counterpane in the hotel bedroom. Beside her on the small wooden cabinet a tray set out with cup and saucer and a pot of weak tea stood untouched. The very thought of it made her stomach churn and a wave of nausea rise in her throat.

Oh Holy Mary, she thought she should have known better than to drink water straight from the tap. Dev had warned her not to. In Adelaide sensible people drank only water that had been boiled or came out of a bottle. The dark brown water from the River Torrens was notorious for causing stomach upsets. But she had been tired and thirsty, drained by her sixth performance in as many days, and she had thought that just this once it would not matter.

It had mattered. She had woken a few hours later wondering vaguely what was wrong with her, raised herself in bed – and then had to rush to the bathroom. Back to bed, dozing a little, and then up again for another dash along the dimly lit corridor. All day it had gone on until she had thought there could not be another drop of liquid in her body and still the slightest movement made her heave. Her stomach ached to the touch and she felt floaty and unreal, dozing off occasionally into nightmare-ridden sleep and waking to worry frantically – whatever shall I do if I am no better tomorrow? I have a show to do – I'll never be able to go on stage like this . . .

Today at least was Sunday. Her one day off from the exhausting round of nightly performances. Dev had called her at lunchtime and when she had told him how ill she was he had sounded concerned.

'You'll be all right tomorrow, will you? You have another week to do here in Adelaide. I don't want to have to replace you.'

462

'I'll be all right,' she had said with more optimism than she was feeling. 'It's probably only a twenty-four hour thing.'

'I hope so! Do you want me to come over?

'No. All I want at the moment is to die.'

'Don't do that. I don't want a dead star.'

She had managed to smile at that. The word could still cheer her, sick as she felt. A star. She was going to be a star. It was the one thing which had kept her going these last months through all the upsets and ructions, the exhausting rehearsals and draining performances, the sheer loneliness of endless hotel rooms. She was going to be a star. At last. The one thing she had ever really wanted!

Now, in the small hotel bedroom overlooking the city parklands, her mind drifted back across the events of the last six months since Dev had come to see her perform in the Charity Concert in Melbourne.

She had known, she now believed, even before she left the Town Hall, what she was going to do. Richard was in Singapore – heaven only knew how long it would be before he came home – and if he could take decisions without consulting her then why shouldn't she do the same? The thought of more months living under his mother's roof with nothing but endless dinner parties and stultifying politeness to look forward to was more than she could bear. Even Margaret didn't really need her – she only slept, wet her nappies and took her feeds, and Nanny made it quite clear she was far better qualified than Tara to look after her. And here was Dev offering the kind of life she had always dreamed of. Margaret is too young to miss me and Richard doesn't give a damn, Tara thought. Why shouldn't I make a life of my own?

That night with the adrenalin still pumping in her veins it had all seemed so easy. But of course it had not been.

First there had been Richard's mother to contend with.

'How can you think of such a thing?' she had asked, shocked, when Tara first told her of her plans. 'It's scandalous – an Allingham on the stage!'

'Don't worry, I won't use your name,' Tara assured her.

'What difference does that make? Oh, I knew we should never have agreed to your taking part in that concert! What will Richard say about it?'

'Judging by your remarks when he went to Singapore it will be a long time before Richard is in a position to say anything,' Tara returned acidly.

'What about Margaret? She needs you.'

'Margaret is well looked after. And I'm not going to the moon, only to do a few dates here in Australia. I shall be able to come back and see her every so often. Anyway,' she added, 'when she's a bit bigger she can travel with me. It's time we had a home of own own. You've been very kind but we can't impose on you forever.'

Only Mrs Allingham's good breeding allowed her to check her temper.

'This is Richard's home and you are his wife. Kindly remember that.'

'Perhaps you should remind Richard of that fact,' Tara said sweetly.

It still hurt, hurt badly, that he should have chosen to go to Singapore rather than come home. Little as she had wanted to believe that he had in fact volunteered, the suggestion had taken root and spread like a cancer in her, fed and watered by her own nagging guilt and her observation of him since their marriage. And the antidote to the pain it caused her was anger.

He was doing good work she had no doubt – his letters were full of suffering of the men he had gone to help. Ragged skeletons he called them, men deprived of nourishment and medical care, forced to live and work under appalling conditions and who now had to be helped back onto the road to recovery. But none of this eased her hurt that he should choose to be anywhere but with her. There were other doctors who could have gone to Singapore, equally well qualified and with fewer responsibilities. Perhaps if she showed him that she too was capable of stepping outside the accepted framework he would take notice of her. Perhaps he would think more highly of her. After all, it had been after he had seen her perform for the first time he had begun to notice her.

And so she had contacted Dev.

As always he had been matter-of-fact. His wry amusement had raised her hackles.

'Good. I'll meet you at the Craigie offices, introduce you to the management and we can discuss contracts.'

'You don't seem very surprised,' she said coolly.

'I'm not. I knew you wouldn't be able to resist, Tara my sweet.'

'I might have done. I'm not only a wife, I'm a mother, too, you know.'

'You – a mother!' Heaven help your child!'

'Sean Devlin, if you continue to be rude to me I might still change my mind.'

'You won't,' he said. And of course she had not.

With the wheels set in motion events had moved fast. Contracts were signed, rehearsal schedules arranged. There were dressmakers, hairdressers and musical directors, all of whom tried to shape and change her. And there was Dev, insisting that she should remain herself, market nothing more and nothing less than the talent which had captivated night club patrons, troops and the entire well-heeled audience in Melbourne.

To begin with she had performed mainly at establishments owned by the Craigies, at hotels and clubs which seemed little more than up-market versions of the Canary. But as time went by theatres were included in her programme. First, the small theatres in small towns, singing to a rowdy but appreciative audience still rooted in the traditions of music hall. And then the bigger ones. Adelaide had been her biggest engagement yet. Outside the theatre she had looked at her name on the billboard with a thrill of pride and excitement. Two whole weeks here and then on to Perth. She had never been to Perth and the prospect started more fires of excitement.

'The sweetheart of a continent' they had billed her – suddenly it had seemed the continent part at least was no exaggeration.

One week in Adelaide down, one to go. And now this. She lay on the bed feeling like death and wondering what would happen if she was not fit to perform tomorrow.

Don't even think of it. You will be fit. You have to be.

A tap came at the bedroom door and she moved restlessly. Could it be room service? Unlikely. She had not ordered anything and when they had brought the tea she had asked simply to be left alone. Dev, then. More possible. It would be very like Dev to come around. Checking on his investment. The phrase made her smile weakly. That was all she was to him these days. She could not remember the last time he had propositioned her. Could not remember when any man had been close enough to proposition her. She was a glamour figure, yes, but cocooned away from the public by a row of footlights, a succession of hotel porters and the professionals who surrounded her, all more interested in her talents on stage than off it. Not that she wanted attention, but it was ironic all the same.

And now here was Dev, come to offer a little sympathy and a lot of advice on how to make it to the theatre tomorrow evening and sparkle under his new revised exotic lighting plan . . .

'Come in,' she called. Her voice sounded weak.

The handle turned but nothing happened. She remembered it was locked on the inside, swung her legs gingerly over the edge of the bed and padded to the door, her head swimming. Unlocking it, she swung the door open – and gasped. Not Dev. Richard.

'Oh!' she said weakly.

His face was like stone. 'May I come in?'

'Yes – yes, of course.'

She stood aside. Her legs felt like jelly. 'I didn't know you were home.'

'You wouldn't, would you, since you are not at home either,' he said icily.

'But you could have written.'

'I did write. Perhaps the letter was delayed.'

Or perhaps your mother did not bother to pass it on to me, she thought.

'Anyway, the fact is I'm here. Pack your things, Tara. I'm taking you back to Melbourne.'

'Now wait a minute . . .'

'Pack your things. There is nothing more to be said. And what on earth is the matter with you? You look dreadful.'

'You're a doctor,' she flared. 'Perhaps if you had been in Australia looking after me I wouldn't be here now – and I wouldn't be ill.'

'Don't be ridiculous,' he said. 'I had a job to do. And if that is what this is all about, a fit of pique, I don't think much of it.'

The anger made her feel faint once more. 'I'm sorry, Richard, I don't feel up to arguing.'

'I can see that,' he said. 'God in heaven, Tara, just what do you think you are playing at?'

'I'm not playing at anything. Just making a life for myself while you were on the other side of the ocean.'

'I was on the other side of the ocean, as you put it, to do my duty as a serving officer in the Armed Forces.'

'Oh, I see.' She crossed to the basin, running the tap and splashing cold water onto her face. 'You mean you didn't volunteer.'

She snatched up the towel and turned, dabbing it to her mouth, just in time to catch his expression. Guilt. Written all over him. So he *had* volunteered. His mother had been right.

'Why?' she said. 'Why did you do it?'

The lines of his mouth hardened. For a moment the expression behind his eyes frightened her. Don't tell me! she wanted to cry. I know I asked, but – don't tell me! I don't want to know. Then his eyes fell from hers and she knew he was not going to tell her anyway.

'Somebody had to,' he said, 'and it was no reason for

you to abandon Margaret and go chasing all over Australia.'

'I did no such thing. She has her nanny and she's too young to miss me.'

'You have deceived yourself into thinking she wouldn't miss you because you couldn't keep away from the stage. You haven't really thought about the implications at all. My mother is terribly upset.'

'Your mother is probably delighted at having something to hold against me at last. She's never liked me.'

'That is hardly surprising when you behave like this!' He looked around the room, saw her suitcase stowed in a corner and threw it onto the bed so that the lid flew open. 'Come on now – pack!'

Beneath the anger she felt the love welling up. She had never seen Richard like this before, so strong and decisive – except perhaps on the terrible day when Darwin had been bombed. Certainly he had never spoken to her like this before. Perhaps it meant he did care. Oh, if he did she would throw it all in, give up any thought of a stage career, go back with him and happily spend the rest of her life simply being his wife. Then she remembered the way his eyes had fallen from hers when she mentioned Singapore and hardened her heart.

'I'm not coming back with you, Richard. I have another week to do here in Adelaide and then some other bookings to fulfil. I couldn't back out even if I wanted to. I have signed a contract.'

'That can be taken care of. Contracts can be broken. Our solicitor . . .'

'No. I wouldn't let them down like that.'

'Letting us down doesn't matter I suppose.'

'I am not letting you down. When the tour is over I'll come home.' Her lip wobbled suddenly. 'If you still want me.'

'Oh, for heaven's sake, Tara!' He gestured helplessly. 'What am I to do?'

She wrapped her arms around herself. She was feeling

weak and ill again; for a little while the shock of his arrival had rallied her, now as the adrenalin drained away she was not sure how much longer her legs would support her.

'You can give me something to clear up this tummy upset,' she said.

For a moment she thought he was going to refuse.

'I don't carry a medical chest with me when I rush across Australia to find my wife,' he said shortly. 'Still, I suppose if you are adamant about seeing this nonsense through I can hardly drag you back bodily.' He fished in one of his pockets and pulled out a prescription pad. 'If you are no better tomorrow when the pharmacists open you can get this made up. It should settle your stomach if it's just an upset. If it continues, you will have to seek other advice.'

Oh cold, so cold! Seek other advice! So professional – doctor and patient, not husband and wife.

'Thank you,' she said primly.

He looked around. 'It seems there's little point in my staying here.'

Again her heart bled. How long was it since she had seen him? How many long months? Oh this was some reunion!

'Richard . . .' she whispered.

His back presented a hard line. 'I hope you realize what you are dong, Tara. We'll talk again at home. When you come to your senses.'

Then he was gone. She almost ran after him, changed her mind and sank down onto the bed. Pointless to say more – she would not change her mind and neither would he. Oh Holy Mary, what am I doing? she whispered. She laid her head against the pillow, too weak even to cry, and the flimsy hotel bed shook with the violence of her trembling.

*

She was still lying there in the half-light when Dev came.

469

'Tara, for Chrissakes, what is the matter?' He had come in through the door left unlocked after Richard's departure.

'Oh Dev!' Her voice cracked.

He sat down on the bed beside her smoothing the damp curls away from her face. 'I didn't realize you were this ill. I'm going to get a doctor to see you.'

'No!' She laughed, weakly hysterical. 'I've seen a doctor. That's mostly what's wrong with me now.'

'What are you talking about . . . ?' He broke off. 'Do you mean what I think you mean?'

'Yes. Richard came . . .' And then it was all pouring out and he was listening, holding her hand, touching her face where the blue shadows lay.

When she finished he was silent for a moment. 'I'm responsible for this.' His voice was low. 'It's my doing, isn't it?'

'No – no . . .'

'Yes it is. Look, Tara, if you think you should go home I'll arrange for you to be released from your contract. We won't make a legal battle of it. God knows, I don't want to wreck your marriage.'

'No!'

'Think about it. He's all you ever wanted, isn't he? All you want now?'

Her breath came out on a shuddering sigh. 'I don't know. Oh Dev, I'm just not sure about anything any more.'

'Well, my love,' he said softly. 'The choice is yours.'

'Oh Dev!' she whispered, turning her face into him. 'I'm in such a muddle!'

Her head was cradled in his lap and he smoothed the tangle of her curls, not speaking. The long minutes ticked by and she felt the first stirrings of awareness run through her, fuelled by need. She raised her head and saw him looking down at her, his face all planes and shadows in the half-light, saw her own deep primeval desire mirrored in his eyes. She moved her hands to his shoulders. The muscular strength of them emphasized her own weakness and made her long even more to lean on him.

'I should have listened to you a long time ago,' she said. Her voice was husky.

'Too right you should.'

'Please hold me,' she said.

He held her.

'Please stay with me.'

His lips were in her hair, the supple firmness of her body against his was rekindling the fires she had begun in him the first time he had seen her.

'Oh Tara,' he said, 'of course I'll stay.'

*

Tara sat staring in near disbelief at the newspaper headline. 'High Ranking Ex-Army Officer on Rape Charge.' The words stood out starkly against the page – words that had made her look and look again. Now, with a sense of mounting horror, she read the account beneath the banner headline and felt herself transported back to Northern Territory, to Adelaide River, and to the night of the concert when an unknown man had attacked her . . .

It was so long ago now – most of the happenings in Northern Territory seemed a little like a dream – yet the horror of that attack was something she had never quite been able to forget, and the fact that she had never known who it was who had violated and beaten her had been one of the aspects which had returned to haunt her. I could meet him again and never know it she had thought and the knowledge had lain dormant in her, making her a little wary of men she knew as well as those she did not in a way she had never been wary before.

She looked again at the baldly stated facts of the newspaper report.

'A highly respected surgeon who saw service during the war as CO of 138 AGH was today sentenced to gaol in a Queensland court after being found guilty of rape of a young SIGS officer. Colonel Frederick Adamson had pleaded not guilty to attacking the girl – a 20-year-old West Australian – after meeting her at a Townsville club. He had made advances to her, the girl told the court, which she rejected. Later, walking home, she was aware that someone was following her. Though she tried to escape the man caught and overpowered her. During the struggle she was able to tear a button from his jacket which later identified him as Adamson.'

So, thought Tara, at last I know who it was. He made advances to me, too, and I rejected him. It must be. It would be too much of a coincidence for it to have been anyone else. But Colonel Adamson – I can't believe it! Oh, he had an eye for me, didn't I know it, but I'd never have thought him capable of . . .

Once more the events of that night played themselves out in her mind's eye but somehow the horror had lessened. She could put a face to the monster who had taken her in the darkness and it was the face of a man she knew.

Well, thank goodness he's been caught, she thought. How he'll hate it in gaol – even more than he hated Northern Territory! But at least he won't be raping and beating any more girls for a very long time. And it never even occurred to her how lucky she was that she could regard the terrible incident in such a philosophical light.

Chapter Twenty-nine

When the final engagement of her first contract was over Tara rushed home eagerly to Melbourne. The tour had been a success, not a doubt of it, but lately she had found herself longing for Richard – and for Margaret. It was one thing to be on stage, the centre of attention, quite another to return to a lonely hotel room. She did not like to keep the late hours some of the theatre people kept – Tara had always needed her beauty sleep – and in any case they were not overly friendly towards her. They resented her overnight success and her friendship with the management in the shape of Dev, she supposed.

When he was around the loneliness was eased, of course, but a great deal of the time he was away on business, touring the various Craigie interests to help set up new technical extravaganzas, and even when he was there she tried to put a certain amount of distance between them. That one despairing night she had needed him desperately, but once it was over she had realized the danger of repeating it. Become too closely involved with Dev and her marriage would be under even greater threat than it now was. In spite of her rebellion, Tara still wanted her marriage and still loved Richard regardless of the gulf that lay between them.

Through the lonely hours she had thought about it and made up her mind. As soon as the tour was over she would go home and make him understand why she had done it. He had volunteered for Singapore – she had done a concert tour. Surely they were even now and could begin all over again with a clean sheet..

She did not think of the barriers that had grown between them because it did not suit her to do so. The small coolnesses which had preceded that last quarrel in

Adelaide were forgotten and she thought instead of the good times they had shared – and the happy future which could still lie ahead of them. She would give up her career if he asked her to – with the 'fix' of performing still sending a high through her veins it was easy to imagine that she could do it. She had tasted success, she thought. It should be enough and now she could return to the reality of life with Richard. Perhaps they could have another child so that Margaret would not have to grow up alone. They could find a home of their own. And she would be content just to be his wife and the mother of his children and forget all thoughts of stardom.

One dream or the other – she could not have both. Richard and a family – or the glamour of the stage. As she travelled home, curled back in the corner of the railway carriage as the train ate up the hours and the miles, she no longer had any doubts as to which it would be. She closed her eyes and saw his face and at the thought of him her arms ached with the need to hold him and her heart raced.

Oh Richard – Richard – I'm coming home – I'm coming home . . . The wheels on the track echoed and re-echoed the words.

It was early evening when the taxi deposited her outside the house. She had told no one she was coming and walking up the drive she felt a qualm. The house looked deserted – if everyone was out what an anticlimax it would be.

On the doorstep she hesitated. Should she ring the bell and have the maid let her in? No – for heaven's sake, she lived here, didn't she? She tried the door and it opened. The hallway was deserted. She looked into the dining room and saw that the table was not set. They were dining out tonight then. Her heart sank. But as she approached the drawing room the murmur of voices reached her.

Richard! She drew up taut for a moment checking the urge to run straight to him. It was so good to hear his voice and what a lovely voice it was – low, firm and cultured . . .

Another voice reached her and adoration and love

474

became tinged with annoyance and disbelief. She had not stopped to wonder who it was Richard was talking to. Now she heard the woman's voice and knew.

Alys Peterson. Trust her to be here, taking advantage of Tara's absence! Tara took a step forward, laid her hand on the door to push it open – and stopped. The door was slightly ajar and Alys Peterson's words carried clearly out to her.

'I promised to marry him, Richard. I can't go back on it now.'

'Alys please – you must. Oh, I know I have no right to ask, but . . .'

'You have every right.' Her voice was soft, laden with meaning. 'But a promise is a promise. For one thing I don't want to hurt him. For another, well, it's a matter of honour. You must understand that.'

A chair creaked as if Richard had risen impatiently. Peeping through the crack in the door she saw him pacing.

'I understand all right. I've tried to do the honourable thing all my life – and look where it has got me. That's why I want to stop you making the same mistake. I honestly believe now there is only one good reason for marrying – and that is because you love somebody so much you can't envisage life without them. Not out of pity. Not out of loneliness. Not even because you believe it is the honourable thing to do. That is a recipe for disaster, believe you me. Don't do it. Please.'

There was a tiny pause. Then Alys said. 'Why are you so keen to dissuade me, Richard? I think I have the right to know.'

Another pause. Tara stood frozen. Her heart thudding horribly in the seemingly hollow cavity of her chest was the only sign of life.

'You know why.' There were savage undertones in Richard's voice. 'You know very well why I don't want you to marry him. Don't make me say it.'

The shock rippled through Tara in waves. Sweet Holy Mary she had come rushing home to hear this. Richard and Alys. Alys and Richard. She had always known, of course. Some small hidden part of her had known – and kept its secret. But it did not detract now from the sense of outrage, the feeling that the ground had been swept away from beneath her feet. She pushed open the door with a jolt and went into the room.

'Very touching. I'm sure.'

They both swung round. Their faces were blank, expressionless.

'Tara . . .' Richard found his voice first. He took a step towards her and she backed furiously away.

'Don't you dare touch me!'

'Tara . . .'

'I suppose you didn't expect me. I suppose you thought I was safely out of the way . . .'

'I think I had better leave,' Alys said quietly.

'Yes, I think you had.' Tara could not look at her.

'I'm sorry . . .'

'Don't be. I'm grateful to you for opening my eyes.'

'It's not really what you think . . .'

'Really? You must think I was born yesterday.'

Alys cast an agonized look at Richard. His face was stricken.

'Well, Richard, it is nice to know where I stand,' Tara said when Alys had left. 'So you married me out of pity, did you? And loneliness? And because you believed it was the honourable thing to do?'

'No – of course not.'

'I just heard you say so with my own ears. Don't bother denying it. Well, let me tell you something. I was coming back to you for exactly the same reasons. So – there you are. See what honesty does? We need not pretend any more, either of us. You can go on persuading Alys not to marry whoever it is she is going to marry and you might even succeed. And I can go back to my career.'

He was white-lipped. 'Tara, do you realize what you are saying?'

'Yes, I do. Something I should have said a long time ago.'

'What about Margaret?'

'Margaret will be all right. I think we shall both make sure of that. But you, Richard . . . you can go to hell!'

*

Tara left next day. She had cried most of the night, angry bitter tears, prompted as much by the knowledge that she had been a blind fool as by the sadness that comes with the end of a dream. For too long she had tried to pretend to herself that Richard loved her; the truth was there now staring her in the face and she could no longer deny it.

When she said goodbye to him he looked as white and shaken as she felt.

'Tara, I would ask you to believe this at least – I have never been unfaithful to you. It isn't much, I know; but . . .'

She snorted. 'There are plenty of ways of being unfaithful as I'm sure you know. Though I agree it's unlikely you have been to bed with Alys. You are too much of a gentleman for that. Heaven knows, half the time you are too much of a gentleman to go to bed with me!'

'Tara, you have a viperish tongue.'

'Well, you won't have to listen to it much longer. I'm leaving.'

'Tara!' He was distressed now. 'I don't want it to end like this. Don't go.'

'Too late I'm afraid. I've already made arrangements. Dev is picking me up.' She saw the pain flash in his eyes and was glad. 'Don't let it upset you, Richard. With me out of the way you will stand a far better chance with Alys. But I should warn you I shall be home as often as I can make it – to see Margaret.'

Saying goodbye to Margaret was another emotional hurdle to be overcome. The baby held onto her hand, giving her a gummy smile, and Tara thought: She's beginning to know me. Now my marriage is over I shall have to work out a way to have her with me.

As she got into the car beside Dev, however, it was only of Richard she was thinking. Holy Mary, was it possible she still loved him? There could be no other explanation for the pain inside. How much can one person take and still go on loving? She sat in silent misery and Dev respected her need for privacy.

He drove her to Adelaide to Duke Craigie's offices. There, fresh contracts were signed and arrangements made. Afterwards Duke Craigie entertained them both to dinner in his suite and as the champagne flowed freely Tara began to relax a little, unable to avoid comparing her ease in this company to the stiff misery she had experienced at Mrs Allingham's dinner parties. Well, they were behind her now. She had shocked polite society and when they knew she had left her husband they would be even more shocked. A bubble of champagne tickled Tara's nose and she began to giggle. Dev glanced at her. She raised her glass and dimpled at him then was struck by the serious caring look on his face and sobered.

By the time he drove her back to her hotel she was in sombre mood again. He drew up outside and turned to look at her.

'Tara, once before you asked me to stay with you. Do you want me to stay tonight?'

She chewed her lip, tasting blood. She could not answer.

'You're in a right old state, aren't you?' he asked.

She looked back at him, seeing the strong lines of his face in the sodium lights of the hotel foyer, knowing that what lay behind his offer was more than just one night of comfort. Dev had always wanted her just as she wanted Richard. She had the power to inflict the same kind of pain on him. And it was not fair. Just because she was lonely and wretched, just because she ached for arms to hold her and lips to make her forget for a little while . . . it was not fair on him.

478

From somewhere she found her voice. 'It's not fair on you,' she said.

A corner of his mouth twisted upwards. 'What in life is fair? You kicked me out once before. I dare say you'll do it again.'

Tentatively she reached out and touched his hand on the steering wheel. His fingers were thick and sinewy, they felt good to her touch. He made no move, just looked at her.

'No ties,' she said. 'No firm promises.'

'I didn't ask for any,' he said. 'I just offered to keep you company. It's going to be a long night.'

She interlaced her fingers with his. 'Sometimes, Dev, I wonder what I would do without you.'

'You'd get along fine. You don't need anybody, Tara.' He laughed softly. 'What am I saying? Talking myself out of a job. With no ties at all, I am going to set out to prove to you just how much you do need me. Right?'

'Right.'

In her room she stood by the window, arms wrapped around herself, looking out at the darkness punctuated by a thousand lights.

'Are you coming to bed?' he asked.

'I don't know . . .'

'Come to bed.' He undressed her and she let him. His lips touched the hollow below her shoulder while his hands rested lightly on the curve of her hips. Then he lifted her in his arms and carried her to the bed. She lay looking at the strong muscular lines of his body as he undressed himself, feeling the dark sweet excitement stir within her yet unable to move. Then he lowered himself to the bed rolling on top of her and taking her head between his hands. 'I am going to make you forget that bastard doctor if I have to burn him out of you. Oh Tara, Tara!'

His weight was crushing her, one knee was between her legs forcing them apart. Still she lay motionless listening to the waves of desire making music in her soul, experiencing darts of fire in every nerve ending. His teeth raked her breasts and she cried out then his mouth covered hers, catching the breath which his body was squeezing from her lungs. And suddenly she was passive no longer. The tiny fires exploded to blazing light and she was devouring his mouth with hunger so great it obliterated all conscious thought. Her nails dug into his back and she arched her hips to him wanting to take him whole into her body. As he entered her it was as if the ocean was washing over them, she let it buffet her with the waves of Desire. Dev . . . Dev . . . each thrust took them to a higher plane and each thrust was his name. When the final roller lifted them she cried out, tensing her body as if to hold the moment forever. Then, as the gentle breakers wafted them towards shore, she relaxed into a depth of warmth and contentment like nothing she had ever experienced before. For a long while she lay with her face against his shoulder and his skin tasted salt beneath her mouth as if the sea really had taken them. And as the mists of sleep began to blur reality she murmured drowsily: 'You were right, Dev.'

'So – I get to stay, do I?' His voice was drowsy too.

'Please. Oh please.' The last word became a whisper of deep even breathing and she was asleep. But it was all she had need to say.

ACT III
Chapter One

The Capitol Theatre, Sydney, fronted onto Parker Street. Within its glass panelled doors two matching staircases swept down from the gilt-wrought balcony leading to the dress circle, the ceiling was painted sky-blue and light from the street-lamp-style lanterns at the foot of the stairs caught the bright gold paint and made it gleam and glint against the deeper blue of the carpets.

Outside the billboards bore the posters and photographs of the starring artistes – a comedian, exotic dancers, a fire-eater. But above them all, larger and more impressive even than the fire-eater with his flaming torch suspended above his open mouth, was the face of a girl, eyes dancing dark behind glossy lashes, lips parted tantalizingly, and the name that dominated the posters was simple and easily remembered.

Tara Kelly.

It had taken a year for her to become a star, a year when she had toured the theatres and clubs, rising gradually in popularity and importance from the first presumptive addition to the posters . . . 'And introducing . . .' to this heady accolade of success. Two recordings, played across the continent, and her photograph on the cover of the sheet music had helped her on her way, and now she stood where she had always known she was destined to stand. Top of the bill at the theatre she had gawped at in open-mouthed admiration as a child. The Capitol, Sydney.

Tara Kelly had arrived.

On the day before the opening she stood on the pavement outside the theatre unnoticed by the crowds of passersby gazing with something like wonder at her own picture, her own name, up there, where so many famous names had gone before. Yet her triumph was tinged with sadness.

She had made it. Not a doubt of it. But, oh Holy Mary, what had it cost her? For a moment success tasted bitter on her tongue and she buried her face in the soft dark hair of the child in her arms.

'See Margaret? Look – that's your Mammy up there. What do you think of that now?'

The child, unimpressed, took hold of a handful of Tara's hair and tugged. Her eyes, blue as Tara's, were wide behind their fringing of lashes, her mouth a pursed up rose-pink button. Tara's heart filled with love. Whatever else it had cost her she still had Margaret. Richard and his mother could do what they liked, they would never take Margaret away from her. Never.

Almost a month she had had her now and in spite of all the problems she felt it had been the happiest month of her life. Why had she waited so long to take Margaret? She should have done it long ago, when Margaret was still a baby. She had always intended to. But in the struggle to reach the top of her profession it had seemed better for Margaret to leave her for a while in the stable surroundings she knew. She had her own room and her nanny and Richard, whatever his failings as a husband, was without doubt a doting father. So Tara had delayed the moment of decision.

Then, a month ago, events had forced the decision on her.

She was playing the Tivoli in Melbourne and at the first opportunity had rushed eagerly out to the Allingham house to see Margaret. The reception had been cool as it always was and she had been annoyed to find Alys Peterson – or Alys Hicks as she now was – there. But it was not that alone which had made up her mind. It was realizing with a shock that Margaret was no longer a baby who simply needed love and care. She was growing up into a little girl who knew and took notice of those around her, responding to them with affection. And the person she seemed most eager to respond to was Alys.

'Does Alys spend much time here?' she asked Richard

coolly when they were alone. 'I would have thought now she is married to John she would have better things to do.'

He held her look. Alys and John had been married six months earlier and Tara never missed an opportunity to needle him about it.

'Not a great deal of time, no.'

'Strange. She always seems to be here when I come. And Margaret seems to know her well.'

A shadow of discomfort passed over his face.

'We sometimes go out to Buchlyvie. It's good for Margaret to get some fresh air into her lungs and she loves the animals too.'

'And Alys.'

'Why keep on about Alys?' he asked a trifle impatiently.

She did not answer. She did not want to remember the way Margaret had held her arms out to Alys to be picked up, any more than she wanted to remember the things she had overheard that night over a year ago. The small gesture had hurt her disproportionately, more even than the fact that the wretched woman still came here on friendly visits in spite of what had happened. She had longed to snatch Margaret up into her arms and say: I'm your mother, not her! – but she had known it would simply sound childish.

Well, perhaps it was time to *show* Margaret – and the rest of them – just who her mother really was.

'I've been thinking for some while I'd like to have Margaret with me now,' Tara said. She saw Richard's face change and felt pleasure. 'She is old enough to miss me and not old enough to be at school. And you are forever accusing me of neglecting her. This will prove I don't.'

'You can't take her away, Tara!' he said harshly.

'Why not?'

'How would you look after her?'

'I'd take Nanny along too.'

'I'm not at all sure she would go. And besides she is my employee, not yours.'

'In that case I'll hire a nanny of my own.'

Their voices were raised; whenever they saw one another nowadays they were quarrelling it seemed. Richard deliberately cooled his tone.

'I won't let you do it, Tara. If you insist on attempting such madness I shall divorce you.'

'Big deal!' she snorted.

'I mean it. And I should warn you I have enough evidence to do it.'

'Then why haven't you already?'

'I haven't wanted to drag your name through the courts. Adultery is a dirty word. And you are Margaret's mother. But if you try to take her from this house I'll do whatever I have to in order to keep her.'

'Indeed. Chivalry stops here.' Tara was beside herself now, the explosive mixture of love and hate which their marriage had become seemed to keep her perpetually on a short fuse. 'I think you would be hard put to it to find a court to take a child away from her mother,' she went on, 'and as for the mudslinging you intend to do I defy you to prove it.' She smiled tightly. 'You won't, Richard. I'll see to that.'

'You can't take her, Tara!' Richard begged. 'She belongs here with me and . . .'

'Alys?' Tara finished bitterly and knew that the hurt was still as sharp and all-consuming as it had been that night when she had come home to find them together. 'I'm sorry, Richard, but I am taking her. Stop me if you dare.'

He had not stopped her. Afraid of the ultimate scene, she thought a little scornfully. Oh, she was beginning to know Richard. But for all his distaste for unpleasantness she took seriously the threat he had made. If he could prove that she sometimes shared a bed with Dev he would use it to take Margaret away from her. And he would probably succeed. There was nothing for it. She would have to make quite certain she gave him no grounds upon which to do it.

The first week Margaret was with her there was no problem as Dev was away in Perth on business and Tara

484

was able to concentrate on more immediate worries – the hiring of a new nanny, and the nagging fear that Richard might arrive at the hotel without warning and take the child away again.

But when Dev returned, blowing in as always like a hurricane, she knew that somehow she had to make him understand that for the time being at least she had to be discreet.

He had come to her dressing-room after the show, bringing with him a bottle of champagne and sweeping her off her feet.

'Tara! It's good to be back. You're looking lovelier than ever. Just wait till I get you alone and I'll show you how good it is.' He felt her stiffen in his arms and held her away, looking down at her. 'What is it? What's wrong?'

'Nothing's wrong, Dev. It's just that things have changed a bit while you've been away . . .'

It was his turn to stiffen. 'Oh my God. You haven't patched things up with the good doctor, have you?'

'No. I've got Margaret with me. She and her nanny are sharing my room so you see I don't see how you and I can . . .'

He laughed, twisting the top of the champagne bottle. 'Quite a novelty I would have thought!'

'Be serious!' she snapped.

'I am being serious. But if it worries you take another room.' The champagne cork popped and froth ran over the neck of the bottle. 'Where are the glasses, Tara?' he asked. 'This lovely drink to celebrate our first night together for three bloody long weeks is all going to waste.'

She did not move except to scrub a little of the carmine greasepaint off her lips.

'You don't understand. Richard has threatened to divorce me. I can't take the risk.'

His mouth tightened slightly. 'Why not? Your marriage is over anyway. Let him divorce you and be damned. Now, where the hell are those glasses?'

Turning quickly he saw the pain flicker across her face

and swore to think that Richard could still hurt her. These last months he had thought, and hoped, that he had shown her a life that was much more to her taste than the closeted role of an upper middle class wife, and opened her eyes to a loving that would make her forget Richard and his restrained passions once and for all.

'Won't you miss me just a little if you kick me out of the bedroom?' he asked.

'Yes, but – I can't help it, Dev. If he divorces me for adultery the court will probably let him have Margaret. But maybe we could – you know – here . . .'

He experienced a moment's triumph. She had more or less admitted she would miss him – in bed at any rate. He concealed the triumph.

'What do you mean, Tara?' he teased.

'Well, if Richard puts private detectives onto me a hotel room or an apartment would be the first place they would look. But here . . .'

'If you think I am so desperate to make love to you that I will do it in any hole and corner place you can find where your husband's private eye won't see us, you can think again!' he told her, mock sternly. 'Oh no, Tara, if you kick me out at the front door don't expect me to come creeping in at the back.'

Her chin wobbled.

'Don't be horrid, Dev, please!'

Quite suddenly, he was angry. 'I am not being horrid, my lovely – though I confess I am jealous and just a little tired of forever playing second fiddle where your priorities are concerned. No, I'm simply telling you where I stand. And if it is your opinion that your young daughter will be corrupted by me being with you in, shall we say, intimate circumstances then I bow to your judgement.'

'Dev . . .'

'No, quite all right, Tara, quite all right.' He picked up his keys which he had tossed onto her dressing table when he had come in and swept her off her feet. 'I'll leave you to your daughter and her nanny. And I hope you all enjoy the champagne!'

She felt bereft when he was gone, lonely and empty and a little frightened. But she was certain in her own mind that she had done the right thing. One day, perhaps, she could afford the luxury of thinking about her own personal life. For the moment she must put Margaret first. Nobody, ever again, was going to be more important to her baby than she was – and nobody was going to be more important to her than her baby!

Melbourne became Bendigo and Bendigo Canberra. She missed Dev more than she would have thought possible, missed the comfort and the loving, missed his arms around her and his lips in her hair, missed the drink they had used to share after the show was done, champagne sometimes but usually whisky, old and good, clinking over the ice cubes from some hotel bedroom refrigerator. But she counted it a small price to pay for her peace of mind. As they left Melbourne behind the shadow of Richard's threats hung less darkly, but she knew she dare not take risks with her reputation. A hint of scandal and Richard would have what he needed – evidence that his daughter was exposed to corrupting influences.

And oh, she could not bear to lose Margaret now! Tara, who had never thought of herself as a possessive mother – or scarcely a mother at all – had discovered the joys and torments of parenthood so suddenly it had taken her breath away.

Margaret was adorable. Curled in Tara's arms her body was firm and rounded – plump almost. (How did a child of mine come to be plump? Tara wondered.) Her hair smelled of scented soap, her finger nails were small pearly-pink shell. She was a bright child, too, already able to speak a few words and point out what she wanted and she had taken her first unsteady steps from Nanny's arms to Tara's. But Tara thought it was at night she loved Margaret most of all. She would come home after a show and hang over the rim of the cot watching her baby sleep and filling up with love.

I don't need anything else, Tara told herself. I have a career and I have Margaret. They are all that is important.

The same thought occurred to her as she stood in front of the Capitol Theatre, Sydney looking at her name in two-inch high letters and pointing it out to her daughter.

You couldn't have it all, Tara. Nobody can. You pays your money and takes your choice. But you got more than most . . .

'Well, Margaret we had better get you home,' Tara said.

She turned – and stopped abruptly. A large black Cadillac was drawn up at the kerb, carelessly defiant of the hooting traffic. The rear passenger window had been rolled down and a man was sitting forward looking out at her. Hook nose. Piercing eyes. Hair blacker than she remembered it, as if it now came from a bottle. But unmistakable nonetheless. Her heart seemed to stop beating, her arms turned to jelly so that she had consciously to clutch at Margaret so as not to drop her.

Red Maloney. It couldn't be. It couldn't be! Yet she knew without a shadow of a doubt that it was.

The first moment of frozen shock became blind panic and it somehow lent strength to her trembling legs. She turned, clutching Margaret tightly to her with no clear idea in her head but to get away – away! But she had gone only a few steps when he caught her. His hand on her arm was like a vice and she swung round, her eyes full of terror.

'Well, Tara, so it is you!' He was smiling, but it was not a nice smile. 'You weren't going to run away, were you?'

Her mouth was dry; she could not speak.

'I think you and I should have a nice little talk. Such old friends and so long since we saw one another.'

Still holding her arm in that vice-like grip he forced her back towards the car. In her arms Margaret whimpered, frightened by the sudden change of circumstances in her safe world – and the communication of her mother's fear. Mesmerized by it, Tara let him push her into the rear seat then his bulk was filling the doorway as he climbed in behind her and it was too late for escape.

'So, Tara, I've found you.' His voice was light, amused almost, but she heard the undertones it concealed and trembled again. 'Did you really think I wouldn't, my dear?'

She could not answer. Over the top of Margaret's head her eyes were clear blue, transparent with fright.

'Where have you been all this time?' he asked.

She swallowed. Perhaps attack would be the best form of defence.

'Where have you?'

He laughed. 'Don't try to be clever, Tara. You know damned well where I have been.' He reached out, touched the switch and the bar glided open to reveal the same array of drinks that Tara remembered. 'Somewhere where good scotch is hard to come by, amongst other things. Would you like one?'

She would have given almost anything for a drink to steady her nerves. Anything but her pride.

'No, thank you.'

'Suit yourself.' He poured a whisky on the rocks and tapped on the smoked glass partition which separated him from his driver. 'Drive around, please. We don't want to risk being picked up for obstruction.'

Tara's heart sank. At least while they were stationary there was always the chance of escape, however remote. His piercing eyes regarded her over the top of his whisky glass.

'You're looking well, Tara. You have done well for yourself. I always knew you were a clever girl!'

The compliment brought her chin up. She was beginning to rally a little, recover from the shock and feel anger that he could kidnap her and Margaret this way.

'What do you want with me, Red?'

He rested his glass on the bar, drew out a fat cigar and lit it.

'You seem nervous, Tara. What do you think I want with you – revenge? Understandable after what you did to me.' His eyes narrowed behind the smoke and she felt a new stab of fear. 'Oh yes, I could have gone for revenge. When I saw your name up there outside the Capitol I thought about it, just as I have been all these years when I've had too much time for thinking. A bullet between those pretty eyes of yours, perhaps. Or an artist to arrange your features so no man would ever want to look at you again. And then I thought – no. What good would that do me? And I got to remembering the good times we used to have before you began cheating on me.'

'I never cheated on you, Red.' she said.

'No? No, that's right you didn't. Who did he turn out to be, that bloke? Some pimp, wasn't he? Friend of your backstreet whore pal.' He saw the anger spark in her eyes and laughed again. 'It's as well you weren't cheating on me, Tara. That is one thing I would never forgive.'

'Where is this all leading, Red?' she asked.

He sipped his whisky, looking at her narrowly through the haze of smoke from his cigar and she recognised the look in his eyes. He still wanted her. More. He was still obsessed by her. The realization gave her heart and frightened her again both at the same time. Red had always been so determined to get what he wanted. Had prison changed him? She doubted it. If anything he was probably harder, more determined.

'What do you want?' she asked again. She felt like the child she had once been, trapped in this black monstrosity, a monument to extravagant living.

'You know the answer to that, Tara,' he said. 'I want you.'

She felt the small surge of power.

'I'm sorry, Red. It wouldn't work.'

He sat motionless but the strength of his personality filled the car.

'I think you learned once before that I am not the man to be refused.'

'Things were different then. I was young and desperate. Not any more.'

The car purred along the block. Under the railway arch, alongside the high stone parapets golden in the sun and covered with creeper. Tooheys Brewery loomed on the left. Memories. So many memories. But she hardly noticed. He glanced at Margaret who was staring fascinated at the gleaming assortment of bottles and glasses in the miniature bar.

'A pretty child,' he said, deceptively casual. 'Yours, I presume.'

She felt a small chill of fear. He reached out and touched Margaret's hair. His ringed fingers looked thick and threatening against the soft dark silk.

'I'm sure you wouldn't want any harm to come to her,' he said.

The chill of fear became a river of ice. She pulled Margaret close into the protective circle of her arms.

'You wouldn't . . .'

He smiled. 'It must be very difficult for you to protect her all the time. Especially with the sort of life you are leading. Come back to me, Tara, and be sure she grows up into a beautiful young woman.' He rapped on the smoked glass partition and the car slid to a stop. 'Think about it. And remember, the more successful you are the more difficult it is to hide.'

Somehow she had the car door open. Then she was standing on the pavement watching the Cadillac glide away and merge into the traffic in the sunlit street. She was shaking from head to foot. She had always known in her heart Red would come back one day. She had just become complacent about it – it was not possible to live with fear forever. Now he was back and it was not just her who was threatened but Margaret too.

Stumbling, the child now a dead weight in her arms, she half-ran along the street. Where to go? Where? back to her hotel – would it be safe there? Red did not yet know where

491

she was staying, did he? No, she had a little while. A little respite, but not long – not long . . .

By the time she reached the hotel exhausted by physical exertion and fear she knew there was only one person she could turn to. She grabbed the telephone and asked for the call to be put through, then waited trembling and praying that he would be there, that she could reach him.

An endless wait, a secretary's modulated tones, and then she heard his voice, wonderfully calming, a rock to cling to in the midst of the torrent of her panic.

'Dev!' she whispered. 'Oh Dev, please could you come over? I have to talk to you!'

And without asking why he gave her his answer.

'Give me five minutes and I'll be with you, Tara.'

*

'Well, Tara, I guess you have two choices,' Dev said.

As good as his word, it had taken him less than half an hour to reach her. Now he stood, back to the window, in her hotel room while she sat distraught on the edge of the bed. 'The first is that you do as he asks and go back to him.'

Her head jerked up. 'No! I couldn't do that!'

'It sounds as though he gave you a good life.'

'He's a hoodlum and a murderer! He had Maggie's Jack shot in cold blood. I couldn't!'

'Your other choice is to go back to Richard. You'd be safe with him.'

She buried her face in her hands. 'I don't think he would want me. I'm not sure that he ever did. And besides – what about my commitments? I have signed a contract.'

'These are special circumstances. I'm sure I could talk Duke into releasing you.'

'But I'm due to open at the Capitol tomorrow night. It's my dream, Dev. The Capitol, Sydney.'

He shrugged. 'Well, if you care more for your career than your safety . . .'

492

'It's not my safety I'm concerned about,' she said impatiently. 'It's Margaret's.'

'Ah-hah. Well then, it's even simpler. You send Margaret back to Richard.'

'Oh!' She was almost in tears. 'I don't want to part with her, Dev.'

He pulled out a packet of cigarettes and lit one.

'Your trouble is you want it all ways, Tara. But life is not like that. You have to make choices. And if Red Maloney is as dangerous as you say he is you had better choose pretty quickly.'

She sat chewing her lip for a moment then stretched out her hand.

'Can I have one of those cigarettes, please?'

He raised an eyebrow. 'You – a singer – smoking? Now, Tara, I don't know about that.'

'Don't moralize with me!' she snapped. 'I'm shaking like a leaf, can't you see that?'

'All right, all right.' He took out another cigarette, lit it and passed it to her. 'Here you are. Don't set yourself on fire.'

She puffed, coughed as the smoke bit at her throat, and sat for a few moments in silence. Yes, she could see the sense in what he said. She had to make a decision; knew already what it must be. Margaret's safety must be put first. She could take no risks with that. Red was a ruthless man and he would have no hesitation in carrying out his threats if he was thwarted. But it was hard. Oh God, so hard. To take her back to Richard and his mother. To give her up.

But it need not be for long, she told herself. Just long enough for Red to forget about her . . .

'I haven't time to take her,' she said, pressing her hands together to keep them from trembling. 'I wouldn't be back in time to open.'

'Your nanny could take her.'

'Yes, but suppose Red . . .'

'I'll take them to the station,' he said. 'He doesn't know

493

me. Or the nanny. And it's unlikely he would recognize Margaret.'

'No, but . . .'

'And I'm sure he won't expect you to act so quickly. Pack her things, Tara. Now.'

'Oh Dev . . .'

He crossed to her and laid a hand on her shoulder. It felt good and reassuring.

'She'll be all right,' he said. 'She will be safe in Melbourne.'

'Yes.' She nodded. 'All right, I'll do it.'

She stood up, turned to him and felt his arms go around her. She clung to him, needing him more than she had ever needed him, wanting to lose herself in the safety of his embrace.

'All I ever seem to be is a present help in time of trouble,' he said ruefully.

'Not this time,' she whispered. 'You are, of course, but you're more too, much more than that.'

He held her a moment longer then put her gently away from him.

'Later, Tara. For now there is no time to waste. Pack Margaret's things. And tell your nanny to pack hers.'

'Yes, Dev,' she said obediently.

Chapter Two

Alys took the sleek bay and rode out across the Buchlyvie paddocks in search of John.

Impossible almost now to see any signs of the ten year drought which had almost desolated the land. The rains had come again on the very day that the Japanese surrender was signed and the withered grass and the dry brown trees had responded by growing with fresh green vigour. Now, the pastures were rich again, the creeks brimming with clear bubbling water, the sky clean washed blue and silver. Peace had returned to Australia and Buchlyvie was prosperous and happy once more.

Well, prosperous, anyway. For the rest . . .

Alys saw the lonely figure dark against the skyline and headed the bay in his direction. God, but the bunnies were having a feast out here, she thought, riding through close-cropped patches. But today she had more important matters than the wretched rabbits on her mind. Today, she had something to talk to John about – and urgently.

He raised his head at her approach, putting down the hammer he had been using to repair fences and pushing his hat to the back of his head.

'What brings you out here, Alys? I thought you were knee deep in accounts. He took in her serious expression and his own face became serious. 'What's happened?'

'I have just had a call from Richard Allingham.'

'Oh.' He picked up the hammer and took a healthy swing at one of the posts. 'What did he want.'

'He has a big problem. He wants our help.'

'And what can we do to help Richard Allingham?'

'He wants us to have Margaret for a while.'

'What on earth for? I thought she was with her mother.'

'Yes, well, it's a long story . . .' Alys dismounted and

stood holding the bay by the reins while she explained. As she finished John's lips pursed into a silent whistle.

'Tara is a girl of many surprises, I'll say that for her.'

'Trouble certainly seems to follow her around.' Momentarily, there was a faraway expression in Alys' eyes. 'Anyway, the point is Richard is afraid this Red character might trace Margaret to his home. The Allinghams are fairly prominent after all. So he is asking if we would be prepared to have her out here for a little while.'

'And what did you say?' John asked.

'That I'd have to ask you, of course.'

'Hmm. If it were left to you what would you say?' His eyes were shrewd.

'I'd say yes. She's a lovely child; she'd be no trouble at all, especially with her nanny to look after her. And if we can do something to help.'

'Yes.' There was a wry note to the monosyllabic reply and she looked at him sharply.

'Why did you say it like that?'

He did not answer her directly. 'Look, Alys you're the one who will be most affected by this. If you think you can cope with having a baby here then just go ahead and say yes. It makes no difference to me.'

She felt a fly tickle her cheek and brushed it away.

'You said once that you didn't think you could stand having children at your age.'

'You make me sound like a grumpy old man!' he laughed. 'No, what I said was I didn't think I wanted to start a family of my own again but since you are not able to have a baby that doesn't arise. No, looking after someone else's child is something quite different. It's for a limited time and you know you can always hand her back.'

'True. Though, quite honestly, I think I could become so attached to Margaret I wouldn't want to hand her back. She's so beautiful and sweet and she's . . .'

'Richard's,' he said. She glanced up at him and caught

the look in his eyes. Half sad, half knowing. 'That makes
her special, doesn't it, Alys?'

She felt the colour rise in her cheeks and turned quickly
to the bay, rubbing his coarse velvet nose in the hope that
John would not notice.

'What a funny thing to say! Richard is a good friend, of
course . . .'

'Of course.' His tone was dry. 'Yes, well, if it will help
out tell them we'll have Margaret here for as long as is
necessary.'

'Thanks, Oh – what time will you be in for supper?'

'The usual time I should think. Make it a good feast.
I'm starving.'

'Right.' The moment had passed. She remounted the
bay and kicked him to a canter. But as she rode her mind
was whirling and her hands trembled slightly on the reins.

He knew. He knew the way she felt about Richard. How
could she have hoped to keep it from him? God what a
mess!

The pastureland was eaten up by the flying hooves of
the bay and still the thoughts whirled round Alys' head.
She loved Richard. It was true. From the first moment
they had met she had known he could be special to her, the
one person who could stir in her the feelings she had
experienced for Race – and make her forget the tragic
ending to that affair. But he had belonged to Tara. Now it
seemed that marriage was all but over. If she was free they
could have found happiness together, perhaps. But she
was not free. She was committed to John. And she would
never do anything to hurt her husband.

That much, at least, she owed him.

*

Tara came off stage with the deafening applause ringing
in her ears. She had made it. A rave success at the Capitol,
Sydney. Everything she had ever dreamed of. But there
was a hollowness deep inside her that she could not for the

moment identify and when she did, wished she had not.

'Dev, I'm scared,' she said.

He had been in the dressing-room waiting for her, not a cramped shared dressing-room now but her own, equipped with a washbasin, easy chairs and a couch and with her shimmering, glitteringly glamorous dresses hanging beneath a plastic cover on a rail in the corner.

'Why scared?' He was stretched out in one of the easy chairs, smoking. 'Scared is what you should be before a performance. You've finished now and you were a great success.'

'I'm scared because of Red,' she said.

She sat down in front of the brightly lit mirror and began wiping off her make-up with wads of cotton wool and Leichner cream. As the greasepaint came off the pallor of her face was obvious.

'Relax,' Dev said. 'You've not heard any more of him, have you?'

'No, and that's why I'm scared. He doesn't give up easily, Dev. He's not that sort of man.'

'Look, be reasonable.' Dev stubbed out his cigarette. 'What can he do?'

'I don't know. Anything. Red can do anything.'

'Correction. He used to be able to do anything. But he's not the man he was. He's been in prison for years. Others have taken up the reins of power. All Red Maloney is now is a lot of empty threats.'

She shook her head. 'He's dangerous. Maybe even more dangerous if he feels weak. I know him. I lived with him, remember?'

A wry smile twisted Dev's mouth. 'How did you explain him to Richard, I'd like to know.'

She avoided the question. 'There's only one way I'll ever feel safe from Red – when he is lying under six feet of earth.'

'So – employ a hit man.'

Her eyes flicked up, full of horror, to meet his in the mirror.

'You're not serious!'

He lit another cigarette. 'Why not?'

'Because it would make me no better than him, that's why not! Killing is a mortal sin.'

He laughed. 'Still the good Catholic girl, in spite of everything. Well, if you won't employ a hit man you could always say a few rosaries.'

She tossed aside the used wad of cotton wool.

'You don't understand, Dev. He's ruthless.'

He stood up and came across to her, putting his cigarette down in the ashtray on her make-up table and placing his hands on her shoulders.

'He's just a man, Tara. Only a man.' He was massaging gently, easing the tension out of her. 'Do you want to go somewhere to eat first or shall we go straight home?'

She sat quite still. His touch was arousing her as well as relaxing her, stirring the longing to have his arms around her, his body close to hers. That way and that way alone she could feel safe, losing herself and her fears in his strength.

She looked up and saw his reflection in the mirror, his swarthily dark face, his eyes brightly dangerous, desiring her, his mouth – the mouth that could make her forget everything else – twisted into a half-smile. She looked at his hands, still spreading and kneading her shoulders, the fingers square and strong, and the need was suddenly a fire in her. No one had ever made love to her the way Dev did. Not Red, experienced and generous though he had been; certainly not Richard, always restrained, always too much of a gentleman to satisfy her totally. But Dev – oh Dev. He had never disappointed her. How was it that men could perform more or less the same actions and yet make it so different? She did not know – or care very much. Only that Dev could make her forget all her fears and worries for a while, lose her in a maze in a strange land where only the responses of her body and his were important.

'Which is it to be then?' Dev asked.

In the mirror her eyes met his. She put her hands up to

cover his, feeling the tiny pinpoints of fusion spark between them like bare electric wires.

'Just for the moment I don't want to do either,' she said.

She stood up, crossed to the door and slid the bolt home. Then she went to the couch, sat down on it and held her arms out to him, knowing that for a while at least the menace that was Red Maloney would be pushed away to the fringes of her consciousness.

*

In the big double bed she shared with John, Alys lay tautly awake, every nerve strained and listening. Beside her John's breathing was still deep and even, interspersed with small comfortable snores, and the warmth of his body glowed out towards Alys beneath the cool cotton sheets. A pleasant sensation. Sometimes when she could not sleep she curled herself around his back enjoying the contact and the knowledge that he, at least, was at peace with the world. Maybe he did know of her deep secret feelings for Richard but at least he did not let them disturb him unduly. He was too wise, too well adjusted for that. Jealousy was for younger, less self-assured men.

But tonight there was no comfort to be drawn from his sleeping body. Tonight, Alys was barely even aware of it. Her own nerves were too tightly drawn, her instincts too busy telling her something was wrong.

What had woken her? She did not know. Some small unconscious part of her remembered a sound that had jarred, something that should not have been, but now all was silence and she did not know what it was. A door slamming somewhere? The creak of a floorboard? I don't know. I don't know. But something . . . it was some-thing . . .

A soft scuffling noise made her tense and she shot up in bed.

'John. John!'

But still his breathing was deep and even. Her hand

hovered over his shoulder then, on the point of waking him, she hesitated. Perhaps she was just imagining things.

'I'll look in on Margaret and see that she is all right,' she thought.

She got out of bed padding barefoot across the rugs which covered the polished board floor and went down the landing towards Margaret's room. A nightlight was burning there, bathing the room in a soft rosy glow. Alys crossed to the cot and looked in.

Margaret was sleeping as peacefully as John. Her curls were dark against the pillow; one small chubby hand lay on top of the covers, the other was bunched defensively against her cheek.

A smile curved Alys' mouth. It was the nanny's day off and she had put Margaret to bed herself tonight, bathing her and revelling in the sweetness of her firm pink body, tickling her toes as she dried them in the downy-soft towel and tweaking each one in turn: 'This little piggy went to market; This little piggy stayed at home . . .'

When she had put Margaret into the cot she had stayed with her for a while, singing softly and not very tunefully until the child's eyelids had begun to droop. There had been no need for her to do it, she supposed. For all that she had been moved from pillar to post throughout her young life, Margaret seemed a very happy child. She did not seem to miss Tara or even her nanny, smiling with her little rosebud mouth at whoever happened upon the horizon. Alys had remained with her even after she was asleep and for almost the first time she had been aware of a sense of deep regret that she would never be able to have a child of her own. What a wonderful feeling it must be to look at a small perfect human being and know that it had been created from your own act of love and born of your body. Lucky, lucky Tara. She had Richard and Margaret. But foolish Tara to spend them so carelessly.

If they were mine, thought Alys, I would never ever let them go.

Now, satisfied that Margaret was sleeping peacefully,

she crept back to the door. After the rosy light in the child's room the landing was a passage of darkness. She was halfway along it when her senses screamed to her something was wrong – something was not as it should be. She froze, twisted, saw the dark solid shadows leap in the blackness, opened her mouth to scream and felt a hand clamp across it.

'Don't make a sound and you won't get hurt.' The voice was low and urgent and above the level of her ear, indicating that the man, whoever he was, was much bigger than she. She tried to struggle and felt the strength of him, massive and immoveably rocklike. The way he was holding her she could not move a muscle except her feet. Wildly she kicked out, felt her heel connect and the hand tightened against her mouth.

'Bitch! Any more of that and I'll break your bloody neck!'

Another form materialized out of the darkness.

'Who is it?'

'Just some bloody sheila.' He shook her. 'Where's the baby, huh? Tell us where the baby is and we'll leave you alone.'

Behind the muffling hand Alys squeaked indignantly, fear and shock dissolving into white hot anger as she realized these were no ordinary intruders but the very men they were supposed to be protecting Margaret from. How in hell had they found her? Oh, easy enough for some enterprising private eye, she supposed. They hadn't exactly hidden her away. But she was amazed that anyone should go to such lengths.

She was throbbing all over now with discomfort and she struggled again but the big man pinioning her merely held her more securely than ever, jerking her against the doorpost so that it provided a straight-jacket down her right side. The rim of the jamb bit into her cheek; if he pushed her harder she thought her cheekbone would splinter.

'Now listen to me.' The second man materialized out of

the shadows moving as softly as a cat. 'We're not going to hurt the kid. We just want to take care of her. So tell us where she is nice and quiet – no noise to wake up the rest of the house – and you won't get hurt.'

Alys' mind was crystal clear now and the thought uppermost in her mind was how close, how terribly close, they were to Margaret. Just a few steps from the door to her room – and that was ajar. If she woke, whimpered, cried out, there was no way they could avoid hearing her. Somehow she had to get them away.

'Right. Tell me now. And remember – any funny business and you'll regret it.' The hand was lifted just far enough to allow her lips to move but ready to clamp down again at the first suggestion she might try to raise the alarm.

'Downstairs,' Alys said. Her voice was muffled.

'Downstairs?' He sounded incredulous.

'Our spare room beyond the living room. Nanny can't manage stairs.' She prayed they did not know the nanny was in her early twenties, the keenest jiver in Victoria.

The hand was over her mouth again. 'See if she's telling the truth!'

One of the shadows moved and she heard the man going down the stairs but her captor held her fast. She had the feeling he was enjoying himself, enjoying her helplessness. The seconds ticked by. Oh God, what now? Any moment and the other man would be back knowing she had lied.

With a superhuman effort Alys jerked her head and as the man's grip slipped slightly she sunk her teeth into the heel of his hand. He tore it away, swearing, and she screamed – 'John! John!'

Oh, let him hear, please let him hear! Surely not even he could sleep through this!

'Bitch!' The man punched her. Her head cracked against the door jamb and both sides of her face went ice cold numb. She screamed again – and saw the light go on in their bedroom.

It seemed then that everything happened at once. Footsteps running back to the stairs; John rumpled from sleep silhouetted in the doorway of their room wearing his blue and white striped pyjamas; something cold and sharp pressing against her throat. And in the quiet of the night Margaret's sudden frightened wail.

'What the hell is going on?' John asked. His words were drowned by the second man's thundering footsteps on the stairs. She saw him emerge from the well, every inch a hoodlum.

'In there,' her captor hissed. 'The baby's there. Get her.' John took a step forward and the blade bit at her throat. 'Keep back you – or she gets it!'

Horror, pure and stark, flooded her. There was nothing they could do. If John interfered her throat would be cut. In that moment she did not care – nothing mattered but saving Margaret – but she knew John would not do it. She was still too precious to him. Helpless, she watched the second man enter Margaret's room to emerge with the terrified child in his arms. At the foot of the stairs he shouted back: 'Right. Clear. Come on – let's go!'

Her captor edged as far as the top of the stairs, the knife still at her throat. Then down, very slowly, step by step. Did they intend taking her with them? She almost hoped so. At least she would be with Margaret.

Halfway down the man pushed her aside and ran. She lay half stunned and saw John racing down towards her, leaping over her tumbled body, giving chase now she was no longer in danger. The man turned, dropping the knife, and she saw the glint of a different metal.

'John – be careful! He's got a gun!' she tried to scream but no words came from her dry mouth.

And in any case her warning would have been too late. The gun cracked, a blue flash in the half-dark, and John was arrested in mid flight. Like a slow motion tableau she saw his hands go to his stomach. He took another step or two and the gun flashed again. He fell, his body crumpling, and went down on his knees. Somehow she was up and beside him, looking down at the stain spreading scarlet on the blue and white pyjamas. And now she had found her voice again and was unable to stop screaming and sobbing.

'John – John – John!'

She dropped to her knees beside him. He was still conscious – just – his face ashen, his eyes full of agony.

'I'll get a doctor. I'll – oh God, what have they done to you?'

With an effort his lips moved. His voice was a curious gurgle yet his words were strong and lucid.

'Never mind a doctor. Too late. Ring the police. Tell them the bastards have got Margaret.'

*

Red Maloney's house in Elizabeth Bay was bathed in morning sunshine. Tara, her eyes red from crying, walked up the front path and rang the bell, remembering the first time she had come here young and desperate. It seemed like a lifetime ago but in reality nothing had changed. Red had won again just as she suspected he would always win.

The doorbell echoed through the house and Tara stood waiting tensely, reliving the horror of the night before. The shrilling of the telephone had woken her from sleep, turning her cold with unpleasant anticipation. She lay rubbing her eyes as Dev got up to answer it, saw his face change, heard his barked '*What*?'

She sat up in bed. 'What is it? What has happened?'

He shushed her to silence with his hand. 'Yes – yes – oh, my good Christ!' He replaced the receiver and turned to her. His face was like stone. 'Tara, something terrible has happened.'

'What?' She was shaking all over. He hesitated and she knew. 'Margaret!' she screamed. 'Something has happened to Margaret! She's dead, isn't she? Oh, my God! My God!'

He took her by the shoulders. 'No, Tara, she's not dead.

But Red Maloney has her. At least we think so. Two of his hoodlums have been out to Buchlyvie.'

'And they let them take her? But they were supposed to be looking after her! Oh, how could they? How could they . . . ?'

'They tried to stop them.'

'Then they didn't try hard enough. Oh Margaret . . .'

'John is dead,' Dev said.

'John?' She looked blankly uncomprehending. 'Oh John – Alys' John.'

'Yes. He has been shot and killed.'

'I don't believe it. This can't be happening.' But she knew it was. Once before she had seen a man gunned down by Red's henchmen. It was real – all too real.

'Tara!' Dev shook her gently. 'The police have been alerted. They will find Margaret.'

She shook her head. 'I doubt it. Red is too clever. Oh, I told you I was frightened, Dev. I told you he was ruthless. Why wouldn't you believe me?'

'Be sensible, Tara. What more could we have done? And they will get her back. They must.'

'And if they do, what then? Red can find us wherever we hide. He's proved that. There's only one answer. I shall have to do what he wants.'

'Go back to him?'

'I don't think I have any choice. I can't take gambles with my child's safety.'

Most of the rest of the night they argued, discussed, tore to pieces the details of the whole ghastly business. And when morning came Tara called a cab and drove over to Elizabeth Bay.

The door was opened by one of Red's minions. He smiled slyly when she told him who she was and a few moments later she was ushered along to Red's gymnasium. History repeating itself, she thought.

In spite of the early hour Red had been working out with weights. As he saw her come in he gave the barbell a last heave then carried it to a shelf and stowed it.

'Well, Tara, what a surprise!' His voice was heavy with sarcasm. 'What can I do for you?'

She faced him squarely. 'I think that you know very well why I am here.'

He reached for a tracksuit jacket and pulled it on over his singlet. With his bulging muscles and tattoos covered he looked only marginally less threatening.

'You tell me.'

'I want my daughter,' she said.

He smiled. It was not a nice smile.

'And I want you. So – do we have a bargain?'

'I despise you.'

'Very possibly.' He smiled again. 'But I seem to remember you came to me under protest once before. It wasn't so bad, was it?'

'Oh Red,' she said softly, 'how can you do this to me?'

'Easily. You better than anyone should know I always get what I want. Come here.'

She took a step towards him. 'I want to see Margaret first.'

'Oh Tara, surely common sense must tell you she is not here yet. Melbourne to Sydney in just a few hours? Oh no. But she is being well taken care of I assure you. You need not worry about Margaret.'

He reached for her, pulling her close. She smelled the sweat fresh on his body from her exertions. Once, almost against her will, he had excited her. Now she felt only revulsion.

'Tara, Tara. In spite of what you did I still want you. You should be flattered.' He bent his head, kissing her full on the mouth. As his tongue parted her lips she fought the urge to push him away. There was no other way. Margaret was all that mattered now. His hands moved over her body, unfastening the buttons of her blouse with practised ease.

'Take it off,' he ordered.

'But . . .'

Sounds of a commotion infiltrated the gymnasium.

Voices raised. One familiar. Tara jerked around as the door burst open.

'Dev!'

Standing there in the doorway, his face dark with anger, he looked every bit as threatening as Red.

'What the hell . . . ?' Red began.

Dev ignored him. 'It's all right, Tara. The police have caught up with Margaret. Alys just telephoned.'

'Oh!' It was a sob of pure relief.

'So come on. There's no need for you to stay here with this bully boy.' He turned to Red. 'I'd watch it if I was you. Be prepared for another stint in gaol. A man has been killed, you know.'

'You bastard – get out of here!' Red stormed towards Dev. 'Tara stays!'

His huge fist shot out connecting with Dev's jaw. Dev reeled then came back at him and the two men were trading blows, rolling and lurching around the gymnasium while two of Red's minions watched in amusement and Tara in terror. First one, then the other seemed to have the upper hand; they were evenly matched. Red's hands were around Dev's throat; Dev fought him off, back against the wall. As Red gave way slightly Dev wrapped his hands around the wall bars above his head, jack-knifed and thrust his feet like twin pistons into Red's belly. The big man staggered back and collided with the shelving where the weights were stored. It rocked wildly.

What happened next seemed to Tara to have been captured forever in a slow motion film imprinted on her mind for all time. The weight Red had been using when she arrived rolled slowly to the edge of the shelf just above his head. Horrified, she screamed a warning and one of the hoodlums started forward. Too late, both of them. The weight shot over the edge of the shelf. Alerted Red glanced up. The barbell caught him full in the face and crashed with him to the ground. For a moment the onlookers resembled a tableau in wax then they rushed towards the man who was pinned to the floor of his own gymnasium.

There was nothing any of them could do for him. It was obvious at the very first glance. The weight had snapped Red Maloney's neck. The moment it hit the ground, he was dead.

*

The two funerals took place on the same day.

Red's funeral in Sydney was a flashy affair, a procession of huge black Cadillacs following the flower-decked hearse. The men all wore black suits, ties and Homburgs, the women tight-fitting black dresses, hats and thick veils.

John's was a simple family gathering and the tears that were shed, though less conspicuous, were a great deal more genuine.

Afterwards, Alys stood alone at the graveside, white-faced and silent, remembering the man who had been her husband. Richard left her for a few minutes, respecting her grief and her need for a private farewell. Then he crossed the turf to join her.

'Alys, I am so sorry. Nothing I can ever say could tell you how sorry I am.'

She nodded, not looking at him. 'He was a good man. It seems so unfair. To die like that.'

'I feel so damnably responsible. If it had not been for us, for Margaret . . .'

Don't blame yourself,' she said. 'No one forced us to have her. We did it because we wanted to.'

'I know. But still. If there is anything I can do, anything at all . . .'

Her eyes were blurred with tears. 'Just be there, Richard. Please – just be there.'

'I will,' he said. They stood for a moment looking down at the coffin with its fresh sprinkling of earth. Then Alys bent, picked a rose from the simple bouquet which lay on the fringing mound of soil and dropped it into the coffin.

'Goodbye John.'

Richard copied her action.

'Goodbye John, and thank you.'

Then he put his arm around Alys turning her back towards the path and together they walked across the firm turf to join the other mourners.

Chapter Three

Tara's show at the Capitol was an even greater success than she had dared hope. The critics raved about her, calling her a new singing sensation, every seat to the end of her run was sold, and some resold at double and treble their original price, and crowds gathered each night outside the stage door to catch a glimpse of the star who could truly be called 'Sydney's own girl'.

Some of her success was due to the insatiable curiosity of the public, Duke Craigie maintained. The dramatic story of the kidnapping of Tara's daughter and the death of Red Maloney had made big headlines and without a doubt some of the audiences had flocked in to see for themselves the woman at the heart of the scandal. But having come as voyeurs they remained to applaud and Duke Craigie congratulated himself on his talent for spotting rising stars and began to make plans for a new venture, a musical show which would sweep across the continent, helping Australians to put behind them the austerities of war and making a household name of its star, Tara Kelly. The most exciting musical director in Australia was working on the score, Dev had drawn up plans for some spectacular lighting effects, lavish costumes such as those that had stunned the world in the pre-war Hollywood musicals were planned and already Duke Craigie was conducting auditions for the forty-strong chorus.

Tara knew she should have been excited by it all, but she was not. One thing alone mattered to her, one question dominated her every waking moment and sometimes invaded her dreams too – how much longer would it be before she could have Margaret with her once again?

As the days passed her impatience grew. Leaving

Margaret with Richard had seemed the sensible answer while the attention of the press was centered on her, but it had not been easy for her. With the terror she felt for Margaret's safety so fresh in her mind she could hardly bear to have her out of her sight and she ached for the feel of the firm little body in her arms and the silky whisper of hair against her cheek.

When the curtain fell on her final performance at the Capitol it seemed to Tara there was no need to delay fetching Margaret a day longer. She had a week all to herself before starting rehearsals for Duke Craigie's extravaganza – plenty of time to go to Melbourne and back. Her heart sang at the thought of it. But she avoided mentioning her plans to Dev until the very last moment – and when she did she was prepared for his expected objection.

They were in his apartment enjoying a quiet drink to round off a pleasant evening spent wining and dining at Angelo's, the most exclusive nightclub in Sydney, and Tara had chosen this moment to break her news, hoping Dev might be mellowed by the potent mix of wine, whisky and good food.

The moment she saw his face darken, however, she knew he was not.

'Fetch Margaret?' he repeated, fumbling in his pockets for his cigarettes. 'I don't think that's a very good idea.'

'Why not?' Tara retaliated sharply.

He found the cigarettes, put one between his lips and looked at her steadily across it. 'Don't you think she's better off where she is?'

'No. Why should she be? Besides, I want her with me, Dev. I've missed her so much . . .'

'That's as maybe.' The flame of his gold cigarette lighter flickered briefly and he drew the smoke into his lungs. 'I think you should consider what's best for Margaret. You love, her, I know. But what sort of a life would she have with you? A gypsy's existence, no real security or roots. Just one hotel room after another, living out of suitcases.'

'It's not that bad! Travel is a good thing. It broadens the mind. And I'd be with her. That's what matters most.'

He turned away and poured more whisky onto the half-dissolved ice cubes in his glass. 'And what is Richard going to say about it?' he asked quietly.

Instantly she was trembling with aggressive reaction. 'What can he say?'

'He'll fight you.' Dev turned slowly, looking at her with the same disconcerting directness. 'And after what happened last time you had her I would think the chances are very good that he would win.'

'Fiddlesticks! I don't see why.' She held out her empty glass and while he refilled it she went on: 'Red is dead now. He can't harm her any more. And I am her mother.'

'A woman alone in a very precarious position.' He handed back her glass. 'A woman on her own.'

She took a quick gulp of the amber liquid and felt it burn her throat. 'I'm not on my own. I have you.'

He shook his head. 'Uh-uh, Tara. No.'

She jerked her glass away from her mouth. Whisky slopped onto her wrist. 'What do you mean – no?'

His gaze was still, steady and emotionless. 'If you go through with this you can count me out.'

'But I thought that we . . .' Her voice was breathless.

He put down his glass and leaned back against the cabinet, hands in pockets. 'I want you, Tara,' he said 'I've always wanted you, you know that. But I'm not prepared to go along with you in this. I believe a child needs a stable background to grow up against. And there's more.' He paused but his eyes continued to hold hers. 'While Margaret is with you, you will still be tied to Richard. I'm not prepared to go along with that any longer, either. It's my opinion that you should let Richard have custody of Margaret and leave him to pair off with Alys. It's what they have both always wanted and they will make a good stable home for Margaret. So there you are. I'm laying it on the line. It's decision time, Tara. Margaret and Richard – or me. I won't compete any longer.'

She had turned white. Angrily she banged her glass down on the table top. 'Margaret is my child, Dev – and Richard is still my husband, whether you like it or not.'

He shrugged. 'Then go to them,' he said coldly. 'But leave me out of it. I've had enough.'

'You don't mean it!' she cried.

'Oh, but I do. For years I have stood by and watched you make a fool of yourself – and me – over that man. Since we have been together you have asked me to stay and sent me packing with equal abandon several times. Well, enough is enough. I am not prepared to go on that way. Either you make a firm commitment to stay with me and me alone, or we are through. Once and for all. The choice is yours, Tara.'

'Don't be ridiculous!' She had never known him to be like this before, so cold and hard. It frightened her and the fear fired her quick Irish temper. 'You can't make me choose to give up all the rights to my own child! It's too much to ask. I won't do it.'

His face was like granite. 'I didn't really think you would. Though after what has happened, I don't believe it's too much to ask. I killed a man for you, Tara. Oh yes I did, even though the official verdict was that it was an accident and God alone knows he deserved to die, but I shall always have it on my conscience – what conscience I have. And further than that I am not prepared to go.'

She was shaking uncontrollably now and could say nothing.

'Go for Margaret if that's what you want to do,' he said harshly. 'But don't expect me to be here waiting when you get back.'

'All right, Dev,' she said. 'Of course you must please yourself.'

She finished her drink in one gulp, reached for her wrap and swung it around her shoulders. But even now, as finality hung coldly in the air with the echo of their angry words, she did not accept that he meant what he said. He couldn't. He loved her, didn't he? When he saw she was serious about having Margaret with her he would accept the situation. For now the most important thing was making a good exit.

'Don't bother to see me down, Dev,' she said. 'I'll take a taxi.'

As she swept out of the door she heard the crash of his glass as he flung it against the wall after her.

*

Buchlyvie was dreaming in the afternoon sunshine.

Since John's death it had continued to tick over and as yet the farm had scarcely missed him. A stickler for detail, he had left everything in apple-pie order and those problems that had occurred had been minor ones, routine matters, easily settled.

'You'll sell the place, of course,' Daniel Peterson had said to Alys on the day of the funeral when the mourners had all left. 'Come back to Toorak. There's always a home for you there.'

Alys had stared at her father uncomprehendingly.

'Sell Buchlyvie?'

'Of course. You can't run a farm on your own.'

Her jawline had tightened a fraction. Sell Buchlyvie? The idea had never occurred to her. It was her home, hers and John's, and she had been happy here. To leave would be to sever the last link with something very precious and would be a betrayal of all they had shared – a betrayal of John himself.

'I can manage,' she had said. She had seen the disbelief in her father's eyes and read his thoughts – the shocking manner of John's death had unhinged her. 'I know what I'm doing,' she had said, smiling slightly. 'You said once you wished you had taken me into the business because you thought I might have been able to make a go of it. Well, this is *my* business and I'm not going to let it go lightly.'

Her father had nodded, patting her arm. 'Perhaps you can do it, Alys. You're my daughter right enough.'

'Yes,' she had said. 'I think I am.'

In those first dreadful weeks responsibility for the farm had kept her going. When she lay sleepless in the big bed she and John had shared, grieving for him and reliving too sharply the horror of the night when Red's thugs had invaded the house and their lives, she turned her mind to the practical problems – how she, a woman with no farming experience, could run a place like Buchlyvie.

Manpower was the most urgent problem to be solved. John had done the work of several hands. So, several hands would have to be hired. That was no problem for there were plenty of returned servicemen seeking employment. Then there was the book work, the accounts and the dealing. Alys could feel only gratitude that she had learned this side of the management so thoroughly with John's help and advice. Much of it now came to her as second nature, though when she had to make a decision or deal with an unexpected problem loneliness could sometimes descend on her without warning so that she sat head in hands at his big desk crying silently to him: 'Oh John, John – what would *you* do? Help me, please!' And often, it seemed to her, he was there. His calm presence would seem to pervade the room so that she could almost feel him, hear him, and gradually the despair would fade to be replaced by a new determination.

Richard came to visit often, bringing Margaret with him, and these were the times Alys loved best. With John dead there was a slight awkwardness between them, as if they both realized that now only Tara prevented them from being together – and Tara was not there. But they were reluctant to make the move that would change their relationship forever – it was too soon, though the love between them was as real as it had ever been. That move, once made, would be irrevocable. They both knew it and shrank from it. And Margaret provided the buffer they needed. When she was there, there was no question of them having to make or avoid physical contact. They could simply take pleasure in one another's company – and in being with Margaret.

Alys adored the little girl – not only because she was Richard's. Somehow, it seemed to her that Margaret was the child she could never have, the embodiment of everything she could have wished for in a daughter of her own. And Margaret returned that love. Her brightest smile was always for Alys, and her warmest hugs. When Margaret was curled trustingly on her lap Alys felt more fiercely maternal than she would have believed possible and her patience with the child was endless.

That warm drowsy afternoon the three of them were on the veranda. It was Richard's afternoon off the hospital and he had brought Margaret to Buchlyvie as was his habit. He and Alys sat in the cane chairs chatting while Margaret played happily with some brightly coloured wooden shapes and a posting box – a favourite game which Alys kept to amuse her when she came to Buchlyvie.

'Are you staying for dinner?' Alys asked Richard.

He stretched comfortably. 'I don't think I should. It'll be past Margaret's bedtime. Why don't you come into Melbourne and dine with me?'

'That would be nice. I must confess it's in the evenings when I really do begin to get a little tired of my own company. But I'm not sure I ought to come to Melbourne, Richard. What would your mother say?'

'About what?' He leaned forward to retrieve one of Margaret's cubes which had rolled away.

'About you keeping company with me, of course. You are still a married man, after all. And your mother is very much a stickler for protocol.'

'That's true.' He smiled, a little wistfully. 'However, you can take it from me that you are in great favour with my mother, whereas Tara . . .' He glanced at Margaret as if for the moment he was afraid she might be able to understand what he was saying, then reached across so that his hand was lying on the arm of Alys' chair. 'My

517

mother never did approve of Tara. I know she thought I married her for all the wrong reasons, and she was probably right – except that she never did know what those reasons really were.' He paused and in the silence Alys thought for a moment that he was going to tell her what had happened in Northern Territory to precipitate the wedding. But Richard was too much of a gentleman for that. Close as he and Alys were there were some things which were too private, and which did not belong to him alone. 'I suppose I believed I was doing the right thing,' he said evenly, 'but they do say, don't they, that the road to hell is paved with good intentions.'

She put her hand out to cover his, but said nothing – some things needed no words.

A small squeal of frustration from Margaret attracted her attention. The child was trying to post one of the cut-out shapes into the box and she could not do it. Alys smiled, rose from her chair and dropped to her knees beside Margaret.

'Look, sweetheart – like this. You hold the piece and push it through there – see?'

Margaret snatched the piece back eagerly.

'Me do! Me do!'

'All right. Like this. Let me show you again . . .'

'Alys.' Richard's voice was quiet but taut. She looked up, surprised, to see him looking down the drive. She turned her head to follow his gaze. Someone was coming up the drive, someone small and dark, wearing a bright yellow sundress. Alys' heart came into her mouth.

'It's Tara,' she said.

*

She walked towards them and knew that the tightening in her throat came from a backwash of pure jealousy. Oh, but they looked like a family there on the veranda – Richard tanned and relaxed in his cool slacks and open-necked shirt, Alys sitting on her heels playing with

Margaret. She had known what to expect, of course. When she had arrived at Richard's home and his mother had told her, in that coldly disapproving way of hers, that Richard and Margaret were at Buchlyvie she had been neither particularly surprised nor dismayed. She had known the situation for a long time and knowing it helped to ease the guilt she felt about the havoc she had brought indirectly into Alys' life. But knowing Richard and Margaret were here was one thing, seeing them all looking so *right* together was quite another.

'Well,' she said, and her voice was harsher than she intended. 'This is cosy, isn't it?'

'What a surprise, Tara,' said Richard. 'We weren't expecting you.'

'I can see that. I'm sorry if I've inconvenienced you. I didn't know I had to make an appointment to see my daughter.' Her face softened as she dropped to her knees beside Margaret. 'Hello, darling. What are you doing? Have you got a hug for your Mammy?'

Margaret regarded her solemnly but made no move.

'Margaret!' Tara coaxed. As she reached for her the child's face puckered mulishly and she turned to Alys.

'Box! Show Magit box!'

'Margaret!' Alys admonished, embarrassed – and to Tara: 'I'm sorry, she's fascinated by those toys. You know what children are.'

'You can hardly expect her to come running to you, Tara.' Richard said coolly. 'You are virtually a stranger to her after all.'

'I'm her mother!' Tara protested.

'And this is the only home she knows. She's probably afraid you are going to take her away again.'

Something cold and hard twisted in Tara. Was that how Margaret saw her – as a stranger to be afraid of, someone who would take her away from the familiar and trusted?

She glanced up to see Richard looking at her accusingly.

'Is that why you are here, Tara?'

She could not answer. All her usual confidence seemed to have deserted her and she was defensive suddenly.

'What if I am?'

'I won't let you do it.' His jaw was set, those narrowed eyes chips of granite.

Tension sang in the air as they glared at one another.

Alys stood up quickly taking Margaret's hand. 'Shall I take her for a little walk while you discuss it?'

Tara looked at Richard sharply.

'It's all right,' he said with irony. 'It's not some plan to abduct her. I intend to keep Margaret with the law on my side. But it's better that she doesn't hear all this, don't you think?'

Tara could only nod, her sense of guilt deepening. What sort of a mother was she to argue about her child's future in front of her? What sort of a mother had she ever been? But then she had been given little chance to be anything else. From the moment she had been born Margaret had been treated as an Allingham. She, Tara, might have been biologically responsible for her, but Richard's mother had made up her mind she should have as little influence on Margaret as possible and that dreadful bossy nanny had been employed to intimidate and keep her at arm's length. The one attempt she had made to be a real mother had ended in disaster.

But, oh God, I love her so! Tara thought in a moment's desperation. She is mine – the only person in the world who has ever been truly mine . . .

'We had better talk this through here and now, Tara.' Richard's voice brought her sharply back from her reverie of guilt and indecision. 'I had hoped it wouldn't come to this but since it has I might as well put my cards on the table. I won't have Margaret dragged around from one theatre to another with no home except a succession of hotel rooms. A child needs stability – to know where she belongs.'

'She needs her mother!' Tara protested. 'Shouldn't I of

all people know that? My mother left me and I never stopped looking for her, wondering if I'd find her again – and why she walked out on me. I don't want that for Margaret.'

'With respect, Tara, your situation was a little different. Margaret has a good home with me.'

Tara's mouth twisted slightly. 'And, I suppose, with Alys.'

For a moment he did not answer.

'You've always wanted her, haven't you? she said and was surprised at how little bitterness there was in her tone. 'Going right back to Darwin it was always her. If circumstances had been different I'd never have stood a chance with you.'

'That's not true,' he said, but it did not sound convincing.

'Oh yes it is. You only married me because you thought I was pregnant. And now you think you can have it both ways – you think you can have both Margaret and Alys.'

For a brief moment she saw some of her own doubt reflected in his eyes. She had hit home, she realized, touched a raw nerve.

'You are in love with her, aren't you?' she said.

He moved impatiently.

'This discussion is about Margaret, not about us. Unless you have changed your mind and want to come home. Is that it? Do you want to try again?'

She caught her lip between her teeth. So the door might still be open to her. In spite of everything Richard would still take her back. For Margaret's sake and probably for the sake of the propriety which meant so much to him. Suddenly, she experienced something close to panic. She had accused him of wanting everything – but wasn't that exactly what *she* was guilty of? Greedy, greedy Tara. Snatching at Richard. Snatching at a career. And now snatching at her daughter.

The time had come to choose. She knew it now, saw it starkly before her. She could go on with her career, fight,

fight and fight again. Or she could come home and try to make something of a marriage which had never really been given a chance. Be a wife to Richard and hope she could make him love her. Be a mother to Margaret and make a home for her. The very thought of it closed in around her like the walls of a prison cell. And she had always been a fighter, hadn't she?

She looked up to see Richard's eyes on her and wondered unexpectedly whatever had happened to the all-consuming passion she had once felt for him. Perhaps, if it had still burned as brightly, she could have turned her back on the new and glittering world. But she had exchanged one passion for another now – an old passion with its roots in her past, in her very being . . .

'It wouldn't work, Richard,' she said softly. 'I'm sorry for what I did to you. But you have Alys now. You'll make one another happy whilst we – well, we'd just end up tearing one another apart.'

She thought, though she could not be certain, that she saw a glimmer of relief.

'And Margaret?' he said.

Suddenly it was all too much.

'I don't know,' she said and the tears were throbbing inside her, the need to decide tearing her apart. 'I love her so, Richard.'

'So do I,' he said quietly. 'I know you think I'm doing this for selfish reasons and perhaps I am. But because I love Margaret I also want the best for her. If I honestly thought she would be better off with you I'd let her go. But I don't. I think she should be here in a proper home environment and I think in your heart of hearts you must realize that too. I know you love her, Tara. But because you love her you must do what is best for her. You must let her stay here.'

She crossed to the veranda steps looking towards the paddock. At its edge Alys stood with Margaret in her arms stroking the nose of one of the ponies. As she watched Margaret stretched out a small hand to do the same and when the pony moved in to nuzzle her she did not pull away.

Tara watched them and the tears slowly blurred her vision. Richard was right. She knew already in her heart what she had to do – but oh, the pain of admitting it! She loved Margaret and because she loved her she had to let her go, to grow up in this world of grace and plenty that was her birthright, with the people she had learned to love and trust. In the end only one thing really mattered – Margaret's happiness and well-being. For the rest . . .

I've survived before and I'll survive again, Tara told herself.

She raised her chin but did not turn around. She did not want him to see her tears.

'If I was to leave her with you, you would let me see her when I wanted to, wouldn't you?'

'Of course.' She heard the eagerness and hope in his voice and dug her nails into her palms to keep from trembling.

'Maybe even let her come and stay with me sometimes – when she's older?'

'Yes.' He was behind her now, cupping her elbows with her hands. 'I know it's the right thing, Tara.'

She stood rigid. 'Just one thing. Please don't let her grow up thinking her mother didn't want her, will you? Please tell her I did it because I love her so.'

His voice was a little thick, a little unsteady. 'Of course I will.'

She leaned her head back against his shoulder for the last time and a tear crept out of the corner of her eye and trickled down to the corner of her mouth.

'That's it then I guess. I'll go out and say goodbye to her.'

'You don't have to go yet,' he said. 'Stay a while longer. Stay overnight if you want to.'

She swallowed the tears, pulled away and set her lips in a tight little smile. 'If I don't go right this minute I might change my mind.'

The sun was bright and warm on the baked earth of the farmyard. Alys had set Margaret down and Tara fell on her knees beside her.

'Mammy is going now.'

Margaret gazed back at her solemnly.

'Next time I come to see you you will be riding that pony I shouldn't wonder.'

'She will indeed,' Richard said.

Tara could not tear her eyes away from the child's face.

'Shall I let you into a little secret, Margaret? Your mammy is scared to death of horses. But you won't be, will you? You'll learn to love them and ride like the wind . . .'

She pulled her close, feeling the firm little body against hers, the soft dark hair silk-like against her cheek. The smell of her, the feel of her pervaded all her senses and drew a deep maternal urge she had not known she possessed from her very soul so that she longed to hold her, run with her, never let her go . . .

The tears threatened again and she set Margaret away from her. Of all things the child must not see her cry.

'Bye, my little love. Be good.'

She stood up, feeling her heart was being torn from her body, and looked one last time at the small pert features, imprinting them indelibly in her mind. As if she could forget! As if she could ever forget . . .

'Goodbye, Richard. Goodbye, Alys. Look after her for me.'

'I will, Tara, I promise.' Alys too looked close to tears.

Tara nodded. There were no words left in her.

Abruptly she turned and walked away across the yard.

FINALE

She sat alone in the corner of the railway carriage watching the Victorian countryside speeding past the window and saw nothing but a blur of green.

The night, spent alone in a hotel room, had been a long one, a night of soul searching and heartache. Yet this morning she had woken and drawn the curtains as if to a whole new life.

Her decision had been made – there was no going back. And in the darkness she had ached for one person only – Dev, who understood her, who had always known her better than she knew herself; Dev whose touch could set her on fire as Richard's never had for all that she had loved him.

Soul mates. That was what she and Dev were – yet it had taken her so long to realize it.

She curled back in the corner of the carriage, half-closing her eyes and imagining his face, the dark swarthy face she had loved to hate and now knew she loved, his careless strength, the sound of his laugh, sometimes mocking, sometimes uninhibited, tearing out from the depths of him. And the way he kissed her and held her, making her forget everything with the power of his loving . . .

Oh Dev, I'll never leave you again, she thought. I'm coming back to you because we are wonderful together in every way. And perhaps the best bit of all is that I don't have to pretend with you. I can be what I am and know you love me for it.

Victoria became New South Wales, the ground rockier and vegetation more sparse. And then just when it seemed the journey would last forever they were drawing into Sydney railway station, into the great glass smoke-blackened dome and she was breathing the air of home.

She took a cab from the station to Dev's apartment.

Hurry – hurry! she wanted to shout to the driver. Hurry! She could not wait now to see him, tell him the way she felt. It was as if a load had been lifted from her shoulders. She had discarded the old life like a snake shedding its skin. Now, at last, she was totally ready to begin the new one.

The cab drew up outside the apartment building. She paid off the driver and ran in, her overnight bag bumping against her side. Dev's apartment could soon be her apartment too. They would live together. Maybe when she and Richard were divorced they might even marry. Mrs Sean Devlin. It had a good ring to it. She wondered why she had taken so long to realize how much she liked it.

The lift ground to a halt. She slid back the gates and rushed along the corridor. Dev's door was ajar. Ajar? Why?

'Dev!' she called. She pushed it open and stopped. Three suitcases stood in the middle of the room. On top of them was Dev's overcoat. Her heart leaped into her mouth.

'Dev!' she called again.

He came out of the bathroom fastening his gold cuff links.

'Well, Tara!'

She ran to him. 'Oh Dev, I've come back. But what are the suitcases for? Where are you going?'

He put her away with a cool casual movement.

'England.'

'England! What on earth for?'

'Duke wants to expand. I'm going to London to set up a British branch of the business.'

'But Dev – you can't go to England! What about me?'

'What about you?'

'I've made up my mind. I'm going to divorce Richard and let him and Alys bring up Margaret. I think it's the best thing for her.'

'The best thing for you I expect you mean. What

happened to make you realize you didn't want a child as a millstone round your neck?'

'What a terrible thing to say!'

'Is it? I think it's probably near the truth. When did you ever think of anyone but yourself, Tara?'

'Dev!' She pressed her hands to her ears. 'It's not that! Oh, I know I'm not the world's best mother – that's why I want something more for her, the security I never had.'

'And Richard?' he said. 'What has made you decide finally to let that poor fish off the hook?'

'How can you be so horrible? I realized I've been making a mistake, that's all. You and I, Dev, we're right together, aren't we? You always said so and now I can see it.'

'Well, good for you, Tara.' He crossed to the mirror and adjusted his tie. 'A little late, I'm afraid.'

'What do you mean?'

'I told you. I'm going to England.'

'But . . . .'

'I also told you that if you went to Melbourne it was the end as far as I was concerned.'

'But you weren't serious!'

'I was never more serious in my life. I've been prey to your moods and whims long enough, Tara.'

'Oh Dev, please – you can't go! What will I do?' She caught at his arm, close to tears now. He shook himself free.

'You'll be all right. You have a musical show to do. You are a star already and you're going to be an even bigger one. You don't need me.'

'But England! It's the other side of the world!'

'The world is getting smaller all the time. It's not so far. I shall enjoy setting up Craigie Enterprises in London. Who knows, one day you may come over yourself.' The telephone rang, he lifted it and nodded. 'Right. My taxi has arrived, Tara. I have to go.'

'Dev!' She wanted to weep, cling to him, but suddenly the old pride was resurfacing and she could not do it. She had thrown herself at one man – and look at the consequences! She would not throw herself at another. 'All right. Bye then, Dev. Good luck. And I'll see you.'

'I expect so.' In the doorway he looked back at her. 'Keep smiling, Tara. Sparkle like a star. You can conquer the world, you know.'

She nodded. Pride or no pride the tears were too close to allow her to answer.

'Lock the door for me when you leave, will you?'

And he was gone.

*

For a long while she stood in the empty apartment too stunned to cry – or to think even. Then she went out, locking the door as he had asked her.

She walked blindly with no clear thought as to where she was going – but her feet needed no telling. There was one place in all of Sydney that she loved above all others, one place where she could forget heartache and loneliness, where the people she had loved and lost faded to a sweet sad echo in her heart. As it came into view she caught her breath and felt the familiar twist of excitement shiver through her.

The Capitol.

Its lights blazed out into the night and music wafted through the partly opened door. Tonight it was a different name in huge letters, different portraits on the hoardings, but once already it had been her name, her portrait, and she knew it would be again.

'I made it, Mammy, you see – I made it!' she whispered, and as if in reply she heard Dev's last words to her.

'Sparkle like a star. You can conquer the world.'

It's true, she thought. I may lose everything else but nothing can stop me from being what I am. And Dev doesn't really mean it's over for good – I'm sure he doesn't. He's just trying to give me a fright, that's all. Maybe if he is in England I can go there and be a star too!

528

She pressed her hands together as she had done as a child, visualizing the future and what it held for her. A star in Australia. A star in London. A star all over the world. And Dev . . . oh Dev, please take me back. Please. It's so very empty and lonely without you . . .

But I'll make it – I will! I know I will!

With the lights of the Capitol brightening her face she knew it was a dream to hold onto.